BY MICHAEL LEVIN

MICHAEL LEVIN

SIMON & SCHUSTER

NEW YORK • LONDON • TORONTO
SYDNEY • TOKYO • SINGAPORE

ALIVE
and
KICKING

SIMON & SCHUSTER
Simon & Schuster Building
Rockefeller Center
1230 Avenue of the Americas
New York, New York 10020

Copyright © 1993 by Michael Graubart Levin
All rights reserved including the right of reproduction
in whole or in part in any form.
SIMON & SCHUSTER and colophon are registered trade-
marks of Simon & Schuster Inc.
Manufactured in the United States of America

10 9 8 7 6 5 4 3 2 1

Library of Congress Cataloging in Publication Data

Levin, Michael Graubart.
Alive and kicking : a novel / Michael Levin.
     p.   cm.
   I. Title.
PS3562.E88965A79   1993
813'.54—dc20   92-21540   CIP
ISBN 0-671-73190-4

"Talk to Her of Love" © 1925 Emil Levin, used by
permission.

FOR ROBERT ASAHINA
My editor, my teacher, my friend

The right of a man to dispose of his property by will as he sees fit is one which the law is slow to deny.

—*Perkins v. Perkins*,
Supreme Court of Iowa, 1902

Where there's a will, there's a way.

—the entire Gaines family

THE GAINES FAMILY TREE

Prepared by Howard Person,
New York Bank and Trust Company

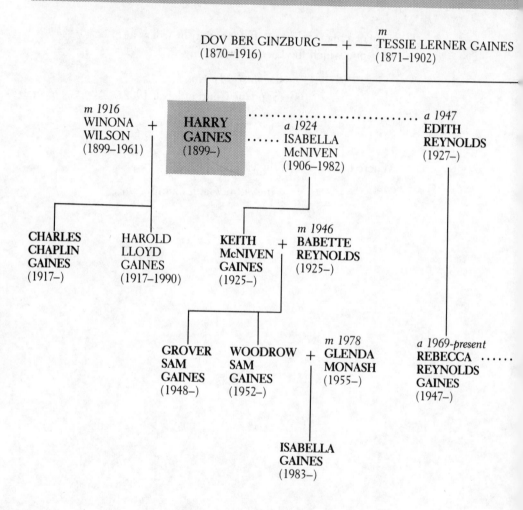

DOV BER GINZBURG— + — *m* TESSIE LERNER GAINES
(1870–1916)   (1871–1902)

m 1916
WINONA WILSON + HARRY GAINES .... *a 1947* EDITH REYNOLDS
(1899–1961)   (1899–)   *a 1924* ISABELLA McNIVEN (1906–1982)   (1927–)

CHARLES CHAPLIN GAINES (1917–)   HAROLD LLOYD GAINES (1917–1990)   KEITH McNIVEN GAINES (1925–) + *m 1946* BABETTE REYNOLDS (1925–)

GROVER SAM GAINES (1948–)   WOODROW SAM GAINES (1952–) + *m 1978* GLENDA MONASH (1955–)   *a 1969-present* REBECCA REYNOLDS GAINES (1947–)

ISABELLA GAINES (1983–)

NOTE: *m* = married   *d* = divorced   *a* = affair
Living relatives are in **bold face**.

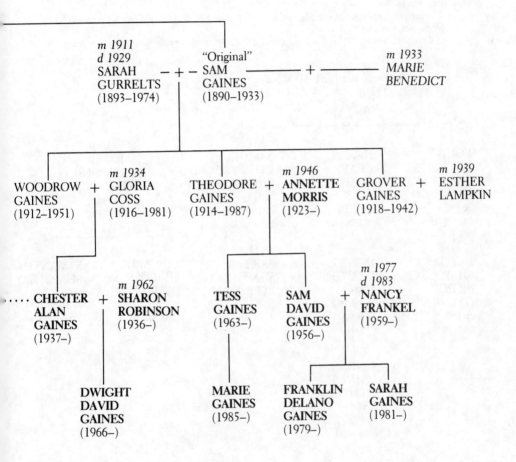

THE SHAPOLSKY FAMILY OF ATTORNEYS

The following traces those Shapolskys who practice or practiced law.

"A" denotes the year of admission to the New York State bar.
OLD SHAP denotes membership in the original firm of Shapolsky and Shapolsky, founded in 1941.
NEW SHAP denotes membership in the more recently created firm of Shapolsky & Shapolsky, founded in 1948.
The members of New Shap replaced the "and" in Old Shap's name with an ampersand (&) for purposes of clarity.
"Of counsel" means "retired but still coming in every so often to see how things are doing."

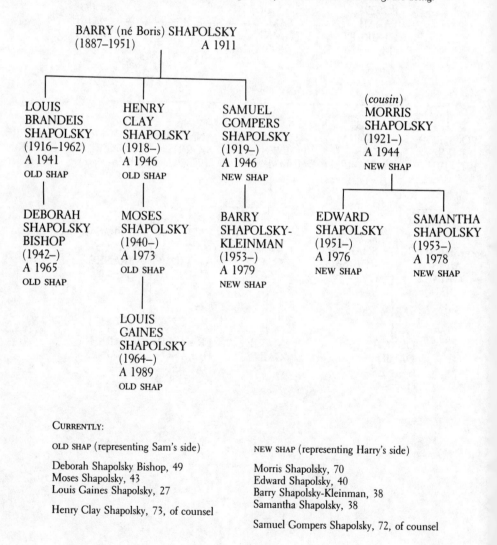

BARRY (né Boris) SHAPOLSKY
(1887–1951)   A 1911

LOUIS
BRANDEIS
SHAPOLSKY
(1916–1962)
A 1941
OLD SHAP

HENRY
CLAY
SHAPOLSKY
(1918–)
A 1946
OLD SHAP

SAMUEL
GOMPERS
SHAPOLSKY
(1919–)
A 1946
NEW SHAP

(cousin)
MORRIS
SHAPOLSKY
(1921–)
A 1944
NEW SHAP

DEBORAH
SHAPOLSKY
BISHOP
(1942–)
A 1965
OLD SHAP

MOSES
SHAPOLSKY
(1940–)
A 1973
OLD SHAP

BARRY
SHAPOLSKY-
KLEINMAN
(1953–)
A 1979
NEW SHAP

EDWARD
SHAPOLSKY
(1951–)
A 1976
NEW SHAP

SAMANTHA
SHAPOLSKY
(1953–)
A 1978
NEW SHAP

LOUIS
GAINES
SHAPOLSKY
(1964–)
A 1989
OLD SHAP

CURRENTLY:

OLD SHAP (representing Sam's side)

Deborah Shapolsky Bishop, 49
Moses Shapolsky, 43
Louis Gaines Shapolsky, 27

Henry Clay Shapolsky, 73, of counsel

NEW SHAP (representing Harry's side)

Morris Shapolsky, 70
Edward Shapolsky, 40
Barry Shapolsky-Kleinman, 38
Samantha Shapolsky, 38

Samuel Gompers Shapolsky, 72, of counsel

ONE

Intimate Relations

1

I T IS BAD FORM to come right out and express one's desire that an elderly relative should stop wasting everyone's time already and pack it in. Those favored with elderly, wealthy relatives, especially if those relatives are perceived in the family as difficult or uncaring, might confess, if they were thoroughly honest, that such uncharitable thoughts have crossed their minds more than once. Even if the bounty awaiting the family on the passing of the dearly beloved does not exceed sixty million dollars, as it did in the case of Harry Gaines, money inherited is money spent a hundred different ways in the imaginations of the beneficiaries before the corpse is cold. If it is a sin that youth is wasted on the young, it follows axiomatically that it is foolish to waste riches on the old.

Harry Gaines, the ninety-two-year-old man whose potential estate occupied the thoughts of his eighteen living relatives, two law firms named Shapolsky, and the management of the Trust Department of the New York Bank and Trust Company, lay quietly in a neatly made bed on the sixth-floor cardiac care wing of Manhattan Hospital, possessed of an advanced case of what normally is later called natural causes. Harry examined with a surgeon's precision the legs of a twenty-five-year-old, painfully (to Harry) attractive new day nurse named Cynthia Crossen as she expertly removed the intravenous tube attached to his person at the right wrist. At this

15

moment, Harry cared only about determining how best to make a pass at her. He lay in bed, passive but not inert, and then he gave Cynthia a stage wink that had gotten the attention of women old enough to be her great-grandmother.

"When I get out of here," Harry promised, his eyes narrowing into a friendly leer, "I'm gonna take you out for a night on the town and buy you the biggest steak dinner you've ever seen."

Cynthia stopped what she was doing and gave her prone suitor a sidelong glance. The night nurse had warned her about Harry. "I'm a vegetarian," she parried. "I don't eat steak."

"Vegetarian, huh?" Harry grunted, sensing an opening. "Then I'll take you out for the biggest cucumber salad you've ever seen."

"I don't *think* so," said Cynthia, not wanting to hurt Harry's feelings, impressed that he did not give up easily, and wondering whether the offer was serious. What would a date with a ninety-two-year-old man be like? she asked herself.

Harry read her mind. "I'll take you to the best nightclub in the city. Champagne and carrot sticks. It'll be so healthy it'll kill you. And then back to my place, and a little more champagne—and a few more carrot sticks. Whaddya say?"

"Uh-uh," said Cynthia, smartly sticking a fresh IV needle into Harry's arm.

Harry winced at the needle and the rejection. "Why not?" he asked, sounding hurt.

"Because *I'm* so healthy," said Cynthia, straightening herself and brushing ever so gently against Harry's shoulder, "that it would kill *you*."

"That's exactly the way I want to die," said Harry, thinking for a moment about the irony of his passing the same way his brother did more than half a century earlier. Just then Harry's attorney, Morris Shapolsky, burst into the room. He had been visiting every day for the past two weeks, ever since Harry had been readmitted, complaining of chest pains.

"What's all this talk about death and dying?" Morris asked nervously. "I don't like it."

"Relax, Morris," said Harry. "This gorgeous nurse creature and I were making dinner plans. Just the two of us."

Morris looked with surprise at the nurse. Had she really agreed to go out with Harry?

"Tell me another one," Morris said, not buying it. "The only dinner date you've got is with that IV in your arm."

"Some friend you are," grumbled Harry. And to the nurse, with exaggerated courtliness: "And when shall I have the pleasure of your company next?"

"Whenever you push that button by the side of your bed, Mr. Gaines. But don't get your hopes up about dinner. My boyfriend wouldn't like it."

"If your boyfriend is jealous of an invalid like me," Harry retorted, "he should be ashamed of himself. At my age, hope is the only thing I *can* get up."

The nurse smiled at Harry and shook her head at Morris as if to say, He's incorrigible. Then she departed.

Morris sat in the chair by the bed and, as was his custom, wasted no time. "We have to talk about the theaters," he said bluntly.

Harry gave him a dirty look and rang the call button for the nurse.

"Cut that out, Harry," said Morris, losing patience quickly. "Don't play those childish games with me."

The nurse entered, her expression reproving. "Mr. Gaines," she said, "you're only supposed to call me when you need me."

"I do need you," said Harry, frowning and crossing his arms. "This man is bothering a patient. I've never seen him before in my life. Throw him out of here."

"Here we go again," said Morris, looking annoyed.

Cynthia played along. The nurses, Harry, and Morris had been through this routine once a day since Harry had reentered the hospital. In that time, Morris's tolerance for Harry's lack of interest in his business affairs had run lower and lower.

"Now, Mr. Shapolsky," she said, as though speaking to a four-year-old, "are you bothering the patient?" She did not know exactly what Mr. Shapolsky did for a living, but she knew it was something important to Harry. She also knew that Morris's presence, as much as Harry sought it, exasperated the normally unflappable Harry. He sat up in bed now, stone-faced.

"Am *I* bothering the patient!" Morris exclaimed. "The patient is bothering *me*! He is *financially irresponsible,* and it doesn't seem to bother *him!*" The emphasis Morris placed on the two long words suggested that Harry's alleged irresponsibility was a condition more grave and less remediable than Harry's problems with his heart. Cynthia did not understand why Mr. Shapolsky was hectoring Harry in this manner. Harry was ninety-two, and the doctors held out little hope for him. Why should Mr. Shapolsky care whether he was financially irresponsible or not?

"This I pay him to come and tell me when I'm trying to get over whatever the hell is wrong with me?" Harry asked Cynthia, seeking her support in his two-week argument with Morris. Actually, the argument went back much further than that. Harry's declining health merely added a new level of urgency to the debate.

"If I don't tell you, then who will?" Morris asked hotly. "Your *farshtunkene* family? For them you can't die fast enough."

Harry could not dispute the observation. He tried to change the subject and pointed to Cynthia. "If she won't go out to dinner with me," he asked Morris, "then what do I have to live for?"

"You don't understand the *seriousness* of this," said Morris, his tone indicating clearly that *he* did. "I hate to put it so bluntly, but you don't have a will, Mr. Wise Guy. Do you know what happens if you die without a will?"

Harry thought it over. "I take it all with me?"

"No, you don't take it all with you," said Morris, his neck starting to grow red. Harry was having fun now. Getting Morris's neck red had been an oft-achieved goal for decades. He often told friends that "pissing Morris off has put ten years on my life."

"They hold a big garage sale?" Harry asked blandly, hoping to further infuriate Morris. Morris, to his credit, tried to remain calm. In fact, Harry admired Morris's steadfastness. For fourteen straight days, Morris had come to the hospital, first to check on his best friend's medical condition and then to importune him to put his financial house in order. *That's what friends are for,* Harry thought happily. *On the other hand,* Harry told himself, *he is billing me for all of the visits, including travel time to and from the hospital.*

"No, they don't hold a big garage sale," Morris told Harry.

"You die intestate—without a will—and you know what your family is going to do?"

Harry knew. He did not want to think about it. He turned to Cynthia. "I once got arrested," he told her, "for bringing a girl across intestate lines."

Cynthia laughed.

"It was a violation of the Mann Act," Harry continued. "That was the best-named law I ever heard of."

"Are you finished?" Morris asked, drumming his fingers on the side of his chair.

"Does my lawyer have a sense of humor, or what?" Harry asked Cynthia.

"If you die without a will," Morris said slowly, "your family are going to kill each other. And you know it. You owe it to them to have some sort of plan to keep them from destroying one another. It's morally wrong to die without a will. Don't you realize that?"

"This is terrific," Harry told Cynthia. "From a lawyer I'm getting a lecture on morals. That's a good joke. For this kind of legal advice I pay two hundred fifty bucks an hour."

"Two hundred *sixty* an hour," Morris corrected him, looking sheepish.

"Two hundred sixty an hour?" Harry repeated, surprised. "Since when?"

"Since last week," admitted an embarrassed Morris. "It wasn't my idea. It was my kids. They heard the top guys in Old Shap were getting two sixty. We had to keep up."

Old Shap referred to the law firm of Shapolsky and Shapolsky, from which Morris's firm Shapolsky & Shapolsky, or New Shap, had broken off in a Shapolsky family disagreement decades earlier.

Harry made a gesture that asked, What can I do? "So you come here and depress me, *and* I'm paying two hundred *sixty* dollars for the privilege?"

"Look, Harry," said Morris, "it's not my desire to depress you. You know that. I'm just trying to get you to think of your best interests."

"My best interests?" Harry said, amused. "What *are* my best interests? What do I have, Nurse, weeks to live? What should I do lying here, spin off a conglomerate? Take myself public? Morris, I put you in charge of my best interests years ago. You just keep on taking care of my best interests and send my estate the bill. Two hundred sixty an hour. Huh."

Morris sighed. "Look. I'm tired of this conversation. We keep having it over and over again, and I'm not going to put up with it. If you don't want to talk about your estate *right now, today*, then I'm walking out that hospital door and you'll never see me again."

Harry blinked twice. Could Morris be serious?

"I'm warning you, Harry," said Morris, sounding awfully serious. Now he waited anxiously for Harry's response. Harry, relishing the drama that placed him at the center, paused dramatically before answering. He pointed an index finger at Morris, opened his mouth as if to give a serious reply, and dropped his hand and turned to the nurse.

"I think he's bluffing, Cynthia," he told her matter-of-factly, in a tone chosen to drive Morris crazy. "What do you think?"

"I—am—not—bluffing!" Morris said, trying to keep from exploding. "You think I'm kidding? Look, I've put up with your *mishugas* for all these years because I love you like a brother. Do you think I want to watch everything you've built up all these years torn apart by those—those *relatives* of yours? I won't stick around to see it! They can find lawyers other than Shapolsky & Shapolsky to sue each other! I will not see everything you created disappear in legal fees, even though I personally would be collecting those fees!"

"Now I think he's serious," Harry told Cynthia.

"Of course I'm serious!" Morris exclaimed.

"You'd really turn them down as clients?" Harry asked, impressed.

"I'd rather see everything you own disappear than be a party to what your family is going to do to each other. Don't you understand that?" Morris asked.

"Frankly, you deserve the estate more than they do," said Harry. "Most of them have been pretty lousy to me over the years. On the other hand, I haven't been much of a relative to them, either."

Harry lay back and thought for a few moments. He hated to

admit it, but Morris was right. If he died without a plan for the disposition of his assets, his family would self-immolate fighting for pieces of the pie. Harry, who had performed for crowned heads of Europe, who had loved more women than he could remember even before his memory began to fail, who had made and spent fortunes, who since the age of seventeen had never denied himself any form of pleasure, no matter how costly or fleeting, bore only one regret. He had never been much of a family man. His family had fought for years over money. He could not have prevented all of the fights, but he could have set a different moral tone in the family. He could have been a presence. Now, at the end of his long life, he wanted to do something good for his family. Leaving a will, making a plan, helping them avoid a family will battle that would consume all of them in hatred and legal fees—this is what Harry suddenly wanted to do.

When Harry spoke again, his tone was so enthusiastic that both Morris and Cynthia could not restrain their surprise. "Okay, Morris," he said briskly. "You win. I'll make a plan. I'll put my house in order. Just tell me what you want me to do."

Morris looked suspiciously at Harry. He did not believe Harry meant what he said. He thought Harry might just have been trying to get him out of the room. Had a man with a lifelong disregard for money and family, even for his own money and his own family, decided to change his ways at the eleventh hour?

"I mean it," Harry said, straightening himself out in bed. "You tell me what to do, and I'll do it."

"I—I—I—" The words lodged in Morris's throat. He felt a profound sense of joy.

"I once saw an act that sounded just like that in Milwaukee," Harry told the nurse. "Trained seals. Nineteen sixteen."

Cynthia was conscious of the change in Harry, of the vanished tension between the two old friends. "I don't understand what you're doing exactly, Mr. Gaines," she said, "but I'm very proud of you."

"So we're on for dinner?" Harry asked, seizing the moment.

Before Cynthia could answer, Morris found his voice. "I want you to meet with someone from the bank tomorrow. A trust officer.

To make a plan. That's all you have to do. One meeting, and then one signature. And then I'll stop bothering you."

Harry looked up at Cynthia. "Did I ever say this man was bothering me?" he asked her. "He's not bothering me. I love this man."

Morris's eyes radiated gratitude. "It's the easiest thing in the world," he said. "Just tell the trust officer what kind of plan you want, and he'll draw it up, and then you'll sign it, and that's that."

"It's got to be a special kind of plan," Harry warned.

"Of course," said Morris. "The best. Only the best kind of plan for a man like you."

"Not just any plan," Harry admonished.

"Certainly," said Morris. And then, nervously: "What kind of plan did you have in mind?"

Harry frowned, deep in concentration. "I want a plan that will do something for my family after I'm gone that I could never make them do while I was alive."

"What's that?" asked Morris, concerned.

"I want a plan that will make them . . ." Harry paused.

"Yes?" Morris asked anxiously.

"That will make them . . ." Harry paused again.

"Make them *what*?" asked Morris, unable to bear the suspense.

"That will make them *get along*," Harry said with finality. "I want a plan that will make my family get along."

Morris swallowed hard. He started to review the state of affairs in the extended Gaines family, but then he made himself stop thinking. It was too depressing.

"*That's* the plan?" Morris asked timidly.

"*That's* the plan," Harry said firmly. He had quickly fallen in love with his newly devised method of social engineering. "If they can get along, they get the money. If they can't get along, even for a little while . . ."

"Then what?" asked Morris, expecting that they would never get along, even for a little while, even for a share of more than sixty million dollars. Harry, after all, owned a majority interest in three Broadway theaters, and sixty million was a conservative estimate of their current worth.

"Then fuck 'em," said Harry, settling back comfortably into the bed. He added with enormous satisfaction: "*That's* the plan."

"What do you mean, 'fuck 'em'?" asked Morris. "What kind of plan is that?"

"I mean they don't get a penny," said Harry. "Nice flowers," he added, looking around the room.

"I'm glad you like them," said Morris. "You paid for them."

"I did?" Harry asked. "When did I buy myself flowers?"

"When your relatives all went to the same florist and charged them to your account."

"Typical," said Harry. He looked across the room to a large bouquet of flowers that contained an American flag. A servicemen's organization had sent it to him, a tribute to Harry's wartime shows for the USO. Harry had an idea. "My family will have one month to make peace with each other," he said. "One month from the reading of the will. If they can't get along after one month, my whole estate goes to the United States Government. To reduce the deficit. This country's been very good to me and my family. If my family can't make peace, then the money goes to Uncle Sam."

"*That's* the plan?" Morris asked, almost dumbstruck. He had expected something a little simpler—this grandchild gets this, that daughter-in-law gets that. He did not anticipate an idea like this one.

"That's the plan," Harry said contentedly. "And if my family doesn't like it, it's too bad. You go tell your trust officer to make me up a plan like this, and I'll sign it."

Morris stood. It really was not what he had in mind, but at least it was a plan.

"I'll call the bank right away," Morris promised. "This plan— it's complicated. It may take a couple of days to draw up. You're not gonna die on me before then, are you, Harry?"

Harry grinned the grin of a much younger man. "What, are you kidding?" he asked. "Now I have something to live for! I have a plan!" He turned to Cynthia. "And I have Cynthia! Now will you go out with me? You see how smart I am?"

"But what about my boyfriend?" Cynthia asked playfully.

"We'll bring him too," Harry declared. "Carrots for *everybody!*"

"This really isn't what I had in mind," said Morris, shaking his head, and he headed out of the room without even saying goodbye. How on earth would all those Gaineses get along? He could practically write a check for sixty million dollars to the United States Treasury. The Gaineses behaving? *No chance*, Morris told himself. *But at least it's a plan of some sort.* He found a telephone down the hall so that he could communicate the wishes of his client to the Trust Department at the New York Bank and Trust Company. *It's really not what I had in mind at all*, he told himself as he dialed the number of Mr. Skeffington. *They'll think I'm as crazy as Harry is.*

"Mr. Skeffington's office," said the secretary on the other end of the line.

"Hello, this is Morris Shapolsky, and I need to speak to Mr. Skeffington immediately. Before my client drops dead or changes his mind."

Clients on the verge of dropping dead or changing their minds were commonplace to Mr. Skeffington's secretary.

"Hold, please," she said.

2

A T ROUGHLY the same moment, in Manhattan's venerable Exquisite Tulip restaurant, an expensive, frilly kind of place that appealed to the very rich and the very old, specializing, as it did, in sandwiches with the crusts cut off, salt-free foods, and young, fawning, and impossibly thin headwaiters, Amelia Vanderbilt, junior trust officer at the New York Bank and Trust Company, glanced at the menu only long enough to determine that it had not changed since her two lunches there the previous week, or the week before that, or the week before that.

Amelia, in charge of the bank's clientele known as DLOLs (Dear Little Old Ladies), smiled warmly at the eighty-six-year-old woman across the table and mentally reviewed her file. Eva Baum, née Berman; widowed three years ago; lives with four cats in a three-bedroom apartment on West Seventy-sixth Street in a brownstone her husband left her; one hip replaced; two children, seven grandchildren, and four great-grandchildren, all living in New Jersey, all conniving to get as much of her money as possible before she goes; a will that leaves half her assets to her family and the other half to a home on Staten Island for cats whose owners move, die, or give up their pets for some other reason. What was it, Amelia wondered, about old women and cats?

Eva needed little time with the menu, as she ate at the

Exquisite Tulip once a month with Amelia and always ordered the same thing. She put the menu down and addressed Amelia.

"I want to talk about my funeral," Eva said, opening her large purse and removing a rolled-up bunch of papers.

Not again, Amelia thought. "All right," she said graciously. "What would you like to discuss?"

"The seating arrangements," Eva said. She smoothed the sheets out on the table. "I finally figured out where to put Max."

"Eva," Amelia said gently, "you don't have seating arrangements at a funeral."

"Of course you don't," Eva responded. "That's why funerals are so tacky. No one knows where to sit. Now look here."

Amelia looked on patiently as Eva showed where she wanted each relative and friend to sit in the funeral chapel, which she had already chosen and for which she had already placed a deposit. Fortunately, the waiter came and rescued Amelia.

"Yes, girls?" he asked.

"I want the cucumber sandwiches," Eva said. "And leave the crusts on, for crying out loud. Crusts never hurt anybody. And some seltzer water."

"Of course," the waiter said. "And the usual for you, Ms. Vanderbilt?"

"Please," said Amelia, and she waited until the waiter wandered off. "Now, Eva, if you're planning your funeral again, then something must be bothering you. Are you feeling okay?"

"I feel fine," Eva said, putting away the seating chart, relieved that the ploy had worked. "It's my granddaughter again."

"Connie?" Amelia asked. Connie lived in Passaic and had wheedled thousands out of Eva until Amelia put a stop to it.

"No, the pretty one, Sandy," Eva complained. Sandy lived in Saddle River and, in Amelia's opinion, gave ostentatious materialism a bad name.

"What does she want now?" Amelia asked. "Last time it was that grandfather clock, wasn't it?"

"She wants a Jaguar," Eva said helplessly. "She says all the other grandchildren have Jaguars and she feels left out."

"How did you get here today?" Amelia asked.

Eva blinked rapidly. She wondered what that had to do with anything. "I took the bus," she said.

"You could have taken a taxi," said Amelia. "You could have hired a limousine."

Eva dismissed the idea. "Don't be silly," she said. "Izzy would never have done anything like that. He'd think I was getting soft in my old age."

Eva was convinced that her beloved Izzy was watching all of her actions through a hole in the sky. Izzy, she believed, paid particular attention to her finances. Amelia had long since given up hope of disabusing Eva of this notion. After all, Eva could be right, Amelia decided.

"Now, Eva," Amelia said patiently, "if you don't even want to spend your money on taxis, your granddaughter doesn't have to have a Jaguar."

"Oh, I know that," Eva said, looking flustered. "I just don't know how to tell her. I can't buy her a Jaguar. I'm not rich."

Oh, yes you are, Amelia thought. *You could buy each of your relatives Jaguars, and your trust fund would never know the difference.*

"Would you like me to say something to her?" Amelia asked, taking out her notebook and writing herself a reminder. "In my family, every week my parents put some money in an envelope that says 'Car' on it, and after three or four years they go out and buy a used car. I always say to them, You can afford a new car; why don't you get one? And they say, Because it's not thrifty. They're so careful with money."

"I wish my children were that way," Eva said wistfully. "Would you mind saying something to Sandy, dear? It's so hard for me to say no to any of them."

"I'll be happy to," Amelia said. "I'll do it this afternoon." Few things in life annoyed her more than grasping children and grandchildren. Playing the heavy on behalf of a DLOL was a regular part of her job.

"And I got this letter from the Income Tax," Eva said, fishing it out of her handbag. "Something about worker's compensation for the superintendent of the building. Will you take care of it?"

"Of course," Amelia said. She noticed that the letter was dated several months earlier. "When did you get this?"

"A while ago," Eva admitted. "I kept forgetting to bring it to you."

Amelia tried to hide her exasperation. "Now, Eva," she said patiently, "when you get a letter from the IRS, you have to give it to me immediately. Don't you remember what happened last time?"

Eva remembered. "I'm always so afraid of bothering you," she said. She looked embarrassed. "I know how busy you must be."

"Eva, my job is taking care of you," said Amelia. "If you don't give me the letters from the IRS, you're not letting me do my job."

"And it's so nice of you to come have lunch with a lonely old lady," Eva said, relieved that Amelia would take care of everything. "You have no idea how much I look forward to seeing you."

"You're sweet," Amelia said. "And *I* love having lunch with *you.*"

"And you look so pretty," Eva said. "Those pearls are perfect, and your hair is so nice, and you're so thin and pretty, and you dress so nicely. . . ."

Uh-oh, Amelia thought. *Here it comes.*

"Why aren't you married already?" Eva asked. "Then you wouldn't have to work in a bank anymore. Can't you get a man, dear?"

Amelia controlled herself. "I have a boyfriend," she said. "And I happen to like to work in a bank. I love my job."

"Then tell me, how have *you* been, dear?" Eva asked. "I wish you were one of my relatives instead of just my banker."

I wish I were one of your relatives too, Amelia thought. *You're worth three point seven million in securities, not even counting the brownstone. If I were related to you, I'd have Jaguars coming out of my ears.*

"Oh, just fine," Amelia said sweetly. "Everything's fine."

"You're from Kansas, aren't you, dear?" Eva asked. "What a funny place to be from."

"Nebraska," Amelia said gently. They went through this routine every month.

"Does your mother still bake those walnut chocolate chip cookies for everyone in your department?" Eva asked.

"It's my grandmother," Amelia said. The large tin of walnut chocolate chip cookies, surprisingly fresh after their voyage from the Plains, arrived weekly at the bank, along with a long letter from Granny Vanderbilt about life in Amelia's hometown of Greenwood, Nebraska. All work in the Trust Department ceased while Mr. Scarpatti, Amelia's next-desk neighbor, would read the letter aloud. Greenwood was a town without dirt, grime, drug problems, the Broadway Local, or sidewalk vending boxes containing the *New York Post*. For the hardened New Yorkers who worked in the Trust Department, it sounded heavenly if slightly boring.

"And your father works on a farm?" Eva asked. "I haven't been on a farm since I was a little girl."

"Actually, he runs a feedlot," Amelia said. She wondered whether Eva would tell the story about how, when she was three years old, she wandered onto a farm a mile from her family's apartment building in Brooklyn and her parents found her underneath a cow. Amelia had heard that story virtually every time they had gotten together for lunch.

"Did you know," Eva began, a faraway look in her eye, "that when I was a little girl, somehow I went down the stairs of our apartment building in Brooklyn and I ended up on a farm? My parents found me sleeping underneath a cow. I suppose the cow thought she was protecting me."

"Is that right?" Amelia asked with interest. She did not mind hearing the same story over and over again. She understood that it felt good for Eva to have someone who would listen. God knows her family would never listen. They were too busy stretching out their palms.

"It certainly is," said Eva, eyes bright at the memory. "When I was a little girl, Brooklyn was all farms and trees and countryside. Just like Kansas, where you come from."

"Nebraska," Amelia said gently.

"Just like Kansas," Eva said. "But then the developers got ahold of it, and now it's disgusting."

"Yes, Eva," Amelia said patiently. The "Brooklyn is disgusting" story usually ran about four minutes. Amelia thought briefly about the rest of her clients. She handled the accounts of twenty-seven Dear Little Old Ladies, all of whom were worth a couple of million, all of whom wanted to go out to lunch once a month at restaurants like the Exquisite Tulip, and all of whom had stories not unlike the "my parents found me under a cow" story and the "Brooklyn is disgusting" stories that Eva told. Amelia wondered how long it would take for Eva to tell her, yet again, the story of how she and her irreplaceable Izzy first met.

Sometimes it was hard for Amelia not to be ever so slightly jealous of the financial security of her clients and their various relatives. And lunches at the Exquisite Tulips of the world all seemed too similar. After all, Amelia often asked herself, just how much tuna niçoise can a girl eat? At the same time, though, the DLOLs served as surrogate grandmothers for Amelia, whose own family was so far away. In many ways, the DLOLs were all the family that Amelia had.

Just then the waiter arrived with lunch. "The cucumber sandwiches," he said, setting them in front of Mrs. Baum. "And for Ms. Vanderbilt, the tuna niçoise. Anything else, ladies? Enjoy your lunch."

"Did I ever tell you about the time I met Izzy?" Eva asked Amelia. "It was at a dance in 1925. . . ."

Amelia prepared to hear yet again the story of how Izzy and Eva came together over a fox-trot. Unless it was a waltz. No, it was definitely a fox-trot. Or it might have been a merengue. Eva always had trouble with that part of the story.

3

T HE NEXT MORNING, Amelia, who knew nothing of the conversation between Morris Shapolsky and her boss, Mr. Skeffington, pushed through the cathedral-size steel doors of the New York Bank and Trust Company, angled her body slightly so that she could run a finger on the wallpaper for good luck, and headed for the Trust Department. The wallpaper was tulle and textured and not like anything she had seen, she often said, growing up in Nebraska. She attributed a certain magic to it. Today, she assumed, would be a day like the rest: a morning spent writing a letter to the nursing staff of an ornery eighty-one-year-old widow who refused to accede to her family's wishes and move to a nursing home; then untangling Eva Baum's worker's compensation mess with the IRS and telling her granddaughter to forget about the Jaguar. After lunch with another DLOL, the afternoon would be devoted to paperwork relating to a slightly larger trust, of which Mr. Skeffington had recently placed her in charge.

The Trust Department consisted of a rectangular, oak-paneled, high-ceilinged room approximately one hundred twenty feet by one hundred forty feet. Twelve identical massive oak desks filled the large room's center. Each desk had a matching high-backed ornate desk chair and a smaller chair for guests. A small pull-out shelf was provided on the visitor's side of the desk, in case a visitor needed to take notes. Surrounding the desks were private offices with large windows, where the men (for they were all men) who ran the department worked. Amelia greeted her co-workers as she approached her own oak desk, where she found, to her mild annoyance, Aaron Blickstein, forty-seven, married twice and divorced twice, an attorney and a member of the bank's Legal Department.

In addition to his work as one of the bank's lawyers, Aaron's legal career included successfully defending himself, on technical grounds each time, in three separate sexual harassment charges brought by women employees at the bank. Aaron had perched himself on the edge of Amelia's desk and was reading—and creasing, Amelia noted disapprovingly—someone's otherwise pristine copy of *The Wall Street Journal*.

"Hi, cutie," he said. He had been after Amelia for about a month now. "How about dinner?"

"Please, Aaron," said Amelia. "I haven't had breakfast yet."

"How about breakfast?" asked Aaron.

"You're not half as charming as you think you are," Amelia told him.

Aaron took the hint. He put down the newspaper and got off Amelia's desk. "My door's always open," he said.

"My mind's always closed," she responded. "Will you please leave before Mr. Skeffington sees you?"

The mention of Mr. Skeffington's name snapped Aaron to attention. Mr. Skeffington had testified as a witness in two of three sexual harassment cases against Aaron and was believed to be eagerly awaiting the day when he could so testify once again.

"You know where to find me," Aaron said, backpedaling out of the Trust Department.

"Under the nearest rock," Amelia said under her breath. She looked disapprovingly at the front page of *The Wall Street Journal* that Aaron had crumpled. What she saw on the address label surprised her so much that she nearly dropped her briefcase. She gasped. It must be a mistake, she told herself. Andre, the department's ambitious if nearsighted delivery person, must have placed the paper on the wrong desk.

No rules—no *published* rules—governed the distribution of

Wall Street Journal subscriptions to bank employees. Many of those who received it never even opened it, but they made a point of conspicuously displaying each day's copy, the address label never obscured, as evidence of their importance in the hierarchy of the bank. Amelia had always wondered how many years would pass before she received a subscription of her own. And now, it seemed, the momentous day had arrived.

Closing her eyes tight, she sank into her desk chair, with hope in her heart, afraid to see whether the paper truly was meant for her. Implicit in its appearance this morning was the promise that it would await her, to comfort her with the very order of its columns, every morning of every business day for as long as she remained at the bank. Quickly she opened her eyes and stole a glance at the private offices to see whether any of the executives who might have been responsible for her *Journal* subscription was watching, enjoying her delight and surprise in seeing the newspaper and perhaps remembering, with fondness and a touch of sorrow for his own long-departed youth, the day when he first found a copy of the *Journal* waiting for him.

Amelia scanned the private offices. No sign of Mr. Skeffington. Mr. Scarpatti was with Mr. Morris in Mr. Morris's office, and both had their backs to Amelia and the rest of the department. The anonymity of Amelia's benefactor was unthreatened. Cautiously, slowly, she prepared herself to look at the address label again, trying to keep her emotions in check, steeling herself for the disappointment that would follow the likely discovery that she had misread the label and the newspaper belonged to someone else. She looked up at the ceiling, and then she lowered her eyes slowly to the desk. To her enormous delight, the address label in fact read AMELIA VANDERBILT. In the Confucian world of the New York Bank and Trust Company, Amelia had finally arrived.

The presence of tall, bespectacled, scrupulously trustworthy Mr. Skeffington, standing over her desk, interrupted her reverie. He held two faxes.

"Handle these immediately," he said, in a tone that suggested no present desire on his part to talk about her new *Wall Street Journal* subscription. "Then come to my office."

"Yes, sir," said Amelia. "Right away."

She accepted the faxes. Mr. Skeffington noticed that she was clutching the *Journal* tightly in her other hand. His face relaxed into a grin as he left her alone with the faxes. She read the first one:

WIRE TWENTY FIVE THOUSAND DOLLARS TO ME
IMMEDIATELY C/O BANQUE D'ANTIBES ANTIBES FRANCE
DWIGHT DAVID GAINES

Gaines? Amelia asked herself. Had Mr. Skeffington put her on the Gaines Trust? The Gaines family was the largest account in the Trust Department. Now Amelia was to be a part of the team handling them. *What a day*, she told herself. *First the* Journal *and now the Gaineses. Unbelievable.* She turned to the second fax.

SIDNEY ARRIVING ASPEN EIGHT THIRTY MOUNTAIN TIME
PLEASE PROVIDE ESCORT
BABETTE REYNOLDS GAINES

Amelia's pride dissolved. She might be handling Gaines family business, but it was Gaines family scutwork, in her opinion. Wiring money to a spendthrift scion? Arranging a limo for some family member taking an unplanned vacation? Was this the promotion that the *Wall Street Journal* subscription signified? A moment of terror struck Amelia: would she have to give up her dear little old ladies to handle such vapid chores for the Gaineses?

"No," she said aloud. "I'm not going to do it. I'm not sending Dwight the money."

She put that fax on the desk, to the side of her *Wall Street Journal*, and she considered the second one. Amelia knew the broad outlines of the Gaines family; everyone in the department had heard the stories of their titanic will contests and their frequent, practically automatic resort to Surrogate's Court, where such cases are decided. The Gaineses, clients since 1925, were the stuff of Trust Department legend.

Amelia considered the request for an escort at the Aspen airport somewhat more reasonable and not unlike the services Amelia frequently provided her DLOLs. The fax failed to specify which flight Sidney, whichever Gaines he was, had taken. She put her resourcefulness to work. From the second drawer of her desk, where she kept a neatly organized collection of reference materials, she pulled out a Pocket Flight Guide, a few months out of date but still serviceable. She found the TO ASPEN section and scanned through the various flights until she found one arriving from Los Angeles at the correct hour. The schedule showed the flight departing Los Angeles at 4:25 A.M., stopping in Denver at six in the morning, and arriving in Aspen at 8:26.

Sidney's got to be on this flight, she told herself. She returned the flight guide to its proper place and called directory information in Aspen for the number of Aspen Limousines. She invented the name, expecting the directory operator would have a similar listing if there wasn't a company with that exact title.

As it happened, there was. Amelia neatly took down the number on a Rolodex card, placed the card in her Rolodex in the precise alphabetical position, and made the call. As she waited for Aspen Limousines to pick up, she wondered who Sidney Gaines was and why he would choose to fly to Aspen at four in the morning. Some kind of wild partier, she told herself, with a measure of distaste. Another Dwight David Gaines, she thought. Dwight David, who had been in the south of France for two years, seeking, on his family's money, to have jet skiing declared an Olympic sport, owned a reputation for spending money that was unequaled among the other clients of the Trust Department.

"Aspen Limousines," said the voice.

"Good morning, this is Amelia Vanderbilt of the New York Bank and Trust Company. A Mr. Sidney Gaines will be arriving at, um, eight twenty-six this morning on Western Airlines flight 644 from Los Angeles via Denver. Could you arrange to have a limousine for him, and could the driver meet him at the gate?"

"Six forty-four, Sidney Gaines, eight twenty-six," the voice repeated. "No problem. We know Sidney well."

"I'll bet you do," Amelia said disapprovingly.

"Huh?" asked the voice.

"Never mind," said Amelia. "Let me give you a credit card number."

"That's okay," said the voice. "The Gaineses have an account with us. Thanks for the call."

Amelia hung up and returned her attention to the fax from

Antibes. She stared hard at it, as if a withering glance might somehow cause the request to vanish, or at least reduce itself. Twenty-five thousand after-tax dollars was just too much, she decided. She rose from her desk, fax in hand, and marched to Mr. Skeffington's office.

"Yes, Amelia?" said Mr. Skeffington, looking up from a memorandum. "All taken care of?"

"I'm not going to do this," she said bluntly.

Mr. Skeffington leaned back in his chair. "You're not going to do what?" he asked, not understanding.

"The twenty-five thousand dollars," she explained. "I'm not going to send it to Dwight David Gaines."

Mr. Skeffington considered her statement. He had been involved, one way or another, with Gaines family matters since his first day at the bank, more than forty years before. In all that time, no trust officer had ever refused to carry out an order related to the Gaineses and the disposition of their wealth. "And why not?" he asked.

"He doesn't need that much money, sir," said Amelia. "He's already spent over a hundred thousand dollars this year, and it's only May."

She was not exactly sure of the figure, but it sounded good.

"But it's his money," said Mr. Skeffington, amused by Amelia's firmness of purpose.

"But it's *wasteful*," she countered.

"Not to him," said Mr. Skeffington. "I'm sure he has what he considers some very good ideas about how to spend that money."

"Oh, sure," said Amelia, her hand on her hip. "More jet ski equipment, and expensive restaurants, and European women. I think that's awful."

Mr. Skeffington sighed. "If you're going to be in charge of the Gaines account, you're going to have to realize some things about them. First of all, they have a lot of money to play with. Second, when Harry dies, they'll have a lot more. Twenty-five thousand may sound like a lot to you or to me, but to them, it's walking-around money. Enough just to keep their wallets filled. It's like—"

Amelia was not listening. She thought she had heard Mr. Skeffington say "in charge of the Gaines account."

"Excuse me, Mr. Skeffington?" she interrupted politely.

"Yes, Amelia?"

"Did you say, 'in charge'?"

"I did," said Mr. Skeffington, who could not meet Amelia's gaze. Instead he shuffled papers on his desk. He felt his throat going dry.

Amelia could not believe her ears. She snuck a glance past Mr. Skeffington so as to look at the wallpaper. Amelia thought the pattern in the wallpaper was smiling at her.

"Mr. Skeffington," she said breathlessly, "I cannot begin to tell you how proud I am that you've given me this account, and all I can say is—"

"Save the speeches," interrupted Mr. Skeffington. "Just get Dwight David his money. And once you've done that, I want you to draw up a trust agreement for Harry Gaines—he's not well, you know. There are some special instructions. I'm sending you a memo that explains everything." He paused and looked at her with the expression of a father giving his only daughter away in marriage to an oft-married and highly disreputable groom. "And Amelia," he added, "for heaven's sake, be careful."

"Yes, sir, Mr. Skeffington, I certainly will be," said Amelia, who did not hear, or did not want to hear, the warning. After all, Stone and Vaccaro, the last two trust officers nominally in control of the Gaines family assets—in truth, no one could be said to be in control of the Gaineses or anything to do with them—had not only left the bank; they had left banking.

"All right, come with me," said Mr. Skeffington. He escorted her to an empty office three doors down from his. Andre, the department's earnest, loyal, and constantly harried messenger, was busy unloading massive boxes of files. Files covered the entire floor of the room, all three of the chairs, and the entire desktop. Amelia looked around the room.

"Are these all of them?" Mr. Skeffington asked Andre.

"These are only half," said Andre, wiping his brow. He had been carrying boxes since 7:00 A.M. "Nineteen twenty-three to nineteen fifty isn't even up yet."

"Which of these are the Gaines files?" Amelia asked, looking dubiously at the large, dusty boxes.

"All of them," Mr. Skeffington said. "Just get Dwight David his money and wait for my instructions about the trust for Harry."

Amelia pondered the massive files. She would much rather have dived into them than sent the wasteful Dwight David any more cash. And after all, she *was* in charge of their money now.

"Do I have to?" she asked. "What if they . . . run out?"

"They'll never run out," said Mr. Skeffington.

"Don't I have a responsibility," Amelia rejoined, "as their new trust officer, to educate them as to, you know, fiscal soundness?"

Mr. Skeffington smiled thinly at her naïveté. "They'll eat you for breakfast," he said. "Think about Stone and Vaccaro."

Amelia thought about them for a moment. One ran a restaurant in Pennsylvania, and the other had never been heard from again. Then she thought about having to send twenty-five thousand dollars to Dwight David. She looked around the room at the endless boxes of files that Andre continued feverishly to unload. "Maybe this family is going to be tougher to handle than I thought," she admitted.

"I think you're catching on," Mr. Skeffington agreed.

4

N UNDEREMPLOYED Broadway actor and part-time law office word processor named Gil Thompson, a striking young man with thick dark hair and sad brown eyes who, unlike many underemployed Broadway actors, bore a striking resemblance to his publicity photo, had spent the last fourteen afternoons in the lobby of Manhattan Hospital, not far from the elevators that communicated with the sixth floor, where Harry Gaines was resting comfortably and coming on to all his nurses, even the unattractive ones. Anyone who noticed Gil would have assumed that he, like so many others in the hospital's lobby, awaited word about an elderly or unwell relative. Anyone who would have made such an assumption would have been wrong.

Gil kept a copy of *The New York Times* in front of him at all times but held it low enough so that he could peer surreptitiously over the top of the paper. Whenever he saw Morris Shapolsky enter the hospital—usually around two in the afternoon—he waited until the elevator doors closed and made a note of the time on the back of a candy wrapper. He did not actually eat the candy, because sugar was bad for his teeth. He would remain in a state of heightened awareness until the elevator doors opened on Morris Shapolsky. Then he would note the time and make a careful observation of Morris's facial expression.

Gil had taken it upon himself, in addition to his assigned duties, to befriend the nursing staff of the cardiology unit. He had convinced several of the night nurses that he was a relative of Harry's and therefore was entitled to all information about his condition. A new day nurse had just joined the unit. Her name was Cynthia Crossen, and Gil had decided to gain her confidence as he had gained that of the other nurses.

During the first thirteen days of Harry's hospitalization, Morris had come and gone with a look of frustration and sadness. Yesterday had been different. Morris had entered the hospital as glum as usual, but he stayed longer and had departed with something approaching joy. Gil, concerned, had made a note of this. As soon as Morris had left the hospital, he rushed to a pay phone. His employer received his reconnaissance with a sharp intake of breath and a request to heighten the surveillance. Above all, find out why Morris was so happy. If Morris returned to the hospital with someone else, find out who that person was. This is serious business, Gil was told. He nodded, looked both ways, hung up, and returned to his post in the lobby.

The memo from Mr. Skeffington read as follows:

To: Amelia Vanderbilt

From: F. J. Skeffington

Re: Gaines

Per my conversation with Morris Shapolsky, Harry Gaines's attorney, please draw up a trust agreement for Harry Gaines's signature ASAP. Use our standard form but come up with a clause that forces the family to get along or the money goes to the federal government. Be creative. Mr. Gaines is very ill. Work quickly.

Skef.

It was midmorning at the bank, and trust officers, reading, doing paperwork, telephoning, or talking with one another, occupied virtually all of the desks on the department floor. Amelia looked up from the memorandum to find Howard Person, an accountant who worked four desks away, standing there. Howard was thirty-two, tall, serious, and an excellent squash player, and he had been Amelia's boyfriend for over two years. Mr. Skeffington disapproved at first of the office romance but eventually accepted its existence for two reasons. First, Amelia and Howard were sufficiently discreet so as not to disturb the work of the bank. Second, Mr. Skeffington recognized that it was difficult for young people to meet each other in a city like New York. In other places, the floridly psychotic and dangerously antisocial tend to dress to fit the part. In New York, they dress and look like everyone else.

Amelia and Howard had gotten close while cleaning out the large Port Chester, New York, house of a recently departed Dear Little Old Lady, who scrupulously had saved virtually every piece of paper with which she had ever come in contact during her eighty-four years of life. Her house was crammed with newspapers, bills, receipts, long-defunct magazines, advertising fliers, junk mail, jam jars, unopened cans of cat food, shopping bags, and balls of string, much of which dated back decades. Amelia and Howard found stock certificates, bearer bonds, and, hidden amidst a collection of New Jersey road maps going back to the 1940s, eleven thousand dollars in small bills. After ten days of such tedious sifting of ancient trash, Amelia and Howard were more than junior trust officer and trust accountant. They were in love.

The only thing that stood between them and marriage, as far as Howard knew, was the inability of their two families to get together. Howard, who came from a very good family in Westchester County, had promised his parents that he would not propose to Amelia until all the parents had met. It seemed like a small formality, but to Howard's dismay, it proved harder to organize than he had expected.

Bringing off such a rendezvous occupied Howard's thoughts just now. He stood at Amelia's desk with a carefully organized file folder of sightseeing tours, Broadway shows, and hotel accommodations. Howard was planning a trip to Manhattan for Amelia's parents, and as befitted his background in accountancy, he was leaving nothing to chance.

"I've got to talk to you for a minute," he said, by way of greeting. "Would your parents want to stay in Manhattan or in

Westchester? If they stay in Manhattan, it'll be noisier, but they won't have to rent a car or take the train in every day."

Amelia, her head full of Gaineses, looked confused. "What are you talking about?" she asked.

"You said your parents are coming to New York next month," Howard explained, surprised that Amelia could have forgotten something so important. "You told me that last week. So they can meet my parents. So we can get married."

"I said that?" Amelia asked, suddenly feeling defensive. "That they were coming?"

"Of course," said Howard.

"But—but my mother just told me her arthritis was acting up again," Amelia said. She really did not want to think about this right now.

"Arthritis?" Howard asked. "I thought she had rheumatism. That's why they had to cancel last time."

"I meant rheumatism," Amelia said, digging herself in deeper. "She was so disappointed."

"So were my folks. But that's not going to happen this time. Look, my folks want to take your folks to a Broadway show. They like comedies, right?"

"Um, no. they like musicals," said Amelia.

"Gee, that's strange," Howard said, scratching his head. "I thought they hated musicals. You told me that last year."

"Well," said Amelia, thinking quickly, "they've never seen a *Broadway* musical. They've just seen little hick stuff. I bet they'd love to see a real Broadway musical."

"Okay," said Howard. "I'll get tickets for a Broadway musical. They'll love it."

"I just hope Granny Vanderbilt's over that car accident she got in. My mother's had to take care of her every day since then."

Howard looked confused. "I thought your grandfather got in the accident, not your grandmother."

"Did I say it was my grandmother?" Amelia asked, embarrassed. "Granny was driving, but Gramps was the one who got hurt."

"Oh, I get it," Howard said, although it did not quite ring true.

"It doesn't matter. The main thing is, your folks are going to come to New York and meet my folks, and then you and I can . . . you know. It'll be great."

"Look, Howard," Amelia began, changing the subject, "I want to tell you about the Gaineses."

"What about them?" Howard asked, disappointed that Amelia did not share his enthusiasm over her parents' upcoming trip.

"You're not going to believe this," she said, unable to contain her excitement. "You're going to be so proud of me. Mr. Skeffington just *gave me their account!*"

Howard looked shocked, disappointed, and angry all at once. "He *what?!*"

"He gave me the Gaines account!" Amelia repeated. "Isn't that great? Aren't you happy for me?"

Howard said nothing. He seated himself at Amelia's desk and shook his head.

Amelia did not understand Howard's reaction. "What's wrong?" she asked, hurt. "I thought you'd be happy for me."

Howard pulled himself together. "Of course I'm happy for you," he said gallantly. "I'm—I'm . . . congratulations."

"What's wrong?" Amelia asked.

Howard struggled to find words to justify his reaction. "Um, Stone and Vaccaro," he said, referring to the two previous custodians of the Gaines wealth. "I don't want to see what happened to them happen to you. That account drove them crazy. The whole family drove them crazy. If they gave me the Gaineses, I'd give them right back."

"That's ridiculous," Amelia said. "You don't turn down one of the biggest clients we have. I think you're jealous because I got a big client and you didn't."

"I have plenty of big clients," Howard said defensively. "I don't need them. They're difficult, and they make the bank do demeaning things we shouldn't have to do for clients. Do you know how much time Vaccaro used to spend just taking care of their *pets?* And the way they go through money! It's—it's depressing! They're so wasteful! You won't be able to sleep at night. You'll just lie there and think about how much money the Gaineses wasted that day."

Amelia thought of the fax from Dwight David requesting the twenty-five thousand dollars. She still had not responded to it. Howard had a point.

"Well, still," she said. "They're clients of the bank, and Mr. Skeffington assigned them to me, so I've got to do the best job I can. Anyway, all I have to do right now is draft this agreement for Harry." She paused. Her honesty forced her to mention the fax. "And I have to send Dwight David twenty-five K," she admitted sheepishly.

Howard gave a knowing look. "That's just what I mean. And tomorrow you'll get another fax, and the next day Sidney has to fly somewhere else—have you met Sidney yet? Do you realize he has more frequent flier miles than most business people?"

Amelia pursed her lips. "Yes, I already met Sidney," she said. "But look, are you going to help me on this trust agreement for Harry, or aren't you?"

"If you were really smart," Howard told her, "you'd go back to Mr. Skeffington and tell him no, thanks."

"If *you* were really smart," countered Amelia, "you'd quit acting so weird and you'd start helping me handle this account. This is the biggest thing that ever happened to me."

Howard read the memo from Mr. Skeffington. He snorted. "That family couldn't get along for five minutes."

"Even for sixty million dollars?" asked Amelia. "That's what Harry's worth, isn't it?"

"Even for sixty million dollars," said Howard. "You just don't understand how deep it is. That family—they just *hate* each other."

"Well, it's their lucky day," Amelia pronounced. "Because I'm going to straighten them out."

Howard gave Amelia a look that said, Fat chance.

"I wish you could have a little more faith in me, Howard," Amelia said, raising her voice. "I'll straighten out the Gaineses. You'll see. And a musical sounds great. My parents'll love it."

Howard glumly took his file folder marked "Vanderbilt Parents Visit—Upcoming" and slunk back to his desk.

"You'll all see," Amelia said, and she returned to her paperwork. Before her lay the fax concerning Dwight David and his request for twenty-five thousand dollars.

She drew up a request for a wire transfer of twenty-five thousand dollars to the Banque d'Antibes in the south of France, as Dwight David had demanded. But she added an original touch. She sent a note along with the money: "Are you sure twenty-five thousand is enough? A. Vanderbilt, Trust Services." Perhaps Dwight David would respond to sarcasm, she told herself. *Maybe Stone and Vaccaro couldn't get anywhere with this family,* she thought. *But now they've got* me *to deal with.* Her twin goals— teaching the family financial responsibility and helping them to put the past behind them and get along—burned within her. She rang a bell on her desk to summon Andre.

He came quickly.

"Take this to Financial," said Amelia, handing him the wire transfer request and the text of her note to Dwight David. "It's got to go out today."

"Yes, Ms. Vanderbilt," said Andre. "Too bad about your getting the Gaineses. Oh, well. It was nice working with you. Got any chocolate chip cookies?"

Amelia looked puzzled. "How do you know I'm going to straighten out the Gaineses?"

Andre ignored the question. He looked both ways, leaned over Amelia's desk, and whispered conspiratorially, "Heard about Scarpatti?"

"What about Scarpatti?" Amelia asked.

"Skeffi gonna fire him," Andre whispered. "He lied on his résumé and the DLOLs are in trouble, too."

Amelia looked horrified. "I don't believe a word you're saying!" she exclaimed.

"Suit yourself," Andre whispered. "Don't tell anybody I told you. Gotta motor." And he was gone.

5

THE CONCEPT seemed so simple, really: "getting along." But what, Amelia wondered, did Harry really mean by those words? Did he mean that the family members had to promise to be nice to each other? Or get together for a family dinner? Or spend a certain amount of time with each other? Or just stop taking each other to court?

And how long a period would the family have to get along before they could get his money—his share of the theaters? How did you monitor something so amorphous? Was the bank supposed to send private investigators to make sure that the Gaineses were treating each other nicely?

Amelia also wondered what would happen if, under the terms of the trust agreement she was to draft, some of the family members got along but others did not. Would the entire family forfeit Harry's estate, or just those relatives who could not play by the rules? Amelia was stumped. She went to Mr. Skeffington's office, where she found him on the telephone. She waited respectfully at the door until he finished his conversation. Then she entered his office and seated herself in the chair opposite the desk.

"Yes, Amelia?" Mr. Skeffington asked.

"What do you mean by 'getting along'?" she asked him.

Mr. Skeffington thought for a moment. "Just what it says," he said. "They have to get along, or they don't get the money."

"I understand that part," said Amelia. "I'm just not sure what 'get along' means. It's so vague. Did Mr. Gaines tell you exactly what he meant?"

"I didn't speak to Harry," said Mr. Skeffington. "I spoke to his attorney, Morris Shapolsky."

"Well, what did *he* say it meant?" Amelia asked.

"He didn't say," said Mr. Skeffington, and nodded. "I see your point. Perhaps you should ask Mr. Gaines himself."

"Me?" asked Amelia, taken aback.

"He's your client," Mr. Skeffington said dryly.

Twenty minutes later, Amelia Vanderbilt found herself in a taxicab on her way to Manhattan Hospital to ask Harry Gaines exactly what he meant by "getting along." Traffic was moderate, and it took her less than half an hour to get from Wall Street to the East Seventies and the hospital. Amelia inquired at the information desk as to the location of Harry Gaines's room. Gil Thompson, vigilant as ever, perked up his ears at the mention of Harry's name and looked surreptitiously over his newspaper to see who was making inquiries about the object of his surveillance. He made a note of the time and of Amelia's appearance and watched her wait for the elevator.

Inside the elevator, Amelia straightened her skirt and brushed back her hair. She wanted to make a good first impression on this, her wealthiest and most important client. The elevator reached Harry's floor, and Amelia asked at the nursing station for Mr. Gaines's room. A few moments later, she found herself before Harry's closed door. She drew in a quick breath, knocked gently, and swung the door open.

The bed was empty. Her first thought was that Harry had died. She was too late. Her panic subsided, however, as she noticed that the room was still full of the personal effects—flowers, magazines, clothing—that the staff would remove upon the death of a patient. Unless he had died in the last twenty minutes. Frozen with fear, Amelia made her way back to the nursing station.

"Is Harry Gaines . . . okay?" she asked timidly.

The nurse laughed. "Okay?" she said. "He's never been better."

"Where is he?" Amelia asked.

"In there," the nurse said, indicating the lounge area. Amelia walked quickly in that direction and heard faint music. A little old man with a plastic oxygen tube in his nostrils leaned forward in a wheelchair, playing a ukulele and singing. His audience consisted of about two dozen patients and visitors, all smiling and all released, for the moment, from the fear and insecurity of being in or having a loved one in an intensive care unit. Amelia, intensely relieved, smiled as she listened to the words of her new client's gentle ballad:

> If in dancing and in prancing
> With a girl who's not entranced yet
> Your dance is for enhancing:
> Just talk to her of love.
>
> With eyes so scintillating
> And the music that is pulsating
> With joy that's stimulating
> She will speak to you of love.
>
> She will grow enthusiastic
> As you trip the light fantastic
> And you'll feel some things quite drastic
> As she looks at you with love.

Harry noticed Amelia. He had been giving pretty women the eye from the stage for decades; he gave her that look now. She blushed and smiled. He did not seem to care that he was old and wheelchair-bound. He sang the last verse directly to Amelia:

> While in your mind debating
> Just what she means by "mating,"
> Beware lest hesitating,
> She will make you fall in love.

He finished the song with a flourish on the ukulele and a big wink for Amelia. The audience burst into grateful applause.

"Okay, show's over, folks," said an orderly, who undid the brakes on Harry's wheelchair.

"Next show at dinnertime," Harry promised. "No cover, no minimum."

The patients and visitors lined up to shake Harry's hand and wish him well. Amelia watched, in awe of Harry's ability to entertain so easily, to lift people's burdens of care.

"No more autographs, Mr. Gaines," said the orderly, starting to wheel Harry away. "Doctor's orders."

"May I come visit you for a minute?" Amelia asked Harry.

"I was hoping you'd say something like that," Harry told her, admiring her good looks. "Have we met?"

Amelia walked alongside as the orderly wheeled Harry back to his room. She noticed the oxygen tank hanging on the back of the wheelchair.

"Not really," she said. "But you have a beautiful voice."

"I wrote that song in 1925," Harry said proudly. "It sold half a million copies of sheet music. That's how they sold songs before records came in."

"That's great," Amelia said. "I'd love to hear all about it."

"I'd love to tell you all about it," Harry said, as the orderly negotiated the wheelchair through the door to Harry's room. "You're not another vegetarian, are you?"

Amelia looked confused. "I beg your pardon?"

"Never mind," said Harry. "Private joke. Okay, Captain, I'm ready."

The orderly nodded and helped Harry out of his wheelchair and back into his bed. Then he left, closing the door behind him.

"I love to sing," Harry said. "Whenever I sing, I feel better."

"You made everybody so happy," Amelia said.

"Thats what an entertainer does," Harry said. "That's what it's all about. What can I do for you, my sweet thing? Are you from the hospital, or are you a civilian?"

Amelia laughed. "I'm a civilian, I guess. My name's Amelia Vanderbilt. I'm from the New York Bank and Trust Company. I'm in charge of your—" Amelia was about to use the word "estate," but she stopped herself in time. "Of your account," she concluded.

The light went out of Harry's eyes. "Then you need to see Mr. Shapolsky, my attorney," he said. "He handles my affairs. All I handle around here is the nurses."

"I just have one question for you," said Amelia, sensitive to Harry's different mood. "I'm trying to write your trust agreement and I—"

"*You're* writing my trust agreement?" Harry asked, surprised. "You're a girl."

Amelia stiffened. She reminded herself that Harry was from the old school and probably meant no harm. "Actually," she explained, "I'm a trust officer at the bank, and I've worked there for quite a few years now. The head of my department assigned me to write your trust agreement, and I just needed one piece of information from you."

"Like what?" Harry asked. The modern world was a wonder to him. Men on the moon. Girls writing trust agreements. Vegetarians. Where would it all end?

"You say you want your family to 'get along.' What exactly do you mean by 'getting along'?"

Harry closed his eyes. When he reopened them, his expression was dreamy. "When I was a young man," he said, "there was this vaudeville act on the Keith circuit called Swayne's Rats and Cats. This fellow Swayne had actually trained these rats to wear little jockey outfits and ride cats bareback. It was the damnedest thing you'd ever seen. They'd have races across the stage."

Amelia waited patiently.

"Get along?" Harry repeated, realizing quickly that Amelia would not be put off by a convenient lapse of consciousness. "What do I mean by 'get along'?"

Amelia nodded. "That's the question."

"You know," said Harry. "They should get along. That's what I mean."

"Sir?" Amelia asked.

"I mean, they should . . . you know. They should get along with each other. That's what I mean by 'get along.' "

"I realize that," Amelia said diplomatically. "But what exactly does that *mean?*"

Harry genuinely did not understand the question. He thought Amelia was being obstinate. "Getting along means getting along," he said, sounding frustrated. "Everybody knows what getting along means."

"Does it mean they have to apologize to each other for things that happened in the past?" Amelia asked, hoping to coax him gently into a more substantial definition.

"They don't have to do that," Harry responded.

"Does it mean they have to . . . call each other on the phone?"

"If they want," Harry allowed.

"Does it mean they have to . . . have dinner with each other?" Amelia asked.

"If they're hungry," said Harry.

"What if some get along and some don't?" Amelia asked.

"That's how it's always been," said Harry, wishing he could satisfy Amelia, feeling frustrated because he could not figure out how. "Some get along and some don't."

"What do you want your family to do?" Amelia asked, hiding *her* exasperation. "What do you want from them?"

Harry looked sadly into Amelia's face. "I only want one thing from them after I go. Just one thing."

"Which is what?" Amelia asked.

"I want . . ." He paused, searching for just the right words.

"Yes?" she asked anxiously.

"I only want . . ." Harry stopped again.

"Yes, Mr. Gaines?" Amelia sat at the edge of her chair.

"I only want that they should . . . *get along*," Harry said.

Amelia sighed. She patted Harry's hand. "Everything's going to be okay," she promised, but she was no closer to understanding what "get along" meant, and knowing how to draft Harry's trust, than when she had arrived at the hospital.

"I think I want to take a little nap," said Harry. The excitement of the singing and Amelia's visit was catching up with him.

"You do that," said Amelia, stroking his hand, wondering about his condition. Would he be all right again? Would he last long enough to establish his trust?

"Care to join me in here?" he asked, with a stage leer. He patted the bed. "Two can sleep as cheap as one."

Amelia, relieved, smiled. "I don't think it's what your doctor has in mind."

"Let my doctor find his own girls," said Harry.

"See you later, Mr. Gaines."

"Girl trust officers," said Harry, nodding off. "What an amazing world."

6

IN SUN-DRENCHED Antibes, twenty-five-year-old Dwight David Gaines, great-grandson of Original Sam Gaines, slept gently in his massive fifteenth-century farmhouse on a small hill overlooking the sea. Beside him cuddled his Danish or perhaps Norwegian girl-friend; he had asked once where she came from and had forgotten what she told him. Elsewhere in the house, somewhere between a dozen and eighteen houseguests, a few of whom Dwight David actually had invited to stay there, were in various stages of sleeping, waking, showering, or rummaging through the refrigerator and the pantry in search of breakfast.

Dwight David considered himself an excellent host. His guests looked at his farmhouse as a youth hostel that did not charge. Dwight David sometimes wondered how all these American, Canadian, Australian, and Scandinavian backpackers found their way to his place. He assumed that he was listed in *Let's Go, Europe* or some similar guidebook. In fact, word spread up and down the beach at Antibes that this "really rich guy" let you stay as long as you wanted, provided breakfast if you didn't mind fixing it yourself, and didn't even complain if you carried off some of the valuable antiques with which the house was rented.

Someone was rapping with a coin at the windowpane. Dwight David awoke, annoyed. He had been dreaming, as he often dreamed, of welcoming Bianca Jagger or some young Kennedy or other to the private celebrities' room in the American Club. The American Theater, one of the three theaters of which Harry was the majority owner, would become the American Club as soon as Dwight David could convince his family of the merits of turning all three theaters into private clubs.

Meanwhile, in Antibes, Dwight David did not mind guests coming and going at all hours, as long as they went about their business quietly. Then he looked out the window and saw a teenage boy wearing the blue jacket and hat of the PTT, the French telegraphic agency. The boy was riding a beat-up three-speed bicycle. He held up a telegram for Dwight David. Dwight David extended a finger, as if to say, Hang on a moment.

Telegrams usually meant good news—another unknown relative popping off and leaving money to Dwight David, or some daughter of an Italian industrial magnate, with about as much money to spend as Dwight David, inviting herself to Antibes for August. He rolled out of bed quietly, so as not to disturb his sleeping girlfriend of uncertain Scandinavian origin, pulled on a pair of shorts and sneakers, and went outside, wondering what the news was.

The messenger had him sign for the telegram, and Dwight David tipped him ten francs. The boy looked on as Dwight David read the cable: "Are you sure twenty-five thousand is enough? A. Vanderbilt, Trust Services."

Dwight David considered the message. He did not recognize the name A. Vanderbilt. His requests for money had previously been handled by someone named Vaccaro, who was a real pain to deal with. Whoever this guy Vanderbilt was, he understood something about being an heir. Dwight David never liked Vaccaro. He never liked Vaccaro's preachy attitude toward Dwight David's spending patterns. The bank was supposed to pay his American Express bills, not call him up—at the family's expense—and give him guilt. And whenever Dwight David needed extra cash, which happened roughly once or twice a week, Vaccaro always sounded so critical. What business was it of Vaccaro's how Dwight David spent his money? It wasn't Vaccaro's money.

Recently, though, Dwight David had noticed that Vaccaro

sounded more and more depressed. Finally, the calls from the bank stopped coming, and whenever Dwight David needed money, it took a few days, but he got it. Now came a cable from someone new. A Vanderbilt. Probably an heir himself, Dwight David thought. Probably worked in the bank as a joke; stuffed his paychecks in his top drawer or signed them over to his secretary. On the rare occasions when Dwight David ever thought about working for a living—extremely rare occasions indeed, unless the thoughts related to his dance clubs—he always thought he would stuff his paychecks in the top drawer of his desk, just to show people he was working only because he felt like it. Dwight David felt a sudden and deep bond with A. Vanderbilt. Finally, he thought, the bank has gotten someone who understands people like me.

Dwight David reread the message: "Are you sure twenty-five thousand is enough? A. Vanderbilt, Trust Services."

"That's so thoughtful," he told the messenger, without first ascertaining whether the lad spoke anything but French. "You know, it really isn't enough. Parlez-vous English?"

"A leetle," admitted the boy, who, like the rest of the townspeople, knew the reputation of the wealthy young American with the farmhouse full of smelly backpackers.

"Give me your pen," said Dwight David. "Pretez-moi ton parapluie."

"Parapluie means unbrelle," said the boy, whose English was barely better than Dwight David's French. He handed Dwight David his pen nonetheless.

"Well, whatever," said Dwight David, who wondered why he was so bad at languages. After all, he had bought an expensive cassette system that promised to have him speaking French like a diplomat in thirty days. On the back of the cable, Dwight David printed: TO A. VANDERBILT, NY BANK AND TRUST CO, NY USA: YOU'RE ABSOLUTELY RIGHT. MAKE IT FIFTY THOUSAND. WELCOME TO THE GAINES FAMILY. DWIGHT DAVID GAINES ANTIBES

"Take this back to the office and send it to New York," Dwight David instructed the boy. "Have I tipped you yet?"

"Non," lied the boy.

"Then here," said Dwight David, and he reached in his pocket and fished out a crumpled twenty-franc note. "Reverse the charges. Comprende?"

"Sí, Señor," said the boy, putting the cable and the twenty francs in his sock. He mounted his bicycle and rode off. Dwight watched him go.

"A. Vanderbilt," he said aloud, as he yawned and wandered back into the farmhouse. "Sounds like my kind of guy."

Half a world away from Dwight David's Antibes farmhouse, a driver in full uniform stood in the air terminal at Aspen, Colorado, and held up a sign that said SIDNEY. After the last of the passengers got off the plane, a flight attendant handed him a cat box containing a complacent, well-traveled, twelve-year-old cat. The driver, a young man who had come to Aspen to work in a ski shop and had stayed on because he could not think of anything better to do with his life, accepted the cat, said, "Hello, again, Sidney, remember me?" He carried him to the limousine parked outside, placed him carefully on the passenger's seat, and drove off.

At the Trust Department of the New York Bank and Trust Company, Amelia Vanderbilt was pacing inside the spare office that Mr. Skeffington had asked Andre to fill with Gaines family files. Files were stacked everywhere. Half of them were buried under or behind other stacks of files. Andre had not put them in any sort of order because the files themselves were not organized or marked at all clearly. Some of the folders did not even have dates on them. They all said "Gaines," though, in a hundred different handwritings. Generations of clerical staff at the bank had devoted not insubstantial portions of their careers to filling these folders with every last shred of paper that had anything to do with the Gaines family and its fortune.

Amelia blew the dust off the oldest-looking files and peered inside. She found letters from the 1930s, bills of sale for long-collapsed Brooklyn apartment houses, tax receipts from the 1920s, old blueprints on architectural paper that cracked at the touch, rent receipts, an early subway map, and a sixty-year-old map of Queens, which identified most of that now populous borough as empty fields. Amelia dug further and removed a large sealed manila envelope marked "S.G.—Personal Effects."

She unsealed the envelope and found inside it ticket stubs from a baseball game played at the Polo Grounds between the New York Giants and the Boston Braves in 1924. She also found stacks and stacks of liquor store bills, several handwritten documents in Russian, and an aged, slightly torn photograph of a mausoleum shaped like the Washington Monument, bearing the words SAMUEL GAINES in stark, almost frightening relief. Fascinated, she reached further into the envelope and felt something smooth yet somewhat metallic. She pulled the object out and realized that she was holding a set of false teeth. Instinctively she dropped everything. The false teeth fell and broke on the office's floor.

Ugh, she thought, and she bent down to collect the scattered pieces.

"Amelia?"

Mr. Skeffington's voice startled Amelia. She practically jumped up to attention.

"I was just going through the files, sir," she said.

"You don't have time for that," Mr. Skeffington said. "I just got another call from Morris Shapolsky. Harry's taken a turn for the worse. You've got to finish that trust agreement in twenty-four hours."

"I found some old letters," Amelia said. "Who was Sam Gaines?"

"Harry's brother," Mr. Skeffington told her. "He died a long time ago. But you don't have time for that now. Just work on the agreement. Did you send Dwight David the money?"

"I did, Mr. Skeffington," said Amelia.

"Well, that's good," he said, and he left Amelia alone in the office again. She straightened up the "personal effects" envelope that had fallen when she dropped the false teeth and looked longingly at the remainder of the dust-shrouded files. She wondered what else about the Gaineses she might discover. She wanted nothing more than to spend the rest of the afternoon digging through the folders, but the trust agreement had to be drawn up. Reluctantly she returned to her desk to begin drafting it.

•

Midnight found Amelia still at her desk, struggling to cast her idea in unchallengeably legal language. The usual meticulous appearance of the desktop had given way to stacks of trust documents, piles of lawbooks, and a dozen yellow pads, covered with Amelia's notes. Also, there was a tin of Granny Vanderbilt's homemade cookies. Amelia had already eaten half of them. The center of all this drafting and eating frenzy, Amelia herself, looked frustrated, weary, and thoroughly overcaffeinated.

Mr. Skeffington had provided her with a temporary secretary to handle the typing as Amelia worked and reworked the critical provisions. Amelia's problems were these: She had to make the document airtight, preventing any legal challenge from a family member. She had to make the terms acceptable both to Harry and to any possible probate or surrogate's court that might be charged with determining its legality.

At least Harry had given her one hint, she told herself. Just before five o'clock, Andre had dropped off on Amelia's desk a memo from Mr. Skeffington based on a letter from Morris Shapolsky delivered to the bank by messenger service. Morris's letter contained a clause for the trust agreement that Morris said Harry had requested. The clause, as it appeared in Mr. Skeffington's memo, read:

"In the event that the family fails to comply with the terms of this agreement, the firm of Shapolsky & Shapolsky is hereby authorized to liquidate the assets of the trustor"—*that's Harry*, Amelia told herself—"and to remit the proceeds, less customary commissions and expenses, to the Federal Government."

That language about the Shapolskys selling the assets and sending the proceeds to the government saved Amelia the enormous headache of figuring out a mechanism for turning the theaters, and Harry's other properties, into cash. She had made a mental note to thank Morris for coming up with the language when she met him, because it saved her several hours of work.

While the temp entered Amelia's microcassette dictation of her eighth draft into a word processor, Amelia felt herself drawn irresistibly to the office converted temporarily into the Gaines file room. It felt eerie to be in the bank alone except for the temp and the young security guard who passed through hourly. Amelia switched on the light in the room containing the Gaines files and felt a shiver up and down her back as she looked again upon the hundreds of massive file folders that no doubt contained all the secrets of this strange and complicated clan.

She returned to the file she had been reading earlier that morning, the one containing the letters and the false teeth. With trepidation, she reached for the file and put her hand inside, holding her breath and wondering what she might pull out. Her fingers closed around two pieces of paper, one stiff and one soft. She slowly removed her hand from the file and saw that she held a letter and a photograph. The photograph showed a smiling young man in a bowler hat, carrying an umbrella. The five-by-seven-inch picture had been printed on thick photographic stock. It bent slightly at the edges. Looking more closely, Amelia realized the subject could be no more than seventeen or eighteen years old. The face bore some resemblance to that of the elderly man she had just met in the hospital. *Could it be Harry?* she wondered.

The subject, unlike so many people in old photographs, seemed at ease. The bowler hat, large for his head, came down to his ears and cast a slight shadow on what little of his forehead it left uncovered. The eyes laughed as they seemed to study the lens. The boy's cheeks—he really looked more like a boy than a man—were full and fleshy. Baby fat, Amelia thought. He smiled in such a way that she could not see his teeth. The grin looked natural, unforced, that of a young man comfortable with laughter. His chin was as fleshy as his cheeks. He wore a dark tie against a white shirt, its collar up in what Amelia presumed was the style whenever the photograph was taken. He was posed slightly away from the camera, his left arm bent at a ninety-degree angle framing the lower-right-hand corner of the print. The way he held the umbrella loosely, just below its ornately carved wooden handle, connoted ease. He looked full of life. *This must be Harry*, Amelia decided.

She turned the photograph over. On the back were two rubber-stamped notations in slightly faded purple ink. The top one read:

HARRY GAINES, COMIC ACTOR
NATIONAL CARDETTES

Supplies Only to the
Profession

THE STUDIOS
840 Broadway
New York

The bottom stamp read:

NEWSPAPERS MAY REPRODUCE
ACKNOWLEDGING UNDERNEATH EACH
REPRODUCTION
PHOTOGRAPH BY NATIONAL, NEW YORK, 1917

Amelia turned the photograph over again and looked at Harry. It was obviously a publicity photograph. She found it difficult to accept that in the morning she would visit the same man, hospitalized and near death, and ask him to sign a legal document relating to the disposition of his estate.

Taking one last look at the photograph, Amelia turned to the other item in her hand, the letter. There was no envelope. It was written—actually, it was typed, Amelia noticed—on two pages of gray hotel stationery stapled together. "Hotel Columbian," Amelia read. Over the hotel's name was a small coat of arms with a crescent-moon-shaped letter C. Below it, in small print, were the words "FELDMAN BROTHERS, Props.," and below that, "SARATOGA SPRINGS, N.Y..............., 19 " had been printed. In the blanks, the date had been typed in: "July 30, 1931." In the upper-left-hand corner, in even smaller print, were the words: "Phone Saratoga 1640/1641." The right-hand corner read: "Opp. Congress Park."

"Dear son"—with a lowercase s on "son," Amelia noted—the letter began. "Hmm," Amelia said, and she gently flipped to the end of the letter to see who had sent it. The last words were:

and will avoid great financial damage.
With kindest regards, I am,

Your loving father,
S. Gaines

"Sam," Amelia said aloud, and felt a shudder. She held in her left hand a photo of Harry Gaines and in her right hand a letter from Sam Gaines. Nineteen seventeen and nineteen thirty-one, the brothers alive again, the world as it was then. For a moment, for Amelia, the bank did not exist, her job did not exist, *she* did not exist. She floated back and forth between the two worlds the photo and the letter conjured up for her.

"I finished the draft," the typist was saying. He handed her four double-spaced sheets. "Do you want to proof it so I can make the changes right now?"

"Um, sure," said Amelia, looking longingly at the file folders that contained God knows what else about the Gaineses. Once again, she would much rather have spent the time digging among the family records than working on the trust. Duty called, however. She accepted the draft from the typist.

"Give me about half an hour," she said. "I want to go over the language one more time."

"Okay," he said. "I'm gonna get some coffee. Want some?"

"Please," said Amelia. She was about to put the letter and the photograph into the file, but then she had a better idea. She took the file, along with the draft of the trust agreement, back to her desk in the center of the Trust Department, and she put the old Gaines material into her briefcase.

She sat down at her desk and rubbed the weariness out of her eyes. Even trust bankers had to put in a few late nights now and then, she told herself. She ran a pencil through the electric pencil sharpener, cleared her thoughts, and began to read.

7

T HE FOLLOWING MORNING, the taxi containing Morris, Howard, and Amelia arrived at its destination, Manhattan Hospital.
Morris gallantly paid, but he waited for the receipt so that he could
be reimbursed. The hospital doors opened to admit the trio.
Unnoticed by them was actor-turned-legal-spy Gil Thompson.
When Gil saw Morris in the company of two corporate-looking
young people wearing serious expressions and carrying expensive-
looking briefcases, he nearly dropped his newspaper. As nonchalantly as he could manage, he observed them waiting for the
elevator. At that moment, he decided to exceed the call of duty.
Casually, he walked up right behind them and listened to their
conversation.

Unaware of their eavesdropper, Morris, Amelia, and Howard
entered the elevator. Just before the doors closed, Gil joined them.
Aware that Harry was on six, Gil pushed seven and stood near the
door, his back to the Gaines party. His ingenuity was quickly
rewarded.

Morris said, "I'm sure he'll sign it. Just leave it to me."

"It's what he wants," said Amelia.

"Of course it's what he wants," said Morris. "He told me so
himself, just yesterday."

Howard said nothing. Amelia wondered why he remained so

upset about her getting the account. He should be happy for her; instead he seemed sullen and withdrawn. Perhaps he knew something about the family that she did not know. She thought for a moment about Stone and Vaccaro.

The elevator doors opened on six. Morris, Howard, and Amelia pushed past Gil, who covered his face with one hand, as he had seen someone do in an acting class when they had been studying spy movies. To Gil's credit, none of Harry's visitors noticed him.

As Gil continued up to seven, Morris, Howard, and Amelia approached Harry's room. The door was closed. The day nurse, Cynthia, recognized Morris.

"Hi, Mr. Shapolsky," she said, her expression and her tone guarded.

Morris worried immediately. "What's wrong?" he asked. "Is he okay?"

"He comes and goes," Cynthia admitted. "It's not great."

Morris, Howard, and Amelia exchanged worried glances.

"It's the painkiller," Cynthia explained. "He's more comfortable, but he's not always lucid."

Morris exhaled deeply. "Can we go in?"

Cynthia motioned to Harry's door, as if to say, Help yourself, but be prepared for what you see.

The three, concerned, entered Harry's room. What they saw was Harry Gaines sound asleep. Howard tried to close the door quietly. To his dismay, it banged shut. Harry awoke.

He squinted at Amelia, unable to place her, and then he smiled.

"Anne Frank," he said comfortably. "I've always wanted to meet you."

"Oh, God," said Morris.

"I loved your diary," Harry said. "And this must be your boyfriend," he added, pointing to Howard.

No one knew how to react. "I'm not Anne Frank," Amelia replied as gently as she could manage. "We met yesterday. My name is Amelia, and his name is Howard. We work for a bank."

The word "bank" had a strong effect on Harry. He sat up in bed and looked at Morris.

"Morris," he said in a firm voice. "These people—did they bring the plan?"

Harry was back.

"Thank God," Morris said under his breath. "I did, Harry," he said, his tone almost jubilant. "They've got the plan right here." And to Amelia, in a stage whisper: "Give me the will."

Amelia stared at Morris. "He can't sign in that condition! He thinks I'm Anne Frank!"

"Give me the will," Morris repeated. "If he stays lucid, he can sign. Harry, who is this young woman?"

"What are you, nuts?" Harry asked. "She's from the bank. She just said so."

"He's perfectly fine," Morris insisted.

"Of course I am," said Harry indignantly. "Give me the goddamned agreement."

"You heard him," Morris told Amelia.

Amelia was torn. She looked at Morris with disgust. He wanted a man who was having visions to sign a will. She thought it was wrong.

Howard could not fail but notice her distress. "If he's lucid long enough," he whispered to Amelia, "it's legal if he signs. It's okay. This may be the last chance."

With misgivings, Amelia opened her briefcase and handed Harry the will and trust.

"Give me my reading glasses," Harry instructed Morris.

"I'm Amelia Vanderbilt of the New York Bank and Trust Company," Amelia said, extending her hand. "We met yesterday."

"Of course," said Harry, grasping her hand and giving it a surprisingly firm handshake. The grip seemed to say, I'm still here.

"You're very beautiful, Amelia," said Harry, all charm. "You're the most beautiful woman I've ever met who worked in a bank. Except for a girl teller in Wichita in 1927. When I get out of here—and, confidentially, I should be out by the middle of next week—perhaps we can have dinner, and you can tell me your innermost thoughts about trust banking."

"He sounds pretty lucid to me," Morris whispered.

Howard did not like the idea of Harry trying to move in on his girlfriend. "My name is Howard Person," he said quickly. "I also work at the bank. I'm an accountant."

As Howard and Harry shook hands, again with great firmness of grip on Harry's part, Harry peered at him from the top of his reading glasses. "Yes, you certainly are an accountant. No mistaking that. Well, who's going to tell me about this whatchamacallit?"

Morris looked at Amelia. She drew a deep breath for courage. "It's basically a will containing a trust agreement," Amelia said. "Under its terms, as you requested, the family has to get along, or they lose everything to the federal government."

Harry grinned. "I got my plan," he said, and he enthusiastically began to read.

Just then the door opened to admit cardiologist Chester Alan Gaines, a grandson of Harry's late brother, Sam, and Harry's personal heart surgeon for twenty years. Chester Alan was surprised to see the crowd gathered around Harry's bedside.

"How's the patient?" he asked, and then he noticed Morris Shapolsky. "Oh, hello, Morris," Chester Alan said warily.

"He's just fine," said Morris quickly. Morris wanted Chester Alan out of there lest he try to change Harry's mind about the trust plan.

"I'm Chester Alan Gaines," Chester Alan told Amelia and Howard. "I'm Harry's cardiologist. I'm also sort of his . . . I'm related to him, but I don't know exactly how."

"I'm Amelia Vanderbilt, and this is Howard Person," said Amelia, shaking hands with Chester Alan. "We're from the New York Bank and Trust Company."

"You're his great-nephew," Howard said helpfully. He was an expert on Gaines family matters.

"Oh," said Chester Alan, taken aback, wondering how Howard knew that. "Really? What's going on?"

"No big deal," said Morris, a little too quickly. "We just need Harry's signature in a couple of places. Just some legal matters."

"Like what?" Chester Alan asked. "Anything I should know about?"

Harry glanced up from the document. "You'll find out soon enough," he told Chester Alan. He went back to reading. Then he said, "I think you misspelled a word."

"Really?" Amelia asked, embarrassed. "Where?"

"Shouldn't this be 'executive'?" Harry asked.

"No, that's 'executor,' " she answered, relieved. She wanted the agreement to be perfect. " 'Executor' is a legal term. It means the person who is responsible for making sure your will gets carried out."

"Oh," said Harry, and he went back to reading.

"That's a will," said Chester Alan, concerned. "Harry, are feeling well enough to be doing that?"

"I feel fine," Harry said. "That's what I pay you for. I'm reading."

"He sounds fine," Amelia admitted quietly to Chester Alan. "But when I came in, he thought I was Anne Frank."

"He's been delusional," Chester Alan whispered. "It's on and off."

"He's okay now," Morris said. "Isn't he, Doc?"

Chester Alan looked at Harry's chart. Everything looked good—blood pressure, temperature, eating, and sleeping.

"You'd have to ask him."

Harry looked disgusted. "Just because I'm in a hospital doesn't mean I'm sick. I feel fine. I'm trying to read this thing."

"Would you like me to read a copy of that?" Chester Alan asked Harry.

"No, he wouldn't," Morris answered quickly. The last thing he needed was Chester Alan explaining to Harry that the family would never agree and he should come up with some other plan. Also, who knew whether Harry would ever be this lucid again? Morris wanted a signature *right now*.

"Let him answer for himself," Chester Alan responded, not liking the way Morris was speaking up for Harry.

"When I'm done," Harry told Chester Alan. "I really feel fine. I'll leave you a copy when I'm done. Let me just finish up with these people, and then you and I can talk."

"Okay," Chester Alan said reluctantly. "I'll stop by later."

"That's wonderful," Harry said. And to the others, about Chester Alan: "He's such a nice boy. My brother's grandson. Brilliant."

Chester Alan, a shy man, found the compliments embarrassing. "Nice to meet you," he told Amelia and Howard. To Harry, he added, "I'll stop by after I finish the rest of my rounds." He glared at Morris and left the room.

Morris was relieved. "How does it look, Harry? Do you want a pen?"

"What's your hurry?" Harry asked Morris. "I have such nice visitors. This man says he's an accountant, and nothing he has done or said since he entered the room has led me to believe otherwise. But this young lady is lovely. I'd like to get to know her better."

Amelia blushed. She found it hard to reconcile the seventeen-year-old boy in the publicity photo with the ninety-two-year-old before her.

"Do you have any questions about the agreement or the will?" Amelia asked, hoping to steer the conversation to safer ground. "Is there anything Howard or I can explain to you?"

Harry grinned. "What, are you kidding? You can explain the whole thing to me. It's all in Legal. I don't speak Legal. That's why I pay him two hundred fifty an hour to read it for me."

"Two hundred sixty," Morris admitted.

"Two hundred sixty," repeated Harry. "Since when?"

"Since last month," said Morris. "I told you yesterday."

"You did?" Harry asked. "I don't remember."

Amelia and Howard exchanged glances. Was Harry losing it again?

"Okay. If you told me, you told me," Harry said, not seeming to care overly much. "This is a true *gonif*," he told Amelia, pointing to Morris. "He steals even from his own clients. Watch him after I go. Watch him *before* I go."

"About the will . . ." Morris said impatiently.

"I told you, Morris," Harry said, enjoying his attorney's obvious discomfort, "I want to speak to my guests. *Then* we'll get to your will. My will. Whatever. Who cares. When I die, they should take everything I own and throw it into the sea."

"If that's what you'd like"—Amelia smiled—"we can arrange that for you."

Harry returned a smile. He liked Amelia. Morris, on the other hand, saw nothing funny in Amelia's comment.

"He's just making a joke," Morris said testily.

"She knows a joke when she hears one," Harry said, laughing. He enjoyed seeing Morris upset. "Actually, I really don't understand how this thing works. Who wrote it, you or the dime-store Indian over there?" He indicated Howard.

"I did," Amelia said modestly.

"They pay you well at that bank?" Harry asked. "Come work for me. I'll double your salary."

Amelia smiled. "What do I have to do for the money?"

Harry gave her a wolfish grin. "We'll think of something."

Now both Morris and Howard were annoyed.

"The will," said Morris.

Harry jerked a thumb at Morris. "Who invited this one to the party? Why can't we slip off somewhere and be alone?"

Amelia had to admit that Harry sounded about as lucid as half the men she met in New York.

"What can I tell you about the will?" Amelia asked, warming to Harry.

"You heard the plan, right?" Harry asked. "My family gets along or they get nothing, right?"

Amelia nodded.

"So how do you get from that plan to this?" He held up the will.

"Okay," said Amelia, and she prepared to launch into an explanation of the trust. She was so busy trying to phrase things properly that she did not notice Harry had stopped paying attention. Morris and Howard noticed, however, and they looked nervously at one another. Was Harry slipping back into incomprehension?

Harry seemed far away. "Did you know that I used to have to follow an act called Swayne's Rats and Cats?" he asked.

"Oh, no," Morris said aloud.

"Damnedest thing you ever saw. This guy Swayne taught these rats to ride on the backs of cats, bareback, in little jockey outfits. They'd have races across the stage. The audiences loved it. Nobody'd ever seen anything like it. There's never *been* anything like it. Swayne was the strangest guy I ever met. All he would talk about was how hard it was to train rats."

The door opened, and Cynthia, the nurse, walked in. She saw the glum faces. Harry was out of it, she surmised.

"This is my wife, Winona," Harry told the others, pointing to Cynthia. "I had to marry her," he explained to Howard and Amelia in a stage whisper. "She was pregnant."

Morris's heart sank. Neither Howard nor Amelia knew what to say.

"Winona, I'd like you to meet Anne Frank."

Amelia and Cynthia, not knowing what else to do, shook hands.

"How do you do," Amelia said quietly.

"I've heard so much about you, Miss Frank," Cynthia said.

"You think it's easy, training a rat to sit on a cat's back?" Harry said. "Especially with an audience laughing and screaming. Women would always scream. I don't know how the hell Swayne does it. I'll ask him. I'm having supper with him after the show."

Amelia, Cynthia, Howard, and Morris exchanged looks of concern.

"Never follow an animal act or another comedian if you can help it," Harry admonished the group. "You'll never go over."

"I'll come back," Cynthia told the others, and she withdrew from the room.

Harry watched her go. "That was Cynthia," he explained, himself again. "She's a hot number. If I weren't ninety-two, I don't know what I'd do."

"I really think we should come back some other time," Amelia said firmly.

Even Morris had to agree. "Harry, this isn't the best time to be talking about these things. Why don't we come back tomorrow morning?"

"Nonsense," Harry said firmly. "I'm sick of paying you all this money to take taxis to visit me here. Two hundred sixty an hour. When I was a kid, if you made two hundred sixty a month, you were a rich man." He turned to Amelia. "Now. You were telling me about the will."

Amelia did not know how to react. She looked to Howard for direction. Howard shrugged. "Give it a try," he whispered.

"Give it a try," Harry repeated, displaying his displeasure at being treated like a small child. "I'm here, I'm alert, and I'm listening. Shoot."

Amelia steeled herself. "It's pretty straightforward under the terms of this paragraph." She showed Harry the relevant language.

Harry read it slowly and carefully, while Amelia, Howard, and Morris held their breath. Finally, Harry asked, "That's it?"

Amelia nodded. "That's it."

"That's my plan?" Harry asked. "I get my plan?"

"You get your plan," said Amelia. "It's completely legal."

Harry looked admiringly at his young trust officer. "You're terrific," he said. "When I made up that plan, it was to get this *yutz* out of my hair. I never dreamed you could actually get a bank to do this legally. Where do I sign?"

Morris lit up like a Christmas tree.

"Just a couple of questions first," Amelia said.

Morris shot her an angry look. Amelia caught it and ignored it. "First of all," she said, "on page two, I included Edith Reynolds as one of your relatives. You never married her, but she did have your child. So I want to know if you want to leave her in."

"Leave her in," Harry said magnanimously. "I've supported her for forty years, haven't I, Morris?"

"Yes, you have," Morris said impatiently. He clearly wanted Amelia to stop asking questions and let Harry sign before his mind wandered off again.

"Okay," said Amelia. "Fine. Now, pick two people from your side of the family."

Harry thought for a moment. "Did I ever tell you about Swayne's Rats and Cats?" he asked, sounding dreamy and far away.

"Oh, Christ," said Morris.

Amelia was resolute. "Mr. Gaines, I'm asking you a question," she said firmly. "I want to know which family members you want from your side of the family on your trust committee. It's very important."

Harry blinked. "Keith," he said. "My son Keith."

Everyone let out a breath.

"And?" Amelia asked. "We need one more."

"Glenda," said Harry. "My granddaughter-in-law."

"Did everybody hear that?" Amelia asked Howard and Morris. "He wants Keith and Glenda. What about from Sam's side of the family?"

Harry frowned. He did not like to think about Sam's side. "Sam David and Tess," he said. "If they can get along, they *deserve* my money."

"Oh, thank God," said Morris. "He's actually going to make it."

"Sign here," said Amelia, indicating the last page of the will.

Harry took the pen that Morris offered him. He signed.

"Now write today's date," she said.

Harry thought for a moment. "Today's the sixth, right?"

"Right," the others chorused. He knew what day it was. But would he get the month and year right, as well? He scribbled a date. Amelia leaned over to look. It was the right date.

"Now I need you to initial each of the pages," she instructed.

"She's very bossy," he told Morris, who just smiled nervously. Morris wanted Harry to stay lucid for just one more minute.

Harry wet the tip of his thumb, flipped to each page of the will, and initialed "H.G." in the lower-right-hand corner. Amelia, Howard, and Morris then signed the will as witnesses. Amelia removed her notary stamp from her briefcase and notarized it.

"One more thing," said Harry.

"What's that?" Amelia asked, holding her breath. Where was Harry? Nineteen seventeen? The present day?

"Who are the two people from the bank going to be?" Harry asked, concerned. "The will says seven people, and so far we've only picked four. No, five, counting Morris."

Amelia looked gratefully at Harry. The question removed all doubts from her as to his capacity to understand what was going on.

"Whoever you want," she said.

"I want you and the Indian," he said, pointing to Howard, who squirmed in reply.

"Then you've got us," Amelia said. "Actually, let me write this down so you can sign it." She removed a yellow pad from her briefcase. She wrote:

I, Harry Gaines, select the following seven individuals pursuant to Paragraph Four of the Will I have just signed:

> Keith Gaines
> Glenda Gaines
> Sam David Gaines
> Tess Gaines
> Morris   Shapolsky
> Amelia Vanderbilt
> Howard Person

She hurriedly handed it to Harry, who read it, nodded, signed, and dated it. "Howard Person," he said. "What a funny name for an Indian."

Morris looked so relieved that Amelia thought he might pass out. Now he wanted to hustle Amelia and Howard away from Harry before Harry could either change or lose his mind.

"Anything else?" Harry asked, smiling brightly at Amelia. Everyone let out a sigh of relief. A lucid Harry had taken care of business.

"Okay, that's everything," Morris said. "Harry, I'm very proud of you. You came up with a very good plan, and now everything is going to be taken care of. Let me take these two people back to the bank, and we'll get it all squared away. Okay? Let's go."

Amelia hesitated. "Just one more thing," she said. Howard and Morris stared at her. They wondered what that thing could be.

Amelia, uncertain of her motivation, opened her briefcase one more time and took out the publicity photo of the young Harry.

"Could I have your autograph?" she blurted out.

Harry looked at the old picture of himself, and his expression softened. "Gee, how do you like that," he said, fondly looking at his younger self. "I haven't seen that picture in years. Where'd you get it?"

"It was in the file," Amelia admitted. She looked at Howard and Morris with an expression that said, Call me crazy.

"I'll be happy to sign it for you," Harry said warmly. "Nobody's asked me for an autograph in twenty-five years."

He took the picture and Morris's pen. He thought hard for a moment, and scribbled furiously on the photograph, and handed it back to Amelia with a grin.

"You just made an old man's day," he told her.

Amelia took his hand. "And you just made mine," she said.

She put the signed photo in her briefcase along with the will. With smiles and handshakes, the three visitors took their leave. Amelia, Howard, and Morris made their way out the door, past the nurses' station, and to the elevator bank. There, trying to look inconspicuous, was Gil Thompson. He tried not to snap to attention when he saw the people he awaited approaching.

"I knew he'd be okay," said Morris.

"I can't believe he signed it," said Morris, relieved. "I thought he'd give us a hard time and make me go back and make changes."

"He liked it just the way it was," Howard said, unable to contain his pride in having developed the Trust Committee idea.

Morris turned to Amelia. "It was very thoughtful of you to ask for his autograph," he said.

Gil was trying to remember every single word of their conversation. The elevator arrived, and all four stepped in. Morris pressed the button for the ground floor, and Amelia removed the signed publicity photo from her briefcase. Gil looked on, interested.

"I can't wait to see what he wrote," she said excitedly. "I'm going to have it framed."

She read the inscription, and her jaw dropped.

"Oh, my God," she said.

"What's wrong?" Howard asked.

Dismayed, she showed the photo to Howard and Morris, saying: "He signed it, 'To Anne Frank.'"

8

GIL HAD no sooner descended with Morris, Amelia, and Howard than he took another elevator back to the sixth floor. There, he engaged Cynthia, Harry's nurse, in conversation, claiming to be Harry's nephew. Cynthia remained the only nurse whom Gil had not yet befriended.

"How's my uncle?" Gil asked. "Harry Gaines?"

Cynthia turned sympathetically. "That sweet man is your uncle?" she asked, her heart melting. "He's stable. But those *people* who came in today!"

She then let loose a four-minute tirade on the "disgusting creeps" and "losers" who were taking advantage of her poor, defenseless patient. Cynthia invented nothing. She simply told Gil, in harsh and frank language, what she had seen: an illucid Harry, an impatient Morris, and two lawyers, or bankers, or whatever they were, trying to push Harry into signing something. Gil listened and looked shocked at the awful treatment accorded his "uncle."

"I hope you do something about those terrible people," Cynthia concluded.

"You bet I will," Gil said convincingly. "I'll tell the rest of my family at once."

"Do you want to see Harry?" Cynthia asked. "I'm sure he'll be happy to see you."

Gil first thought to decline the offer. Then he said, "Of course I'd like to see him. That's why I came."

"What's your name?" Cynthia asked. "I'll tell him you're here."

Gil had to think of a name. He looked around for an idea. On the wall in the hallway was a travel poster of Sydney, Australia.

"Sidney," said Gil. "Sidney Gaines. I'm his nephew."

"Sidney," said Cynthia, looking gratefully at Gil. Here was a relative of Harry's who cared enough to visit and who shared her indignation over Harry's ordeal. "Be right back."

Cynthia knocked gently on Harry's door, pushed it open, and disappeared inside. Gil hung back, barely breathing, waiting for the results of his ploy.

A minute later, a distressed Cynthia emerged from Harry's room. "He says he doesn't have a nephew named Sidney," she said. "He said Sidney is a cat."

Gil tried to look stricken. "I didn't realize he was that far gone," he said. A *cat?* he wondered.

"I'm sorry," said Cynthia. "He's delusional. It must be the painkillers."

"Maybe I should come back later," Gil said, trying to sound disturbed and understanding at the same time. "What's your name?"

"Cynthia Crossen," said Cynthia. "You can call the nurses' station and ask for me anytime."

"Thank you, Cynthia," said Gil, trying to look appropriately sad. He held back nonexistent tears. "I'll—I'll call you," he said, with a catch in his voice.

Gil and Cynthia exchanged a long look of mutual sympathy and support. Then Gil headed for the elevators.

"What a nice guy," Cynthia murmured after Gil left. "And after Harry goes, he'll probably be rich. Unless those lawyers stole everything." Her indignation stirred again, and she resumed her duties on the floor.

In the hospital lobby, Gil ran to a telephone and called his employer.

"I've got a lot to tell you," he said. "Big news. I'll be right over."

Fifteen minutes later, Gil Thompson found himself in a conference room at the firm of Shapolsky and Shapolsky, or Old Shap, explaining to the gathering of attorneys all that he had done and seen in the hospital. Present were Deborah Shapolsky Bishop, Moses Shapolsky, Louis Gaines Shapolsky, and Henry Clay Shapolsky.

". . . So after I overheard their entire conversation in the elevator, I was convinced that Harry was completely out of his mind when he signed the agreement. So then I figured, I can get the nurse on our side even more if I tell her I'm a Gaines and I'm here to see my uncle."

"Beautiful," said Louis Gaines Shapolsky, admiring Gil's ingenuity. Placing the firm's receptionist and chief word processor in the hospital lobby had been Louis's idea.

"So I make up a name. Sidney. Now, I know Harry's got no relative named Sidney, because you gave me a list of relatives and their pictures. So she goes into his room and says Sidney's outside. So he's gonna say, Sidney Who? I don't have any relatives named Sidney. So now she thinks that Harry's really round the bend. And I convinced her I'm Harry's nephew, and I really care, and all that, so now I can call her anytime and find out what's going on."

"It's very devious," said Deborah Shapolsky Bishop.

"I like it too," said Moses Shapolsky.

Henry Clay Shapolsky, the seventy-three-year-old son of the firm's founder, Barry (Boris) Shapolsky, stirred in his chair and emitted a growling noise. "Mm-haugh. Have we really gotten to the point where we're spying on Harry, and Morris, and the rest of those people?"

The younger members of Old Shap squirmed in their chairs. Gil looked nervously at the floor.

"I'm afraid so, Father," said Moses Shapolsky.

Henry Clay nodded. "Good," he said. "I never liked those sons of bitches."

Everyone was relieved. Deborah continued questioning Gil Thompson.

"Did you get any sense of what the document contained?" she asked. "And are you sure he signed it?"

Gil shook his head. "I never saw it," he said. "Neither did Cynthia, the nurse. But when I was in the elevator, those people— Morris and the other two—they said he signed it. That guy Morris looked really happy about it too."

"I'll bet," said Deborah. "Morris has got to be up to something. He can't be that happy just for Harry. He can't be that happy for someone other than himself. It's just not like him."

"Did Morris say why he was so happy?" Moses asked. "Morris's happiness is the key to this whole business. If he's smiling, it's going to come out of *our* pockets."

Gil shook his head. "I have no idea," he admitted. "It's not like I could lean over in the elevator and say, 'How come you're so happy, pal?' See what I mean?"

The Old Shap lawyers nodded.

"You've done brilliant work," said Louis Gaines Shapolsky. "We're giving you a raise. Call Cynthia and give her your phone number. Tell her if anything happens to call you immediately. Establishing that relationship with the nurse was a great idea."

"Thank you," Gil said modestly. "Actually, I got the idea from this Equity Waiver thing I tried out for but the part went to some other guy because they needed somebody who could look older. I told them I could look much older and I can do my own makeup and hair and everything, but they said—"

"That's okay, Gil," said Moses. "We really don't care. Just keep on doing what you're doing. You're doing just fine."

"Yes, sir," said Gil, who really wanted to finish the story, because it was funny in the end. In fact, the other guy got the part but was hit by a beam during a dress rehearsal, and he had to leave the show. But these stuffy lawyers would never know. "Thank you, sir," Gil said, trying to sound appropriately humble to his employers.

"The really great thing about what you did," said Moses, "is that if we don't like whatever Harry signed, we can challenge it on the grounds that he wasn't lucid when he signed it. And now that we've got his nurse in our pocket, we have the perfect witness to the fact that Harry was bonkers and that Morris made him sign it."

"We could get Morris disbarred!" Deborah said excitedly.

The others paused to consider this delicious possibility. Coercing an elderly, delusional client to sign something was definitely grounds for sanctions. Things were looking better and better for the members of Old Shap.

"I think you should go back to the hospital and hang out in the lobby," Louis G. told Gil. "In case you see anyone else. Okay?"

"Okay," said Gil, once again transformed into his role as undercover investigator. "I'm on my way."

He left the room.

"He's kind of a jerk," said Moses, "but I like him."

"What do you think Morris is up to?" Deborah asked.

"We'll find out," said Louis G., proud of his protégé. "They can't keep it a secret for long. Whatever Morris is up to, we'll beat him. I promise you. We'll beat him."

Word spread quickly throughout the Gaines family that Harry might finally be slipping away. Most of the adult members of the family had designs on the three Broadway theaters of which Harry had majority ownership. If they were to see those designs turned into reality while Harry was still alive, now was the time to act.

And certain of them acted. That afternoon, as Harry slept peacefully in his room at Manhattan Hospital, Gaineses arrived. They came bearing not gifts but plans and blueprints. In the lobby, Gil, hidden behind his increasingly ragged *New York Times*, observed them all. Sam David Gaines, grandson of Original Sam and the family's real estate mogul, arrived first, accompanied by his M.B.A. assistant, Richard Bickle. Bickle struggled under the weight of three scale models of skyscrapers to be built on the sites of the three theaters. Under Bickle's arms were architects' renderings of how the buildings would look from street level. They would look immense and overbearing, and they would darken the streets they dominated. They also looked to Sam David like money machines. In fact, they were. Sam David, hurtling through the lobby, afraid that some other Gaineses would beat him upstairs, urged Bickle to walk faster. Sam David carried an assortment of flowers he had purchased in haste from a street vendor. Sam David and his assistant, Bickle, disappeared into an elevator.

Gil surreptitiously made a note: *Sam David—buildings.* Just then he heard a familiar voice from behind. It sounded as though someone was addressing him.

"Sidney?"

He froze.

"Sidney!" the familiar voice repeated. Gil turned to look. It was Cynthia. "You're the dearest man! Do you want to sit in your uncle's room? Visiting hours are over, but I'll give you a pass."

"That's okay," said Gil, thinking quickly. "That would be . . . too painful. Has he woken up at all?"

"Not once," said Cynthia. "You know, there's a coffee shop on the second floor. You could sit there. You'd be more comfortable."

"You don't say," said Gil, looking over Cynthia's shoulder at another potential Gaines heading to the elevator. It was Charles C. Gaines, Harry's oldest remaining son, empty-handed. He looked tired to Gil, and he was muttering to himself.

"Well, if you need me," Cynthia said sympathetically, "you know where to find me. I get off at eight, if you want to grab a bite. You must be very upset about your uncle."

The offer surprised and delighted Gil. Developing Cynthia's trust could be crucial to his employer's case. "That would be fine," he heard himself say.

"Great," said Cynthia. "I'll see you at eight, right here."

Gil tried to look appropriately forlorn as he said goodbye. He motivated himself by remembering a scene from an acting class in which he had to play a squirrel on Mount St. Helens just before the explosion. He watched her go, and then he made another note: *Charles C. Gaines—grumbling.*

No Gaineses came or went for the rest of the afternoon. Then finally, at seven o'clock, Keith and Babette Gaines arrived straight from the airport. Keith, Harry's son by his first mistress, carried plans and models for his proposed Harry Gaines Vaudeville Museum under his arm. Like Sam David's creation, the vaudeville museum was so big that it would require the use of all three theaters. Gil, back in the lobby, recognized Keith and Babette immediately but could not determine what they were carrying. He wrote: *Keith and Babette Gaines—I don't know what.*

The couple made their way to Harry's room, where they met Cynthia. She explained that Harry had been unwell in the morning and had slept since lunchtime. She invited them to go into the room and leave for Harry whatever it was that they were carrying. Keith and Babette entered Harry's room and were dismayed to find Sam David's three skyscrapers positioned side by side at the window, complete with tiny scale models of people, cars, trees, fountains, and even dogs at street level.

Keith and Babette watched Harry sleep for a few minutes, until Cynthia came in and rescued them. Her experience with family members had long ago taught her that some people could not leave the bedside of an unconscious relative until a nurse in effect gave them permission to do so.

"He's had a few visitors," Cynthia said, pointing to Sam David's models. "I don't know what all of this stuff is," she added. "Oh, by the way, Sidney is in the lobby," she said. "He's been there all day."

"No he hasn't," said Babette. "He flew with us from Aspen in his little cage."

Cynthia looked confused. Then she decided that Babette was feeling the strain of losing Harry. She gave a worried smile. "Well, I guess you folks are tired from your trip," she said. "I'll tell Harry you came by the minute he wakes up."

"Thank you," Babette and Keith said in unison, and they left the unit. As they entered the elevator, Cynthia could hear Babette telling Keith, "You're lucky he was sleeping. Otherwise you'd never have gotten in to see him."

At eight o'clock, Cynthia finished her shift and met Gil in the lobby. They went to a coffee shop around the corner and ate a quiet dinner, during the course of which he told Cynthia many things about Harry's life, all of which Gil had invented. By the end of the meal, she trusted him completely and invited him home with her. He accepted the invitation.

The Gaineses from France to California waited for their patriarch to awaken. On the sixth floor, however, Harry never woke up again. At 10:57 P.M., surrounded by scale models, financial projections, and flowers, Harry Gaines, ninety-two-year-old alumnus of an East Side orphanage, vaudeville star, lover of many, father of four, and majority owner of three Broadway theaters, peacefully and dreamily slipped from this world into the next.

TWO

Undue
Influence

9

H ARRY HAD LEFT no instructions for the disposition of his remains. Morris had considered asking him what he wanted but never got around to doing so because to ask a hospitalized man whether he wants burial or cremation is to suggest that one has better information about the patient's condition than does the patient. Harry made only two comments to Morris about "Getaway Day," as he euphemistically referred to it. Several years earlier, Harry and Morris had gone to the funeral of a vaudeville colleague of Harry's, and as they watched the coffin being lowered into the ground, Harry told Morris, "On Getaway Day, don't let them bury me with my brother."

Morris had nodded and promised himself he would see to it, if he survived his client and friend. When Harry's estranged wife, Winona, died thirty years earlier, Morris had taken the trouble of buying the adjacent plot in the New Jersey cemetery where she was buried. Morris assumed, although Harry had never once spoken of it, that Harry wanted to be buried beside her, because otherwise people would talk.

The only other comment Harry ever made to Morris, or, as far as Morris knew, to anyone else, about death or dying conveyed his desire to be buried wearing clean new socks. This predilection became known to Morris only a week before Harry died, during the sole and brief moment that Harry actually spoke of his impending death. Harry told Morris that he had a drawerful of socks of different colors in his apartment and that he wanted Morris to see to it that whatever suit they chose to lay Harry out in, a matching pair of socks from that drawer would go with him. Morris, wondering whether Harry was making a sick joke, agreed. The day after Harry died, Morris went to Harry's apartment, opened a drawer, and found the socks. He brought them all to the New York Bank and Trust Company, which was in charge of the funeral arrangements for Harry, as it had been for every Gaines who had died since Woodrow, forty years earlier.

The bank made funeral arrangements for Gaineses because that way no one in the family had to do it, and because Mr. Skeffington and his predecessors meant what they said when they said their service was cradle to grave. The task of organizing Harry's affairs devolved upon Amelia, who had a measure of experience in the field as a result of her devotion to her aging population of dear little old ladies. Amelia, her desk covered by socks, alerted the New Jersey cemetery to Harry's arrival the following day. She determined in telephone conversations with Harry's remaining sons, Keith and Charles C., that he had no favorite rabbi. Instead she engaged an unctuous rabbi from an East Side synagogue who had a reputation for burying celebrities. She hired a funeral chapel, limousines, and all the other trappings of American burial. She declined, however, to have the affair catered.

Phone calls, a short article accompanied by a grinning 1964 file photograph, and death notices in the obituary section of *The New York Times* alerted colleagues and friends to Harry's passing. Amelia had taken the largest possible chapel at the funeral home because Harry had known people from so many walks of life. But Harry, dying at ninety-two, had simply outlived most of the people he had ever known. Those who attended—wizened ex-vaude-villians, a few old friends who had not given up New York for Florida, and family members—looked scattered and swallowed up in the huge hall.

Amelia and Howard sat in the back of the chapel. Amelia thought for a moment of Eva Baum's seating plan for her funeral and repressed a smile. An aggressive-looking man, dressed perfectly in an elegant funereal black business suit, entered the chapel and took a seat three rows ahead of Amelia and Howard. He was in his mid thirties, and Amelia thought him handsome.

"Who's that?" she whispered to Howard.

"Sam David Gaines," Howard whispered back. "Harry's great-nephew. Sam's grandson. He manages the family real estate business."

A woman in her late twenties, bearing a strong family resemblance to Sam David, entered and took a seat at some distance from him.

"Who's that?" Amelia wanted to know.

"Tess," Howard whispered. "Sam David's sister."

"Why aren't they sitting together?"

"They aren't speaking."

"Oh."

"What about those two?" Amelia whispered, indicating Gil and Cynthia. "Isn't that Harry's nurse?"

Howard squinted at the couple. "I don't know who he is, but you're right about her." Then Howard nodded toward a woman who appeared to be in her mid sixties. She had the look of a woman who had been very beautiful in her youth. "That's Edith Reynolds," Howard whispered. "She had an affair with Harry in the forties. They had a daughter, Rebecca. She's sitting up front."

Amelia turned toward Howard with surprise. "You really know this family, don't you?" she asked.

Howard shrugged. "You could say that," he said evenly. "Here."

He reached into the inside pocket of his suit jacket and handed Amelia two folded pieces of paper.

"What are these?" Amelia asked, unfolding them.

"Family trees," Howard explained. "Of the Gaineses and their lawyers, the Shapolskys. If you're handling the Gaineses"—his throat went dry—"these'll be helpful."

"Thanks!" Amelia whispered, studying the family trees. "There are so many of them! Gaineses *and* Shapolskys."

"You'll get used to them," Howard said.

As Amelia studied the family trees, the Gaineses spaced themselves out in the front three rows like checkers on a checkerboard. All the living Shapolskys and their various spouses and children also attended. They sat behind their various Gaines family clients. Members of New Shap did not speak to members of Old Shap, except for young Louis Gaines Shapolsky, who asked his uncle Morris in the men's room whether Morris's meter was running. Morris looked extremely offended but did not respond; in point of fact, it was.

Cynthia Crossen, Harry's nurse at the end, sat in the back with Gil Thompson, whom she still believed to be Sidney Gaines.

"Don't you want to sit with the rest of your family?" Cynthia asked.

"No," Gil/Sidney answered quickly. He had already thought this part through. "I'm not on great terms with them. They won't even talk to me. They'll pretend they don't know who I am."

Cynthia took another look at the Gaines family. They revolted her.

At that moment, Sam David recognized Gil and went over to say hello. Sam David wanted to reinforce Cynthia's belief that Gil was a Gaines and therefore entitled to any information she might possess about Harry's will.

"Hello, Sidney," Sam David said warmly. A warning call from Old Shap had prepared Sam David to assist in Gil's ruse. "A sad day, isn't it?"

Gil, not prepared for this, rapidly swung into character anyway. He recognized Sam David from his frequent and heated visits to the Old Shap offices.

"Hello, Sam David," Gil said sadly. "It's a sad day for the whole family."

"I know," said Sam David, watching Cynthia. Cynthia was buying it. "I know how close you were to Harry."

Gil wiped away a nonexistent tear. "Thank you, Sam David. Lunch next week?"

"Absolutely," said Sam David, who squeezed Gil's shoulder with remarkably genuine feeling, looked deeply and sadly into Cynthia's eyes, and then walked off.

Gil watched him go. These Gaineses were good actors, he decided. Sam David's stratagem reminded him of Fredric March and Ida Lupino in *Family Affair*.

The rabbi, who had never met Harry, gave a warm and flowery eulogy about Harry's love for his family, the pride he took in playing the role of family patriarch, and how much he loved his little great-granddaughter, Isadora, as the rabbi mistakenly called Isabella. Everyone present, with the exceptions of Cynthia and Gil, knew that all this was total fiction. Harry had never shown the slightest interest in the role of family patriarch and had met Isabella only twice, on both occasions giving her a pat on the head and a twenty-dollar bill. For all Harry knew, her name might have been Isadora. The rabbi told old vaudeville stories that he ascribed to Harry's life; a few weeks earlier, he had told the same stories and said they had happened to someone else.

The service eventually ended, and the family members now had the difficult task of leaving the chapel without bumping into one another and having to say something. One by one, they made their way into limousines. All went to the grave site, as did the New Shap lawyers. The Old Shap attorneys went out to lunch instead, feeling that they had done enough already.

Babette turned to Keith as they sat in their limo. "It was pure bullshit," she said. "Just the way Harry would have wanted it."

Keith glared at her. There was nothing he could say.

Amelia paid the rabbi, paid the chapel, and took the guestbook, which all those present had signed. She and Howard rode in the last limousine in the procession to New Jersey. Howard had brought a briefcase full of work. On the way, she flipped through the guestbook as Howard crunched numbers. Each of the Gaineses, Amelia noted, except for the married couples Keith and Babette and Woodrow Sam and Glenda, had affixed their signatures to different pages.

"This family," Amelia said, shaking her head. Howard did not look up. She looked at names she did not recognize. "Harry's friends," she said. One name struck her, that of Henry Swayne.

"Swayne," Amelia told Howard as the limousine entered the Lincoln Tunnel.

"So what?" Howard asked, as he switched on the reading light above the back seat. He feared he would lose a whole afternoon of work to this funeral.

"Remember Swayne's Rats and Cats?" Amelia asked. "Harry was talking about it in the hospital. Do you think he's related?"

"I have no idea," Howard mumbled. Amelia looked at him disappointedly. She wanted to talk, and he wanted to work. "Oh, well," she said, and she returned to the guestbook.

At the graveside, the relatives spaced themselves around the rabbi so that they would not have to speak with one another. The service went off uneventfully except for an unseemly rush on the part of certain of Original Sam's descendants, who wanted to be the first to dump a spadeful of dirt on Harry's coffin. Howard had remained in the limousine, busy with numbers. Amelia left the service midway through, to go to the cemetery office and pay the bill.

Her experience with DLOLs had taught her to recognize a padded cemetery bill when she saw it; she saw one now. They had charged the estate for a casket far more expensive than the plain pine box in which Harry had been laid to rest; they had charged for embalming services that Amelia had specifically demanded not be performed and which in fact had not been performed, and they had charged for half a dozen other frills that had not been ordered.

"I'll get the manager," the office attendant told Amelia, and she disappeared behind a closed door. Amelia studied her surroundings. Around her were tasteful photographs of fields of tombstones and artists' renderings of a massive mausoleum under construction, for which "pre-need" deposits were now being discreetly taken.

A young man in his twenties walked in, wearing neatly pressed blue jeans, high-top sneakers, a white shirt, and a fish tie. Amelia glanced at him. He looked vaguely familiar.

"You work here?" he asked.

"No," said Amelia, vaguely offended that anyone might think she worked in a cemetery. "Do you?"

"No," said the young man. "I'm here for a funeral."

"Oh," said Amelia, and she looked away. *That's quite a way to dress for a funeral*, she thought. She wondered what was taking so long with her bill.

The young man noticed her disapproval of his attire. "This old guy in my family died," he told Amelia, who hadn't asked.

"I'm sorry," Amelia said, coolly polite.

"Does anybody work here?" he asked, looking at his watch. "I've got to find out where this funeral thing is."

"There's someone inside," Amelia said, avoiding his gaze. She felt that he was appraising her looks. She noticed something appealing about him despite his gross lack of taste in terms of dressing for a burial. He was sexy in an unassuming sort of way. "She'll be back in a minute."

"What's your name?" he asked, sensing her curiosity about him.

"My name is Amelia," said Amelia.

The young man put a hand out. "Nice to meet you, Amelia. That's a really pretty name. My name is Dwight David."

Amelia's eyes widened. "You're Dwight David?" she asked. "Dwight David Gaines?"

"How'd you know my name?" he asked, surprised. "Are you, like, psychic?"

"I thought you were in France," she said, staring at him. She felt revulsion for Dwight David, showing up late to his own great-granduncle's burial and wearing tasteless clothes to boot. She was appalled at herself for finding him attractive. Her expression did not betray her feelings, however.

"I *was* in France," he said, "but when I heard Harry died, I took the Concorde. I got here as fast as I could."

Just then the door opened and an oily-looking man stepped out. He wore a little badge that said "Mr. Bassano, Mortuary Services."

"Are you the one here about Harry Gaines?" he asked Amelia. "Because we made a mistake on his bill."

"Who *are* you?" Dwight David repeated.

"He wasn't supposed to be embalmed," Mr. Bassano apologized, looking at the bill as though it were an errant child. "That was a mistake."

"What are you doing with Harry Gaines?" Dwight David asked, his surprise evident.

"I'm paying his bill," said Amelia, trying to remain unruffled in the presence of two people of whom she strongly disapproved: an ungrateful, slovenly heir and a cemetery manager bent on overcharging her clients by thousands of dollars.

"He didn't have the K-17 coffin, he had the pine box," said Mr. Bassano. "That was a mistake too."

"Who *are* you?" Dwight David repeated.

"I work for the New York Bank and Trust Company," she calmly told Dwight David while trying to listen to Mr. Bassano.

"You do?" Dwight David asked.

"You did want the Perpetual Evergreen Aftercare, didn't you?" said Mr. Bassano.

"Is that the thing where you do the special landscaping on the grave site every year?" Amelia asked.

"Precisely," said Mr. Bassano. "It's our highest level of care."

"What do you do at the bank?" Dwight David said. "I use that bank too."

"I know you do," Amelia said. "I send you money." And to Mr. Bassano: "Look here, Mr. Bassano. You nearly overcharged my late client four thousand dollars for his burial. I think that's pretty disgusting. I'll make you a deal. You give us five free years of Perpetual Evergreen Aftercare, and my bank won't take you to court."

Mr. Bassano weighed his options.

"What's your last name?" Dwight David asked Amelia.

"Three years," said Mr. Bassano.

"Vanderbilt," Amelia told Dwight David. "Make it four," she told Mr. Bassano.

"Deal," said Mr. Bassano, stretching out his hand. Amelia shook it.

"Write it up right now," she ordered. Mr. Bassano immediately took out a piece of paper and memorialized their agreement.

"*You're* A. Vanderbilt?" Dwight David asked.

"I am," said Amelia, casting a disrespectful eye on Dwight David's attire. "This was a funeral," she told him. "The least you could have done was worn your nicest clothing."

"This *is* my nicest clothing," said Dwight David, hurt.

Mr. Bassano finished his note to Amelia and signed it with a flourish. Amelia examined it and paid a revised version of the cemetery bill. Dwight David watched with awe.

"I want a typed copy of this agreement on my desk tomorrow morning," she told Mr. Bassano. Then she took another look at Dwight David's attire.

"Did you fly on the Concorde dressed like that?" she asked.

"Yes," said Dwight David, not seeing anything wrong with that. He was not a boring businessman. He was an heir.

"I don't normally encourage you people to spend money," said Amelia, digging into her purse, "but in this case I'm going to make an exception." She removed ten hundred-dollar bills from a small manila envelope and handed them to Dwight David as he and Mr. Bassano looked on, openmouthed. "There's going to be a meeting of the family tomorrow at the bank at ten o'clock, to talk about the will. Between now and then, I want you to buy some respectable clothes."

Dwight David looked at the money, and then he looked at Amelia, and then he looked at Mr. Bassano.

"I think you better do what she says," Mr. Bassano told him.

Dwight David nodded silently.

"And you should be ashamed of yourself," Amelia told Mr. Bassano. "Trying to rip off a dead man."

Amelia left the office without another word. Then she stuck her head in the doorway. "Ten o'clock tomorrow, Dwight David. And you'd better be there on time and dressed properly."

She strode off. Mr. Bassano and Dwight David looked at each other and shook their heads.

Amelia went back to the limo. Howard did not even look up from his work. "How'd it go?" he asked.

"They tried to overcharge us, but I didn't let them," she said. "I met Dwight David."

"The one from France?" asked Howard, punching numbers into his calculator.

"The one from France," she said. "He flew in on the Concorde, looking like a slob. He missed the whole funeral."

"Well, what can you expect?" Howard asked, concentrating not on Amelia but on his numbers. "That's how they are."

Amelia thought about Dwight David showing up late and

dressed like a slob, and she felt infuriated all over again. She looked at her boyfriend. "Kiss me," she said, surprising herself and Howard.

"Now now," said Howard, pretending to be engrossed in his numbers. He found himself hating the Gaineses. "I'm depreciating."

"I'll say," said a disappointed Amelia. Why couldn't Howard be just a drop more romantic? she wondered. He didn't have to be like Dwight David, wearing jeans and high-tops on the Concorde. But it would not kill Howard to get his nose out of his spreadsheets once in a while. Amelia looked out the window of the limousine, to see the rest of the Gaineses returning to their cars. "This family makes me sick," she told Howard, who, in any event, wasn't listening.

10

At TEN the next morning, the Gaines family gathered in an auditorium in the lower level of the bank for a reading of Harry's will and an explanation of the trust agreement. Perhaps "gathered" does not give a clear picture of the situation. Once again, they spread themselves out through the large room like high school students taking a college entrance exam. Harry's relatives occupied the right side of the hall; Sam's filled the left. The only Gaines missing, Amelia noted, was Dwight David.

Two phalanxes of Shapolsky attorneys, meters running, glared at each other from the rows of seats behind their clients. The Old Shap lawyers remained convinced that Morris had pulled a fast one on Harry, on Sam's descendants, and on themselves. The question remained—just what had Morris done? For no one present among the Gaineses believed that whatever Harry had done could have been Harry's idea. For too long he had demonstrated a lack of interest in his finances or those of his relatives. If such had been the case during his lifetime, why should things be any different now?

Within half an hour, the entire family and their lawyers, except for Morris, sat in stunned, shocked silence as they contemplated the terms of the will that Amelia had crafted and that Harry had signed. Mr. Skeffington read the will aloud in his usual quiet, dignified manner.

According to paragraph one, Harry revoked all wills and codicils that he had previously made.

According to paragraph two, Harry was currently unmarried, his wife, Winona Wilson Gaines, having died in 1961. He had three children now living: Charles Chaplin Gaines, Keith McNiven Gaines, and Rebecca Reynolds Gaines. He had one deceased son, Harold Lloyd Gaines. He had eighteen living relatives—nine on his side of the family and nine on his late brother Sam's side.

According to paragraph three, he left his personal effects— jewelry, clothing, furniture, and "other tangible articles of a personal nature"—to his three children, in equal shares as they should agree.

The fourth paragraph was the one that mattered.

According to the fourth paragraph, Harry placed his majority interests in the American, the Classical, and the Walker theaters in a trust to be held by the New York Bank and Trust Company, the bank that employed Amelia, Howard, Mr. Skeffington, and their colleagues.

The whole family and their lawyers leaned forward at this point. What kind of trust did Harry create?

According to subhead one of the fourth paragraph, a Trust Committee of seven members would manage the assets of the trust and determine the manner in which the assets of the trust were to be invested or distributed.

According to subhead two of the fourth paragraph, two members of the Trust Committee were to come from Harry's side of the family—specifically, Harry's son Keith McNiven Gaines and his granddaughter-in-law Glenda Monash Gaines. Two members of the committee were to come from Original Sam's side of the family—Sam's grandchildren Tess Gaines and Sam David Gaines.

Those relatives not appointed to the Trust Committee stared blankly at those relatives whom Harry had chosen.

According to subhead three of the fourth paragraph, two members of the Trust Committee were to come from the Trust Department of the bank—specifically, Amelia Vanderbilt and Howard Person.

All present stared at Howard and Amelia.

According to subhead four of the fourth paragraph, the seventh member of the Trust Committee was to be "my trusted attorney and friend, Morris Shapolsky."

All present, especially the various Shapolskys, stared at Morris.

According to subhead five of the fourth paragraph, the Trust Committee would have thirty days to decide on the disposition of the trust. A majority of four votes would be necessary to make any such decision. Moreover, any beneficiary who contested or attacked the will in court was automatically cut out of the will. This was a standard "in terrorem" clause.

According to subhead six of the fourth paragraph, "In the event that the Trust Committee is able to agree, by majority vote, as to how to dispose of all the assets of the Trust, the Trustees shall divide among all of my relatives as enumerated above alive at the time of such decision the entire Trust, on a share-and-share-alike basis."

Lawyers and Gaineses alike realized that if the seven members of the committee agreed on what to do with the theaters, and the rest of Harry's assets, all of Harry's living relatives would get one share of the pie. The committee had a month to do its work. But what would happen, everyone wondered, if the committee could not agree in thirty days' time?

According to subhead seven of the fourth paragraph, "In the event that the Trust Committee is unable to agree as to the disposition of the Trust, the Trustee is hereby instructed to donate the proceeds of a sale of all assets of the Trust, as conducted by the law firm of Shapolsky and Shapolsky, less appropriate commissions and fees, to the Federal Government as a gift to reduce the Federal Deficit."

This was the heart of Harry's plan. If the representatives from his side of the family—Keith and Glenda—could not agree with the representatives of Sam's side of the family—Tess and Sam David— then all three theaters went to the U.S. Government.

The language of the subhead came from Morris's pen. Because the will was read aloud, Morris did not notice that the ampersand in the name of his firm, Shapolsky & Shapolsky, had accidentally been transposed to the word "and." No one present, Morris included, paid any attention to such niceties. The entire family and all its many lawyers were slowly digesting the information that they essentially had thirty days in which to get along, or they would suffer the loss of Harry's entire sixty-million-dollar estate.

They were not pleased.

The family practically ignored the remaining paragraphs of the will, which were, after all, mere boilerplate. Paragraph five said that any beneficiary who challenged the will in court was automatically dropped from it. Paragraphs six, seven, and eight said nothing of importance. Paragraph nine said: "I am of sound mind as I read and sign this Will and Trust. I understand all of the provisions contained herein. I sign this Last Will and Testament of my own free will, and no one has sought to exercise undue influence on my thinking."

No one in the family who was still paying attention believed a word of paragraph nine.

Paragraph ten made Morris Shapolsky the executor of the will.

Neither Amelia nor Howard paid any attention to the reaction of the family during Mr. Skeffington's reading of the will. Howard worked on a spreadsheet, while Amelia concentrated on her latest discovery from the Gaines file room: Harry Gaines's personal datebook from the year 1915. The pocket diary measured five inches by two inches and was covered in purple leather. The personal identification page was written in pen and ink, in turn-of-the-century penmanship:

> NAME: *Harry Gaines*
> RESIDENCE: *74 East 114th Street*
> MY HOME PHONE IS
> In case of accident please notify *Mr. Barry Shapolsky*
> My weight   My height *5 feet 5½ inches*

Amelia considered the data. In 1915, he would have been sixteen years old, she calculated. At sixteen, he was a vaudeville actor with his own apartment in Harlem. *Amazing*, she thought. She turned the page and found the following:

Fri Jan 1. Orpheum Theatre. 2nd Ave. and 8th St. Went big. Went on a spree.

Sat Jan 2. Orpheum Theatre. Still going big. Held for another day.

Feeling a surge of pride for Harry, she turned the page and the next few pages and saw that Harry had made daily entries for the next month and a half. As the banker read the will to a rapt audience of Gaineses, Amelia continued to trace Harry Gaines's January 1915.

Sun Jan 3. Last day at the Orpheum. Supposed to go to Poughkeepsie. Did not go.

Why not? Amelia wondered. It wasn't fair. This notebook was raising questions to which no one alive had answers.

Mon Jan 4. Unique Theatre. Ave. A and 6th St. Did not go good. Could not get wise to my gags.

Tues Jan 5. Still at the Unique. A frost. Wish it was over.

Stupid audience, Amelia thought.

She lifted her eyes from the diary. Mr. Skeffington had just gotten to the formation of the Trust Committee. From one side of the auditorium to the other, Gaines mouths hung open. Amelia returned to 1915.

Sun Jan 10. Unique Theatre. Sunday concert. More fun than Brownie's.

Mon Jan 11. Supposed to go to Kingston and Poughkeepsie but did not go.

Wed Jan. 13. Not working. Went to HIAS to meet Sam. No Sam.

What's HIAS? Amelia wondered.

Thurs Jan 14. A.M.—Back to Hebrew Immigrant Aid Society. Still no Sam. Quick skidoo to Asbury Park, Main St. Theatre. Went big.

Amelia realized what HIAS stood for. She wondered what business Sam and Harry had there.

Sun Jan 17. Went to N.Y. Went to a friend of mine. Played poker. Lost $6.00.

Tsk, tsk, Amelia thought.

Mon Jan 18. Not working. Went to Star Theatre. Tomorrow deadline at HIAS for money for Father—where is Sam?

He couldn't stay away from the theaters, Amelia thought. *And where* is *Sam?*

Tues Jan 19. Not working. Went to Olympic. Took Miss Lorene Webster along. Deadline for Father passed. Sam never showed. What gives?

Aha, thought Amelia, cocking an eyebrow. *I wondered when we'd get to the ladies. But what's this about Sam?*

Wed Jan 20. Went to Murray Hill. Refused admission. Went home.

Amelia grinned. She imagined young Harry turned away from the box office. A vaudevillian himself, he expected to be admitted gratis. Rather than pay to see other performers, he left. Amelia liked that. She liked his pride.

Sun Jan 24. Last day in Yorkville. Brought Hazel Miller to work with me.

Hazel Miller, Amelia mused. She wondered what Hazel looked like. She also wondered what Harry meant by "work." Did he saw her in half, as in a magic act? Or was she his straight woman? Was Hazel Miller still alive? In a nursing home? Using a walker? Dead for decades? Amelia wanted to know, but she realized that no one could tell her. She looked up. Mr. Skeffington had reached the last few sections of the will.

The Gaineses appeared stupefied, Harry's children most of all. Charles C., Keith, and Rebecca seemed hurt, mystified, and angry, all at the same time. Amelia shook her head. She tried to make out a few words at the bottom of the entry for January 28: "Found Sam, who won't apologize for not helping Father. His mind is made up."

What's *that* about? Amelia was wondering, when she felt Howard elbow her gently in the ribs. She looked at him. He looked in the direction of Mr. Skeffington, who had finished the reading of the will and was calling Amelia's name.

She stood, embarrassed. "I'm sorry," she said, sounding flustered. "I was reading something."

"Amelia, if you're not too busy, perhaps you could come down to the microphone and answer some questions about the will."

"I'd be happy to," she said. She climbed over Howard and reached the aisle, still holding Harry's datebook. She made her way to the front of the room, reached the microphone, adjusted it downward, cleared her throat, and brushed the hair out of her eyes. She was about to address the Gaines family for the first time, and at a most inopportune moment. All of them realized the improbability of a trust committee of relatives barely on speaking terms, each with his or her agenda for the future of the theaters, coming to agreement. All of them saw sixty million dollars flying out the window toward the Federal Treasury in Washington, D.C.

The only people present who looked even remotely happy were Morris Shapolsky and the rest of the New Shap lawyers. Morris, in fact, sought unsuccessfully to suppress a grin. Louis Gaines Shapolsky, the youngest member of Old Shap, took note of Morris's barely contained glee and wondered what it meant. He nudged his father, Moses, who elbowed his sister, Deborah, who woke up a slumbering Henry Clay. They all studied Morris for clues.

"My name is Amelia Vanderbilt," she said, an opening that she considered safe enough. "I guess you've all heard Harry's will. Mr. Skeffington put me in charge of the Gaines account. I'm replacing Mr. Vaccaro, who is—who is no longer with the bank. Howard Person, the deputy chief accountant in the Trust Department, is here. Howard, could you stand up for a minute?"

Howard grudgingly stood up and sat down again.

"Howard and I are going to be on the committee, as you've just heard, along with four of you from the family—Glenda, Keith, Sam David, and Tess—and Mr. Morris Shapolsky. So if you have any questions about the will or the trust or the committee, or anything at all, I guess I can try to answer them for you."

An uncomfortable silence followed. None of the Gaineses wanted to be the first to speak, and no one wanted to be the first to ask or say something that could be used later by another Gaines in litigation.

Finally, Sam David put up his hand. Amelia, relieved, motioned to him.

"What I want to know is this," he said, and he looked extremely displeased at the prospect of the terms of the trust. "Who put Harry up to this? Was it you, Morris?"

Morris stopped grinning. "Absolutely not," he shot back. "It was Harry's idea from the word go."

"Then what are you so happy about?" cracked Louis Gaines Shapolsky, speaking for the firm of Old Shap.

"Who says I'm happy?" Morris asked, trying to look appropriately glum. "I just lost my client and my best friend, and you think I look happy?"

As a performance, it was almost convincing. Harry would have been proud.

"As I understand it," Amelia said, "it was Harry's idea to create a trust that would bring his family together. It was also Harry's idea that the money should go to the federal deficit if the family cannot agree."

"I heard he was out of his mind when he signed it," said Annette Morris Gaines. Annette was Tess's and Sam David's mother and the oldest living relative, if by marriage, of Original Sam. "Doesn't that make it illegal?"

Amelia paused before she answered. She wondered how Annette could have heard that, since only Morris, Howard, and Amelia had been present for the signing. She also thought about her autographed picture from Harry to Anne Frank.

"I was a witness to the will," Amelia said. "And I have to admit that there were moments when Harry wasn't all there. But he was as clear and lucid as any of us when he made up his mind to sign it."

"As lucid as any of us?" Tess repeated sarcastically. "That's not saying much."

"I won't lie to you," Amelia said, choosing her words carefully. "There were moments in there when I thought we should have come back another time. But I am convinced beyond a shadow of a doubt that when Harry signed this will, he knew exactly what he was doing."

Keith put his hand up. "Did Harry really think we could get together on this?" he asked, raising a question that was on the minds of many Gaineses present. "Wasn't he just trying to stick it to us, watching us fight each other for thirty days and then we lose the money anyway?"

Amelia looked pensive. "I guess the person who can best answer that is Mr. Morris Shapolsky."

Morris stood up. "I think my client was misunderstood in his lifetime," he began. "He didn't hate his family. He loved you all very much. I don't like to speak ill of the dead, but I think it's true to say that Harry never worked very hard at making that love clear to you. To any of you. Look, he didn't know how. I'm not going to tell you the whole story of his upbringing and coming from Russia and never knowing his parents and the orphanage and the rest of it. You just have to realize that Harry was a creature of his times. It was a different world back then."

Morris paused for a moment. *Of course it was a different world back then*, he told himself. *I was broke.* He continued:

"I was there when he had the idea for this will. He truly hoped that his money could do something after he was gone that he never knew how to do in his lifetime. And by that I mean make you people forget about all the old fights and will contests and everything else and realize that life is short and that you have each other and you have to get along. I think that's what Harry's intent was. No. I *know* that's what his intent was."

Morris sat down again. The Gaineses, a hard audience to reach, were visibly moved. Even the Old Shap lawyers, Morris's bitter enemies, reached for their handkerchiefs.

"If that's the case," said Amelia, sensing the changed atmosphere in the room, "could we convene our first meeting of the committee at two o'clock this afternoon, right here?"

Sam David considered the matter. He did not want to lend the committee any validity. On the other hand, if he did not show up, the others could outflank him and outvote him. He could not take that chance.

"I'll be there," he said.

"I'll be there," said Glenda, thinking of the strategy she would employ to gain control of the theaters for herself.

"Me too," said Keith. He, Babette, and Sidney, their cat, would remain in New York for as long as it took to secure his vaudeville museum.

"So will I," said Tess. She had to be at the bank this afternoon anyway, for a meeting with her own trust officer, so the first Trust Committee meeting would hardly inconvenience her.

"Of course I'll be there," said Morris, amazed that his words had had such a powerful effect on the Gaineses. He had to watch himself, he decided. If he wasn't more careful, he could inadvertently bring the Gaines family together.

"Howard and I will be there," said Amelia. "Two P.M. I guess if there are no more questions, that's it."

No questions followed. Everyone stood up to leave. Amelia was amazed that the Gaineses had accepted the terms of the will so easily. She did not know that they had not really accepted anything—they were simply in too much shock and anger to express their true feelings. And of course, the will contained a clause saying that anyone who challenged it would automatically lose his or her share.

She still held Harry's 1915 datebook, and she wanted nothing more than to go back to her desk and read through the rest of it. The Trust Committee would work out a quick compromise, and the money would stay with the family—and with the bank. Amelia just knew it. As she watched the Gaineses depart, however, she noticed that none of them were speaking to each other. They were even waiting for one another to clear the room so that they would not get stuck on an elevator together. Amelia may have felt hopeful, but no one else appeared to share her optimism, except, she noted, for Morris.

Amelia realized that someone was standing beside her, waiting quietly for her attention.

"I'm Annette Gaines," she said, introducing herself. Annette, approaching seventy, looked anxious. "Tess and Sam David's mother," she added, assuming correctly that Amelia would not be able to place her without some help.

"How do you do?" said Amelia.

"Fine, thank you," she said. "You know it's a free country and people should be allowed to do whatever they want to do."

"I agree with you," Amelia said, wondering what Annette was talking about.

"No one in the family has ever interfered for a minute with Rebecca and Chester Alan," Annette said firmly. "Not for a minute."

Amelia looked bewildered.

When Annette realized that Amelia in fact did not know what she was talking about, she gave an embarrassed smile. "Nothing, dear," said Annette, and she gave Amelia a little wave and strolled off.

"This family is too strange," Amelia said, wondering for the first time whether Howard might not have been right about them. She saw Morris talking with another Shapolsky, and she went over to speak to him.

"How come Harry waited until now to get involved with his family?" Amelia asked.

Morris gave her an appraising look. "How much do you know about him?" he asked.

Amelia shrugged, as if to say: Not much. She handed him the diary. Morris opened it and turned the pages with fascination. "Where did you get this?" he asked.

"From the file," said Amelia. "There's all kinds of stuff in there."

Morris closed the diary and tapped the front cover. "Nineteen fifteen," he said. "That's years before I met him. But this is how he was when I knew him. Always working. Family came second to him. That's just how he was."

Amelia frowned. "But shouldn't he have been more involved with his relatives?" she asked.

"What is 'should'?" Morris asked. "There is no 'should.' You have to take people as they are. It's true in my business. It's true in yours. Look, Harry preferred the theater. That's all you can say."

Morris handed back the diary. He squeezed her hand, smiled benevolently, and left. Amelia, vaguely dissatisfied with Morris's explanation, watched him go.

11

AMELIA RETURNED to her desk to find Dwight David standing beside it, dressed decently if off-the-rack, munching on one of Granny Vanderbilt's large chocolate chip cookies, and absentmindedly reading some papers on her desk. Amelia's initial reaction alternated between surprise at seeing Dwight David at the bank, since he had skipped the will reading, and pleasure and even pride in the way he looked. He wore gray wool slacks, a pale-blue turtleneck shirt, and a navy blazer. Wing-tip shoes replaced his high-tops. *Howard* never dressed that elegantly. Dwight David noticed Amelia's approving look.

"Where were you?" she asked. A pink message sheet on her desk caught her eye. The name on the message was Elizabeth Herder. Amelia gasped, quickly regained her composure, crumpled the message slip, and threw it in the wastepaper basket under her desk. She returned her attention to Dwight David. "You knew the meeting was at ten."

"Stores don't open till ten," Dwight David replied. "I had a choice of showing up looking like I did yesterday or skipping the meeting. What happened?"

Amelia summed up Harry's will. Dwight David looked philosophical.

"Well, I figured it would be something like that," he said. He reached for another cookie. "You know the number for Air France?"

"Not offhand," said Amelia, reaching into her second drawer for her Pocket Flight Guide. "Why?"

"Well, if those four people have to agree on something, I might as well go back to Antibes. So much for my hot, happening nightclubs. It's a good thing I'm rich."

He accepted the Pocket Flight Guide from Amelia and flipped through it. "I can probably still get on today's Concorde if I hurry." He considered the way he was dressed. "I can drop this clothing off at Tess's homeless shelter. My friends in France wouldn't recognize me, looking like this."

"I think you look very nice dressed like that," said Amelia, surprising herself.

"You do?" Dwight David asked, finding the Air France number and dialing it. "Thanks." And into the phone: "Hi—it's Dwight David. I need one seat on the Concorde to Paris. . . . I'll hold."

Amelia found herself wishing that Dwight David would not leave so quickly. "Aren't you going to stay and try to help the Trust Committee get along?"

Dwight David just grinned. "I really don't think you understand us," he said. "Good cookies."

"They're from my grandmother," said Amelia. "She bakes them and sends them to me."

"Really?" asked Dwight David, impressed. "I've never heard of anything like that in my life. A grandmother who actually does stuff for you. Radical." And into the telephone: "Yes, I'm still holding."

"Couldn't you just stay one day," Amelia asked, "and try to help out with your family? Everybody must be so sad about losing Harry."

Dwight David looked perplexed. "Are we talking about the same family?" he asked. "Look, first of all, except maybe for Keith and Rebecca, and people like that, I don't think anyone in the family really cares that Harry's gone. All they care about is the money. All *I* care about is the money. . . . Sold out? Is there a waiting list? . . . Dwight David Gaines." He put his hand over the mouthpiece. "Can I give your number here?" he asked Amelia. She nodded. Maybe Dwight David wouldn't be leaving so quickly.

Dwight David read off the phone number to the Air France person. "Real full, huh?" he said, sounding discouraged. "A birthday party? Wow. Now that's what I call rich. Thank you." He hung up. "Some French dude rented the Concorde as a birthday party for his girlfriend. That's impressive. I should do something like that sometime."

"You do that just once, and you'll spend the rest of your life riding Trailways," Amelia told him.

"What's Trailways?"

Amelia looked at Dwight David as though he had descended from another planet. "It's a bus company," she said. "It's for people who can't afford planes."

"Hey, I didn't grow up in this country, so don't get on my case if I never heard of Trailways," said Dwight David, a bit defensively. "And besides, now you're starting to sound like Mr. Vaccaro."

The mention of Amelia's predecessor got her thinking. "Will you tell me something?" she asked. "How come Mr. Vaccaro stopped handling your family?"

"We're completely unmanageable," Dwight David said cheerfully. "We can't get along. We only see each other as a family at funerals and in courtrooms. Frankly, I give you only six months before we drive you crazy too."

"Forget it," Amelia said firmly. "Things'll be different from now on. You'll see."

"You're right about that," said Dwight David. "This committee thing has zero chance. So in thirty days we'll be flat broke. That'll be *very* different. It's a good thing my father's got lots of money. Otherwise I might have to, you know, get a job, and stuff like that."

Amelia looked at him. "Dwight David," she said, "I don't think you're dealing in reality."

"I think reality is overrated," he said. "I have a better life than anyone I've ever met. I spend my whole time partying in France. So what if I don't live in the real world? You can't have everything."

"You know what people in Nebraska would call someone like you?" she asked.

"Yup," he said. "*Lucky*. I have lots of money, and they don't. So what? At least I know how to have a good time."

"Don't you have any, you know, conscience about just being a bum?" Amelia asked. She had never met anyone quite like Dwight David before. "Doesn't it bother you that all you do is spend money you didn't earn?"

Dwight David smiled pleasantly. That was his answer.

Amelia, about to criticize him, stopped in midbreath. "You really are different," she said.

"Well, I'm going to get out of these clothes," Dwight David said. "I've got some shopping to do. You can't get good Snickers bars in Antibes. They call them Snickers bars, but it's some kind of European chocolate. The texture's all wrong. It was nice meeting you, Ms. Vanderbilt. I'll be in touch. Good luck with my family. And I hope you find another client thirty days from now, when the Gaineses're all flat broke. Well, maybe not flat broke. But too broke to afford a bank like this."

He picked up another cookie, waved it at her, and headed away.

"Wait!" she said abruptly.

He turned around.

"I could use your help," she said. "Maybe I—maybe I really don't understand your family. Maybe you could give me a few pointers before the first committee meeting."

"Are you inviting me to lunch?" Dwight David asked.

"Um, I guess I am," said Amelia, surprised at herself.

"Okay," said Dwight David. "But you're buying, right?"

Amelia thought about it. "Actually, your family is buying," she said. "It's a business expense, so I'm charging it to your family."

"Now you're talking," said Dwight David, grinning. "I'm glad I'm all dressed up."

"Don't get so excited," said Amelia. "I'm taking you to the bank cafeteria."

"Oh," said Dwight David, suddenly sullen.

"But the food is pretty good," said Amelia. "You'll like it."

Dwight David had his doubts. He had not eaten in a cafeteria since his third and final first semester of college. He grabbed a handful of walnut chocolate chip cookies as insurance, and the two of them made their way to the elevator. Amelia had an idea. She went back to her desk and found the Gaines family tree Howard had given her. Perhaps Dwight David could shed some light on the family over lunch.

The elevator took them to the fourth floor and the large, cheery bank dining hall. Its oak-paneled, thick-carpeted solemnity pleased Dwight David, who had feared that he would be eating from a plastic plate in a mean, fluorescent-lit subbasement room. The bank provided the highly subsidized, top-quality dining hall as a perquisite. The bank had its reasons. Employees who ate in were more likely to get back to their desks more quickly, to talk business during lunch, and to deepen their sense of family ties to the bank.

Amelia and Dwight David looked around for an empty table. There were few. Nine tables were taken up with Shapolskys and Gaineses. On the left side of the room sat members of Old Shap with members of Sam's side of the family. Deborah Shapolsky Bishop sat with Tess Gaines, Moses Shapolsky with Sam David Gaines, Louis Gaines Shapolsky with Chester Alan Gaines, and Henry Clay Shapolsky, the old man of the firm, with Annette Morris Gaines, Original Sam's only remaining daughter-in-law.

Across the room sat members of New Shap with members of Harry's side. Morris Shapolsky sat with Woodrow Sam and Glenda, Edward Shapolsky with Keith and Babette, Barry Shapolsky-Kleinman with Rebecca and Grover Sam, Samantha Shapolsky with Edith Reynolds, Harry's second mistress, and Samuel Gompers Shapolsky, along with Morris the co-founder of New Shap, sat with Charles Chaplin Gaines, Harry's oldest surviving son.

"I think that pretty much tells you all you need to know about our family," said Dwight David. "Nine lawyers, nine tables."

Amelia sighed. It did look daunting, all that disunity. Did she really expect to ride herd on this family? Did she really expect to have any sort of effect on them? If anything, she felt sorry for them. They might not have been the friendliest bunch in the world, but they were on the verge of losing a fortune, simply because they could not get along. As she stood with Dwight David at the edge of the dining hall, one by one the Gaineses and Shapolskys noticed them.

"That's her," she heard repeated at table after table. "She's the one."

The Gaines family apparently had decided to hold Amelia responsible for Harry's plan. It wasn't fair of them, but fairness was not in Gaines genes.

"Maybe we can find someplace else to eat," she told Dwight David, feeling self-conscious.

"I heard some good things about an Italian place a few blocks from here," murmured Dwight David. "Where there won't be so many relatives hanging around."

"I think that's a good idea," Amelia said quietly.

They turned and left the dining hall.

12

FIFTEEN MINUTES later, Dwight David and Amelia found themselves seated in a Wall Street expense-account-type Italian restaurant called Il Sabatino. Dwight David looked happily at the inflated prices. "This is the kind of restaurant my father takes me to when I come to New York," he said.

"Do you come often?" Amelia asked. She found herself hoping that he did.

"Not really," admitted Dwight David. "My father is so successful that it makes me feel like a real fuck-up. I see my mom a lot, though."

"Does she live in France too?" Amelia asked.

"Africa," said Dwight David, buttering a roll. "She writes for *Time*. We're pretty close."

"That sounds unusual for the Gaines family," said Amelia, watching and wincing slightly as Dwight David got crumbs all over the tablecloth.

"Well, she's not really a Gaines," he said. "But what are you going to tell me—your family doesn't fight?"

"Actually," said Amelia, "it doesn't. My family gets along very well."

Dwight David looked up from his bread. "Really?" he asked, a touch of envy in his voice. "That must be great. I've never heard of anybody's family getting along."

"Mom and Dad have a very strong marriage," said Amelia, not without pride. "And Granny and Grampa Vanderbilt have been married for sixty-one years."

"Incredible," said Dwight David, looking at Amelia with new respect. "Harry was married a long time, you know, to Winona and everything, but they never saw each other more than a couple of times a year. I always thought that was the key to a successful relationship. Not that their marriage was successful or anything."

"Doesn't it bother you to come from such an insane background?" Amelia asked, giving voice to a question that she had thought about since meeting Dwight David.

He pondered the matter and popped another piece of buttered roll into his mouth. "Until I met you," he said, "I never knew anybody who came from a happy family. I always realized we were crazy, but I figured, so was every family. Your parents really like each other?" he asked, wanting to believe it.

Amelia smiled. "They're crazy about each other. They're like newlyweds. After twenty-nine years."

Dwight David looked at Amelia as though she were a goddess. "That's the most beautiful thing I've ever heard of in my life," he said, visibly moved. "I was never going to get married, but now I want to. I want to be just like your mom and dad."

He had an idea. "Hey, look," he said. "I can't get on the Concorde until tomorrow. How'd you like to go out to—where are you from?"

"Nebraska," said Amelia, more than slightly alarmed. "Greenwood, Nebraska."

"Yeah, great," said Dwight David. "Greenwood, Nebraska. What is that, like a small town or something?"

"Real small," said Amelia, afraid of where this was leading.

"Come on," said Dwight David. "I can charter a plane and we can go there. I want to meet your parents. A happily married couple. My girlfriend would never believe it. *I* would never believe it. I want to take their picture, so I can show it to people."

"I just don't think so," Amelia said nervously. "I mean, it's a difficult time for them—the farm and everything—"

"Your parents live on a *farm*?" Dwight David shook his head in amazement. "And they love each other? I can't believe you! I just—what *century* is it in Nebraska? It's unbelievable! It's so—" Dwight David groped for the right word. "It's so *authentic*," he proclaimed.

"Yeah, well," she began, "they're really busy with the farm and everything, and I've got to stay here for the Trust Committee meeting for your family. I can't be running off around the country right now."

"Well, maybe over the weekend?" he asked. "They're not going to be having meetings over the weekend, are they?"

"Well, no," Amelia began. "But aren't you flying back to France tomorrow?"

"Oh, no," said Dwight David. "I'm staying for this. A happily married couple. When they die, they should get stuffed for some museum someplace, so that people from later generations can come and see it. Oh, I'm sorry. I don't mean to be talking about your parents that way."

Amelia was surprised to realize how happy she was that Dwight David wanted to postpone his plans.

"It's okay," she said. "I know you're just kidding around."

"I am, but really! A happily married couple. Wow. So you're, like, well-adjusted and everything, huh?"

Amelia blushed. "Well, I'm—"

"And you probably have a totally normal boyfriend and everything?"

"Well, yes, I—" Amelia bit her lip. For some reason, she did not want to admit to Dwight David that she was seeing someone.

"And he's probably got a totally normal job, like, um"—a Belgian accountant he had met in Antibes came somehow to mind—like an accountant?"

Amelia's throat went dry. She gave a small nod.

Dwight David's eyes widened. "He *is* an accountant! I can't believe it! And the two of you have this completely responsible relationship, am I right?"

Amelia shrugged. She could not bring herself to lie. They did.

Dwight David just shook his head. "You're so . . . *young* to be so . . . *normal*," he told her. "I've never met anybody like you."

"I've never met anyone like you, either," Amelia said, telling the truth.

"There's so much you can teach me," said Dwight David. "This may sound crazy, because I'm such a, you know, kid from a crazy background and everything, but all my life there's something I've always wanted to be."

"What's that?" Amelia asked.

Dwight David looked at the tablecloth and noticed that it was covered with crumbs. He brushed at them with his knife, which caused them only to jump up, multiply, and leave the area in front of him more filled with crumbs than before. Then he looked straight at Amelia with a level of honesty in his eyes that she had not seen before.

"*Normal*," he said plaintively. "I want to be normal. I want to do whatever normal people do. Dress normally. Live normally. Not waste money. Finish my education. Get a job. Maybe work in a supermarket, or a drugstore. Just something totally normal like that."

"Well, you don't have to go *that* far," Amelia said.

"I had one relative who was pretty normal," Dwight David said, a far-off look in his eye. "His name was Grover. He would have been my great-uncle."

"What makes you think he was normal?" Amelia said, and then she added quickly, "I don't mean anything by that."

"I have this article about him," Dwight David said. "He was a baseball player in the thirties, and then he went into World War Two. It sounds so, you know, all-American. It sounds really normal to me."

It sounded rather normal to Amelia, as well. "What happened to him?" she asked.

Dwight David looked at Amelia. "He was killed in the war." He added ruefully, "I have a very nice girlfriend and everything, but I don't think she's normal."

"Why not?"

"Well, she's in love with me, for one thing. I mean, how normal is that?"

"Oh, Dwight David, you shouldn't feel that way about yourself," said Amelia. "Just because you're very rich doesn't mean you can't be lovable."

"Really?" he asked, wanting to believe her.

"Really," she said. Just then the waiter arrived.

"Do you have any off-the-menu specials that we should know about?" Dwight David asked. Then he noticed a faint look of disapproval from Amelia. Dwight David cleared his throat. "Maybe I'll just have a steak, medium rare," he said quietly.

"Certainly, sir. And for the lady?"

"Can I get a tuna niçoise salad?" Amelia asked.

"Certainly."

The waiter made notes, took the menus, and left. Dwight David looked thoughtful. "Is salad more normal than steak?" he asked.

Amelia pondered. "I really don't know," she said. "Steak is okay. It's just that I've got to go back to work, and so I wanted something light."

"Oh, work," said Dwight David, a look of comprehension in his eyes. "I see."

Amelia unfolded the Gaines family tree. "Maybe you can help me," she said.

"Wow, look at that," said Dwight David, taking the genealogy and studying it. "Wow. Check out Harry. He did okay with the women."

"And the obstetricians," said Amelia. "Now look. Just take Sam David and Tess, right?"

"Okay," Dwight David said agreeably as he buttered another roll. He noticed that Amelia was watching him. He gave a look that asked: Am I doing something wrong?

Amelia bit her lip. She did not want to be criticizing him all the time. "If you use a bread plate and only butter the part of the roll you're going to eat, you won't get crumbs all over everything. You're getting butter on the family tree."

"Oh, I'm sorry," Dwight David said quickly, wiping away the smudge and accidentally making it bigger. Embarrassed, he folded up the genealogy. "Now, what about Sam David and Tess?" he asked.

"They're brother and sister, right?"

"Right," said Dwight David.

"So they ought to have some kind of decent relationship, right?"

"Um, not exactly," said Dwight David, trying to be delicate about it. "They don't exactly get along."

"Well, why not?"

"Look here," said Dwight David, opening the family tree and pointing to the entry below Tess Gaines. " 'Marie Gaines, 1985'— that's Tess's daughter. Now, do you see a father anywhere here for little Marie?"

Amelia studied the family tree. Little Marie had no father listed.

"Well, we don't know who he was," said Dwight David. "Tess never told us."

"Oh," said Amelia, trying to understand. "Theodore didn't like it?"

"Understatement," said Dwight David. "He hated it. She just wouldn't say who the father was. But that's how Tess is. So Theodore cut Tess out of his will."

"*Really?*" asked Amelia, shocked. "Just because she had a baby without getting married?"

"This could never have happened in Nebraska, right?" Dwight David asked. "There's one more thing. Look at the name of Tess's kid."

Amelia looked at the chart. "Marie," she said.

Dwight David nodded. "Do you see the name Marie anywhere else on this page?"

Tess scanned the family tree for another Marie. She found one in the upper-right-hand corner. She read aloud the relevant data: "Sam Gaines m. Sarah Gurrelts 1911, div. 1929. 1933—m. Marie Benedict."

"Marie Benedict Arnold," said Dwight David. "That's the family joke. Don't you see what happened? Original Sam divorced Sarah—that's Theodore's mother, now, we're talking about the guy's mother—and he took up with this Marie chick. She did something in the Saratoga baths Sam used to go to. I think she was the one who basically covered you with mud when you went up for a treatment. My great-grandfather was into mud baths for health. "So Sam left Sarah. He went out with Marie, this bimbo spa attendant. The mud girl. Sam's son Theodore thinks Sam is an asshole. Then he has a daughter, Tess, who gets pregnant without getting married. And Theodore is old-fashioned and thinks it's a terrible idea. So what does Tess do, just to piss her father off even more?"

"She names the baby Marie," said Amelia, putting two and two together. "After the spa attendant. The one who seduced Theodore's father. According to your version."

"According to what happened," Dwight David insisted. "You know what 'denial' stands for?"

"What?" Amelia asked.

" 'Don't Even Notice I Am Lying,' " Dwight David explained. "The battle cry of the Gaineses."

"And so Theodore was enraged by Tess naming her daughter Marie," Amelia surmised.

Dwight David nodded encouragingly. She was beginning to get it.

"So much so," Amelia concluded, "that he cut her out of the will."

Dwight David's nodding grew increasingly vigorous.

"So why don't Tess and Sam David speak?" Amelia asked.

Dwight David stopped nodding. "I don't know," he admitted.

"Uhh," said Amelia, slumping onto her elbows. "I came so close to understanding."

"It's not like Greenwood, Nebraska?" asked Dwight David.

"It's not like Greenwood, Nebraska," Amelia agreed.

The waiter arrived with lunch. "Can we stop talking about my family?" Dwight David asked. "It really messes up my appetite."

"Sure," Amelia said absentmindedly as they set to their meals. "Tell me about Antibes."

"You'd love it," Dwight David said, setting to his steak. "Maybe you'll come visit."

"Maybe I will," Amelia said. After all, he was her client. What would be the harm in that?

13

THE FIRST MEETING of the Harry Gaines Trust Committee convened at precisely 2:00 P.M. The four family members of the committee—Keith, Glenda, Sam David, and Tess—filed into the boardroom and chose seats as far apart from one another as was humanly possible. Morris Shapolsky took a seat up front, next to Howard Person. Howard thought it odd that Amelia would have lunch with Dwight David on the very day the committee began its work. It did not seem entirely professional to him that she should do such a thing.

Amelia arrived last, prepared for the tension between Tess and Sam David, which was considerable. She also accepted the acrimony between Tess and Sam David on the one side and Keith and Glenda on the other. She did not know why Keith and Glenda had chosen to sit so far from each other. She wondered whether there was bad blood between them, as well. At the center of the table sat a large silver chafing dish filled with Granny Vanderbilt's walnut chocolate chip cookies. So far there had been no takers.

Okay, Amelia thought. All eyes turned to her. She had expected Morris to take the lead role, but he merely looked at her, as did the others. Amelia sucked in a breath and said to herself, *Well, here goes.*

She cleared her throat. "I welcome you," she began, "to this first meeting of the Harry Gaines Trust Committee, as provided by his last will and testament. Our purpose is—"

"We know what our purpose is," Sam David interrupted. "I think the whole thing is a sick joke."

"What are you talking about?" asked Morris, who looked offended, although he secretly agreed.

"There's no way in hell the four of us could agree on anything. Not in thirty days and not in thirty years."

"I agree with Sam David," said Keith. "I think we have no shot of reaching an agreement."

"My sentiments exactly," said Glenda.

Tess nodded. "I feel the same way."

"What I think we're all trying to say," said Sam David, "is that Harry never intended any of us to get a nickel of his estate. He knew we all had all kinds of different plans for the theaters, and he knew we're not exactly a family given to compromise. I think he constructed his will so that we could have at it like scorpions in a bottle, or, in this case, a boardroom, and fight and scream and carry on and make asses of ourselves—*and lose the money anyway.* I think the whole thing was just a crazy joke on Harry's part, and I don't even know why I'm in here."

What little Amelia had learned of the Gaines family in action made her wonder whether perhaps Sam David understood Harry's intentions perfectly.

"May I say something?" asked Morris.

"You're a member too," said Glenda.

"Look, I encouraged Harry to come up with some sort of way of distributing his assets. If it weren't for me, he would have died without a will."

Keith gave him a withering stare. As one of Harry's three surviving children, Keith would have received a large chunk of the estate had Harry died without a will. No one could have challenged it. He could have fulfilled his lifetime ambition and built the grandest vaudeville museum the world had ever seen. If one looked at the will strictly in terms of winners and losers, Keith, his half-brother, Charles C., and his half-sister, Rebecca, were the biggest losers of all.

Morris continued. "I understand that some of you may not like the terms of the will—"

"None of us like the terms of the will," said Tess, thinking of the expanded homeless shelter she would never get to construct. Tess devoted her life, and the income from her own sizable trust fund, to a homeless shelter of her own creation, one that was constantly strapped for funds. She had been eyeing the theaters for years as expansion sites for her shelter.

"But I give you my word of honor," Morris went on, "as Harry's lifelong friend, that he truly regretted not playing more of a role as a family leader. I know he seemed distant at times. I know he seemed not to care. But as my kids sometimes say—"

"Get to the point," ordered Sam David.

"Sorry," said Morris. "I'm trying to say that Harry loved his family, even though he didn't show it outwardly. This is not a joke on his part, this committee. He truly wanted to help his family get together and put the past behind them. And it's my job to try to help that process with all my heart," he said, ending on a rather sanctimonious note.

"That's very generous of you, Morris," said Sam David. "Why is it that whenever you get generous, I feel like reaching to make sure my wallet is still in my back pocket?"

Morris replied hotly. "Why is it that after I shake hands with you, I feel like counting my fingers?"

"Morris, please," said Howard, speaking up for the first time. "Sam David. Look, I understand this family hasn't always gotten along so well, but could you please at least make an effort to take this process seriously? There's a lot of money at stake, and it doesn't affect just the four of you. It affects the whole Gaines family. From Annette Morris Gaines down to little Marie Gaines. Okay?"

The Gaines family members, as well as Morris and Amelia, looked at Howard with a measure of respect. He had certainly done his homework.

"Let's just go around the room," said Amelia. "Let's see whether there's any common ground here. Maybe the whole process could be easier than you all think. Sam David, what would you do with the theaters if you had control?"

Sam David looked at Amelia as though she had finally said something sensible. "I would do the one thing that would maximize profits for this family. I would tear those stupid theaters down."

"Over my dead body," snapped Glenda, who was not about to let a descendant of Sam rob Harry's side of the family of their rightful inheritance, and who was especially not about to give up her own dream of running three Broadway theaters.

"Glenda's got that one right," said Keith, who did not intend to surrender without a battle his dream of creating a memorial to Harry and vaudeville.

"I'm with the two of them," said Tess, who could not abandon entirely her dream of a larger homeless shelter.

"You people have no conception of money," Sam David told his relatives. "What would you possibly do with those properties that would net a greater return than sixty-story buildings? Tell me. I'm listening."

Silence. Keith, Glenda, and Tess all realized that from a strictly financial point of view, Sam David was right.

"Well, what about some of the others?" Amelia asked. "Tess, what would you do if you could choose?"

Tess stared at Sam David as she spoke. "I would turn those buildings into the best-quality homeless shelters this city has ever seen."

Sam David snorted. Keith nodded slowly. "I understand your philanthropic impulse, Tess," he said, "but isn't sixty million dollars a lot of money to spend on the homeless? Especially when you consider that that's the bulk of this entire family's patrimony?"

"This family could give up the sixty million," Tess responded, "and we'd still be okay. You have your own fortune in real estate, and so does my brother. Chester Alan makes a half million a year as a heart surgeon, and Dwight David's trust funds make even more money than *he* can spend. I don't exactly see how those sixty million dollars are essential to the well-being of this family."

Amelia found herself surprised by her reaction to Tess's comments about Dwight David's spending habits. She was feeling protective of him.

"But is that what Harry would want?" Glenda asked. "He built theaters. *Broadway* theaters. Do you really think he would want unemployed people sleeping in them?"

"In the first place," Tess responded, "unemployed people sleep in them now! You know and I know that the only people who go in those theaters today are drunks and bums."

It was true. The theaters, once grand palaces, had fallen on rough times and offered third-run, martial arts, and soft-core pornography films to an audience often sorely lacking in sobriety or even enough money for a bed for the night.

"If Harry minded unemployed people," Tess continued, "he could have kicked them out of the theaters years ago. So I think a homeless shelter is not all that far from what the theaters have turned into. And in the second place, not all homeless people are unemployed. Many of them have jobs but just don't have a place—"

"Please don't lecture us on the homeless," Sam David said acidly. "On the other hand, if you want to tell us about unwed mothers, I think we'd all be willing to listen to your expert testimony."

Tess glared at him. "You're such an asshole," she said. "I wouldn't vote with you if my life depended on it."

"Please," said Amelia, hoping to head off a disaster. "What about you, Keith? What would you do?"

Keith cleared his throat. "For many years," he began, as though he were making a speech to hundreds instead of a comment to the other members of the committee, "for many years, people have forgotten about vaudeville and its contribution to the American theater. People are also forgetting about the role played by our illustrious relative Harry Gaines, one of the pioneers of vaudeville comedy."

"Oh, Christ," said Sam David, looking at the ceiling. He noticed the molding for the first time. He liked it. He wondered how much it would cost to have such a molding installed in his office.

Keith glared at him. "I didn't interrupt you, did I? So please don't interrupt me. Anyway, people are starting to forget Harry Gaines."

"And the sooner the better," cracked Sam David.

"I'll ignore that," Keith said graciously. "I would use the theaters to construct a museum of vaudeville dedicated to my father's memory. I think no nobler use—"

"If I can't lecture on the homeless, you can't lecture on nobler uses," Tess interrupted.

Keith looked dismayed. "I'm just trying to answer Amelia's question," he said.

"We've only got thirty days," said Sam David. "We can't waste twenty-nine listening to you rattle on about your father. This isn't some group of idiots. We all *knew* Harry. Don't try to lie to us."

"Thank you, Keith," Amelia said firmly, trying to shut Sam David up. "Now, Glenda, how would you use the theaters?"

Glenda's expression suggested that there could be no question. "I'd use the theaters as theaters," she said. "Regular Broadway theaters. That's what they are, aren't they? Look, I agree with the rest of you—let's clean them up and get the drunks and bums and everyone else out of there. Those are Broadway theaters in the Broadway district. They've got history. You can't just tear them down. I think Harry would love it if regular Broadway audiences were coming back to his theaters, night after night, for great shows. Comedies, dramas, musicals, everything."

"And just who would run these Broadway theaters?" Sam David asked.

"Well, I would," admitted Glenda.

The meeting dissolved in snorts and derisive laughter.

"What's so funny?" she asked. "I'm the only one in the room with Broadway experience. I've acted in sixteen plays. I *know* the theater."

"You're not even a Gaines," said Sam David.

The comment stung the sensitive Glenda. She half expected that Sam David would accuse her of carpetbagging. "You're barely related to Harry yourself," she snapped back. "And at least when I got married, I stayed married."

"My condolences to Woodrow Sam." Sam David grinned.

"Okay, please," said Amelia. "Now we've each had a chance to hear what the others would do if they were in charge. Does anyone have an idea that could be the basis for some kind of compromise?"

The others, Morris and Howard included, looked at Amelia as though she were insane.

"Well, neither do I," she admitted. "Look, we've gotten through a whole discussion, and we were able to talk like, well, like normal people about it. I think it's a good sign. I think if we all try really hard, we can get an agreement in the next thirty days."

"I think you're on drugs," said Sam David.

"Well, maybe I am," said Amelia. "I'd just hate to see you lose the sixty million. Today is Tuesday. What if we met again here next Monday, six days from now—would that be okay? Two o'clock? Just to see if there's any movement?"

The Gaineses present nodded grudgingly. "Morris?" Amelia asked. "Is that okay for you?"

"As if he has any other clients at all," snapped Sam David.

Morris gave Sam David a sarcastic look. "I think my calendar will permit me to be here."

"It means I have to stay in New York," said Keith. "Frankly, I think the whole thing is impossible. I want to go back to Aspen."

"Sixty million dollars,' said Howard. "Your museum of vaude-ville."

Keith reluctantly agreed. "I'll be here," he said.

"We'll see you all then," Amelia concluded. The Gaineses, looking no happier than when they had entered the boardroom, filed out, one at a time, the avoidance of conversation their highest priority. Morris departed next. Only he, of all seven committee members present, had a slight smile on his face. Amelia and Howard were left.

"I got the tickets for *Bliss*," Howard said, once they were alone. "We're twelfth row center."

To Howard's surprise, the news seemed to startle Amelia. "Isn't *Bliss* a musical?"

Howard nodded, confused.

"But my folks hate musicals," Amelia said nervously.

Howard thought of the money he had laid out for the tickets. "You said your folks wanted to see a musical," he said. "You just told me that."

"I did?" Amelia asked. "Are you sure?"

"Of course I'm sure," Howard insisted. "I mean, I think I'm sure."

"Can you take the tickets back?" Amelia asked nervously. "I mean, they must be expensive."

"I can try," Howard said, looking at Amelia and trying to figure her out. Perhaps the Gaineses were already taking their toll on her. "Do you—are we on for dinner?"

Amelia looked sadly at Howard. "I can't," she said. "Dwight David was going to give me some more background on the family."

"Dwight David," Howard repeated evenly. "The number-one cash drain on the Gaines family fortune."

Amelia glanced sharply at Howard. "That's the one," she said.

Howard drew together the papers before him. "He's the worst of all," he said.

Amelia grinned. "You're jealous," she said.

"I am not jealous of Dwight David Gaines," Howard said, and he strode out of the boardroom.

Denial, Amelia thought: Don't Even Notice I Am Lying. The Gaineses obviously weren't the only ones who acted that way, she decided.

14

At LEAST one pair of Gaineses loved each other deeply, treated each other with kindness, and could not bear extended periods of time during which they could not see each other. Unfortunately, they were not married to each other.

Chester Alan Gaines, at fifty-four the grandson and oldest relative on Sam's side of the family, worked as a cardiologist at Manhattan Hospital. Rebecca Reynolds Gaines, Harry's youngest child and only daughter, worked in the same place, as a cardiac nurse. Their romance was the stuff of hospital legend, taking place as it did in unoccupied patients' rooms, large supply closets, darkened operating theaters, and suites reserved for the families of wealthier patients. For many years, Chester Alan and Rebecca believed that no one, in or out of the hospital, knew of their passionate assignations. They were wrong; everyone knew. Sightings of the pair *in flagrante delicto* had brightened the day of numerous of their colleagues over the past twenty-two years.

On the top floor of Manhattan Hospital are eight luxury suites rented out to visiting families of extremely wealthy patients. Doctors with the status and pull of a Chester Alan could command these suites for themselves during those periods when a string of patients required their attention all at once. Chester Alan used his leverage with the hospital administration immediately after hearing of

125

Harry's death. He arranged to have a suite booked for him for a full week.

As Rebecca waited in the suite for Chester Alan to finish his day's rounds, she placed the last of twenty-two candles in a black forest chocolate cake, Chester Alan's favorite, that she had baked late the night before, to celebrate the anniversary of the commencement of their affair. Their celebration, of course, would be muted by Harry's recent passing. Rebecca finished with the candles, and her thoughts turned to the trust agreement her father had created and the various relatives who stood to benefit under it.

Until his eighty-seventh birthday, Harry would invite Rebecca to dinner on all those nights when she was not dining or otherwise engaged with Chester Alan. Many thought that Harry was in love with Rebecca in a suitor's sense and not just a fatherly sort of way. Harry would not have denied it, although he would never have acted upon such impulses. The daughter of his middle age was faultless in his eyes, and he could not spend enough time with her. He would sing her old songs from vaudeville. He would tell her the stories about life on the road in the teens and twenties that Keith, Charles C., and Harold Lloyd would have loved to hear. He told her about the women he met and slept with decades ago, remembering for her all the details—how they smelled, whether they were married, what line or approach he had used, whom he went back and saw every time he returned to a town.

Rebecca could be said to be the only person, male or female, who truly interested Harry. The details of his own life meant little to him. He could wear a suit until it was shiny or shoes until they looked so bad that women gave him a look of dismay. He missed appointments, meals, dates, and, occasionally, court appearances, but he had never failed to show, on time and ready to roll, for any booking throughout his career. He treated his relationship with Rebecca in the same careful way. Even had he not favored Rebecca financially and emotionally, her brothers would have been jealous merely of the fact that when Harry told her he would meet her somewhere, he invariably was there, on time if not ten minutes early, pacing, and carrying for her a little gift he had picked up on the way.

Once, to the consternation of her mother, Edith, and everyone else in the family, Harry took Rebecca to Rockefeller Center on the first day of a school vacation during ninth grade, got her a passport, taxied to Idlewild, as JFK was then known, and flew her to France with nothing more than the clothes on their backs. They had dinner in Paris, went to the Folies Bergère, bought a change of clothes, sneaked into the Luxembourg Gardens at two in the morning (Harry pointing out a bench behind which he had copulated at two in the morning thirty years earlier), and flew home the next day. Edith had to be almost forcibly restrained from bringing kidnapping charges against the father of her daughter. Why Harry's sons talked her out of it is something Edith never understood. Harry, incidentally, never thanked them for doing so.

Rebecca sighed and checked her watch. Chester Alan would be there soon. She lit the twenty-two candles, but she hardly felt like celebrating. A few moments later, precisely on time, Chester Alan knocked softly at the door. He entered and they embraced. Chester Alan gazed at the cake and the blazing candles on top.

"We've lasted longer than most marriages," he said, blowing out the candles. "I love you very much, darling. Nothing could ever come between us."

"I guess the secret is not to get married," Rebecca said. "I love you too. I just miss Daddy."

"Me too," said Chester Alan, pulling her close and stroking her hair. "And they just admitted Charles C. is doing worse. Harry's death was a real shock to him."

Charles Chaplin Gaines, like his father, had suffered the odd heart attack or two over the years. Chester Alan had discovered the cause of but not the cure for the heart ailments that had afflicted many of the men of the family over the years. He attributed it to a slight hardening of heart tissue; in honor of his research, the disorder had been named Gaines's syndrome.

Charles C., unlike his father, refused to let Chester Alan treat him. Except for his friendship with Tess, Charles C. punctiliously observed the rift between relatives of Harry and relatives of Sam.

"What's his status?" Rebecca asked.

"A three," said Chester Alan. Manhattan Hospital, like many

hospitals, summed up its patients' health in a code about which families were not informed. Patients were fives, fours, threes, or twos. Fives and fours could count on going home soon. Threes could look forward to relatively long hospitalizations. Twos were not expected to survive.

"That's not so good," she said. "Maybe you can just stop by his room and say hi."

Chester Alan gave her a rueful look. "You think he'd even talk to me?"

Rebecca sighed. "This family," she said. "You'd think something like losing Harry would bring people together."

"Maybe *you'd* think that," said Chester Alan. "What did you hear about the Trust Committee?" he asked.

"I heard plenty," Rebecca said. "Keith and Glenda both called. I haven't heard from them in years. They want me to lean on you to lean on Sam David and Tess."

"That's funny," said Chester Alan, laughing for the first time since Harry's funeral. "Sam David and Tess called *me*. They want *me* to lean on *you* to lean on Keith and Glenda."

"What a family!" Rebecca said, shaking her head.

"But where does that leave us?" Chester Alan asked.

"I don't know where it leaves us," Rebecca said gingerly, disengaging from Chester Alan's embrace. "It leaves *me* screwed."

"What are you talking about?" Chester Alan asked, surprised. "Harry was just trying to bring the family together."

"With my money," Rebecca said, a trace of bitterness in her voice.

"With *your* money?" Chester Alan asked. "When was it ever your money?"

"Until Morris got to Daddy and gave him that stupid idea about getting along! I swear, he had to be delusional when he signed that thing."

"He was not delusional," Chester Alan insisted. "I was there."

Rebecca stared at him. "*You were there?*" she asked, stunned. "You let him just sign away my inheritance? To people like Sam David and Annette?

"What was I supposed to do?" Chester Alan asked, hurt. "Take the pen out of his hands? Tear up his will? And you don't have to attack Sam David and Annette. They're my relatives, for chrissake."

"Oh, now you're on their side!" Rebecca exclaimed. "They treated Daddy so badly—they treat *us* so badly! Annette's been so mean to both of us! You know that!"

"Yes, but—"

"Yes, but nothing! Now that you're all gonna get a piece of Daddy's money, you turn into one of them!"

"I am not 'one of them'!" Chester Alan retorted, raising his voice. "Don't say that! I love you! We're in this together!"

"Yeah, sure," said Rebecca, turning away. "You're just Sam David with a stethoscope!"

"Don't you ever say that to me!" he exclaimed. Then he calmed down a bit. "Look. Maybe you're just upset about losing Harry."

"Maybe I am," Rebecca said, unsure whether she was more upset at Harry's will or at Chester Alan's thinking that the will was a good idea. She turned back to face Chester Alan.

They stared at each other. Nothing in twenty-two years had caused so serious a disagreement between them. A long moment passed.

"I think I better go," Chester Alan said quietly. "This isn't productive."

Rebecca made no effort to stop him. Chester Alan, stung by Rebecca's words, left the suite and closed the door softly behind him.

15

JUST A FEW more minutes," said Sam David Gaines's harried secretary. Amelia had already spent twenty-five minutes camped outside the door to his office. She had chosen the young real estate mogul as the first committee member to visit privately in order to discuss the possibility of compromise. True, she had arrived without an appointment, but she assumed that Sam David would be willing to see her at least for a short while.

The news about the will must have plunged Sam David into a foul mood, because Amelia could hear him yelling and sputtering through the closed office door. Sam David's secretary, a maternal sort named Mrs. Perkins, noticed Amelia's reaction to the muffled but unmistakable expletives.

"He must be upset," she said apologetically.

A few expletives later, Amelia and Mrs. Perkins could hear the dead bolt on Sam David's door slide into place, and all was silent. Amelia saw Mrs. Perkins roll her eyes.

Amelia looked at her watch again and wondered how long it might be before Sam David deigned to see her. Then she remembered she had in her bag the 1931 letter from Sam David's grandfather Sam Gaines to Sam's son Woodrow. She took it out, unfolded it carefully, and began to read.

July 30, 1931

Dear son,

　　I have received your special delivery letter
and am very much disturbed about the condition
of the unfinished business. Of course, it
requires our personal attention at the present
time, since Pocini must be evicted. On the
whole, it requires *your* personal attention,
especially the collection of rents.
　　About Pocini. You must see to their eviction
immediately. He has been a terrible tenant, with
violent tendencies, and a drunk to boot. We have
received many complaints from his neighbors both
within and without the building, and from the
police.
　　As far as your vacation is concerned, I
wouldn't like to spoil your plans, but for me to
go back to the city at this time is almost an
impossibility, because, as per the doctor's
instructions, I am taking mud and mineral
treatments, and by returning to the city now,
practically all these treatments I have taken
would be wasted, as I feel that they are doing
me good.

"You creep!" Amelia said aloud to the letter. Mrs. Perkins
glanced at Amelia and then returned to her typing. Amelia read on:

　　Dear Woodrow, as much as I am very anxious and
very much uneasy about the present condition of
our office, I am compelled to take this step on
account of my ill health.

"Yeah, sure," Amelia said, staring at the letter, wondering why
she was taking Woodrow's side over Sam's. She continued to read:

　　We made a bad mistake in not arranging matters
so that the business would not suffer.
　　It is advisable that you settle with the old
superintendent to leave the premises at once, as
it is bad policy to have the old

As Amelia turned the page, she noticed something odd—the
letter was a carbon copy. Sam, ostensibly on his vacation in
Saratoga, was writing to his son, but he had typed the letter instead

of putting it in his own handwriting. Typing seemed so formal and distant to Amelia, as did the letter's tone. But then, on top of all that, Sam had seen fit to make a carbon copy of the letter. Why would he do that? You only made copies of things if you needed legal proof that you wrote the things you claimed you wrote. Did Sam believe he needed to create legal proof about what he had written to his own son? Did he trust Woodrow that little? Or was Woodrow untrustworthy, and was this the only way Sam could write to him?

Amelia shook her head slowly. She reread the last sentence of the first page and turned to the second page of the letter:

```
superintendent there when the new superintendent
is installed and in charge.
     I believe that your personal attention is
very urgent and would suggest that you postpone
your vacation for another week. I can't rest
here, since we intend to take steps in obtaining
assignments of rents, and the foreclosure of
mortgages. I believe that about the 10th of
August, everything will be in good shape and
myself in better health and that would be a good
time to start your vacation.
     I regret interfering with your plans, but I
believe I am justified. By canceling your
vacation you will be doing justice to both the
business and myself, and will avoid great
financial damage. Finally, at the risk of seeming
repetitious, you certainly should not leave
without handling Pocini promptly, as failure to
do so would have serious consequences for the
108th St. property.
     With kindest regards, I am,

                         Your loving father,
                         S. Gaines
```

Amelia looked at the signature. Sam had not signed this copy of the letter. He had not even left enough room for a signature. *What kind of loving father was that?* Amelia asked herself. *No wonder this family is so screwed up.*

Amelia heard the sound of the door being unbolted. She looked up just in time to see a blur rush past her into Sam David's office. The blur was a recently graduated M.B.A. from one of

America's leading business schools, a young man with carefully parted hair, a heavily starched shirt, and highly polished shoes. He went to stand before Sam David with his report, nervously awaiting Sam David's questions. His name was Richard Bickle. Amelia decided to eavesdrop.

"Sit down, Bickle," Sam David said. "You've done a good job."

Bickle, who had not been to bed for three straight nights, sighed mightily.

Sam David regularly chewed out his staff, whether they deserved it or not, because he believed that yelling at people on a regular basis was good for them. Bickle had prepared himself for the inevitable dressing-down.

Ever since Harry had been hospitalized, Sam David's entire business had gone on its highest level of alert. Bickle knew that upon Harry's death, Sam David would have to act fast to grab Harry's three theaters from his less far-thinking relatives. It was for their own good, of course.

"Thank you, sir," said Bickle, who had anticipated being yelled at if not fired. Sam David paid his M.B.A.'s extremely well, which gave him all the more reason to believe that he could yell at them whenever he felt like it, which was most of the time.

"Just a few questions," said Sam David.

Bickle sat timidly, awaiting the worst. The numbers on the cash flow chart Bickle had provided so tickled Sam David, however, that he could not even bring himself to raise his voice to the young man. Amelia had to strain to hear the conversation. She held open a magazine so as to disguise her eavesdropping from Mrs. Perkins.

"These numbers are fine," said Sam David. "Say I got control tomorrow. What would keep me from starting demolition on the theaters?"

"Oh," said Bickle, and he cleared his throat. He had expected Sam David to ask this question. "The first challenge might come from the theater community," he said. "They would probably resent somebody tearing down three historic theaters at the same time. Or even one at a time."

"Do they have to find out?" Sam David asked.

"It's hard to hide that many wrecking crews in the middle of Times Square," said Bickle.

"Mm," said Sam David, agreeing. "Well, can't we do it at night? Sneak 'em in?"

Bickle looked horrified. "Demolition at night is against the law, sir. Didn't you get a suspended sentence for that building you tore down on East Sixteenth Street?"

"That was a long time ago," said Sam David, scratching his head. "I was hoping maybe people would have forgotten."

"Those theater people can make an awfully big stink," said Bickle. "My research shows that the last time they tore down two Broadway theaters, around 1978, fifty Broadway stars and producers came to the scene and got themselves arrested. It was terrible publicity for the developer."

"What do you recommend?"

Bickle flipped through his notes and offered Sam David two pages of computer printout, stapled together. "I took the liberty of drawing up a list of theater organizations and asking people there how much of a contribution they might accept in order to— ahem—overlook our little demolition project. I was very surprised. We can buy them off for a lot less than I thought."

Sam David scanned the list and read a few entries aloud. "Hmm. Theater Appreciation Fund, eighty thousand dollars. Actors' Benevolent Fund, fifty thousand dollars. Broadway Historical Society, twenty-five thousand dollars. You mean if I donate"—he flipped to the second page and the bottom line—"four hundred grand to these groups, then I won't get a single actor or director picketing the wrecking crews?"

"Yes, sir," said Bickle, blushing slightly with pride in his accomplishments.

"Won't the media find out about these gifts?" Sam David asked suspiciously. "They'd play them as bribes. I'd look terrible."

"Not if you made them in cash, sir," Bickle suggested respectfully.

Sam David looked at his young assistant with a measure of admiration. "Good *thinking*, Bickle," he said. "Go to work on it. Get this money distributed by the end of the week."

Bickle's blush deepened. "Yes, sir," he said. "Thank you, sir."

"What's the next problem?" Sam David asked.

Bickle consulted his notes. "It relates to the size of the buildings," he said. "They're too big for the area. The parcels were zoned for much smaller buildings. Apparently the parcels were zoned in the late nineteenth century, before people even imagined buildings as tall as these."

"So what?" asked Sam David. "Can't we get a variance?"

Bickle paused before he spoke. "I checked with our Legal Department, sir. They said that the zoning commission isn't giving out any more zoning variances in the Times Square area."

Sam David's eyes narrowed. "Well, why the hell not?"

"It has to do with light and air, sir."

"Light and air?" Sam David asked.

"Yes, sir. Every time there's a new skyscraper in Manhattan, it reduces the amount of light and air that is available at ground level."

"That's ridiculous," said Sam David. "Nobody comes to West Forty-fifth Street to work on their tan."

"That's what I told Legal, sir," said Bickle, feeling more and more at ease in the presence of his usually difficult boss. "They said forget about it."

"Well, what do *you* say?" asked Sam David, putting young Bickle to the test.

"Well, sir, if the zoning board won't give us a variance, the only way to get one is to apply to the City Council and the Mayor's Office. I—I happened to notice that the entire City Council is up for reelection next year, and I took the liberty of—of contributing sixty thousand dollars to each of the incumbents."

"In my name?" asked Sam David, eyes wide. "If it looks like I'm trying to bribe the City Council, I could be crucified."

"Well, sir, I thought of that, sir," said Bickle. "I took the liberty of making the contributions through a shell corporation that you control that no one in the city except your legal staff and you and I know that you control. It's actually a limited partnership run through a Bahamian offshore leasing corporation that theoretically donates mattresses to the city for use in homeless shelters. The corporation is called the Homeless Rescue Foundation."

"Who set it up?" Sam David asked.

"I did," Bickle modestly admitted.

"We don't actually donate mattresses to the homeless shelters, do we?" Sam David asked.

"Oh, no, sir," Bickle replied, demonstrating shock at even the thought of it. "I know how you feel about homeless people."

"Does anyone else know we don't give any mattresses to the homeless?" Sam David asked.

"Oh, no, sir," said Bickle. "That's our little secret."

Sam David gave Bickle a broad smile. "Bickle, you're a smart young man."

"Thank you, sir," Bickle said, blushing again. "Anyway, I called up each City Council member and told him or her that the sixty thousand dollars from the Homeless Rescue Foundation actually came from you, but you didn't want anyone to know because you wanted to remain unknown in your efforts to help the homeless."

"Help the homeless?" Sam David laughed. "I *hate* the homeless!"

Amelia put down the magazine and made no pretense of not listening. So did Mrs. Perkins.

"Yes, sir," said Bickle. "All of us who work for you know that."

"The homeless don't pay taxes, Bickle," said Sam David.

"I know that, sir," said Bickle. He could tell that Sam David was in a good mood. Whenever Sam David started to condemn the homeless, it meant that he was in a good mood.

"The homeless don't hold steady jobs," said Sam David.

"I know that, sir," said Bickle, waiting it out.

"The homeless detract from the ambience of the city and therefore hurt real estate values," said Sam David, his voice rising.

"I know that, sir," said Bickle, wondering how much longer this would go on.

"The homeless don't—" Suddenly Sam David's tone softened. "The homeless," he said quietly, "*make me feel guilty.* I *hate* feeling guilty."

"Yes, sir,' said Bickle, daring to interrupt. "Anyway, sir, in my opinion, as a result of your generous and anonymous contributions funneled through the Homeless Rescue Foundation, I think the

City Council would be kindly disposed toward any sort of request for a zoning variance that you might make."

Sam David stopped thinking about the homeless and considered Bickle's conclusion. "I think you're right," Sam David said, and nodded. "Good work."

"Thank you, sir," said Bickle.

"I wish I could start tomorrow," Sam David said. "The only problem is the rest of my family."

"Yes, sir," said Bickle. He, like everyone else who worked for Sam David, had often heard Sam David rail at the other members of his family, who, as Sam David saw it, did not appreciate all the hard work and creativity that Sam David brought to bear on behalf of the family real estate holdings. In Bickle's opinion, Sam David thought only slightly less of the homeless than he did of his family.

"I got a message from Old Shap," Bickle said, quickly and deftly changing the subject. "It's about Morris."

"What about Morris?" Sam David asked suspiciously.

"He visited Harry every day in the hospital, sir," said Bickle.

"And?" Sam David asked. He knew that much already.

"And the day before Harry died, when Morris left the Hospital, he was smiling."

"Morris was smiling?" Sam David asked. His eyes narrowed. He did not like the sound of that at all. In the anteroom, Amelia wondered how Morris could smile when his client and closest friend was so clearly *in extremis*.

"Yes, sir, he was smiling," said Bickle. "According to my information, he was 'grinning contentedly and looking relieved as he left the hospital at two forty-three P.M.' "

Bickle trembled slightly, finding himself in the unpleasant position of conveying bad news to his employer. On the other hand, no one else in Sam David's office had the courage to bring the news to the boss. He looked up at Sam David, bracing himself for an explosion.

Sam David merely nodded. "Bickle?" he said.

"Yes, sir?" Bickle asked, rising.

"Find out why Morris was smiling."

"Yes, sir."

"And then find out what it's going to take for me to wipe that smile off his face."

"Yes, sir." Bickle, sensing that the discussion had ended, walked to the office door.

"And Bickle?"

"Yes, sir?" He held his breath.

"About those contributions," said Sam David, and then he nodded and gave the thinnest of smiles. "Good work."

"Thank you, sir!" said Bickle, overjoyed, and he went off to try to find out why Morris had left the hospital smiling.

As Bickle left, Mrs. Perkins buzzed. "Ms. Vanderbilt is still here," she told him.

Sam David grunted and came to the doorway. "I'm very busy," he told Amelia, by way of greeting.

Amelia noticed that Sam David had decorated his workplace in a silver-and-black Massive Power Trip motif. A photograph of Sam David's grandfather, Original Sam, dominated the office. The photograph, looking like something from the 1920s and blown up to twenty by thirty inches, reflected in Original Sam's expression the same combination of self-satisfaction and insecurity that Amelia had noticed in Sam David. One odd thing about the photograph was its dimensions. It looked considerably narrower than a conventional rectangular photograph. The original shot was of two men, Amelia realized, not just one. Part of an elbow and half an ear were plainly visible to the right of Sam Gaines. For some reason, Amelia believed that the elbow and ear belonged to Harry.

"I just want to talk to you for a moment," Amelia said, appalled yet not surprised by his rudeness.

"Talk about what?" snapped Sam David, blocking the doorway. "That lovely idea you gave Harry?"

"I didn't give him the idea!" Amelia exclaimed. "It was his idea! You can ask Morris!"

"I don't think I'd like to ask Morris," Sam David said. "I don't think I trust Morris."

"You're really not being fair to me, Mr. Gaines," said Amelia. "I'm just trying to do the best job I can. I really don't think you can blame a trust officer for carrying out a dying man's last request."

Sam David softened. "I guess I am shooting the messenger," he said. "But if you've come over here to see if there's grounds for compromise . . ."

Amelia held her breath. This was exactly why she had come over.

". . . you better forget about it. I'm not compromising with Tess. Or Glenda. Or Keith. I don't even speak to them, let alone compromise with them."

"I just thought—" Amelia began.

"I'm sorry," said Sam David. He turned and closed the door on her.

Amelia looked crestfallen.

"You get used to it," Mrs. Perkins said, and she went back to her typing. Amelia sighed and prepared to return to the bank.

16

Less than an hour later, at the firms of Shapolsky and Shapolsky (Old Shap) and Shapolsky & Shapolsky (New Shap), two meetings had begun, with the purpose of analyzing the results of the first meeting of the Harry Gaines Trust Committee.

At Old Shap, attorneys to Original Sam's side of the family, the discussion went this way:

"I still think Morris has an angle," said Moses Shapolsky.

"Like what?" asked his first cousin Deborah Shapolsky Bishop. "He's in as much trouble as we are."

"Then why didn't he looked troubled?" young Louis Gaines Shapolsky asked. "Sam David said he was the happiest guy in the room. Morris doesn't exactly have a poker face. When he's in deep shit, everybody knows it."

"He must have an angle," Moses repeated.

"If Morris has an angle," reasoned Henry Clay Shapolsky, the seventy-three-year-old dean of the firm, "if I may use the indecorous language of my grandson, then it is *we* who are in 'deep shit.'"

"You know, Grandpa," Louis G. began, addressing Henry Clay, "if your old man, Barry, had taken a piece of the business instead of legal fees, we wouldn't be the Gaineses' lawyers. We'd be their partners."

Barry Shapolsky, the progenitor of the firm, had grown up in the same orphanage as Harry and Sam Gaines and had represented them in their real estate transactions. Sam chose the land to buy, and Harry contributed his sizable vaudeville income.

"Partners with the Gaineses?" Moses, incredulous, asked his son, Louis G. "Are you out of your mind?"

"How can you speak that way to your son?" Deborah, appalled, asked Moses.

"Think of it," said Louis G., undaunted. "Even if they sued us, we'd still have a piece of that sixty million. Instead of just crumbs."

"Morris must have figured out how to get more than crumbs," said Henry Clay.

"But how?" asked Moses.

"Beats me," said Louis G.

"Same," said Deborah.

"We've got to find out how," said Moses. "And quickly."

All nodded in somber agreement. The members of Old Shap were not about to let themselves be screwed over by anyone, let alone by the members of New Shap. It was a matter of Shapolsky family honor.

Across town, the atmosphere in the offices of New Shap, Morris's firm, was decidedly more cheerful. The reason for their great glee could be found in the seemingly innocuous language of section four, subhead seven, of the last will and testament of Harry Gaines. That subsection read: "In the event that the Trust Committee is unable to agree as to the disposition of the Trust, the Trustee is hereby instructed to donate the proceeds of a sale of all assets of the Trust, as conducted by the law firm of Shapolsky and Shapolsky, less appropriate commissions and fees, to the Federal Government as a gift to reduce the Federal Deficit."

"Tell me again how you came up with the idea," Barry Shapolsky-Kleinman asked his beloved uncle Morris.

"It was nothing, really," Morris said modestly. "Look, Harry had his idea that his family should get along. I knew it would be impossible. And I started thinking I've done a disservice to this firm, to my own flesh and blood. Because under his plan, all his money should go to the government. I'm an old man. I can retire. But the rest of you, you'd have to make a living, like regular lawyers. Without the Gaines money to fight over, where would any of us be?"

A collective shudder passed over the members of the firm.

"So I thought," Morris continued, "boy, that's gonna be one big real estate commission somebody's gonna get when they sell Harry's theaters. To give the proceeds to the government. And *then* I thought, Why should somebody else get the commission? Why shouldn't *we* get it? We 've been representing Harry for forty years. Why should someone else get that money?"

"Are you sure this thing is legal?" asked Samantha Shapolsky, Morris's daughter and a proud member of the firm since 1978.

"Of course it's legal," said Morris, shocked that his own daughter would even ask such a question.

"How much are the theaters worth?" Samantha asked.

"Sixty million bucks," said Morris. "Give or take."

"What's the real estate commission on a sale of sixty million dollars' worth of property?" asked Samantha.

"I don't know," Morris said. "I don't have a calculator—"

"Well, I do," said Barry, and he removed a calculator from his shirt pocket. He pushed buttons as he spoke: "Sixty million dollars times six percent equals—oh, my God."

"Equals what?" Morris asked.

"Equals three point six million dollars!" Barry exclaimed. "If this firm sells the theaters to liquidate Harry's estate, then we get three point six mil, the government gets fifty-six point four mil, and Old Shap—you know what they get?"

"Nothing?" asked Samantha, brightening.

"They get nothing!" said Barry. "They're completely screwed! There's no more money in the family, so they lose their clients from Sam's side. Harry's wishes have been carried out to a T! And you, me, Dad, Edward, and Samantha split three point six million dollars!"

"Are you *sure* it's legal?" asked Samantha, as the brief training in legal ethics that she had received fluttered across her mind.

"It is if we say it is," said Barry. "Look. The family's going to lose the money. There's no way they're going to get along, right?"

"Right," said Samantha.

"And the federal government isn't expecting anything," Barry continued. "Then, all of a sudden, it's getting a check for fifty-six million four hundred thousand dollars. They're not going to say, We wanted the whole sixty! They won't even know! All they know is, they're getting a gift out of the blue. Do you really think that Harry would want the law firm that represented him for all these years not to get its fair share of the pie?"

"Harry wouldn't want that, no," said Samantha.

"Let's be honest," Morris said sanctimoniously. "I want nothing more than to see them patch up their old differences and get along, and inherit Harry's money."

"I feel just the same way," Barry said, equally sanctimoniously.

"But in case they can't do that," Morris explained, "then we have to be protected."

"Absolutely," said Barry.

"We can't have some second-rate real estate firm sell the theaters," said Morris. "They might not be able to get the full sixty million for them."

"That's right," said Barry. "They might only get fifty million."

"Exactly," said Morris, "or only forty million."

"Or only thirty-five," said Samantha, trying to assuage her own doubts.

Morris put his arm around Samantha's shoulder. "We're doing our civic duty," he said soberly. "We're protecting the interests of the federal government of the United States of America!"

"We're doing a beautiful thing for our country," said Samantha, hoping to convince herself.

"I've never felt so patriotic in my life," Morris admitted. "And you should have heard them in that meeting. They wanted to take each other's heads off."

The members of New Shap exchanged delighted expressions. They were going to be rich, and Old Shap was going to be left out in the cold.

"So you don't think they can reach an agreement in thirty days?" Samantha timidly asked.

"Thirty days?" repeated Morris. "Not in thirty years! As God is

my judge, I swear to you. It's in the bag. You hear me? In . . . the
. . . bag!"

"I hope you're right," Samantha said. "Are you *sure* this thing
is legal?"

Morris threw up his hands in mock frustration. The rest of the
firm grinned. "Where did I go wrong with you?" Morris asked his
daughter. "Of *course* it's legal! We're *lawyers!*"

17

AFTER HER unsuccessful conference with Sam David, Amelia returned to the Trust Department. On her desk she found a plain manila envelope marked: HAND DELIVER—URGENT.

"What's this?" she said aloud. She opened the envelope and found a photocopy of a court case. An unsigned typed note stapled to the case read: "Chester Alan is not the saint everybody thinks he is."

"How bizarre," said Amelia. She read the case:

82-134983

January 11, 1983

Surrogate's Court, PAUL MARTLAND III, Surrogate Judge

Deborah Shapolsky, Shapolsky and Shapolsky, New York, New York, for petitioner Chester Alan Gaines.

Barry Shapolsky-Kleinman and Morris Shapolsky, Shapolsky & Shapolsky, New York, New York, for respondent Keith McNiven Gaines.

Moses Shapolsky, Shapolsky and Shapolsky, New York, New York, for intervenor Sam David Gaines.

JUDGE MARTLAND: By Gaines standards, this is an easy one. Isabella McNiven, decedent, left her entire estate to her only son, respondent Keith McNiven Gaines. Keith's relative, petitioner Chester Alan Gaines, has brought suit in this Court to challenge the right of the late Isabella to leave her estate to her son Keith. It should be noted that pending before this Court and this judge is *Gaines et al. v. Chester Alan Gaines*, 81-390874, in which the situation is reversed. In that case, Keith, among others, has brought suit to stop Chester Alan's late mother from leaving her assets to her son Chester Alan.

We do not believe that it takes a law degree to recognize that physician Chester Alan is trying to give his relative Keith a taste of the same medicine.

Sam David Gaines, Chester Alan's first cousin, has sought leave from this Court to intervene on Chester Alan's behalf in this matter on the ground that he, Sam David, believes that the case of *Gaines et al. v. Chester Alan Gaines*, 81-390874, is strictly the business of the side of the Gaines family descended from the Original (as his family refers to him) Sam Gaines.

I hereby rule that Sam David Gaines has no right to intervene in this case and I dismiss his petition seeking leave to intervene. I further dismiss this entire suit and remind both Chester Alan and his attorneys, who surely ought to know better, that spite and revenge are insufficient grounds for the bringing of lawsuits. I warn them, and I warn the rest of the family, that any further such suits may result in the imposition of sanctions against the parties as well as procedures before the Bar Association for the suspension of various Shapolskys' right to practice law.

Case dismissed.

PAUL MARTLAND III, Surrogate Judge

Amelia called Howard over. She handed him the case and the typed note. He glanced at them and gave them back to her.

"I got the same thing," he said.

"Who would do this?" she asked.

"Beats me," Howard said. "He's not even on the committee."

"I thought you were the big expert on the Gaineses," Amelia said, teasing him.

"I guess I don't know everything," Howard admitted.

She then remembered she had a meeting shortly with Tess, and she decided to return to the file room to find some more background information on her. She rummaged until she found the court decision in the battle over Tess's father's will. This is what she found:

Gaines v. Gaines, et al.	× in the Surrogate's Court
	× New York County
In re Estate of	× New York, New York
Theodore Gaines	×

Morris Shapolsky, Shapolsky & Shapolsky, for petitioner Tess Gaines and intervenor Charles Chaplin Gaines.

Moses Shapolsky, Shapolsky and Shapolsky, for respondents Annette Morris Gaines and Sam David Gaines.

"I don't believe it," Amelia whispered. Tess had actually gone against decades of family policy and had brought in Morris Shapolsky's firm to sue her own side of the family. No wonder she and Sam David were on the outs. Amelia had not been handling Gaines affairs long, but she knew by now that you simply didn't go using the other side of the family's law firm.

July 7, 1988, PAUL MARTLAND III, SURROGATE JUDGE, PRESIDING

This is hardly the first time this particular family has come before me in these chambers. If memory serves, I have personally heard challenges to the three previous last wills and testaments of members of this extraordinarily litigious family. Records of this Court indicate that my predecessors, sitting in this very Court, often were called upon to settle will and trust disputes of this difficult family, and were I a betting man, I would imagine that future Gaineses will come into this same courtroom with the same purposes in mind long after I retire from the bench. While there are certain blessings in continuity, I cannot find anything beneficial in this family's constant recourse to the law.

This case involves the will of the late Theodore Gaines, who died in 1987. His last will and testament, duly probated, provided for the orderly transfer of half his assets to his wife, the respondent Annette Morris Gaines, and the other half to his son, the respondent Sam David Gaines. Comes now the petitioner Tess Gaines, daughter of the deceased, to challenge the last will and testament of said Theodore Gaines on a number of technical and public policy grounds.

Another member of the Gaines family, one Charles Chaplin Gaines, first cousin of the deceased, has sought leave of this Court to intervene on petitioner Tess Gaines's behalf. (Owing to the fact that all parties to this action share the same last name, I shall hereinafter refer to the parties by their first names without any diminishment of respect intended.)

As far as this Court can determine from Charles's testimony, his only reasons for seeking to intervene in this case are, first, a long-standing dislike of his cousin Sam David Gaines and, second, an unseemly enjoyment of will battles as sport. Neither of these reasons even approaches sufficiency; therefore I rule that Charles Chaplin Gaines is not given leave to intervene and is dismissed as a party to this action.

Next I shall dispose of the technical challenges petitioner Tess set forth. Through counsel, Morris Shapolsky of the firm of Shapolsky & Shapolsky, Tess alleges that the will is invalid because of improper witnessing, three typographical errors, and various violations of the requirements for the safeguarding of wills in New York State. I have examined all of the evidence, and I find as a matter of law that none of the technical challenges set forth by petitioner have merit. Such challenges are hereby dismissed.

Finally, we come to the heart of petitioner Tess's argument. She sets forth two reasons for overturning her father Theodore's decision to leave nothing to her under his will. Tess first urges the Court to recognize that a father has no right to disinherit a daughter simply because he disapproves of her life-style. Tess brought evidence in the form of witnesses who are also Gaines family members (and whose testimony is therefore suspect) that Theodore was furious when he learned that his daughter had a child out of wedlock, that she refused to marry the father of the child or even to inform her family as to the child's father's identity, and, finally, that she named said child Marie.

As a matter of law, a testator has absolute dominion over the disposition of his assets. *Sigmund v. Grossbaum*, 37 U.S. 429 (1923); *Brown v. Rudliff*, 319 N.Y.S. 47, 51 (1961), aff'd mem. op. 321 N.Y.S. 427 (1962). By "absolute dominion" it is meant that a person has the right to include or omit anyone from his or her will. Disgruntled relatives may not agree with a testator's decision to leave money to others but not to them, but the law is extremely clear on this point. If a person wants to omit even a child or a grandchild from his will, as is the case here, no court will interfere.

Tess argues that her father's disapproval of her choosing to have a child with an unnamed male amounts to a deprivation of her constitutional right of free assembly. She further argues that her father's disapproval of her decision to name the child Marie amounts to a deprivation of her constitutional right of freedom of speech. This Court disagrees strenuously with both arguments. Tess, like any woman, is free to have a child with whomsoever she chooses and she may call that child any name that good taste permits. As so many would-be heirs have learned before her, however, actions have consequences. If her actions have the consequence of disappointing her father or leading to his disapproval, then she must bear the results. It is not the purpose of this Court to arbitrate family disputes, as much as the Gaineses have tried to force us to do so over the years. As a matter of law, I find that the testator Theodore Gaines was entirely within his rights when he chose to exclude his daughter Tess from his will.

Petitioner Tess advances a second argument in support of her contention that she should be awarded a portion of Theodore's estate despite his clear desire to the contrary. Tess argues that at the time her father crossed her name out of the will, he was legally insane. She brings evidence of this claim in the form of testimony from Theodore's personal physician, who alleged that Theodore died from liver disease, alcohol poisoning, and depression. Tess then brought expert witnesses to testify that insanity can often result from advanced cases of alcoholism. Tess contends that her father at the end of his life was under the influence of alcohol to such a great extent that he was unable to reflect lucidly on family events and crossed her name out of the will in such a moment of insanity.

I shall refrain from commenting upon the tastefulness of seeking to prove that one's father is legally insane so as to collect an inheritance. Suffice it to say that such allegations have been a staple of Gaines will litigation in this Court over the decades. This Court takes notice, however, of testimony developed by counsel for respondents Sam David and Annette, the son and wife of the decedent, to the effect that although Theodore was in fact depressed throughout much of his adult life, and although he did suffer from chronic and untreated alcoholism, at the time that he made the decision to omit Tess's name from his will, he was perfectly lucid.

Respondents' testimony, which Tess did not seek to rebut, showed that Theodore had been threatening Tess with removal from the will if she did not apologize for her behavior. While Tess was entitled to behave the way she did, her father was entitled to make the choices he made. And, contrary to Tess's final argument, a parent eliminating a child from a will does not, in and of itself, present a prima facie case of insanity on the part of the parent. *Robinson v. Robinson*, 237 N.Y.S.2d 211, 219 (1957), *Norton v. Norton*, 324 N.Y.S.2d 43, 44–45 (1963). *See also* my decision in *Gaines v. Gaines and the Fund for Grizzly Bears et al.*, 422 N.Y.S.2d 436 (1980).

"The Fund for Grizzly Bears?" Amelia asked herself.

In sum, I find that Theodore Gaines acted in sound mind, in keeping with the public policy of this State, and in technical compliance with this State's laws of wills when he chose to remove his daughter Tess from his will. While no one can take pleasure in the thought of such domestic disharmony, the law provides no recourse for aggrieved heirs in the position of Tess Gaines.

Her motion is hereby *dismissed* and the last will and testament of the late Theodore Gaines is hereby admitted to probate. Costs to be born by Petitioner.

PAUL MARTLAND III, Surrogate Judge

Amelia put the decision back in the file. She shook her head slowly. Dwight David was right—Tess actually tried to prove in a court of law that her father was insane. *Nice family,* Amelia thought. Maybe the others were right. Maybe trying to bring unity to the Gaineses was a lost cause.

She dug into the file again and found a lengthy typed letter on the stationery of Theodore Gaines addressed to his by then adult children, Sam David and Tess. It was dated January 15, 1982—five years before Theodore's death and three years before the birth of young Marie, Amelia calculated, making use of the family tree that she had begun to carry with her at all times. In block letters, the letter began: NOT TO BE READ UNTIL AFTER MY DEATH.

Amelia shuddered. "How morbid," she said aloud. Before she could even begin the letter, the voice of Andre the messenger echoed in the file room.

"Mr. Skeffington wants to see you, " Andre told her. He moved on, pushing the mail cart in front of him.

"Thanks, Andre," Amelia called after him. "Tell him I'll be right there."

She looked at her watch. Tess's meeting with her bankers had begun five minutes before. She put the letter in her pocket and headed for the client conference room on the second floor.

Amelia let herself in quietly and listened as Thomas Young-blood, Tess's personal financial adviser at the bank, lectured Tess on the sorry state of her trust account. Youngblood acknowledged Amelia's presence with a glance and continued his speech.

"The other traders at the bank laugh at us," Youngblood was saying. "They call us Team Granola. We're completely hamstrung. You won't let us invest in arms manufacturers, companies that pollute, companies that trade with South Africa, companies that, in your opinion, take advantage of people in the third world—"

"It's not just my opinion," Tess said quietly, her eyes flashing.

"Well, whatever," said Youngblood. "You make me take positions in what you call 'environmentally sound' companies. Well, a lot of them are financially *un*sound. Don't you realize that?"

"So if I sell out, they'll be financially better off?" Tess asked cynically. "Is that it?"

Youngblood sighed. He hated this aspect of his job almost as much as he admired Tess. "I understand why you're doing what you're doing," he said. "It's just that you don't realize how much money it's costing you."

"I really don't care how much it's costing me," Tess said. "I'm sure there's lots of money left."

"Well, there is," Youngblood admitted. "But at the rate you're going into capital, there won't be a lot for long."

"How bad is it?" Tess asked.

"Look for yourself," said Youngblood, pushing a computer printout across the desk. Tess picked it up, but Youngblood could not resist telling her himself. "You can spend money on your homeless shelter at the current rate, and in three years you'll be completely wiped out. You won't even have enough to pay your own mortgage."

Tess herself could not quite say when the idea had come to her, but somewhere in her childhood she developed the belief that being an heiress to a large family fortune gave her certain responsibilities to society. She read once that people like the Rockefellers viewed themselves not as possessors of wealth but as stewards of it. Everyone else in the family assumed that Tess was just going through a phase. Eventually, they believed, she would stop bothering with poor people and would settle down to grab and spend her share of family money on herself, just like the rest of her relatives.

With a six-year-old daughter, Marie Gaines, to raise single-handedly and with no other sources of income, Tess, despite her considerable trust fund, found herself in the most difficult financial position of all the Gaineses. Until Tess opened the Gaines Shelter for Women and Children, the only shelters the Gaineses cared about were those related to taxes. Tess always meant to apply for federal or state grants to aid the shelter. She considered the questionnaires from the various government agencies too intrusive, however. They also took too long to complete. Half-finished grant applications always came in second behind more pressing problems, such as a backed-up toilet at the shelter or not enough diapers.

The last time Tess and Sam David had spoken, Sam David, trying to be helpful, urged her to get some state or federal funds. Running a homeless shelter out of one's own pocket was absurd, he said. The conversation degraded into a shouting match when Tess snapped that Sam David had no right to tell her how to run her business.

"Do I tell you how to buy low-income apartment houses so you can tear them down and build skyscrapers for rich people?" Tess had shouted.

"You're such an ingrate," Sam David retorted. "If it weren't for people like me, you wouldn't even *have* any homeless people."

Amelia thought Tess was beautiful. She had long, dark hair, dark eyes, and a resoluteness to match her brother's. Tess slid the printout across the desk to Youngblood.

Amelia spoke up for the first time. "Your share of the sixty million would go a long way to helping the homeless," she told Tess.

Tess considered Amelia and her statement. "I don't want a share of the sixty million," she said. "I want the theaters. I know it's not realistic, but I want all three theaters."

"If you know it's not realistic . . . ," Amelia began.

"Then I should be prepared to compromise," said Tess. "But I just don't *like* compromises."

Amelia pondered Tess's words. "You don't *like* compromises," Amelia reasoned, "but you're not opposed to them? Is that what you're saying?"

"Every human being is only seventy-two sleepless hours from decompensating," Tess said. "Decompensating is a psychiatric term for going nuts, babbling, like the street people you see every day. My shelter keeps sixty people a night from going crazy. I wish I could help more people. If I had even one of those theaters, I could have a shelter for five hundred people. A model shelter, a safe place without drugs or violence. Or men. I could *possibly* compromise. I guess Mr. Youngblood thinks I'm too doctrinaire even to think about compromising."

Youngblood's expression suggested that he agreed with Tess.

"But if there's some way to compromise," Tess admitted, "I suppose you could count me in. I just don't see how my brother and I can see eye-to-eye on anything."

Amelia thought about Sam David's outpouring of vitriol toward the homeless. She wondered whether the homeless were simply surrogates in his war against his sister.

"There's got to be a way," Amelia said.

"You find it and I'll sign on," said Tess. "But I'm not holding my breath."

Amelia nodded and left the conference room. A Gaines amenable to compromise. Perhaps Glenda and Keith might be of a similar mind. Perhaps there was hope.

18

WORD OF THE first Trust Committee meeting leaked out in typical Gaines fashion—quickly and inaccurately. Harry's relatives feared that Glenda and Keith would cave in to Sam David's presumed toughness. Sam Gaines's descendants feared that Sam David and Tess would let Harry's relatives carry the day. After all, Keith was Harry's own son and therefore could claim a filial right to decide about the disposition of the theaters.

A second, nastier set of rumors followed closely upon the first. According to these untruths, Sam David and Tess (if one belonged to Harry's side) or Glenda and Keith (if one belonged to Sam's) were seeking to buy the votes of the theoretically impartial committee members, Amelia, Howard, and Morris Shapolsky. Even members of Harry's side who frequently used Morris as their lawyer believed emphatically that Morris could be bought. After all, he *had* gone over to represent Tess in the Theodore Gaines will battle. This meant that Sam David and Tess, or, if one preferred, Keith and Glenda, had only to "buy" the vote of one committee member from the bank, Amelia or Howard, in order to prevail. In fact, no bribes had been offered, and given the natures of Amelia and Howard, none would likely be accepted.

Or would they? The thought certainly had crossed Sam David's mind. He had been paying bribes for years. Rampant corruption at his construction sites in New York City had inured him to making quiet cash payments. There was the skyscraper in midtown where the elevator operator on the scaffolding required a twenty-dollar bill in order to be convinced to leave the ground. There was the convention center in New Jersey where Sam David had to hand out hundred-dollar bills to keep workers from pouring concrete into the plumbing the day before the scheduled opening. Such payoffs were a way of life in his business. Sam David's favorite joke went this way: "How many Teamsters does it take to change a light bulb?" Answer: "Twelve. You got a problem with that?"

With this sort of business experience behind him, Sam David, when he had not been expressing opinions or criticizing his relatives, had spent the first Trust Committee meeting studying Amelia and Howard. Sam David's stated position was firm—he wanted all three theaters so he could tear them down and build office towers. He had inherited his grandfather's genes for shrewd negotiating, and like any smart bargainer, he already knew his fallback position. This consisted of two office towers for him and one theater for Keith and Glenda. What they chose to do with it was their business. As for Tess, Sam David sensed that there would be no compromise with her. If Sam David could find three more votes for his position, he would have to cut a deal with Keith and Glenda, and he could do this if he tossed them a theater. Any theater of the three. Sam David's strategy was this: appear hard-nosed and uncompromising until the last minute, offer Keith and Glenda a theater, and pick up one of the neutral votes. Two office towers were better than none. And then he would be a worthy successor, in his own mind, at least, to his namesake and fallen hero, Original Sam.

Sam David munched on one of the walnut chocolate chip cookies he ordered his secretary to bake for him three times a week. (He had gotten the idea from Amelia's grandmother's shipments of cookies.)

The question for Sam David remained how to get one of the three swing votes for himself and his compromise plan. Morris was the first choice. If Sam David stood to clear a minimum of forty million dollars by gaining control of two of the properties, then two million dollars amounted to only five percent of the deal. Say Sam

David tucked away two million in a Swiss bank account for Morris. Could Morris say no to that? Not likely.

What if Morris said no? After all, one of the other three committee members, Keith, Glenda, or Tess, could get to him first. It struck Sam David as distasteful to enter into a bidding war for the services of the same attorney that he and his side of the family had been fighting for years. Paying off Morris was especially galling, considering Morris's involvement on Tess's side in suing Sam David and Annette in the Theodore Gaines will case. Morris was an option for Sam David but not necessarily the best option.

Sam David briefly considered Howard Person. Underneath that stolid, unexcitable accountant's facade, beat there the heart of a wild man? Could the promise of a million dollars, up front, in cash, numbered Swiss account, no questions asked—could that tempt him from his spreadsheets and calculator and computer printouts?

No.

This left Amelia.

Sam David bit into another cookie and pondered Amelia. She was young and smart, but she gave Sam David the sense that she did not want to be a trust banker all her life. Sam David accurately sensed that Amelia wanted something undefinable from life, some kind of excitement beyond that obtainable in cutting checks for beneficiaries and heirs. As he thought back to the Trust Committee meeting and her subsequent unexpected visit to his office, something bothered Sam David about Amelia. She was almost too perfect. She was almost too nice, too well-organized, too *kind*. Whoever heard of a trust officer bringing her grandmother's cookies to a client meeting? In Sam David Gaines's world, no one ever did anything to be nice.

Sam David remembered the one time in his life when he had sought to do something for nothing. It happened shortly after his graduation from college. Sam David had just learned to cook, completing a month-long seminar in three days, in his usual haste. He invited his parents to his little apartment, one he was about to abandon for a large three-bedroom condominium he had craftily seized in a fire sale of a belly-up New York construction company.

Unfortunately, the condominium had an occupant, an elderly man who had lived in the building for forty-two years prior to its condo conversion. Sam David pulled some strings in the city and had the tenant declared mentally incompetent. He would leave the apartment as soon as he exhausted his life savings on court appeals. Until then, Sam David lived in a much more modest apartment, a one-bedroom with a view of an air shaft and three other one-bedroom apartments.

Sam David asked his parents to dinner just because he thought it would be a nice thing to do. In the cramped kitchen he served up steaks, broiled vegetables, and curried rice. He had gone to the trouble of stopping at a gourmet dessert place to buy Boston cream pie, his father's favorite. He even had bought a cappuccino machine and spent a feverish afternoon trying to figure out how it worked.

Accompanying dinner was polite conversation among Annette, a relatively sober Theodore, and a business school classmate of Sam David, a woman named Nancy Frankel, whom Sam David would shortly marry and six years later, after the birth of two children, Sarah and Franklin Delano Gaines, acrimoniously divorce. At that moment, though, all was peaceful in Sam David's world. He was about to take over the family real estate business, he had fallen in what he took for love, and the old guy was almost out of what would soon be his new condo. Dinner was excellent. Theodore loved the pie. After the cappuccino, however, there was a nervous scraping of plates as Theodore and Annette looked at each other, cleared their throats, and said to Sam David four words that echoed in his head for years thereafter: "What do you need?"

"What do I need?" Sam David had responded, not understanding. He needed nothing, and he said, "Nothing."

Theodore and Annette looked confused. Why would someone cook them dinner if that person did not want something from them?

"Oh," said Theodore, still waiting for the other shoe to drop. "Well, in that case, how about some more of that delicious Boston cream pie?"

Sam David thought about that dinner whenever he received an invitation to some charity ball or political fund-raiser. He had internalized the lesson that being "nice" came with a price.

And this Amelia was so nice, he thought. Too nice. Something was askew here. Perhaps there was something for Sam David to exploit. He stood, crossed his massive office, closed his office door, and quietly bolted it shut. He glanced, unnecessarily perhaps, out of the picture windows to make sure that none of the office workers in the nearby skyscrapers were watching him.

He then removed from behind a bookcase a life-size photograph of a tall, fortyish, handsome, sandy-haired man emerging from a helicopter, holding a portable telephone in one hand and draping his free arm around a beautiful younger woman with blond hair. In the distance, beyond the helipad, could be seen the outline of a large Atlantic City casino.

Sam David dropped to his knees.

"O Donald," he prayed. " You are my hero. I want to be like you in every way. I have a business proposition. It's about Harry's will. Sixty million big ones. Don't let me fuck up. Help me choose the right person to offer a large cash bribe. Show me what you would do in the same circumstances. Guide me in the Art of the Deal, All-Seeing One."

Meanwhile, in the outer office, Richard Bickle, bearing documents for Sam David's signature, made his way to Sam David's door.

"You can't go in there," said Sam David's secretary. "He's praying to Donald again."

Just then the bolt slid out of the lock and Sam David emerged, looking pleased with himself. Donald was back in his space behind the bookshelf.

"Bickle, get in here," ordered Sam David, unaware that his staff knew of his religious orientation.

"Yes, sir. Did I fuck something up, sir?" Bickle asked plaintively.

"Not this time," said Sam David. "I want to talk to you about Amelia What's-her-name, the girl in charge of our trust."

"Vanderbilt, sir," said Bickle, and the two men entered Sam David's office.

"That's it—Vanderbilt," said Sam David. "Is she a real Vanderbilt? You know, a society Vanderbilt? That might explain her being nice. If I had Vanderbilt money, I'd be pretty nice myself."

"She's not to my knowledge, sir," said Bickle. "I believe she's from Nebraska. We got a letter from Mr. Skeffington at the bank when she took over the account." Bickle searched his memory. "I believe she's from a town called Greenwood, Nebraska, sir."

"Good work, Bickle," Sam David said admiringly. He liked the way Bickle managed to keep track of small, seemingly unimportant details. "What else do you know about her?"

"Um, nothing, sir, except that she had lunch with Dwight David at Il Sabatino."

"That's not nothing, Bickle," said Sam David, leaning forward. "Why did she have lunch with Dwight David?"

Bickle thought. "I suppose it might be to discuss Dwight David's plan to turn the three theaters into discotheques and private clubs," he responded.

"How do you know he wants to do that?" Sam David asked, surprised at both his nephew's plans for the theaters and Bickle's knowledge of those plans.

"He told us, sir," said Bickle. "He had a meeting with us about a year ago. You weren't interested."

Sam David's eyes narrowed. "I am now," he said. "I may need Amelia, Bickle. I think I can buy off Keith and Glenda with a theater. If I get Amelia's vote—"

"You'd have a majority of the committee's votes, sir," said Bickle, "and you'd get to determine the disposition of the proper-ties."

Bickle's understanding of things pleased Sam David. "I think we have two angles of attack on this Amelia Vanderbilt," said Sam David.

"Sir?" Bickle asked.

"First is the Dwight David route. Say she falls in love with Dwight David. It could happen. He's rich, she's poor. He has a fun life, she works in a trust department. She lives in a crummy apartment in Manhattan, he lives in a farmhouse in Antibes. Follow?"

"Yes, sir," said Bickle, who wished that Dwight David were a woman so that he, Bickle, could fall in love with him instead of Amelia. Dwight David sounded pretty good to Bickle.

"If she falls for Dwight David, then she'll do anything to make him happy, right?"

"I suppose," said Bickle, a step behind Sam David's logic.

"And Dwight David wants to build discos, right?"

"Yes . . . ," said Bickle, still not caught up.

"Well, couldn't we put discos into our buildings, Bickle?"

"Sure, but—"

"All we have to do is tell Dwight David that if he can influence Amelia to vote my way, he'll get his discos. He'll get his discos, Keith and Glenda get a theater, and I get two prime West Side locations for office towers. Pretty good, huh, Bickle?"

"Yes, sir, it *is* pretty good," Bickle said admiringly. It was at moments like this, when he got to see a brilliant real estate mind in action, that Bickle knew it was worth putting up with Sam David's temper and sharp tongue. After all, had he gone with Douglas Elliman or Sonneman and Blick, or any of the other enormous New York real estate outfits, he would probably still be drafting boring commercial subleases and having to behave honestly.

"By the way, Bickle, what were you doing eating lunch at Il Sabatino?" Sam David asked. "That's a pretty pricey restaurant for someone like you."

"I was taking the borough president's personal secretary to lunch," Bickle explained nervously. "It's his favorite restaurant, but he can't afford it on what the city pays him. Eating there makes him more kindly disposed to you, sir."

"Excellent," said Sam David, and he looked thoughtful for a moment. "There's one more angle of attack on Amelia," he said at last. "You know, she's just too nice."

"Yes, sir."

"I don't trust nice people," said Sam David, and he thought of that dinner he cooked for his parents.

"No, sir," said Bickle.

"Neither should you, Bickle," Sam David told his assistant.

"Oh, no, sir. I don't, sir."

"Good. Now. I want you to go to Nebraska."

"Now, sir?" Bickle looked alarmed. Sam David had saddled him with far too much work for him to even contemplate a trip to Nebraska.

Sam David noticed his assistant's pitiable expression and changed his mind. "Actually, I need you here in New York. You're too important. Find someone unimportant and send him to Nebraska. Get that actor from Old Shap to go out and snoop around. Find out something about this Amelia Vanderbilt. Let's get some dirt on her. She's just too nice. I don't believe in nice."

"Yes, sir," said Bickle. "Is that all, sir?"

Sam David thought for a moment. "That's all."

Bickle hastened from Sam David's office. Sam David looked at the three scale models of the towers he wanted to build on the sites of the theaters. He then pointed to each in turn, saying, "Eeny, meeny, miney, mo', catch a tiger by the toe . . ." When the verse ended, he took the model of the office tower he was pointing at and threw it in the trash.

Down the hall, Bickle was on the telephone to the offices of Old Shap. He explained to Louis Gaines Shapolsky about Sam David's ideas. Louis G. thought both ideas were inspired. Louis G. then telephoned Gil Thompson, unemployed actor turned legal spy. Three hours later, Gil, accompanied by his new girlfriend, Cynthia, were on their way to Omaha.

19

MEANWHILE, IN MANHATTAN, Amelia squinted in the darkness of the dingiest off-off-Broadway theater she had ever seen. The Theater Del Tuna, on the west side of the Bowery, half a block north of Canal Street, was located three subway stops from Amelia's office and, it seemed, a million miles from Broadway. Actors cannot be choosers, and a role is a role. When actress Glenda Monash Gaines, wife of Woodrow Sam and granddaughter-in-law of the late Harry, found herself cast as a witch in an Equity production of *Macbeth*, naturally she accepted. So tawdry were both the theater and the production that she had not even bothered to invite friends or family to the opening, three days away.

Decades earlier, during the golden age of Yiddish theater, the Del Tuna had been the Royalty Theatre, and virtually every star of that era had headlined there. As Amelia squirmed in her uncomfortable seat and her eyes adjusted to the dim light, she considered the torn red carpeting, the fusty odor, and the broken glass over the fire exit signs, and she decided that in the time since the golden age of Yiddish theater, the Del Tuna must have been cleaned thoroughly at least once. She would not have put money on it, however.

Who came to productions in theaters surrounded by a sea of drunks? Who ran this theater? Could they possibly make enough money to pay themselves a decent salary, or was the whole thing a labor of love? On her arrival, Amelia had expected a stage manager to impede her path, but the stage door was unoccupied, save for a few middle-aged men sleeping quietly under the rear marquee. Amelia seated herself in a back row of the auditorium and waited for the director to call a break in the rehearsal so that she could talk to Glenda, on stage and in full witch's costume and makeup. Glenda and the two other witches leaned against their caldron while the director lambasted Macduff for forgetting a bit of blocking.

Amelia found herself entranced. She had never seen a rehearsal before. True, she was starting at the bottom with this particular theater and company, but she had never seen actors on stage and not acting. The director and another man began a lengthy conference on whether to rewrite or omit six lines. The actors sat or stood or leaned on the stage furniture while the lighting man played with gels and effects, perhaps out of boredom. Amelia's initial interest turned to frustration. She did not want to spend all afternoon waiting for a chance to speak to Glenda. She checked her watch, and then she remembered she had the two 1931 letters from Woodrow to Sam in her purse. She took them out and began to read.

August 6, 1931

Dear Pa,

Having a good time here—and a very good rest. No noise and that sort of thing. Spent most of time fishing—and actually caught a bass of [Amelia had trouble for a moment making out the words] more than a pound and a half.

Hope you are well and continuing to enjoy good rest. No need for you to worry about the office—because Miss Levine writes me about all details. Pocini has been evicted. It seems to me you can stay even longer than the 10th unless something unforeseen turns up. Why not write her and ask if anything important needs your immediate attention.

With hopes that you're having a good rest without worry,

Your loving son,

Woodrow

Amelia rubbed her chin for a moment, and then she unfolded the other letter. She noticed that it was dated eight days earlier.

July 29, 1931

Dear Pa,

To-morrow (Thursday evening) I am leaving for my vacation with Grov as I had planned. You can't understand how tired and worn out I really feel. The dreadful heat we've had the past few weeks has left me nearly exhausted at the end of each day requiring me to run out to the buildings and at the same time attend to the office and all. I don't mean to exaggerate—but I feel that I need a rest and a vacation very badly. Incidentally, for the past week I have been living here alone—Mother having gone with her sister to Ellenville. She will probably stay until about Aug 15th. (over)

2.

The reason I'm writing you this is because I want you to decide whether you ought to come back to New York now instead of waiting until next week. These are the conditions. My new property man and superintendent have moved into the four room on the ground floor of Jackson Heights. To-morrow I shall notify Mitchell, the old sup't, to vacate immediately. The new man is not acquainted with the tenants and may have difficulty in collecting rents from the tenants. Furthermore, I don't want to send him to collect rents in the other buildings—because I have not as yet procured his bond (which he is to

3.

pay for). There are several rents still uncollected at 108 St including Pocini (those tenants with whom it was better policy for me to wait, than to put out).

Put out? Amelia asked herself. *Does he mean "evict"?* She read on:

I hope that you will understand my position. I am really fatigued—and need a short vacation. I really don't want to spoil yours—but you have already had an opportunity

4.

to refresh yourself. You [the ink was blurred here, but Amelia could make it out anyway] should feel strong enough, Pa, to come home now, if you feel you should, and take care of things while I'm gone. I have a very competent clerk who'll attend capably to any legal work you'll give him such as foreclosures, dispossesses, etc. You also will have a first-class property manager and mechanic to care for the buildings and collections. Your job then for the next two weeks will not be hard. You will just have to supervise. Everything else is in proper shape and condition.

I really think you would want to come back now for this short period—and then when

5.

I get back you again can take a good long vacation. From my point of view, all I can say is that I need a rest right now—if I stay here for another week, it will not only be too great a strain on me, but it shall absolutely break up the plans of Grov and this other friend which were made more than a month ago.

6.

I shall commence the Pocini foreclosure if necessary and have the Receiver appointed by the first. So, if you decide to stay for the extra week you may do so—and I've instructed Miss Levine to notify you at once if anything needs your very immediate personal attention.

I hope, Pa, you understand that I am not trying to neglect anything. I really have worked hard while you've been away, and things are in fair shape at the buildings.

Let Miss Levine know what you intend to do. I shall, of course, write you from where I am.

With real regret for disturbing your vacation, I yet remain,

Your loving son,

Woodrow

On stage, the director continued his conference with the unidentified man, while the rest of the cast sank deeper into torpor. Amelia examined the dates on the three letters—the two from

Woodrow to Sam and the one from Sam to Woodrow—and tried to put the puzzle pieces together. She reread the second letter from Woodrow to Sam: "Having a good time here—and a very good rest. No noise and that sort of thing. Spent most of time fishing—and actually caught a bass of more than a pound and a half." She noted the date, August 6, and compared it to Sam's letter: July 30. Sam wanted Woodrow to stay in New York and collect rents and evict people until August 10, but Woodrow went on vacation anyway and had been away for at least a few days by August 6. He was there long enough to get some rest and catch a bass. "Good for him," Amelia said aloud. "He went anyway."

She was surprised by the depth of her satisfaction, knowing that Woodrow had followed his desires instead of his father's orders. The fact that these events had taken place sixty years earlier did not matter to Amelia. They seemed as real to her as events that were unfolding on the stage of the Del Tuna. She pictured Original Sam, covered with mud, cocked to the gills, furious that his son had disobeyed, and she saw Woodrow, relaxing in a rowboat, listening to the gentle sounds of a lake in August, tenants, superintendents, evictions, and his father's anger a million miles away.

She could not help but feel some compassion for Woodrow, who seemed to be trying so hard to obey his father's will despite the exhaustion he felt. Amelia wondered whether the summer of 1931 in New York City was particularly hot. She reread parts of the longer letter, and she wondered what Woodrow really wanted—did he want his father, Sam, to come home and take care of the buildings, or did he want Sam's permission to go on the trip, or did he want one thing and then another, or did he not know what he wanted?

"I thought that was you," said Glenda, in full witch costume and makeup. Amelia quickly rose to her feet.

"Do you have a second?" Amelia asked.

"I might have more than a second," Glenda said. "This company's so cheap, they're thinking about doing *Macbeth* with one witch. I might just have all the time in the world."

"I came down to see you because—"

"You wanted to see the glamorous world of show business for

yourself," Glenda interrupted. She struck a ballerina-like pose. "Pretty wonderful, huh?"

"Well, any theater production is exciting," Amelia said diplomatically. "Especially Shakespeare—"

"Shakespeare on the Bowery?" asked Glenda. "How exciting is that? Look, this theater is a dump. The production company is a joke. The director thinks his rewrites are better than the original dialogue. And they've got to decide whether they're going to pay the actors' salaries or the rent. How do you think I feel? A classically trained actress?"

"Unhappy?" Amelia guessed.

"You got that one right," said Glenda. "Look. I shouldn't be in this stupid Del Tuna—I should be *up there*, running Harry's goddamned theaters. Cleaning them out, refurbishing 'em top to bottom, and then putting in first-class productions. Not *Macbeth* with one witch. Real *theater*. That's what those buildings are. *Theaters*. They aren't homeless shelters or vaudeville museums or any other goddamn thing. They're theaters, and we as a family owe it to Harry's memory—and to Sam's, I might add—to restore them to their former glory. It's that simple."

"I'm just wondering," Amelia said cautiously, "whether there might be any room for"—she could barely get the word out—"compromise."

"Sure," Glenda said caustically. "No problem. Have the homeless waiting outside every night until the show's over, and let 'em sleep in the lobby. . . . I'm sorry. That makes me sound heartless or something. Look, I admire Tess. I think she does a lot of good works. But these theaters aren't—I don't know—big *sheds* or something. They're *Broadway theaters*; they're part of the cultural heritage of this city—and of this *family*. I don't exactly understand how you can compromise between a homeless shelter and—and *Macbeth*."

"But if you all can't make some sort of decision—" Amelia began.

"Then we lose the whole thing," Glenda rejoined. "And we've got you to thank for that."

"No you don't," Amelia said, stung. "I was just carrying out Harry's instructions."

"We need the witches on stage," crackled a voice over an ancient public address system.

"Well, did you have to do such a good job?" Glenda asked. Then her tone softened. "I know," she said. "It isn't easy, working with the Gaineses. But you'll get used to us."

"Not if you can't all compromise," said Amelia. "Then I won't have to get used to you at all. But I promise you, I'm not going to let that happen."

Glenda chuckled. "I love naïveté. I haven't seen any in such a long time. I've got to get back to my caldron. While I still *have* a caldron."

The conference involving the six lines of dialogue had resolved itself—Macduff would use the director's rewrite. Amelia watched the actors rehearse, and then she checked her watch again. With a start, she realized that Mr. Skeffington was probably still waiting for her. She left the Del Tuna and headed back to the bank.

20

LATER THAT AFTERNOON, Mr. Skeffington wore the expression of a man charged with delivering bad news. Amelia, engrossed in Gaines affairs, did not seem to notice.

"The Trust Department is changing, Amelia," said Mr. Skeffington, sounding remorseful, removing a bent paper clip from the otherwise pristine surface of his desk. "I'm not happy with the direction in which we're going. I think it's a very bad idea."

"I agree with you," Amelia said.

"What do you mean, you agree with me?" Mr. Skeffington asked. "I haven't said anything yet."

"I mean, I don't like the direction the whole thing is going," said Amelia. "So far Tess is the only one talking about compromise, but I don't see how Glenda or Sam David can possibly compromise with her. Maybe she's just talking compromise even though she knows it's impossible."

"I'm not talking about the Gaineses," said Mr. Skeffington. "I'm talking about the department."

"The Trust Department?" Amelia asked with surprise. "What about the department?"

"We've been under new management for the past year or so," said Mr. Skeffington. "And until recently they've given me a fairly free hand in running this department as I always have. With a

170

family feeling for the clients whose families we've served for decades."

"I understand that," said Amelia, suddenly fearful.

Mr. Skeffington looked grave. "I've been given a directive." He tapped a letter on bank stationery on his desk. "We've been ordered to let go of all accounts under five million dollars."

"But those are all the DLOLs!" she exclaimed. "Not one of them is worth five million dollars!"

"I know that as well as you do," said Mr. Skeffington. "But each one takes up almost as much bank time as a much larger account. The new management wants to reposition itself and go after bigger fish, like the Gaineses, who generate large fees. The DLOLs simply do not."

He stood up and put his hands on the desk. "You've been in charge of the DLOLs for the past four years. I hate to ask you to do this, but you must contact each of them and tell them that we can no longer service their accounts. You may assist them in establishing banking relationships with some of our competitors. But we can't represent them anymore."

"Mr. Skeffington, you can't do that!" Amelia said, alarmed.

Mr. Skeffington sighed. "It wasn't my decision. I'm sorry."

She left his office. The idea of giving up the DLOLs, of cutting them loose, of never again having tuna niçoise at the Exquisite Tulip with the Eva Baums of the world, was too much for Amelia. Although the bank was abandoning the DLOLs, Amelia herself felt abandoned. Tears formed in her eyes. She steeled herself and tried to suppress the feelings. She was not going to take this lying down, she decided. Perhaps the decision was not final—perhaps she could fight it, go over Mr. Skeffington's head, take her case even to the president of the bank. Or to the newspapers. She had visions of the DLOLs circling the bank building, wearing signboards and protesting loudly, while traffic backed up and television news cameras transmitted the event live. Mr. Skeffington would have a stroke. Well, maybe she wouldn't take it that far. But Amelia told herself that she would sooner give up her job than give up her DLOLs, her graying army of surrogate grandmothers.

"We'll see about this," Amelia said aloud. In the meantime,

the letter from Theodore beckoned. It offered distraction from the sudden loss of her beloved clientele and it promised a few more clues into the nature of Gaines-style family conflict. Amelia unfolded the letter and began to read.

January 15, 1982

```
NOT TO BE READ UNTIL AFTER MY DEATH
Dear Children,
     After my passing, it will be necessary for
you to understand the exact nature of our family
business. Probably there will be a challenge to
my will, as seems to have been the case with so
many members of our family. This is a habit we
should not be proud of, but forewarned is
forearmed. I intend to set forth an explanation
of where our real estate properties come from,
who owned then when, where they are now, and so
forth. This information will be valuable to you
in the event that you must defend a will suit
from one of the other relatives.
     I'll get to the businesses momentarily. I
need to put in writing some things about myself
and the family.
     Now that I am gone, or will be gone by the
time you read this, I don't mind telling you
that your grandfather had a very terrible
drinking problem. We have a picture somewhere of
him in Saratoga or Florida, holding up two
bottles of booze. This was taken during
Prohibition. Prohibition never stopped your
grandfather from finding a drink. Nothing ever
stopped your grandfather from finding a drink,
including the best efforts of my mother and my
brothers.
     I don't want to make my life sound pitiable
or anything like that. I don't think I was
unhappy then. And Father was never violent, nor
did he use foul language, around myself or my
brothers. I don't think he was aware of me much
after he brought Woodrow into the business. God,
he was hard on Woodrow. He wouldn't even let
Woodrow take vacations.
```

Father, of course, meant Original Sam Gaines. Amelia thought about the 1931 letters between Sam and Woodrow.

```
     First I want to tell you a little about
myself. Did you know that Woodrow got into
```

Harvard? But Father would not let him go. Father
wanted him to stay in New York and run the
business. If he had told me not to go, I
probably would not have gone. Father was a very
strong-willed man.

I'm afraid that my going to Harvard placed a
very large strain on my relationship with my
older brother, Woodrow. It's safe to say that he
and I were never close after that. I got what he
had wanted so much. He died very young. He was
thirty-nine. One of his tenants might have had
something to do with it. This was in the summer
of 1951.

"Pocini," Amelia said aloud. And then she wondered: *How
much did Theodore really know?*

After college, I sent most of the money I
earned to Woodrow to invest in the family
business. This turned out to be a very bad idea,
because Woodrow was very neglectful in his
management of the buildings and I lost a lot of
money with him. I tried to make suggestions, but
he was not interested in them, and as a result
it is safe to say that we grew further apart.

After a few years working for a corporation,
I opened my own laboratory in Brick Township,
New Jersey. With typical Gaines modesty, I
envisioned myself the next Thomas Edison. I even
had a certain amount of luck inventing things
for the war effort. Also, thanks to my
laboratory, I met your mother. I was 32 and she
was 23. She was my lab assistant. She studied
chemistry at Rutgers and was very smart. People
also pointed out to me later that she was very
pretty. I never talked about Father with her.

After Father died, I was a fairly wealthy
young man. Father left half his estate to Mother
and one third to each of the three of us,
Woodrow, Grover, and myself, on condition that
Woodrow should manage the properties. Woodrow
would have loved to get out of the real restate
business, and he could have sold out. We advised
him to do so because staying in it was not what
he wanted. Woodrow got as far as making a verbal
agreement to sell the buildings to Barry
Shapolsky, Father's partner and lawyer. At the
last minute, though, Woodrow canceled because he
just could not bear to let go of his father's
buildings. If only Woodrow could have sold. He

would have been so much happier. He probably would have lived longer.

I think I was very hurt that my own brother would be so closed about the family business, which we in fact owned together. You might say that I could have been more assiduous in forcing Woodrow to get a proper accounting. In fact, I tried. I did everything I could, including threatening legal action, to get Woodrow to pay more attention to the business.

After Woodrow died, in 1951, I owned the lion's share of the family business. I cannot explain how it happened, but the same paralysis that struck Woodrow struck me as well. I lived so much in fear of Father when he was alive that to own the buildings he once owned brought back all those terrible feelings of inadequacy and all the memories of his drinking. Please do not think your poor father is crazy, but I swear to you, I saw Father—my father, Sam—in dreams, telling me not to sell the buildings. And I never could sell those buildings. This is why when you, Sam David, took over the business not too long ago, we owned exactly what we had owned in 1951.

Only then did I realize what Woodrow was up against. Certain of Father's original properties, such intelligent investments for the 1920s and even the 1930s, were now dreadful things to own. I, primarily through passivity, had become a slumlord. The properties were too expensive to maintain and too undesirable to sell. The buildings were old and decrepit beyond their years because of Woodrow's and then my policies of neglect. This has been an awful thing to live with. I only hope that you, Sam David, need no encouragement to sell everything you want to sell. Please, please, do not think that just because these buildings have been in the family for sixty years we must keep them. Get rid of everything while you can.

Do I have any regrets about my life? I wish that after Woodrow died I had instructed Louis and Henry Shapolsky to sell everything immediately. I also wish that Father could have seen all the wonderful things I accomplished in my laboratory. Did you know I created the first wheelchair with adjustable foot-holders and a brake? Did you know I invented an extremely successful hearing aid? Did you know I developed the forerunner to the modern catheter? I

licensed these devices to industry and gave much
of the royalties to veterans' organizations in
memory of Grover. I wish Father could have known
about these things.
    I know that you will hear talk about what
your grandfather Sam did to his father, Dov Ber.
I don't know what to tell you about that. Maybe
some things should be left unmentioned. I'm sure
that guilt over this action contributed heavily
to Sam's alcoholism and early demise. I'm sure
he regretted it. Without a doubt, the guilt must
have destroyed him. The whole problem in our
family is our inability to forgive each other,
or ourselves, for actions long past.
    Please do not judge Father, or Woodrow, or
even myself, harshly. I am sure that in the ways
that young people judge their elders, certainly
in the way that I judged mine, all three of us
are terrible and conspicuous failures. Please
remember that I loved you, and that Woodrow and
Father would have loved you, had they lived long
enough to know you. Stand up for yourselves and
be proud to be Gaineses.

                    Your loving Father,

                    T. Gaines

Several aspects of the letter puzzled Amelia. She went over to
Howard's desk. He put down his calculator and looked up at
Amelia.

"What does this mean?" she asked, holding the letter open to
the last page. "What did Original Sam do to Dov Ber?"

Howard took the letter and flipped through it. "I've read this,"
he said. "But I've got no idea."

"I'm amazed," Amelia said, smiling. "There's something you
don't know about the Gaineses. Wait'll I tell Mr. Skeffington."

Howard shook his head. "Mr. Skeffington said you might be
getting . . . too close with the Gaineses," he said.

Amelia felt defensive. Why would Mr. Skeffington confide in
Howard about her approach to her work? "I disagree," Amelia said.
"I mean, I used to agree, but I'm . . . starting to get to know them.
They're not all that bad."

"Especially Dwight David?" Howard asked cynically.

"Just because I had lunch with him—" Amelia began.

"And dinner tonight?" Howard asked.

Amelia shrugged. "And dinner tonight. It doesn't mean anything. He's just giving me advice about the family."

"Well, just as long as that's *all* he gives you," Howard said darkly.

"Howard Person!" Amelia exclaimed. "I'm meeting five Gaineses today! How come you're jealous only of Dwight David? Maybe I'm really interested in Sam David, or Keith."

"Don't be ridiculous," said Howard, and then he brightened. "Well, it's only dinner. After thirty days, we'll never even see them again. There's no way that family will ever agree on anything." Then he added nervously: "Will they?"

"Highly doubtful," said Amelia. "Hey, I got some bad news. From Mr. Skeffington. They're cutting loose the DLOLs."

"I heard," Howard said sympathetically. "You must feel awful."

Amelia nodded. "Mr. Skeffington says they don't generate enough fees," she said sadly. "You can't cut a bunch of eighty-five-year-old women loose! What are they supposed to do? Find another bank?"

"Ask Mr. Skeffington," said Howard. "Where are you going now?"

Amelia stuffed some Gaines-related papers into her handbag and checked her watch. "I've got to go meet Keith, and then I'm meeting Dwight David. Don't take everything so hard. It'll all work out okay."

Howard sighed. He had heard as much from Stone and Vaccaro. "Dinner tonight is definitely out?" he asked plaintively.

Amelia looked compassionately at Howard. "Afraid so," she said. "And don't worry. It's *just* going to be dinner. I'll pretend he's a DLOL."

Howard snorted. "That's a laugh," he said. "I just don't want to lose you to that family. That's all."

"Oh, Howard, you're so dramatic," said Amelia. Then she bit her lip. "There's one more thing. I forgot to mention it. . . . I called my folks. I told them I'd be really busy with this new account and everything. I asked them not to come just now."

"You asked them not to come?" Howard asked, stunned. He

could not have been more hurt if Amelia had announced that they were breaking up. "Why'd you do that?"

Amelia could not meet Howard's disappointed gaze. "I just thought I ought to get settled in with the Gaineses," she said lamely. "If my folks are here, we'd be entertaining them and everything, and I—I couldn't get all my work done. It would be too, you know, distracting. Do you mind terribly?"

"Of course I mind," said Howard, plans of a wedding next June going directly out the window. He had known it all along—the Gaineses, without even meaning to do so, had found a way to come between Amelia and himself. He resented the Gaineses all the more. "Sometimes," he said, with a trace of bitterness, "I get the feeling you don't want me to *meet* your family."

Amelia looked away quickly. "Oh, Howard," she said, "that's foolish. You'll meet them soon. I promise. It's just the wrong time right now."

Howard sighed. "Okay, I guess," he said. "I guess it'll all work out in the end."

"Of course it will," Amelia said reassuringly. Then she looked both ways. No one seemed to be watching them. In a violation of bank tradition, and in complete disregard for their usual conservative practice, Amelia did the one thing that might help convince Howard that he was not losing her to the great, mighty, and powerful Gaines family. She kissed him.

21

THIRTY-FIVE MINUTES into Keith McNiven Gaines's exhaustive description of his Harry and Sam Gaines Museum of Vaudeville, complete with maps, blueprints, charts, graphs, proposed temporary and permanent exhibitions, and a plan for entering into a single computer database information about every theater, actor, actress, trained seal, monologue, and joke that ever had anything to do with the world of vaudeville, Amelia, whose eyes had glazed over during approximately the eighteenth minute of the presentation, came to realize that finally she had found a member of the Gaines family more obsessed with his conception of what to do with the theaters than she was obsessed with the Gaineses themselves.

This discovery alarmed her. Yet Keith seemed unlikely to slow down, let alone to halt his outpouring of hopes and dreams. Amelia looked hopefully across their hotel suite to Keith's wife, Babette, but she sat implacably on the sofa, doing needlepoint. Her cat, Sidney, sat on her lap and pawed at the yarn. Babette ignored Keith with the patience of a wife who loved her husband, pitied his single-minded and, to her, pointless dream, and felt glad for him that he had an audience, however unwilling that audience might be, to hear the whole story. Amelia had no choice. She had made the appointment with Keith and Babette, had asked him for his views on how the family ought to develop the theaters, and had no choice now but to await the end of his monologue. Babette knew from experience that Keith had another twenty or so minutes to go.

Babette and Keith lived as quiet, wealthy retirees in the mountain community of Aspen, Colorado, where they played golf, worked with charities, and fought over Keith's dream of a vaudeville museum. Amelia noticed that Keith strongly resembled Harry, his looks somewhere between those of the young Harry in the publicity photograph and the old Harry in his hospital bed.

Keith and Babette had come to New York the day before Harry died, Keith said, suddenly interrupting himself, because he was convinced that his father's most recent heart attack would be his last. "I wanted to come sooner, but *she* wouldn't let me." He pointed at Babette.

Sidney looked condescendingly at Keith.

"What would have been the good of that?" Babette asked, relieved that Keith had abandoned his speech. "He was comatose. Even if he'd woken up, he would have given you five minutes and thrown you out of the room. That's what he always did."

"That's not true," Keith said. "He always made time for me."

"He made time for the nurses," Babette said. "Not for family. Even Sidney knows that. Don't you, snookems?" She buried her face in her cat's fur. Sidney looked bored.

"How can you kiss that thing?" Keith asked, repulsed.

"Sidney's nicer to me than Harry ever was to you," Babette retorted. "Admit it."

"I will admit no such thing," said Keith.

Amelia squirmed. "I could come back later," she began.

"No, no, no," said Keith. "All right. It's all spilled milk. Anyway, that's what's going to be happening in building one of the museum. Now let's talk about buildings two and three. . . ."

Amelia looked to Babette to rescue her, but his wife had no intention of shutting Keith up. Babette believed that talking about the vaudeville museum was therapeutic for her grieving husband. After another twenty minutes of lecture, Keith appeared to be nowhere near the end of his monologue. Finally, Amelia politely excused herself. She did not want to be late for her dinner with Dwight David.

•

Keith's older son, Grover Sam Gaines, stunt car driver extraordinaire, loved to visit New York, partly because he could always find a party somewhere and partly because it was the one city in the world where people considered it perfectly acceptable, and even preferable, not to have a valid driver's license. Upon learning of his grandfather Harry's death, Grover Sam left the downtown Los Angeles law firm where he worked as a temporary word processor and caught a flight for New York. Unlike his brother, Woodrow Sam, and his sister-in-law, Glenda, and unlike the majority of word processors in the city of Los Angeles, Grover Sam claimed as his true calling not acting but stunt driving. Unfortunately, due to certain untoward circumstances, Grover Sam no longer possessed a driver's license. This made stunt driving for the movies much more difficult and made his word processing job much less temporary.

From a strictly legal standpoint, one does not need a driver's license in order to work as a motion picture stunt driver. Driving on a closed set, or a closed stretch of highway taken over temporarily by a film crew, is not the same thing, in the eyes of the California motor vehicle code, as driving on public thoroughfares. Insuring unlicensed stunt drivers is another matter, however. Grover Sam had lost his driver's license as a result of a spate of mysterious accidents that had given his jeeplike vehicle the appearance of one of those cars that finish, or fail to finish, the race from Paris to Dakar. Grover Sam had no explanation for these accidents; they just seemed to keep happening.

Grover Sam's career had begun promisingly enough. By his twenty-fifth birthday, he could be seen, blurred and in the background, in a variety of extremely successful action-adventure films. He developed a reputation for going along with whatever a director might suggest. This attitude helped him get a lot of work. It also put him in some extremely dangerous situations. Ensuing accidents were blamed not on his driving skills but on his gung-ho attitude. If anything, the fact that he crashed cars on the sets showed just how hard he was working.

Or so people told each other. After a while, word got out that if you had an extremely expensive car and a cheap car at your disposal, give Grover Sam the cheap one and hope you get what you need on the first take. He wrecked Porsches and Pintos with equal abandon. Mercedeses and Mercurys flamed out at the same dizzying pace. If a script called for him to get into a tailspin, he could get into one but he could never get out. Grover Sam, shrugging and smiling (like his grandfather Harry) in such a manner that people could not get angry at him, cost more film crews more downtime than any other stunt driver in the history of their union.

Word spread in the tightly knit stunt-driving community. Other drivers' agents required language written into their clients' contracts to the effect that Grover Sam would not appear in any scenes in which they might be driving. Work dried up for Grover Sam. He stopped going to stunt driver union affairs after nearly running over the left foot of a stunned valet parking attendant. And then came the mysterious series of accidents on public streets, which culminated in the loss of his license.

The only work that Grover Sam could find, apart from his word processing job at the massive downtown firm of Tower and Gates, involved movies shot directly on videotape. The proud world of Hollywood stunt drivers considered these movies impossibly déclassé. The videos had little plot and consisted mainly of car chases and car wrecks. Such work suited Grover Sam's talents to a T. He drove for films like *Totaled Strangers, Accidents Will Happen, Fifty-five and Barely Alive, Wreckless Endangerment*, and his most unforgettable and enduring legacy, *Roadkill*. If you have never heard of these epics, it is because you do not frequent the 7-Elevens in certain Deep Southern states where they are distributed. They were never shown on theater screens because no one would be stupid enough to pay to see them in movie theaters, not even people in the Deep South.

Screenwriters for such movies did not specify directions for drivers. Instead a certain improvisational spirit informed the proceedings. The script would say only: "Grover Sam does his thing." The videotape would roll, and Grover Sam would smile pleasantly, strap himself into some old bomb of a car, usually the sort that auto wreckers would turn up their noses at and refuse to tow away, even if you offered them fifty dollars. Grover Sam would then "do his thing," and the car would shortly be in pieces or in flames. Without question, there were no retakes.

Grover Sam did not want to process words, especially legal words, forever. A realistic sort, he understood that an entire generation of film directors—and insurance adjusters—would have to die or retire before he would be given the wheel again in a major motion picture. This assumed, of course, that Grover Sam would be able to square things with the California Department of Motor Vehicles. This confluence of events might be a long time coming. Grover Sam for several years had looked east, specifically to New York City, specifically to three Broadway theaters in New York City, whence might come his professional salvation.

Grover Sam did not want to act in those theaters. Nor did he want anyone else to act in them. He wanted to create in those theaters a museum of filmmaking that would pay tribute not to actors or directors but to the people behind the scenes—the gaffers, the best boys, and, yes, the stunt drivers. And what better buildings—which translated to the question: what *cheaper* buildings—could Grover Sam find when he considered himself partially heir to the three theaters in midtown Manhattan? Until he arrived for Harry's funeral and the reading of the will, however, it had never occurred to him that other relatives might have other ideas for the same buildings.

Grover Sam liked New York partly because he had grown up there and partly because he considered himself on equal footing with Manhattanites, who often took enormous pride in never even having to learn to drive. Driving was for out-of-towners, for "bridge-and-tunnel people" from the mysterious, vast, and irre-deemably unappealing outer boroughs, and for the unpronounce-ably named foreigners who came to New York to make their livings in taxicabs. Better New Yorkers did not drive. They did not need to drive, because there were subways and buses and taxis and, most proudly, their own two feet.

True New Yorkers consider cars nuisances. One must either pay extortionate rents in garages or be slave to alternate-side-of-the-street rules. Cars on the street suffer constant break-ins, despite all the clever little "No Radio" signs New Yorkers tape to their car windows. Rare is the morning when one can walk down a street even in the most elegant parts of the city, the East Sixties and Seventies, for example, without encountering piles of gleaming bits of smashed green glass reflecting the rising sun in a thousand jagged angles. Comedians joke that the best way to have one's trash removed during a New York City garbage strike was to gift-wrap it, place it on the seat of one's car, park the car anywhere in Manhattan, and lock the doors.

And gas costs fifty percent more in Manhattan than anywhere else in the country. And gas stations provide even the most threatening and dissipated of panhandlers with a steady and captive audience. And then there is the Department of Motor Vehicles down by the Criminal Court Building in lower Manhattan, where lines move with glacial speed and everything takes two hours. Most New Yorkers would rather spend two hours at the morgue.

No, not for good and true New Yorkers was driving: exorbitant, dangerous, unnecessary, trouble-ridden. In New York, the unlicensed Grover Sam was one with the majority, and he liked it that way.

Woodrow Sam, Grover Sam's far more serious-minded younger brother, had spent the last sixteen years of his life dedicated to taking matters a step further: he wanted to ban all private cars from Manhattan streets. He had even formed a group, CONY, which stood for "Cars Out of New York," which sought to quadruple tolls on existing bridges and tunnels, introduce tolls on those bridges—like the Queensborough or the Brooklyn—that currently allowed free access for cars into Manhattan, jack up parking taxes, and ban all on-street parking.

The beauty of a place like New York is that any organization, no matter how foolish, can always net a few dozen to a few hundred vigorous adherents, and such was the case with CONY. The movement had gotten exactly nowhere despite all its handbills, protests, and letter-writing campaigns to the City Council and the Mayor's Office. One of its biggest supporters, by which is meant that he actually provided fifty dollars a year in dues to CONY and allowed the group use of his copying store on Macdougal Street in Greenwich Village, had come unglued, for various personal reasons that did not relate to CONY, and become convinced that his telephone was tapped by the American Automobile Association, which vigorously opposed CONY and all it stood for.

CONY did provide Woodrow Sam with an outlet for his creative energies, which was a good thing, because his acting career, unlike that of his wife, Glenda, had not taken off. Neither Woodrow Sam nor Glenda was a household name in New York, but Glenda did get speaking roles in Off Broadway and occasionally in Broadway productions. She also did many local commercials. She and Woodrow Sam lived primarily off her residuals, with a little help from the smallish trust fund that Keith had established for his two sons at their birth. Woodrow Sam and Glenda sometimes viewed that trust fund as a self-fulfilling prophecy that he would never be able to earn his own way in the world. This was not exactly true. Woodrow Sam, like his brother, always had money problems. Fortunately, his wife's income could always bail him out.

Woodrow Sam spent part of his trust fund money on psycho-analysis. His analyst listened to his ruminations on his inability to get work on the stage and his subsequent channeling of his efforts into CONY. The analyst made the mistake of wondering aloud whether ecology and a faster-moving New York were really Wood-row Sam's reasons for seeking to ban private cars from Manhattan Island. Perhaps the real reason, he suggested, was that by fighting cars he was subconsciously doing battle with his car dealer father and his stunt-car-driving brother. Woodrow Sam responded to this bit of insight by firing his analyst.

After the first Trust Committee meeting and her desultory *Macbeth* rehearsal, Glenda invited Grover Sam to dinner. She cooked leg of lamb, Grover Sam's favorite dish, while Woodrow Sam and Grover Sam made forced conversation. Of the three, only Glenda, whom Harry had appointed to the committee, was in anything approaching a good mood.

As they ate dinner, the three of them steered clear of the topics of Harry's estate and the Trust Committee. They talked about nothing of great importance, even though they were all bursting with comments and opinions about the committee. They were simply following a time-honored Gaines tradition: if something was painful, just pretend it wasn't happening.

Over coffee, Grover Sam asked his brother and his sister-in-law whether they wanted to watch one of his videos, which he happened to have with him. Woodrow Sam was not interested, but Glenda said, "Absolutely!" and the three sat and watched *Roadkill* on the VCR. Grover Sam proudly showed them the box it came in, on which was printed in large letters one of the highest bits of praise Grover Sam had received since entering the crash video field: "NO ONE ELSE DRIVES THIS BADLY THIS WELL"— CHATTAHOOCHEE JOURNAL.

The crashes, explosions, and impossibly dangerous accidents had on the three Gaineses a peaceful, calming effect. One could take nothing seriously after ninety-three minutes of "smash and burn." Their minds soothed into numbness by the repeated explosions—Grover Sam fast-forwarded past anything remotely resembling plot—they found themselves ready to discuss their feelings about the Trust Committee in an atmosphere free of rancor or resentment.

"Aren't you scared, driving that way?" asked Woodrow Sam, an air of wonder and grudging respect in his voice.

"A little," admitted Grover Sam. "But it's either that or type." He turned to Glenda. "How did the meeting go today?" he asked.

Glenda sighed. "Not so well," she said. "I'm not very hopeful."

"Too bad," said Woodrow Sam. "If it weren't for that committee idea, Harry would have probably just split the money between Father and Rebecca and Uncle Charles." And, Woodrow Sam did not need to add, one day part of it would have flowed to him.

"What would you have done, if you had the theaters?" Woodrow Sam asked his brother, who dug into his second slice of pie.

"Oh, I had this idea for a kind of film museum," Grover Sam said, and he briefly outlined his plans to his brother. "But now it'll never happen. What about you?"

Woodrow Sam eyed Glenda before he responded. His desire conflicted dramatically with hers, and they both knew it. "Well," he began diplomatically, "I'd like to see regular Broadway plays in them again, like in the old days, when Grandpa and Original Sam built them. I'd sell them to one of the chains. Glenda doesn't exactly see it that way. She wants to run them herself."

"What's wrong with that?" she murmured, as she poured more coffee.

"Nothing's wrong with it," said Woodrow Sam, "except you don't have any experience."

"I've been in the theater for twenty years," Glenda said.

"Auditioning doesn't count," Woodrow Sam said tartly.

"I get more work than you do," responded Glenda.

"I mean experience running things," said Woodrow Sam. He added, to his brother Grover Sam: "We have this same argument all the time."

"I think I can learn how to run a theater," she said. "I think I can pick it up pretty quickly."

Grover Sam sat and pondered things. "Well, we all want all three theaters, right?"

"Right," said Glenda and Woodrow Sam.

"You know, we could . . . compromise," Grover Sam said. The word "compromise" had a foreign sound coming from the mouth of a Gaines.

"Compromise? How?" Glenda asked cautiously. As a Trust Committee member, she felt she had the most to lose.

"Well, there are three theaters and three of us. What if, you know, we each took one theater?"

"So Glenda manages one," said Woodrow Sam, "we sell one to the Shuberts, and you get the third for your film museum?"

Grover Sam shrugged. "Yeah, kind of," he said.

The three thought about the idea. For each, it represented a comedown. Glenda saw herself as an instant theater chain. One theater hardly a chain of theaters made, she realized, but one theater was better than the proverbial kick in the head. As long as she got the eleven-hundred-forty-seat Classical Theater, largest of the three owned by the family, she might be amenable to such a compromise.

Woodrow Sam wanted to sell all three theaters to a chain because such a sale would net the family sixty million dollars. Selling only one theater would bring in only twenty million. Still, twenty million was twenty million. If they sold the Classical, however, they might be able to net twenty-five million. If they sold the Classical, he would go along.

Grover Sam pondered the compromise he had suggested. Maybe his film museum could make do with only one theater. Provided, of course, it was the biggest theater.

"It's not a bad idea," Glenda said carefully.

"It's worth further study," said Woodrow Sam.

"I'm glad I thought of it," said Grover Sam.

"There's just one problem," said Glenda. "I'm only one vote. You need four votes."

The lapsed into silence again.

"There's Morris," said Woodrow Sam. "We could count on him."

"That only makes two votes," said Glenda.

"What does Father want to do with the theaters?" Grover Sam asked Glenda. It struck him as odd that he had to ask his sister-in-law what his own father had in mind, but such were relationships among Gaines fathers and sons.

"He wants to create this memorial to Harry," said Glenda. "As if Harry'd ever been a father to him."

"What kind of memorial?" Woodrow Sam asked.

"A museum of vaudeville," said Glenda. "He says there's nothing like it in New York."

"That's because nobody cares about vaudeville anymore," said Grover Sam. "It's dead as a doornail."

"Well, Keith cares, and he has one vote."

Once again, the three fell silent.

"I could see my film museum being a Film and Vaudeville Institute," said Grover Sam.

"That's extremely generous of you," said Glenda. "Do you mean it?"

Grover Sam shrugged. In a minute he had seen his three-theater complex become a one-theater complex, and now he was on the verge of giving away half of *that*. Still, they needed Keith's vote. Finally, he nodded. "But it would have to be the Classical," he said. "That's the only way I would do it. Otherwise I won't have enough space."

Glenda bit her lip. She tried to imagine herself making do with the Walker or the American.

Woodrow Sam looked pained. The proceeds from his theater

sale had dropped from sixty million to twenty-five million and now fell another five million dollars. He decided that he had better agree before the sale price sank any lower.

"I could go along with that," he said at last.

"I guess I could too," said Glenda, shifting her thoughts to running the American or the Walker. The Classical was too big and drafty for stage plays anyway, she decided.

"So if Father goes along, that gives us three votes," said Grover Sam. "Where do we get the fourth vote?"

Glenda thought back to the meeting that morning. "I don't know," she said. "Maybe the accountant from the bank, Harold or Howard or something."

"What about him?" Woodrow Sam asked.

"You should have seen the way he was glaring at Sam David," said Glenda. "If looks could kill."

"Why was he glaring at Sam David?" asked Grover Sam.

"I don't know," said Glenda. "I just got very strong feelings about it. I think he doesn't like him. I think he thinks Sam David is an asshole."

"Suddenly I'm gaining respect for accountants," said Woodrow Sam.

"Do you think you can work on him?" asked Grover Sam.

She thought for a moment. "It's worth a try," she said. "Anyone for more coffee?"

"Please," said Grover Sam, feeling better than ever. His film museum might just happen after all. He started to think about the invitation list for the opening.

"Definitely," said Woodrow Sam, whose mood had also improved. Maybe there was hope.

22

AT THAT MOMENT, Gil Thompson—who by now had decided to give up acting for a career in law enforcement—accompanied by his new girlfriend and assistant, Cynthia Crossen, was changing planes in O'Hare Airport in Chicago, en route to Omaha and then Greenwood, Nebraska. The whole thing was an enormous adventure for Gil. It reminded him of an old movie he had seen once—*Under Cover of Darkness*, with Gregory Peck, or it might have been Ronald Colman.

"I still don't understand why we're doing this, Sidney," Cynthia complained as she tried to keep up with Gil's purposeful strides. She had taken several valuable sick days and had gotten other nurses to cover for her, and she therefore believed she was entitled to an explanation. "I mean, what's in Nebraska anyway?"

"Not so loud," Gil/Sidney cautioned her. "I think we're being followed."

They were not being followed, but Gil, given to overdramatizing things, wanted to think they were. They reached the gate for their Omaha connection without mishap, which somehow disappointed Gil. While Cynthia wondered why he was acting so strangely, Gil bought a *Chicago Tribune* and sat with the newspaper in the manner that he had perfected in the lobby of the hospital while watching Morris and the Gaineses.

"It's like this," he whispered to Cynthia, never taking his eyes off the passing crowd. He was not sure how to recognize whoever was supposed to be following him. He knew, though, that he would recognize that person when the time came. "You remember that woman who made my poor uncle Harry sign that will?"

"Of course!" said Cynthia, bristling at the memory of Amelia.

"Well," said Gil, watching a suspicious person go by, and then a second, and then a third. For Gil, the kind of New Yorker who believed you needed a passport and shots to cross the George Washington Bridge, everyone in the Midwest looked suspicious. "The law firm that represents my uncle Harry's interests has hired me—has hired *us*—to go to that woman's hometown and get the scoop on her."

"*Really!*" said Cynthia, impressed. So her new friend, Sidney, was a spy. "Well, I hope we get something good on her. I think she's terrible."

Gil/Sidney put down his newspaper and gave Cynthia his most sincere look. The whole thing was working out extremely well for him. His work for Old Shap would net him his largest and steadiest paycheck in years, he got to travel out of the city, all expenses paid, even if it was only to Nebraska, and he had the admiration and company of a most attractive woman.

"I feel the same way you do," he said with great gentleness. "I know we'll get something."

"Can I ask you one thing, though?"

"Sure," Gil/Sidney said.

"How come our tickets say Mr. and Mrs. Gil Thompson? Your name is Sidney."

"Just a precaution," said Gil, thinking quickly. "In case the other side finds out about this trip."

"Oh," said Cynthia, impressed.

A few hours later, they landed in Omaha, rented a car at the airport, checked into a nearby hotel, and drove west twenty-seven miles along Interstate 80 to Greenwood. They drove along the small town's main street, Gil peering through the windshield for clues about the Vanderbilts. None were forthcoming. They passed a small honky-tonk bar called Grand Central Station. The name appealed to the Manhattanite in Gil, and he slowed to take a better look. Pickups predominated in the parking lot. Gil pulled in.

"What are we doing?" asked Cynthia, looking doubtfully at the bar.

"We're going to get a drink," said Gil.

"But I'm not thirsty," said Cynthia.

Gil gave her a knowing look. "Neither am I," he said. "We're going to order something and ask the bartender about the Vanderbilts. Bartenders know everything in a small town. Didn't you ever see *The Third Olive*, with George Raft and Ida Lupino?"

"N-no," admitted Cynthia.

"Well, if you had, you'd understand. Come on."

They parked their rental car, the only vehicle in the lot without a shotgun rack, and made their way inside. Cynthia, who had feared the worst, was disappointed. A bunch of exceptionally nonviolent, rather bored individuals, all males, sat around, hunched over their drinks, giving a quick look at the strangers as they entered and just as quickly ignoring them. Two young men in jeans and black T-shirts played pool in the corner. An aging jukebox near the pool table quietly played country music.

"Great local color," Gil said admiringly.

"Sidney, this place is creepy," said Cynthia, holding his arm.

"A job's a job," he said, trying to sound tough, although he agreed with her. They made their way to the bar. The bartender was disappointingly young and pleasant. Gil had been hoping for someone older and harder, the kind of bartender people poured out their troubles to, like Audie Murphy in *Last Chance Saloon*.

Gil and Cynthia seated themselves at the bar and tried to look inconspicuous. The bartender approached.

"Boilermaker," said Gil, not knowing what a boilermaker was but hoping that ordering one made him sound tough. Then he remembered that he did not want to drink and drive, because it was dangerous and against the law. "Actually, make that a 7-Up."

"Same," said Cynthia.

The bartender gave them an odd look and went off to get two glasses. Gil cocked an eyebrow at Cynthia. He studied the bartender, who looked to be college age or slightly older. He was extremely good-looking and seemed out of place among the roughnecks of Greenwood.

"A dollar sixty," the bartender said, placing the drinks in front of them. Gil reached for his wallet, pulled out a twenty-dollar bill, and placed it on the bar beside his drink, just as he had seen Bruce Dern do it in *Vagrant from the West*. As the bartender took it, Gil whispered, "You can keep the change if you can tell me about the Vanderbilt family."

The bartender, who was saving money to leave Greenwood and go to New York or Hollywood and study acting, had lived in Greenwood all his life and never heard of the Vanderbilt family. Still, it was not every day that a couple of strangers walked in as though they were in some kind of spy movie and offered eighteen dollars and forty cents in tips just for a little information. The bartender decided to play along and see what this was all about. Something about Gil and Cynthia reminded him of George Raft and Ida Lupino in *The Third Olive*.

He looked both ways before answering. When he finally spoke, he did so in a dramatic whisper, keeping his eyes off his interlocutor.

"Who wants to know?" the bartender asked.

His tone sent a tingle up Gil's spine. Obviously they had come to the right place, and there was something extremely suspicious and terrible to be learned. Old Shap would be so proud of him, he told himself. He saw himself traveling around the country, going into bars, getting information on behalf of wealthy and distressed clients, befriending a network of bartenders, maybe getting plastic surgery every few months in case people were hot on his trail, and Cynthia at his side all the while. Maybe Cynthia would get plastic surgery too.

The bartender took the twenty-dollar bill, went to the cash register, rang up the sale, and pocketed the eighteen dollars and forty cents change. He returned to Gil and Cynthia.

Gil squinted before he answered. "I'll tell you who wants to know. Some interests out of New York."

The bartender nodded slowly and comprehendingly. "New York, huh?" he said, just like Leo Gorcey in *I Kill for Money*.

Gil nodded just as slowly. He did not want to betray his

excitement. Clearly this bartender knew more than he was saying. Gil noticed a display of beer nuts behind the bar. In a loud voice, he said, "How 'bout some of them beer nuts?"

The bartender understood. It was simply a dodge to make the other customers believe nothing unusual was going on. No point in alarming the regulars. The bartender turned to reach for a package of beer nuts. It seemed appropriate; this stranger, whoever he might be, was a nut case.

"Fifty cents," said the bartender.

Gil took out his wallet and extracted another twenty. "You can . . . keep the change," he said, just like John Wayne in *Look Out for the Cactus*. Cynthia watched the transaction, wide-eyed. This was serious money.

The bartender rang up the sale, pocketed the nineteen dollars and fifty cents change, and returned to his position across from Gil and Cynthia.

"Why do you need to know about the Vanderbilts?" asked the bartender, hoping to sound cagey.

"That's between me and my client," Gil said firmly. No bartender was going to drag critical information like that out of *him*. "Got a straw?"

"Huh? Oh, sure," said the bartender. He reached for a straw and handed it to Gil, who put it in his soda and had a sip, maintaining his extremely serious demeanor all the while. Cynthia, watching the exchange, veered between fear for their physical safety—obviously they were about to learn something horrible—and admiration for Sidney/Gil, who was clearly a professional.

"I've got information on the Vanderbilts," the bartender whispered, wiping a clean glass with a dirty bar towel, "that could blow this town wide open."

Gil slurped his soda. "That's what I need," he said.

The bartender nodded understandingly. He wondered what he could say that might pry another twenty loose from the wallet of his strange customer. "We speak the same language," he said. "But tell me what you're looking for. I want to make sure we're talking about the same thing."

Gil decided he could take the bartender into his confidence.

He had already proved his trustworthiness. "We've developed some information that makes us think the Vanderbilts are involved in a scam with old people and their wills. You know, getting them to sign things when they're drugged up and out of it."

Cynthia bristled at the memory of Amelia and the others taking advantage of poor, defenseless Harry.

"I know about it," lied the bartender, wiping the clean glass.

"They do it here too?" Gil asked, looking up quickly.

"All the time," said the bartender, barely able to keep from cracking up. "Um, they did it to a whole nursing home once."

"That's terrible," said Cynthia, disgusted.

"Yes, ma'am, it certainly is."

"I think we've got what we came for," Gil told the bartender. He peeled another twenty from his wallet. "Don't talk to anybody else. And if anybody asks, you never saw us." Just like Ronald Reagan in *I Get in Gunfights*.

The bartender cleared away their half-finished 7-Ups. "My lips are sealed," he said.

Gil glanced at Cynthia. They stood and prepared to leave, Gil keeping his eye all the while on the unremarkable pool players. "Say, do you have a phone?" Gil asked the bartender.

"Outside," said the bartender. And then, more quietly: "If I hear anything else, I'll keep it for you."

Gil nodded appreciatively. This bartender was okay. Maybe Gil would hire him once he got his detective agency started.

Gil and Cynthia left the bar, full of excitement over what they had learned. They went to the telephone, and Gil called information.

"What are you doing?" Cynthia asked.

"I want to find out where these Vanderbilts live," he said. "I think we should just cruise by their houses, see if we can learn anything."

"Do you think it's safe?" Cynthia asked.

Gil pondered the matter. "Probably not," he said. "Maybe you ought to wait here in the bar till I get back." Barbara Stanwyck had waited in the bar for Fred MacMurray in *Really Dangerous*.

"I want to stay with you," said Cynthia, thinking of the pool players.

"Okay," said Gil. "I don't blame you." And into the telephone: "Yes, in, uh, in Greenwood, may I please have the number for John Vanderbilt."

"How do you know his name is John?" Cynthia asked.

"I don't," admitted Gil, placing his hand over the mouthpiece. "But the operator'll tell me their real names that way."

Cynthia looked admiringly at Gil for the tenth time that day. He seemed to know everything about detective work.

"No John Vanderbilt?" Gil asked into the phone. "What about a different first name? . . . No Vanderbilts at all for Greenwood? Are they unlisted at the customer's request? . . . You don't have *anybody* named Vanderbilt in Greenwood? . . . What about, you know, other towns nearby? . . . The whole Omaha area? . . . Not one? . . . Wow. Uh, thanks anyway."

A pensive Gil hung up. "There aren't any Vanderbilts anywhere around here."

Cynthia gave Gil a quizzical look. "What does that mean?"

"I think they knew we were coming," said Gil. "I think they got out of town just ahead of us. We'll check this out tomorrow. I think we should go back to Omaha," he said importantly.

"Okay," said Cynthia. They returned to their car and drove off. From inside the bar, the bartender watched them go. He reached into his pocket and pulled out the agglomeration of tens, fives, ones, and loose change. "This is great," he said. "I'm fifty-eight dollars closer to acting school." He wiped off the bar and wondered whether perhaps he had just been on Candid Camera.

23

THAT SAME EVENING, a few minutes before midnight, Dwight David and Amelia, unaware of the inquiries regarding Vanderbilts being made half a continent away, left a crowded coffeehouse at the corner of Bleecker and Macdougal streets in the Village and walked a few blocks uptown. The two had eaten dinner in a French restaurant nearby, had gone to hear a set at a jazz club where the manager knew Dwight David and seemed extremely happy to see him, and had ended up in the coffeehouse. Amelia had never been to places like these before. She liked seeing new things, and she felt just pleasantly buzzed enough to wonder whether this had to do with the good luck promised by the wallpaper at the bank.

They turned the corner and found themselves on the south side of Washington Square Park, opposite the arch. Dwight David indicated the building to their right.

"NYU Law School," he told Amelia. "All the Shapolskys went here."

"Really?" Amelia asked, turning from the arch to look at the law school.

Dwight David nodded. "It's a tradition, going back to Barry Shapolsky. They're big donors too."

"I find that hard to believe," Amelia said. "The Shapolskys don't exactly strike me as generous people."

Dwight David grinned. "Well, there's a reason," he said. "They give all the money in case one day there's a Shapolsky who's too stupid to get in on his grades. They're just thinking ahead."

"That makes more sense," said Amelia.

"They've given a ton of money," said Dwight David. "I guess they don't have a lot of faith in future Shapolskys."

Amelia laughed. "I don't have too much faith in current Shapolskys," she said, and she looked at her watch. "It's getting late," she added, her tone regretful. "I'd better be getting back."

"You live on the East Side, right?" Dwight David asked. "That's where I'm staying. I can have the cabbie drop you off."

"It's not really necessary," said Amelia. "I can take the subway."

"I've never been on the subway," said Dwight David. "I hear it's noisy."

"You get used to it," said Amelia. "What's it like being so rich?"

"You get used to it," he said. "Hey, you're a Vanderbilt: you should know."

"Yeah, I guess I should," said Amelia, as a cab pulled up.

"Come on, I'll drop you off," said Dwight David. They piled into the back seat. "Where do you live?"

Amelia gave her address to the driver, who possessed a nationality that even the cosmopolitan Dwight David had never heard of.

"That's practically right around the corner from my father's place," said Dwight David.

"Chester Alan?" Amelia asked.

Dwight David nodded.

"You stay with him while you're here?"

"Sort of," said Dwight David. "He's got the top floor of this building, and he keeps a two-bedroom apartment on the ninth floor. He lets me use it while I'm in New York."

"Must be nice," said Amelia.

"It is," said Dwight David. "Want to see it?"

"Not tonight," said Amelia, who wanted to see it and to stay out with Dwight David, but also felt disloyal both to her boyfriend,

Howard, and to her employer, the bank. If she stayed out any later, she would be tired the next day at her desk. Writing to the DLOLs and saying goodbye would require a great deal of energy. That thought depressed Amelia. Then she remembered the letters between Woodrow and Original Sam.

"Hey, can I ask you something about your family?" Amelia asked as the taxi careened uptown.

Dwight David snorted. "That's the only thing you talked about all during dinner."

It was true. Amelia had used the evening to pump Dwight David for information about his family, its members' accomplishments, and the reasons for their failure to get along.

"I'm sorry," said Amelia, not sorry in the least. "It's just my job to know about you people."

" 'You people'?" repeated Dwight David, obviously not in love with the phrase. "You make us sound like, I don't know, some kind of ethnic tribe."

"Well, you are pretty different," said Amelia.

"I guess," said Dwight David. "But I think if you gave any family as much money as we have, they'd turn out pretty much like us."

The cab pulled up at a red light, and Dwight David looked out the window. He noticed a cluster of shabbily dressed men sitting on the front steps of a church. "Look at all the homeless people," he said. "Tess would love it." The cab started up again, a few moments before the light turned green.

Although Dwight David was talking about his family, he was thinking about how he could draw Amelia back to his apartment. Then he remembered something that might work. "You know, I have that article about Grover," he said. "The baseball player. He was my great-uncle or something."

Amelia looked up quickly. "What kind of article?" she asked.

Bingo, thought Dwight David. "It's from a veterans' magazine."

"Can I come over?" Amelia asked suddenly.

"Are you sure it's okay?" he asked, sounding innocent. "I mean, since you're from the bank and everything?"

"It's okay," Amelia insisted. Anything for another clue to the Gaineses.

Dwight David told the cabbie to forget the first address and to take them instead to Seventy-third Street and Fifth Avenue.

"Nice address," said Amelia.

"It's near the hospital," said Dwight David. "That's why Dad lives there."

The cab pulled up at a large apartment building overlooking Central Park. A doorman in uniform came out to the cab to open the door for Amelia and Dwight David. Amelia had never experienced this sort of treatment before.

"Good evening, Dwight David," said the doorman, an avuncular fellow in his late sixties.

"Hi, Ernest," said Dwight David. "This is Amelia. Um, do you have any money?"

Ernest handed him a twenty. "Your father told me you were in town," he said. "Pleased to meetcha, Amelia."

"He'll pay you back," said Dwight David, and he gave the bill to the cabdriver, who made change. Dwight David grinned. "Tell him it was a limo and you gave me a fifty."

"Oh, Dwight David, I could never do that." In point of fact, he did it all the time.

Two minutes later, Dwight David was unlocking the door to the apartment his father let him use. The first thing Amelia noticed was the view. Floor-to-ceiling windows dominated the living room and gave a shimmering view of Central Park, the buildings across the park on the West Side, and midtown. The apartment overlooked the tree line.

"If they grow any higher," said Dwight David, indicating the trees, "this place will lose half its value."

Amelia pulled herself away from the view and admired the exquisite taste and large amounts of money that had gone into furnishing the apartment. Sumptuous carpeting, large sofas, expensive lamps, and what looked like original and expensive artwork lined the walls. Amelia peeked into the kitchen and saw all sorts of marvelous and expensive devices, all untouched, except for some Pop-Tart wrappers and crumbs around the toaster-oven.

"It's just empty most of the time?" Amelia asked. "I'd rent it."

Dwight David laughed. "I'll ask Father. He keeps saying he'll sell it, but he hangs on to it because he knows if he keeps it, he'll get to see me when I come to New York. It's kind of sad, actually. Want something to drink? I didn't have a chance to go shopping. All there is is water. And Snickers bars."

"The article," said Amelia, suddenly conscious that she had accompanied a client back to his apartment late at night. Mr. Skeffington would never approve. Then Amelia decided that Mr. Skeffington need never know.

"Oh, yeah, the article," said Dwight David, remembering. "I think it's in the closet. Give me a minute."

Dwight David returned a few minutes later, not with the article, but with a mug of Kahlúa and hot chocolate laced with whipped cream.

"Breakfast of champions," he told Amelia. "It's hot."

"Thank you," she said, touched by his thoughtfulness. He left the living room to go look for the article. Amelia wondered whether he was trying to get her drunk or was simply being a good host. After all, as he had told her over dinner about his farmhouse in Antibes, "I live for hospitality." Either way, she felt happy. Dwight David wasn't as bad as she had thought. The Gaineses were not as bad as she had thought. Nothing was as bad as she had thought. Howard could be a drag sometimes, but that was about it. Amelia went back to the window. In her Kahlúa-induced mellowness, the city had never looked more elegant. Entranced, she stared at the view as the minutes passed.

"I almost couldn't find it," said Dwight David, appearing with a yellowing newspaper clipping in his hand. "It was under this pile of stuff."

She practically grabbed it from him and in so doing tore it slightly.

"Hey, careful, it's old," Dwight David protested.

"Sorry," she said. Amelia read the name of the newspaper: *Jewish War Veterans of America Newsletter*. It was dated July 18, 1953.

"I'm getting a Snickers bar," said Dwight David. "Want one?"

"No, thanks," said Amelia.

"Let me know if you need anything," he said, on his way to the kitchen, but he knew she was already too engrossed in the article even to hear him.

She yawned, forced herself to focus on the article despite her fatigue, and began to read:

GROVER GAINES,
JEWISH BALLPLAYER AND WAR HERO

by Lieutenant (j.g.) Marcus Cohen, USN (ret.)

Grover Gaines surrendered his life in a tragic accident on board the U.S.S. *Saratoga* on April 17, 1942, as it steamed toward combat at Corregidor. America's Jews lost a fine young man, a war hero, and one of the best Jewish baseball prospects since Hank Greenberg.

Friends recalled him last month at a big reunion of Jewish war veterans from the Bronx, N.Y., where Grover grew up. His friends remembered that he was a big baseball bug and he had a wonderful arm. All the neighborhood children would pick him to pitch. Baseball then was a different game for children. There were no Little Leagues and no organizing principles other than the idea that the two biggest boys would be captains and they would choose up sides. Children would play from dawn until dusk, racking up as many as fifty at-bats in a single day.

Grover was invariably picked first if he was not made a captain. He would pitch six games a day and always bat leadoff. His eye was legend in the Bronx. In an era when schoolyard toughness dictated hitting the first pitch, no matter how wild or how far from the strike zone, Grover practically pioneered among his pals the idea of always, always taking the first pitch, watching it, and with his incredible eyesight he could see the seams turn as the ball made its way to the plate. He invariably drove the second pitch for a home run.

Grover came from a wealthy and some say an unhappy family in the Bronx. That family money came in handy, because he was forever paying to replace broken windows or buying new baseballs to replace the ones he socked out of the schoolyard.

Friends reminisced that Grover spent more time out of school than in it. He just played ball, followed the Yankees, and played more ball. He used to catch hell from the truant officer, but he did not care. That truant officer gave him his first big "break." He was a good Irish fellow, and he happened to play for a semiprofessional team in the Bronx. The league consisted of police precincts, firehouses, school professionals including janitors and truant officers, and meat packers from the slaughterhouses that existed in that day.

Grover was five foot nine inches by the time he was fourteen, tall enough to pass for sixteen, and the truant officer, who had seen him pitch, invited him to try out for the Department of Schools' team.

Grover's tryout was a sensation, and they tapped him to pitch the following Sunday, a blazing summer day in 1932. He wired his father, by then in Saratoga, that he would pitch a semipro game and that he hoped his father might return to New York to attend. Grover's hopes were dashed by a wire that came the night *after* the game. It read: "Never knew Jews played baseball." The lads who knew Grover growing up remembered that Grover's father was from the old school.

Right field was bounded not by a fence but by railroad tracks. Every Sunday afternoon, when Grover pitched, a freight train would slow down, not because a ballplayer was coming too close but so as to afford one of the trainmen a better look at the boy. The trainman's brother was a scout in the Red Sox organization. At age seventeen, Grover was signed to a minor league contract.

Grover could not have been happier to leave New York, his buddies remember. It was not one of those happy homes, apparently. He spent three years in the minor leagues, pitching and winning at Wilkes-Barre, Bradenton, Florida, and finally Pawtucket. He was brought up to the majors during the last week of the 1938 season and got in two games. He pitched a total of five scoreless innings against the Cleveland Indians and the St. Louis Browns. He started the following season with Boston and became a relief pitcher and, because of his keenly developed batter's eye, an occasional pinch hitter.

He was married that May at the ballyard in Providence, old McCoy Stadium, to a waitress he met in that town, an eighteen-year-old girl named Esther Lampkin. His manager was his best man. Along the way, his un-Jewish-sounding last name protected him from the sort of bench riding that other Jews, even greats like Hank Greenberg, suffered. Occasionally his ethnic identity would surface, and some big Southern boy playing for another team, or even one of his own teammates, would say, "I didn't know Jews could play baseball." Grover would never get angry. He would just say "That's what my father said," and turn his back on his accuser.

He pitched for parts of two years in the majors, compiling a career record of seven wins and two losses. His earned run average was 2.79, and he struck out roughly twice the number of batters he walked. As a pinch hitter he was no less successful, garnering eighteen hits in fifty-two times at bat. He was especially good at drawing walks and at prolonging his at-bats, patiently fouling off pitch after pitch, waiting for the one that strayed from the strike zone. You can, as they say, look it up.

The Red Sox were on the verge of converting Grover to a starting pitcher for the beginning of the 1941 season, but he injured a knee during spring training and missed the first four months of the season. The Sox sent him down to Pawtucket for August and brought him back up as a reliever in September, although he saw no action. That winter came Pearl Harbor. He promptly enlisted in the Navy, shipped out to the Pacific, and, as I sadly noted earlier, gave his life when a boiler exploded on the ship. He left a wife and no children. Grover Gaines, *t'hay m'nuchaso b'gan eden*—may his rest be in Paradise, and may his curve ball fool the hitters there, as it did so well on Earth.

Amelia finished the article and shook her head sadly. She yawned—it was late and she had had several drinks more than was her custom. "What a family!" she said.

Dwight David was watching her. "He must have been a good guy," he said. "Real normal. I wish I could have known him."

"Can I ask you a question about your family?" Amelia asked, for what seemed to Dwight David to be the eleven thousandth time since dinner.

"Can you *not* ask me a question about my family?" he countered. "Can you go *five minutes* without talking about my family?"

Amelia ignored him. "If you were to characterize your relationship with your father in a single word," she began, "what would the word be?"

Dwight David thought for a moment. "Distant," he admitted. "I mean, I like the guy, but I guess I hardly know him. Know what I mean?"

Amelia nodded. "And how would you characterize your father's relationship with his father? Chester Alan with Woodrow? Or Woodrow with Original Sam? Or Grover or Theodore with Original Sam?"

"Distant, I guess."

"And what about the relationship between Theodore and Sam David?" she asked. "Or Theodore and Tess?"

"Um, distant," said Dwight David. "Why?"

"Don't you see the pattern?" Amelia asked.

"Pattern? What pattern?" asked Dwight David, playing dumb. "I don't see what you're getting at."

"Stop it," said Amelia, recognizing that Dwight David was pulling her leg. "That's why I think Harry's plan is such a great idea."

"It is?" asked a surprised Dwight David. To his mind, a great idea would have been an outright bequest.

"Sure it is," said Amelia. "He's making you all talk to each other."

"You make that sound like a good thing," said Dwight David.

"Anyway, thanks for letting me see this article," Amelia said, stifling a yawn.

"I found something else you may want to look at," he said.

"What's that?" Amelia asked, yawning with conviction this time. It had been a long day. "I'm sorry I'm yawning," she said.

"It's okay," said Dwight David. "Here."

"What *is* this?" Amelia asked, examining a small booklet from which dangled a tiny pencil on a pink string. The booklet itself, two inches across by three inches down, was printed on stiff ivory-colored paper, was gold around the edges, and read, in gold script: "Order of Dance."

"It's a dance card," Amelia said, fascinated. "I've never seen one of these before."

Gingerly she opened the front cover. Inside, a smaller inner page, printed on lighter ivory stock, read, in elegant Gothic print:

Annual Dance
of the
Alpha and Beta Chapters
of the
Lambda Gamma Phi Sorority
Ritz-Carlton Hotel
March seventh
nineteenth twenty-four

"Wow," Amelia said soberly, out of respect for the date. She gently turned the page. Inside were twenty lines, numbered one through twenty. On half of the lines were names or initials. "H.G.," read the first line. Two was blank. Three read: "Larry." Four, "Blanche." Five was blank except for an asterisk in the margin. Six read: Ruth. Seven, Isabella. Eight, Isabella. Nine was blank. Ten read: Big Blanche. Eleven, Dave. Thirteen, Izzy Baum and Eva Berman. Fifteen, Hank Jaffe. Sixteen, Sylvia Halfer. The rest were blank.

"It's a dance card, right?" Amelia asked. "Whose was it?"

"You're the Gaines family expert," said Dwight David. "I was hoping you could tell me."

"You mean you don't know?" she asked.

Amelia reread the names, looking for clues. "Isabella," she said. "That could be Isabella McNiven."

"Who's that?" asked Dwight David.

"Keith's mother. Keith McNiven Gaines. Let me see." Amelia got out the family tree from her purse. She found Isabella, two names away from Harry. "Born 1906," she read. "So in 1924 that would make Isabella eighteen. I guess Harry met her at this dance."

"Cool," said Dwight David, fascinated by this woman so fascinated by his family.

"Wait a minute," said Amelia, going over the names again. "I recognize this name—Eva Baum. I mean, she was Eva Berman then, but she's Eva Baum now. She's one of my clients. I just had lunch with her."

"Really?" asked Dwight David, surprised. "You *know* her?"

"I arranged Izzy's funeral," Amelia said. "He had intestinal cancer. I can't believe they knew Harry. Can I show this to Eva?"

"If you want," Dwight David said, losing interest in the Baums. "Look at the back."

"Huh? Oh, sure," said Amelia, and she closed the booklet and read the faint print on the back.

Taxi (75¢ & 75¢)	$1.50
Tip	.10
Socks	1.00
Tailor	1.50
Tip	.10
Tip	.30
[Illegible]	.10
	6.20
Tux	2.00
[Illegible]	.20
	4.20

Amelia concentrated on the figures. Despite her deep fatigue, she added the numbers. Harry's calculations were far off the mark. They simply made no sense. She laughed and yawned at the same time. "It has to be Harry," she said. "He never had any concept of a dollar."

"Really?" Dwight David asked happily. "Then I'm not the only one in the family like that?"

"From what I've seen of Harry's spending patterns," said Amelia, "you're still an amateur. On the other hand, he actually *made* the money he spent."

"Oh," said Dwight David, disappointed. "Still, it's nice to know I come by my spendthrift traits honestly. Look inside it. The inside back cover."

"Huh?" asked Amelia, carefully opening the dance card again. "What's this?"

Someone had written something in script—a long poem, perhaps. The handwriting looked familiar to Amelia. She thought for a moment, went to her handbag, and pulled out Harry Gaines's diary for 1915. She opened it to the section listing his whereabouts for January and February. The handwriting on the dance card and in the diary were identical.

"It's Harry, all right," she said. "Look."

Dwight David looked at the handwriting in the diary. There was no doubt. "I always wondered who this belonged to," Dwight David said. "Read what he wrote."

Amelia squinted. The writing on the dance card was half the size of the writing in the diary. Much of it was first draft material—there were cross-outs and changed words everywhere. She read carefully aloud:

> "If in dancing and in prancing
> With a, um, a girl who's not entranced yet
> Your dance is for enhancing:
> Just talk to her of love."

She smiled at Dwight David. "It's cute," she said. Then she remembered she had heard it before. Harry had sung it in the waiting room of the cardiac care unit. She felt a chill.

"Keep going," he urged. He was standing right beside her. She nodded, and this time she began to sing the words, remembering the melody as best she could and improvising the rest.

> *"With eyes so scintillating,*
> *And the—and the—"*

"Music," Dwight David said.

> *"And the music that is pulsating,*
> *With joy that's stimulating,*
> *She will speak to you of love."*

"It's so corny," said Amelia. "It's sweet."
"Keep going," said Dwight David, coming closer.
"Okay," said Amelia.

> *"She will . . ."*

"Grow," Dwight David offered. Amelia nodded.

> *"She will grow enthusiastic,*
> *While her something something fantastic . . ."*

"I can't read that word. Or the next line."
"Let me see," said Dwight David, his head on Amelia's shoulder. She knew it, and she did not halt it. "I can't make it out," he said.
"Well, whatever," said Amelia.

> *"She will grow enthusiastic*
> *While her something something fantastic,*
> *Something some things quite drastic,*
> *As she looks at you with love."*

Dwight David had slipped his arm around Amelia's waist and had begun to rock her gently, in the same rhythm as the lyrics she read:

> *"While in your mind, um, debating* [Amelia sang]
> *Just what she means by 'mating'* [she giggled],
> *Beware lest hesitating,*
> *She will make you fall in love."*

Amelia slowly lowered her hands to Dwight David's waist. Still clutching the dance card in one hand and Harry's 1915 diary in the other, she put her arms around Dwight David's back, carried away by the alcohol and the magic and the city outside and the corny rhythms of Harry Gaines's imagination coming to life again after sixty-six years. Dancing slowly to music that only the two of them could hear, they both imagined themselves at the Annual Dance of the Alpha and Beta Chapters of the Lambda Gamma Phi Sorority at the Ritz-Carlton Hotel, awhirl in the dance, the orchestra sweet and dated, the other couples young and naive.

They kissed and they danced and they danced faster and they kissed again and again until Amelia dropped the diary and the dance card and held Dwight David as close as she possibly could, waltzing—for it had to be a waltz that they heard—all the while. And they both sensed the other couples parting for them, the way the other couples always part in the musicals, so that one couple can have the center of the floor all to themselves, and they sensed the eyes of all the other couples on them as they danced and kissed, they sensed the orchestra leader, his hair slicked back the way men did that in 1924, watching them dance, conducting over his shoulder, the musicians ignoring him, smiling at their own private jokes. Amelia Vanderbilt, small-town girl come to New York to seek fame and magic, found it now in the arms of Dwight David. The music stopped. They kissed again, and Dwight David gently, in a gentlemanly fashion, led Amelia off the dance floor and to the second bedroom of the apartment, the one he had not been living in since his arrival from France several days earlier, the clean one.

THREE

Lucid

Intervals

BICKLE, GET IN HERE!" thundered Sam David Gaines into the office intercom.

It was morning.

Richard Bickle raced into Sam David's office, stealing a glance at his watch as he entered. It was 7:45 A.M., early for Sam David. Usually he did not holler until eight.

"Yes, sir?"

"I just got some unsettling news, Bickle," said Sam David.

"Yes, sir?" If one had examined Bickle closely, one would have found him to be shaking slightly.

"It's from Louis Gaines Shapolsky at Old Shap. He got a call from Gil in Nebraska. There are *no Vanderbilts* in Greenwood, Nebraska. None! Do you hear me, Bickle?"

"Yes, sir," said Bickle. It would have been hard not to hear him. It would have been hard for people several blocks away from Sam David's office not to hear him.

"Do you know what that means?" Sam David asked.

"N-no sir," Bickle offered timidly, wishing to Christ that he in fact did know what it meant.

"Well, neither do I, goddammit!" shouted Sam David.

Bickle felt flooded with relief.

"I have no idea how to understand this information," said Sam

David, calming down. "We have a trust officer in charge of Harry's committee. She claims to come from a town called Greenwood, Nebraska. She claims to receive cookies from her grandmother, whom she refers to as Granny Vanderbilt, who lives in this same town of Greenwood, Nebraska. But we send a man to Greenwood, Nebraska, and we find that there are no Vanderbilts in Greenwood, Nebraska, and there never have been *any* Vanderbilts in Greenwood, Nebraska! Do you get the point, Bickle?"

"Yes," said Bickle, but then he quickly changed his position. "No. No, sir, I don't."

"But you will," said Sam David. "Why would this Amelia Vanderbilt claim to be from Greenwood, Nebraska, if she's not from there? Has she got something to hide? If she does, Bickle, we have something to *exploit!* It's leverage, Bickle, leverage! There's something about her that doesn't add up! She's too *perfect!* She's too *normal!* Cookies from her *grandmother!* If we can find out what she's got to hide, we've got her vote! And we can probably make the accountant Harold vote with her!"

"Howard," said Bickle.

"Whatever," said Sam David. "I don't like him."

"No, sir," said Bickle.

"So that's three votes, and I'll only need one more."

"Yes, sir," said Bickle.

"Get out of here," said Sam David. "Find Amelia, and follow her."

"Aren't the people from Old Shap going to be following her too?" Bickle asked. "Can't we rely on them?"

"No, we can't rely on them," said Sam David. "Old Shap represents Tess as well as myself. Anything they'll tell me they'll tell her."

"But do you really think Tess would try to blackmail Amelia?"

"If she could screw me over in the process," Sam David said darkly, "absolutely."

"I'll get right to work," said Bickle.

"Good man," said Sam David, who had just thought of something else. "And get me Morris Shapolsky on the phone."

"*You* want to talk to Morris Shapolsky?" Bickle asked, his jaw dropping. Did the Hatfields ever want to talk to the McCoys? The Montagues and the Capulets? The Kremlin and the Pope?

"Not really, but I have to," said Sam David. "I'll need his vote. Set up a lunch for him and me at the most expensive restaurant in the city. Now get out of here."

"Yes, sir," said Bickle, and he sped out of his boss's office.

At the moment, Gil/Sidney and Cynthia were flying back to New York. Gil felt extremely proud of himself for his undercover work. He did not understand why Louis Gaines Shapolsky, his "handler" at Old Shap, did not share his fascination with the Vanderbilts' drug and prostitution links in the greater Omaha area. Instead Louis had seemed to care only about the fact that Gil could not locate any living Vanderbilts in the telephone directory or through directory information. Gil could have learned that without leaving New York.

"What are we going to do when we get to New York?" Cynthia asked.

Gil studied her. He wondered, for a moment, whether she was entirely trustworthy. Perhaps she was a plant, someone sent to seduce him by . . . the other guys. Perhaps she was feeding information to the other side as quickly as he could learn things. Suddenly Gil hated his spy work. It drove a wedge between himself and his feelings for Cynthia. Perhaps, if they had met at another time, a safer time, a time when he was not engaged in a multimillion-dollar espionage case, things between them could have worked out. Perhaps they could have fallen in love, gotten married, and left the steamy city for a small town somewhere, perhaps even Greenwood, Nebraska, where they could buy a little house surrounded by a white picket fence and equipped with a massive burglar alarm system.

They could live in quiet contentment, borrowing cups of flour and sugar from the polite, friendly neighbors, the way Gil heard people did things in small towns. Or they'd have the guys from work or the bowling team over for a barbecue on the patio. Or he could teach Junior all about ham radio in the basement. But now, Gil realized, none of those things could happen. As likely as not, Cynthia was a plant. A counterspy. Gil had no alternative. He would have to kill her. Just like the young Robert Stack in A *Bullet for Your Thoughts*.

"Sidney, I'm talking to you," said Cynthia.

"Huh?" Gil/Sidney said, emerging from his homicidal reveries. He couldn't kill Cynthia. It was against the law. He had no alternative. He had to trust her.

"What are we going to do in New York? What did your boss say?"

Gil/Sidney looked both ways up and down the aircraft before he spoke. Could the stewardess be trusted? Would he have to kill her too? And if he did, who would serve coffee and dessert?

Gil whispered to Cynthia. "We're supposed to follow Amelia Vanderbilt. The trust officer. We're supposed to find out everything we can about her. It's pretty fishy, saying you come from one town and not having any relatives there. We're to spend the next couple of days trailing Amelia."

Cynthia nodded. This sounded exciting. She would call in sick at the hospital. Just like Tallulah Bankhead in *Nurse on the Lam*.

"You can count on me," she told Gil/Sidney, taking his arm.

"I hope so," responded Gil. Cynthia would never know how close his suspicions about her had brought him to doing her grave physical harm. "I certainly hope so."

Meanwhile, at Manhattan Hospital, cardiologist Tom Braunstein peered at the sleeping figure of Charles Chaplin Gaines, oldest surviving son of the late Harry Gaines, checked the intravenous drip, examined the medical records, and listened to his breathing. "I don't like it at all," he murmured to the duty nurse. "Keep your eye on his temps. If they spike again, I may want to operate. He's a three?" he asked, referring to the four-three-two system of grading patients' chances of survival.

The nurse checked her records and nodded. Dr. Braunstein shook his head. "Make him a two." He looked at Charles C.'s records again. "Says here in case of trouble I'm to call his cousin Tess Gaines and his trust officer at the New York Bank and Trust Company. A. Vanderbilt. Call them and tell them he's slipping."

"Yes, Doctor," said the nurse, taking down the names and telephone numbers, and they left the room of the sleeping patient.

25

AMELIA VANDERBILT, object of speculation and espionage, arrived at the office mildly hung over and twenty minutes late. She had awakened in the arms of Dwight David thirty minutes earlier, looked at his watch, said, "Omigod," kissed him quickly, struggled into her clothing, and practically sprinted for the elevator. She ran the four blocks to her own apartment. In her haste, she did not notice Chester Alan, in jogging attire, returning to his building after a run in the park. He recognized Amelia immediately.

"How do you like that?" he said to himself. "Dwight David's a fast worker."

Amelia reached her own building, flew up the stairs, showered and changed in under fourteen minutes, ran outside again, and grabbed a cab. In the back seat, stuck in traffic, she calmed her racing heart and applied a little more makeup than usual to cover the shadows under her eyes. She paid the cabbie a block before they got to the bank. She raced inside, whispered a quick "Thank you" to the wallpaper, and hurtled to her desk, the top of which was barely visible beneath a sheaf of pink message notes, including two more from Elizabeth Herder, and her personalized copy of *The Wall Street Journal*. Her head throbbed. Then the details of her late night returned to mind. She grinned. Then she looked up. Howard, veering between concern and reproach, stood over her.

"Where were you last night?" he asked.

"What are you talking about?" she asked, the grin fading.

"I tried to call you."

"I told you I was out," she said.

"I know, with Dwight David. But there were a lot of developments on the Trust Committee. I needed to talk to you."

"Couldn't it have waited for this morning?"

"I called your apartment every half hour from ten o'clock until one in the morning."

I was still dancing at one in the morning, Amelia thought.

"Why were you checking up on me?" she asked, a bit more accusingly than she intended.

"I wasn't checking up on you!" Howard protested. "And besides," he whispered, sounding hurt, "I *thought* I was *supposed* to be your boyfriend!"

Guilt seized Amelia. "Can we talk about it later? I was just out with Dwight David. You know, we were just, oh, whatever."

"He's a *client*," said Howard. "You're on his family's trust committee! It doesn't look good!"

Dwight David looked pretty good last night, she thought, but she certainly did not say as much to Howard. "Okay," she said. "Now, what happened last night that was so important?"

"We got calls," Howard began, "from a bunch of different Gaineses. They all want us to come on board with them and vote their way. They want us to meet them and hear them out."

"Like who?" Amelia asked, stifling a yawn.

"Like Tess, who wants us to vote with her and Morris. And Glenda, who wants us to vote with her and Morris. And Sam David, who wants to pay us a million apiece for our votes. He just came out and said, 'How much is your vote going to cost me?' I said, 'Mr. Gaines, my vote is not for sale. I am a certified professional accountant.' "

"He was probably very impressed," Amelia said wryly.

"I think so," said Howard, unaware that Amelia was teasing him. "That's when he said he'd give us a million apiece for our votes."

A *million dollars,* Amelia thought. She'd be rich. Unless, of course, she got caught.

"What did you say to that?" she asked.

"I said no," Howard replied, surprised at the question. "So he came back with two million."

"Wow," said Amelia.

"Anyway, we're having lunch with Tess, coffee with Glenda, and then dinner with Keith."

"When?" asked Amelia.

"Today," said Howard. "They all want to meet today."

Amelia thought for a moment. "What time are we going to be finished with Dwight David—I mean, dinner?" she asked, instantly regretting the slip.

"Early," said Howard, his feelings hurt. "I suppose you're seeing Dwight David again afterwards?"

"We're just friends," Amelia lied. Now she felt truly awful.

"Anyway," said Howard. "Tess is meeting us at that Italian place next door around one o'clock. Is that okay? No plans to duck out with Dwight David for a little romantic lunch?"

"Howard, please!" Amelia said firmly. "Can we please separate our work lives from our private lives?"

"I can," he said. "Can you?" And with that he turned and walked stiffly away.

I've never seen him like that, Amelia thought. She stared impassively at the messages. Elizabeth Herder. Tess Gaines. Sam David Gaines. Glenda Monash Gaines. Keith Gaines. Babette Reynolds Gaines. Chester Alan Gaines. Dr. Tom Braunstein. *Who's that?* she wondered. She read his message: "Charles C. Gaines condition worsening." Amelia looked around on her desk for her Gaines family tree, in order to learn when Charles had been born. She could not find the family tree. Then she remembered— she must have left it at Dwight David's. She sighed. She felt wonderful and awful at the same time, pleased with herself and terribly guilty for hurting Howard. And now she would have to face him in three different meetings with Gaineses. She swept aside the messages, not wanting to return any of the calls just yet. Underneath them lay the decision from *Gaines v. Gaines,* the battle over Theodore's will.

Amelia flipped through the decision again until she came to the line that read: *"See also* my decision in *Gaines v. Gaines and the*

Fund for Grizzly Bears et al., 422 N.Y.S.2d 436 (1980)." She pondered the sentence. Then she stood up and left her desk, carrying the decision with her. She walked to the elevator and went up one flight, to the offices of the Legal Department. There, she was met by the lecherous Aaron Blickstein of the legal staff. Dealing with Aaron, Amelia realized, was the price for deciphering this legal secret code.

She knocked on his door and firmly announced her presence. "Don't even think of coming on to me," she informed Aaron. "Just find me this case."

She showed Aaron the line in the decision. He snorted. "The Fund for Grizzly Bears," he said. "I remember that one. Come on."

Aaron led Amelia into the large office that the Legal Department used as its law library. Encircling the walls were series of tan-and-blue volumes with large black numbers printed on the spines. "I'll show you how to do it," said Aaron, taking Amelia's no-nonsense attitude to heart, at least for the moment. "This '422' means volume 422. These letters mean this set of books, New York Supplement, 2nd Series." He pointed to a large set of volumes that covered six shelves. He pulled volume 422 from the wall. "This next number is the page number. Four thirty-six." He flipped to page 436 of volume 422. As if by magic, two thirds of the way down the second column, in small, heavy black print, read the magic words "**Gaines v. Gaines and the Fund for Grizzly Bears et al., 74-38297. March 17, 1980.**"

"Wow," said Amelia, impressed that the Gaineses' lives should be recorded in so important a place as lawbooks. "How come they printed it in here?" she asked.

"It's a precedent," said Aaron. "In case there are any other families like the Gaineses."

"Impossible," Amelia said flatly. "What's this number?" she asked, pointing to the seven digits that followed the title of the case.

"That tells you what year the case was filed: 1974. It wasn't decided until 1980. It dragged on for six years."

"Can I read this?" Amelia asked. Reading about hysterical Gaineses appealed more to her than talking to them on the phone.

"Help yourself," said Aaron. Then he added, with a leer: "And if you ever decide to be unfaithful to Howard, I hope you'll think of me."

Amelia gave him a wan smile. His timing was better than he knew. He waggled his eyebrows at her and went back to his office. Amelia pushed all thoughts of Howard and Dwight David from her mind and began to read:

SURROGATE'S COURT,
PAUL MARTLAND III, JUDGE

Deborah Shapolsky Bishop and Moses Shapolsky, Shapolsky and Shapolsky, New York, New York, for petitioners Theodore Gaines, Annette Morris Gaines, Gloria Coss Gaines, and Chester Alan Gaines.

Morris Shapolsky and Samuel G. Shapolsky, Shapolsky & Shapolsky, New York, New York, for petitioners Charles C. Gaines, Keith McNiven Gaines, Babette Reynolds Gaines, and Rebecca Reynolds Gaines.

Henry Clay Shapolsky, Shapolsky and Shapolsky, New York, New York, for respondent, the estate of Sarah Gurrelts Gaines.

Andrew Seidel, Newburgh & Warfield, Aspen, Colorado, for respondents The Fund for Grizzly Bears, The Chipmunk Society, The Aquatic Mammals Protection League, and Birdwatchers of Arizona, Inc.

Martha Brown, Brown and Sunbeck, Bismarck, North Dakota, for intervenors Friends of the Spotted Owl and the Egret Conservancy.

JUDGE MARTLAND: This case, ostensibly brought as a challenge to the last will and testament of Sarah Gurrelts Gaines, widow of the late Sam Gaines, long ago devolved into a grudge match, pure and simple. On one side are the family members, united in their quest to overturn decedent's will because they were shut out of it. On the second side are four animal rights groups, the beneficiaries of the will, arguing strenuously in favor of their right to take under it. On a third side are two more animal rights groups, the Friends of the Spotted Owl (hereinafter "Owl") and the Egret Conservancy (hereinafter "Egret"), which also had been beneficiaries until the decedent chose to eliminate them from her will.

It is the position of petitioners (decedent's relatives by marriage as well as her relatives descended from her late husband's brother, Harry Gaines) and it is the position of the intervenors (Owl and Egret) that at the respective times when decedent chose to eliminate them from her will, she was insane. It is the position of the will's stated beneficiaries (Bears, Chipmunks, Aquatic Mammals, and Birdwatchers) that she was not.

Decedent's will reads, in pertinent part:

. . . THIRD. I give, devise, and bequeath all of my estate, both real and personal, of every nature and wherever situated, of which I may die seized or possessed, including, without limitation, all property acquired by me or to which I may become entitled after the execution of this will, to the following six groups on a share and share alike basis:

1. The Fund for Grizzly Bears

2. The Chipmunk Society

3. The Aquatic Mammals Protection League

4. Friends of the Spotted Owl

5. Birdwatchers of Arizona, Inc.

6. The Egret Conservancy

I shall first dispose of the claims of intervenors Owl and Egret. These groups have argued strenuously during the six years in which this case has been before me that decedent, although of sound mind at the time she wrote and signed her will, was mentally incompetent at the time she modified her will by striking out with a pen the references to these groups. Owl and Egret further suggest that her failure to change the words "the following six groups" to "the following four groups" indicates a failure to act coherently and clearly with regard to changing the beneficiaries. According to this line of thought, only a mentally incompetent person would fail to make such a correction.

Finally, Owl and Egret argue that decedent must have been acting upon a desire to eliminate all flying creatures from her will, yet she retained as a beneficiary Birdwatchers of Arizona, Inc. (Birdwatchers). Owl and Egret adduced testimony from friends of the decedent to the effect that in her declining years she lost interest in all but land- and sea-based animals. Her failure to remove from her will all three bird-related charities, Owl and Egret argue, offers further evidence of her mental incapacity at the time of the revision of the will.

An egret is a heronlike bird with a long white plume. *Webster's New World Dictionary* (1970) 178. Decedent, Sarah Gurrelts Gaines, developed her interests in matters ornithological at a tender age, according to testimony unchallenged by petitioners, intervenors, or respondents. She was born in the year 1893 to a family of prestige and influence in New York City. Her happiest memories of youth involved nature walks in the wilds of the then-untamed boroughs of New York City. Turn-of-the-century Brooklyn and Queens were home to forests, some farms, and a large and thriving population of flora and fauna. In those unhurried times, a favorite occupation of young people was to organize themselves into nature parties and go off and wander through the animal kingdom that once was New York. At a time before widespread popularity of automobiles and "dating," social activity among young people tended to take place in groups. This is to say that the nature walks often had a "romantic" aspect to them. Winchell's *Social History of New York* (1937) at 110–112.

The young Sarah Gurrelts, having profited from the best possible education available to a young girl in Manhattan, frequently led such nature tours, according to testimony at trial. She was extremely knowledgeable about geological matters as well as the deer, wild turkeys, and other animals that then called Brooklyn and Queens home. Her knowledge of the relative merits of land, as well as, we assume, her shapely form and sharp mind, brought to her semimonthly nature tours at least one young man who was interested in learning about Sarah as about other wonders of nature. That man was to be her husband, Sam Gaines.

The late Mr. Gaines today would be considered an early real estate mogul. He bought with foresight and managed with deftness a real estate empire that, had he lived longer than his forty-three years, might today have been one of the most valuable in the City of New York. (Testimony of Theodore Gaines, trial transcript at 857.) Nature in all its primitive glory brought young Sarah and young Sam together. It transcended the class lines that had separated them, Sam having immigrated to the United States from Russia as an orphan at age ten and Sarah having grown up in then fashionable East Harlem. Nature, sad to say, also tore the marriage apart. Sarah was aggrieved to watch Sam use the information she provided him, both on the walking tours of their youth and in subsequent years of their brief and increasingly unhappy marriage, as the basis for real estate speculation and subsequent development of what once had been wooded tracts. (Testimony of Gloria Coss Gaines, trial transcript at 1249.)

According to uncontroverted testimony, Sarah Gurrelts Gaines watched in horror as her husband converted pristine woods and forests into apartment housing, freshwater streams into sewers, and ecologically delicate meadowlands into shopping centers. When Sarah realized that the knowledge of nature she provided her husband was leading to the destruction of the very areas in which she and he had walked as innocent teenagers, she developed a lifelong sense of guilt and betrayal for the world of nature that she so very much loved. (Testimony of Gloria Coss Gaines, trial transcript at 1261; testimony of Chester Alan Gaines, trial transcript at 1004.)

She frequently remonstrated with her husband over his policy of real estate development. Decedent's late husband told his son Theodore that he blamed his drinking problem on his wife's incessant criticism of his business practices. Sam Gaines often called his wife a hypocrite for chastising his real estate interests yet living off the fruits of those same extremely lucrative interests. (Testimony of Theodore Gaines, trial transcript at 871.) The stormy marriage, begun in 1911, ended in divorce in 1929 when Sarah Gurrelts Gaines pleaded extreme mental cruelty on Sam Gaines's part with regard to certain marital infidelities, the recounting of which has no place in this decision. *See generally In re Gaines*, 167 N.Y. 329 (1934).

Although Sam Gaines remarried, Sarah Gurrelts Gaines never did. Instead she expended on the world of nature her considerable energies and no small part of her extremely large divorce settlement and the income from trusts established by her parents on her behalf. She did so because she wanted to atone for the violence she inadvertently did nature as a result of marrying Sam. For more than three decades, from the years 1930 until 1963, Mrs. Gaines was truly a *vox clamanti in deserto*, a voice crying in the wilderness of a wasteful society on behalf of nature and its speechless inhabitants. She traveled the country to speak to libraries, women's clubs, and Rotary groups about the importance of conservation, ecology, and recycling, at a time when these words were foreign to the lips of most Americans. As with all prophets ahead of their time, Mrs. Gurrelts, as she called herself, met with little success and also faced criticism from her family members. (Testimony of Charles C. Gaines, trial transcript at 2076.) She helped to prepare the ground, as it were, for environmentalists of our generation.

The 1962 publication of Rachel Carson's environmental classic, *Silent Spring*, coincided with Mrs. Gurrelts's first stroke and her subsequent retirement from public life. She devoted the years between those events and her subsequent removal to a nursing home in 1971 to cataloguing her vast library of books on nature and conservation. In 1971, she donated her collection, which included several early and valuable Audubon folios, and which numbered approximately nine thousand books, to the New York Public Library. The gift stipulated that a large portion of those books should be distributed to children's departments in the Library system so that city children could be exposed to the delights of nature if not in their own backyards then through reading about them. ("Pioneer Naturist Donates Rare Collection to Library," *New York Times*, January 18, 1971, at 27, col. 6–8.) In that same year, Mrs. Gurrelts prepared and signed a will leaving her extremely large and well-managed estate [Amelia felt a surge of pride at this, because she knew Sarah Gurrelts Gaines had been a lifelong client of the bank] to the six animal and nature groups named *supra*. Somewhere between the February 3, 1971, date of the will and Mrs. Gurrelts's death on July 19, 1974, the names of the Owl and Egret groups were crossed out. It is this will and these cross-outs upon which this Court now passes judgment, after six long and tortuous years of trial and delay.

I have rehearsed the life of decedent with such great detail in order to demonstrate that this Court is firmly convinced that Mrs. Gurrelts's interest in nature and animals was no passing fancy, no sudden passion of her later and declining years. Too often this Court has been dragged into family controversies in which a testator seeks to leave all of an estate to their pet, to an animal shelter, or to a pet cemetery. See, e.g., *Curtis Family v. Bowser*, 327 N.Y.S.2d 649 (1952). This is not one of those cases. Mrs. Gurrelts's passion for animals and nature was lifelong and deeply held. The question before this Court, narrowly put, is, was she of sound mind at the time of making her will, and was she of sound mind when she sought to change it (eliminating Egret and Owl)?

"The right of a person to dispose of his property by will as he sees fit is one which the law is slow to deny. No mere weakening of his mental powers—no mere impairment of the facilities—will invalidate a will executed in due form, so long as he retains mind enough to know and comprehend in a general way the nature objects of his bounty, the nature and extent of his estate, and the distribution he wishes to make of it." *Perkins v. Perkins*, 90 N.W. 55 (Iowa 1902). All sides in the instant matter—petitioners, respondents, and intervenors—brought witnesses to testify as to Mrs. Gurrelts's mental capacity in the first months of 1971, when she signed her will. Evidence was introduced that Mrs. Gurrelts at that time was "real lucid" (trial transcript at 855), "all there" (trial transcript at 1933), "just like you or me" (t.t. at 907), and "fine" (t.t. at 2381).

On the other hand, witnesses also testified that in February of 1971, Mrs. Gurrelts was "agitated" (t.t. at 421), "nervous, just very nervous" (t.t. at 502), and, perhaps most tellingly, "afraid her family was going to pack her off to a nursing home, tell a judge she'd gone wacko and grab all of her money" (testimony of childhood friend and retired physician E. P. Mooney, trial transcript at 196).

Counsel for petitioner family members made much of these last three statements, especially that of Dr. Mooney, as evidence of Mrs. Gurrelts's incapacity at the time of the making of the will. Given the litigious nature of the Gaines family as a whole, this Court finds that if Mrs. Gurrelts feared the worst from her family, she was entirely justified. This family has a history of seeking to prove the insanity of its recently deceased members when those family members' wills have been entered into probate. See *Actors Home for the Aged v. Gaines et al.*, 271 N.Y.S.2d 421 (1961), *Gaines v. Gaines et al.*, 149 N.Y.S.2d 34 (1951), *In re Estate of Grover Gaines*, 329 N.Y.S. 401 (1942), *In re Gaines*, 187, N.Y. 329 (1934), and *Essex Street Orphanage v. Gaines*, 122 N.Y. 173 (1916).

It goes without saying that should petitioner family members prove Mrs. Gurrelts insane at the time of the making of her will, she would be declared to have died intestate, or without a valid will. In such case, New York State's laws of intestate succession would come into play. That is to say, her family would inherit her vast wealth, and the animal rights groups would take nothing.

If Sarah Gurrelts Gaines expressed a fear to friends, her physician, and others that her family might seek to prove her insane and steal her money, this Court most emphatically finds that such a fear demonstrates on her part an unquestionable demonstration of her lucidity and accurate understanding of events. This Court finds as a matter of law that Sarah Gurrelts Gaines, at the time she made her will, was legally sane. The challenge of her family members to that will is hereby dismissed.

We turn next to claims of Egret and Owl, that Mrs. Gurrelts, at the time she changed the will by striking out their groups, was insane. Testimony was adduced from the staff of the nursing home in which Mrs. Gurrelts passed the final three years of her life, and her medical records from that period were also entered into evidence. Without belaboring the point or causing needless embarrassment to the memory of Mrs. Gurrelts, there were times during her stay at the nursing home when she would not have been considered legally competent to manage her own affairs. The question thus becomes: at the time that Mrs. Gurrelts amended her will, excluding Egret and Owl, was she sane or was she insane?

It is well established in this State that a testator either must be lucid or, in the case of a testator who veers between sanity and insanity, must be enjoying a "lucid interval" at the time that a will is written, signed, or changed. *Delafield v. Parish*, 25 N.Y. 22 (1873). The burden of proof that a testator was not lucid at the writing, signing, or changing of a will falls upon the party seeking to challenge that writing, signing, or change. *Robinson v. Stuart*, 29 N.Y. 144 (1891). No one was able to testify in the case before me to the exact date upon which Mrs. Gurrelts changed her will to exclude Owl and Egret. Although counsel for Owl and Egret have established with a great deal of certainty that Mrs. Gurrelts's mental health was, regrettably, in decline during her nursing home years, said counsel has failed to meet its burden of showing that Mrs. Gurrelts was illucid or insane on the day that she changed her will. Therefore I hereby dismiss Owl's and Egret's challenge to this will.

This is not the first time that the Gaines family has come before me in this courtroom. I can only express my hope that I never see any of them, or of the most contentious Shapolsky family of lawyers, again, so long as I remain on the bench. The will is hereby entered into probate and all challenges by petitioners and intervenors are hereby DIS-MISSED.

PAUL MARTLAND III, Surrogate Judge

"Fat chance," Amelia said aloud, responding to the judge's forlorn hope at the end of the decision.

"Isn't that something?" asked Aaron, standing over her. "Here. I've got some more for you." He pondered the shelves of New York State law reporters, pulled out a volume, and flipped to a page marked with an index card, and then he pulled out a second volume.

"More Gaineses?" Amelia asked.

"More Gaineses," said Aaron. "Do you realize how much they've paid the Shapolskys over the years? Morris and the rest of them must be loaded."

"Give me the cases," Amelia said, reaching for them.

Aaron teasingly snatched them away from her. "First promise me you'll have dinner with me."

"Aaron, I wouldn't have dinner with you if hell froze over," Amelia said sharply. "Gimme those books before I tell Mr. Skeffington you're harassing me."

Aaron looked wounded. "Aren't *we* touchy?" he said. Then the telephone rang. Aaron answered it. "Legal," he said. Then: "Yes,

Mr. Skeffington. She's right here. I sure will." He hung up. "He wants to see you in his office immediately."

"Another Gaines must have freaked out," Amelia said. "Leave these out for me. I'll be back later."

She looked longingly at the lawbooks. She would much rather have stayed and read on about the Gaineses. Instead she headed back to the Trust Department, wondering what on earth Mr. Skeffington had found so important.

26

EVERY MAN had his price, Sam David believed. The only problem was that not enough took Visa or MasterCard.

By virtue of his importance as a fairly well-known dealmaker and the manager of a large if not enormous family real estate empire, and by virtue of the fact that he was a heavy but not overly generous tipper, Sam David, when he wanted to conduct a business meeting over lunch, could get either the best table at some of the second-best restaurants in town or the second-best table at some of the best restaurants. The trick for his assistant Bickle was to gauge which sort of table at which sort of restaurant would be most appropriate whenever he had to make a luncheon reservation for his boss. For the lunch meeting between Sam David and his longtime legal enemy, Morris Shapolsky, Bickle opted for the second-best table at one of the best restaurants in the city, a restaurant he figured that Morris probably had never entered.

Bickle was right. Le Serviette was the sort of restaurant Morris avoided, featuring, as it did, linen tablecloths, a sure sign of excessive expense, grasping headwaiters, and ten-dollar appetizers. As the two men were ushered to one of the second-best tables in the house, Morris looked around disapprovingly.

"Eat here often?" he asked Sam David, who was rubbing, for good luck, a wallet-size photograph of the man with the sandy brown hair and the portable phone.

"Only when I have to impress someone," Sam David admitted in a flash of candor.

"I'll be more impressed when I see you pick up the check," said Morris, also speaking from the heart.

The captain himself seated the two men, who stared at each other across mountains of silverware and decades of legal enmity. It could not be said that such a lunch represented the lion lying down with the lamb. Neither man qualified for lamb status. Rather, it did bring together two men who had not seen each other out of a courtroom or a funeral chapel for a very long time. Both men sought to seem conciliatory—Morris because he believed he could afford to and Sam David because he needed something from Morris. Sam David, of course, needed Morris's vote and was prepared to go to great lengths to get it. Morris needed less. His goal, at this lunch, was to give the impression that he wanted the Trust Committee to succeed and come to an agreement as to the disbursement of Harry's assets. Such, of course, was the last thing Morris wanted. If the committee could agree, it would be goodbye sale of the theaters by the firm of Shapolsky & Shapolsky and goodbye three point six million dollars.

The two men settled in. Sam David looked around. He looked in the direction of the best tables, where men who looked slightly more important than himself were just sitting down to do deals that were probably slightly more important than the deals he did. Sam David secretly believed that if only he could eat at the best tables in the best restaurants, instead of the second-best tables at the best restaurants or the best tables at the second-best restaurants, his life would be entirely happy.

Sam David and Morris both found themselves a bit ill at ease to be in each other's company, after so many years of lawsuits and countersuits. Their conversation, somewhat forced, reflected their discomfort.

"Ah, Sam David," Morris began, feeling sentimental, as he tucked his linen napkin into place and thought about how much the food must cost in a place like this. "I've known you since you were a baby."

"You've been suing me since I was a baby," said Sam David, giving Morris a little smile. Sam David's smile interested Morris.

Morris was very surprised to look inside Sam David's mouth and see only one row of teeth.

"I attended your *bris,*" said Morris, referring to Sam David's ritual circumcision.

"You were there to serve papers," said Sam David.

"What else could I do?" Morris responded, chuckling. "Your father avoided me like the plague."

"Why shouldn't he have avoided you?" Sam David asked. "Plague is contagious." Then he gave Morris another little smile, just to show that he was kidding and that all was sweetness and light. The trouble was that Sam David was not kidding, and unless he could get Morris's vote, all would be sour and dark.

"How's your sister Tess?" Morris asked.

"She's *your* client," Sam David replied tartly, referring to Morris's role as Tess's attorney in the battle over the will of their late father, Theodore. Sam David found it hard to be anything but sardonic in the presence of his most persistent legal and financial nemesis. "*You* tell *me* how she is."

"She was only my client that one time," said Morris. "You know that."

"Of course," said Sam David, a bit more graciously. "She's a lovely woman. If only we knew who the father of her child was." He took a gulp of his ice water.

"I am," Morris said. "I'm the father."

Sam David barely avoided spitting his water all over the table.

"A little humor there," said Morris, smiling. "Just a joke."

"Some joke," said Sam David, galled at the idea that he might be uncle to half a Shapolsky. And then he regained the full extent of his social graces. He laughed lightly. "Ha, ha, ha, Morris. Good one. And how are Edward and Samantha?"

"Fine, thank you," said Morris.

"And Samuel G. and Barry?" Sam David asked politely.

"Just fine, thanks," said Morris, who made some rapid calculations: if Sam David was sucking up to him this much, then Sam David needed something important from him. It had to be Morris's vote on the Trust Committee. That vote was not for sale, though. Unless, of course, Sam David was prepared to make a very good offer.

"It's quite an idea of Harry's, this Trust Committee thing," said Sam David.

"It certainly is," said Morris, as the waiter brought the menus. *It's going to make me rich,* he thought, studying the menu.

"It was really Harry's idea?" asked Sam David, glancing at his menu. He always had the same thing when he came here, steak with catsup. He was the only customer in the restaurant permitted catsup, and only because he had heavily tipped the chef. Sam David just liked catsup.

"A hundred percent," said Morris. "I admit, I pushed him into coming up with some kind of plan. I didn't want to see him die without a will of some kind. But the idea about getting along was strictly his."

"Do you think it can work?" Sam David asked. "Do you think someone can get four votes?"

Not if I can help it, Morris thought soberly. "Of course," he said.

"Well, I've got my doubts," said Sam David. The captain came and took their orders. In keeping with business lunch tradition, the two men made small talk throughout the meal, discussing real estate trends in New York City and some of the latest decisions to come down in Surrogate's Court, the Gaines and Shapolsky families' second home. The meal tasted expensive to Morris, but he liked it anyway, especially because he did not have to pay for it and because his meter was running. Finally, over coffee, Sam David nudged the conversation in the general direction of his main concern as delicately and gently as he could.

"Let's cut the bullshit, Morris," said Sam David. "How much money do you want for your vote?"

Morris decided to play it cute. "My vote?" he asked. "For President of the United States?"

"Your vote on the Trust Committee," said Sam David, stating the obvious. "I want to buy your vote. I'll pay more than anyone else is paying. I want to know what your best offer is so far, and then I want to know how much more you'll take to sell it to me."

"I'm not sure I understand," Morris said, sounding as perplexed as he could. Of course, he understood perfectly. "Are you trying to bribe me?"

"You got a problem with that?" Sam David asked.

"Well, it's most unusual," Morris said, trying to sound surprised by Sam David's bluntness.

"The whole committee thing is unusual," said Sam David. "If it were up to me, Harry should have died intestate and we could have duked it out in court, same as always. But he made a committee, and I'm on it and you're on it, and I want to know how much money you want for your vote."

"I'm a little troubled by the morality of it," Morris admitted.

"Do I hear a Shapolsky talking about morality?" Sam David asked.

"You're asking me to violate the integrity of my late client," Morris protested.

"That's exactly what I'm asking you to do," Sam David replied, removing his checkbook from his jacket pocket. "The only thing we're discussing is how much it'll cost."

"My vote's not for sale," Morris said firmly. "It would take an awful lot of money to make me even think of violating Harry's trust."

"A hundred thousand dollars?" Sam David asked.

Morris ignored him. "Can I get some more coffee?" he asked.

A good sign, Sam David thought. *That means he wants to stay and bargain.* He snapped his fingers, and a busboy came running. "More coffee for the gentleman."

The busboy went off for more coffee.

"Three hundred thousand," said Sam David.

"I am not about to sell my loyalty to my late client Harry for a paltry three hundred thousand dollars," said Morris. "And in any event, from you I would require a certified check."

Sam David, offended, put his checkbook back in his pocket.

"Half a million," he said as the busboy poured coffee for Morris.

"Do they have Sweet'n Low here?" Morris asked. The busboy went off in search of Sweet'n Low.

"Six hundred thousand," said Sam David.

"I shouldn't even drink coffee," Morris admitted. "It's bad for my heart, my doctor says."

"Seven hundred thousand," said Sam David, not batting an eye. He had been up against tougher than Morris before. Actually, he had been up against Morris before.

"This is a nice restaurant," said Morris, looking around. "A bargain at half the price, but a nice restaurant."

"Eight hundred thousand," said Sam David, and he thought he noticed Morris's eyes narrow for a brief moment. He stopped the bidding so as to discern, if possible, what was going on in Morris's head.

Morris, calculating rapidly, understood that Sam David had just passed the $720,000 threshold. That figure represented Morris's share of the three point six million dollars his firm would realize in real estate commissions from the sale of the theaters. Morris now had to decide between selling out his clients and selling out his relatives.

"Nine hundred thousand dollars," said Sam David, studying Morris for a reaction.

Morris looked for a waiter. "Do you think maybe I could see a dessert menu?"

"Of course," said Sam David, ever the gracious host. He gave a slight nod to the waiter, who watched Sam David's every move, alive to the fact that the timeliness with which he responded would be reflected, positively or negatively, in the eventual tip. The waiter rushed over.

"A dessert menu for the gentleman," said Sam David, as warmly as he possibly could, which was, to be honest, not all that warm even by New York standards.

The waiter nodded and went off to get a dessert menu. Meanwhile, Sam David had accurately assessed matters—he had come into Morris's price range, and Morris was considering accepting an offer.

"What kind of desserts are good here?" Morris asked nonchalantly.

"I don't know," Sam David admitted. "I never eat dessert."

"Is that how you stay so thin?" Morris asked.

"I only eat one meal a day," Sam David explained, thinking also about the occasional walnut chocolate chip cookie he would snack on at work. "Saves time."

"Ah," said Morris, who could not possibly relate to eating one meal a day, or even just one meal in any given four-hour time period. The dessert menu arrived, and Morris chose something with a French name that he mispronounced. He chose it only because he had never seen a sixteen-dollar dessert item on a menu before and he wanted to know what kind of dessert you got for sixteen dollars.

"You'll like that," said Sam David.

"I thought you don't eat dessert," said Morris.

"I don't, but little Marie does," said Sam David, referring to his six-year-old niece, Tess's daughter.

"Do you bring her here?" Morris asked, impressed at Sam David's handling of his role as uncle. The most expensive meal Morris had ever bought his nephew, Barry Shapolsky-Kleinman, came with your choice of mustard or relish and usually could be eaten standing up.

"Once in a while," said Sam David.

"That's very nice of you," said Morris.

"Nice has nothing to do with it," said Sam David. "In twelve years she'll be eighteen. I'm introducing her to the business."

"But she's only in first grade!" said Morris.

"Better that she should start learning from me. I don't want to see her subpoenaed and not know why. A million dollars."

Sam David was back to business. Morris gulped. A million dollars could be his right now. He would not even have to go to the trouble of selling the theaters. All he would have to do was vote for Sam David.

"Do you think the votes are secret ballot?" Morris asked.

"That could be arranged," said Sam David, closing the net. "A million one hundred thousand."

Morris had not expected to hear numbers like this. His collar felt tight all of a sudden. Dessert arrived. To Morris's untutored eye, the sixteen-dollar Delice St. Something-or-other looked distressingly like a bowl of ice cream served with a thin, triangle-shaped cookie. If Sam David could throw his money around restaurants like this, then he could probably go a lot higher than a million one. Morris dug into the ice cream with a soup spoon that an errant busboy had failed to retrieve and regained a measure of composure.

"You're asking me to sell my clients down the river for a lousy one point one million dollars?" he asked. "I don't know what's worse, that you're trying to bribe me or that you're trying to bribe me so cheaply."

Sam David tried to hide his delight. For all Morris's bluster, Sam David could sense a weakening of his resolve.

"I'm not trying to make you sell your clients down the river for a million one," Sam David said soothingly. "I want you to sell your clients down the river for a million two."

"That's a lot of money," Morris admitted, wondering how high Sam David would go. The ice cream disappeared at great speed. "But my clients' honor is more dear to me than my life."

Don't make me sick, Sam David thought. "I respect that impulse in you," he said.

"Thank you," said Morris, his tone dignified. He ate the wafer. *Sixteen dollars indeed*, he thought.

"A million three," said Sam David.

"Can you get seconds here?" Morris asked, looking around for a waiter.

"Of course," said Sam David, not surprised by Morris's great appetite. He motioned to the waiter to return to the table.

"Another Delice for the gentleman," said Sam David.

"And you can leave off that cookie," Morris told him, hoping not to hurt his feelings. "I don't really think it adds anything to the flavor."

"Oui, messieurs," said the waiter, who went off to get Morris another dessert.

"Where were we?" asked Sam David.

"A million three," said Morris. "I had just turned down a million three." *What am I doing, turning down a million three?* he asked himself. *What am I, crazy?*

"A million four," Sam David said coolly, noting the faint look of alarm on Morris's face.

"A million four," repeated Morris. The whole thing was

getting out of hand. He had expected only to have lunch with Sam David, bill Harry's estate for the time, and turn down some chintzy little five-figure offer for his vote. He never dreamed that Sam David would go this high.

"A million five," said Sam David, who was prepared, of course, to go as high as two million dollars. Two million to get control of sixty million? Chicken feed.

The ice cream arrived, but Morris had lost his appetite. Beads of sweat broke out on his forehead.

"A . . . million . . . five," Morris said slowly, thinking about how nice his life would be with a million five hundred thousand in the bank. He would never have to sue a Gaines again as long as he lived. He himself could become a client at the New York Bank and Trust Company. People like Amelia would be sending *him* checks. What about Samuel G., and Barry, and his own children, Edward and Samantha? his conscience asked him. *Let them earn their own livings*, Morris quickly told his conscience.

"A million six," Sam David said, watching Morris sweat. He sensed that he would not have to go as high as two million. Morris would crack at any moment.

A *million six*, Morris thought. He could give the others a hundred fifty thousand each and still clear a million. No, that would be a million before taxes. Forget about giving them a hundred fifty thousand. That would only make them suspicious. After all, it would be a secret ballot. No one would ever know.

Without realizing it, Morris had eaten all of his ice cream.

"A million seven," said Sam David, turning up the pressure.

Morris made a little gurgling noise. A million seven was a lot of money.

"A million seven," Sam David repeated, "deposited in your name in an offshore numbered account in the Bahamas. Or Switzerland. Or wherever you want. A million seven, tax free."

"Tax free," Morris muttered.

"A million eight," Sam David said firmly. "That's as high as I go. Pierre, the check."

Pierre, hovering discreetly, handed the check to Sam David, who did not even look at it. Instead he casually pulled two hundred-dollar bills from his wallet and told Pierre to keep the change.

"But, Monsieur," Pierre began apologetically, "there isn't any change."

"Huh?" asked Sam David. *Those Delices add up*, he thought. *And Morris did have two entrées.* He took out another hundred and passed it to Pierre.

"Merci, monsieur!" Pierre said delightedly. The bill had come to two hundred and four dollars and eighty-one cents. Sam David had cemented his grip on this, the second-best table in the house, and if he kept up this sort of tipping, he was headed for number one.

"One point eight million dollars?" Morris asked. This was exactly half of what his whole family would have netted from the sale of the theaters. All for him, and all tax free, and no one would ever know.

Sam David nodded.

"This would remain secret forever?" Morris asked. "My family will never find out?"

"I'll take the secret to the grave," said Sam David.

"And the sooner the better," muttered Morris.

"I beg your pardon?" Sam David asked.

"What nice weather," Morris said, recovering deftly.

"Do we have a deal?" Sam David asked. "One point eight million, tax free and top secret?"

Morris hesitated. "I need a little time to think it over," he admitted.

Sam David looked at his watch. "You have sixty seconds. Go."

Morris looked cross. "Cut that out, Mr. Big Shot," he told Sam David. "You need me as much as I need you. If you don't get my vote, you're dead in the water."

"Not so fast," said Sam David. "If I don't get your vote, there are five others. And confidentially, I think I can already count on one of the votes from Harry's side of the family."

This was a complete fiction, but Sam David took hardball negotiating seriously.

"*Really?*" Morris asked, amazed. "Who?"

"I'd rather not say just yet," Sam David said smoothly. "You'll see."

"I need three days," said Morris.

"I'll give you two," said Sam David.

"Two and a half," said Morris. "I'll tell you dinnertime two days from now."

Sam David considered the offer. "Done," he said.

He and Morris shook on it, stood up, and headed out of the restaurant.

"Delicious meal," said Morris. "Thank you."

"Excellent company," said Sam David, who could afford to be generous. He was convinced that he had Morris's vote in his pocket, and it had cost him two hundred thousand dollars less than he had been prepared to spend.

"Likewise," said Morris.

A moderately fawning restaurant staff bade the two men farewell.

"Top secret?" Morris repeated, as they reached the front door, held open for the two men by the son of the owner. "The whole thing?"

"Top secret. Dinnertime, two days from now," said Sam David. "Call me."

"You have my word," Morris said soberly, wondering whether he should buy the Greek island or the condo in Monaco or both.

They nodded at each other, former enemies brought together by a common love of cash. They shook hands again, and Morris departed.

Bickle, who had been sitting at the table behind that of Morris and Sam David, came out of hiding now to congratulate his boss.

"You did it!" Bickle exclaimed. "It's in the bag!"

"I think you're right," said Sam David, pleased with himself.

"I'll call Moses Shapolsky and tell him where things stand," Bickle volunteered. "Maybe they can go to work on Tess."

"Not so fast," said Sam David, thinking quickly, as the two men left the restaurant. "Let's keep this to ourselves for now, okay?"

"Okay," Bickle said slowly, wondering exactly what his boss had in mind.

MR. SKEFFINGTON, waiting for Amelia to return from wherever she had gone off to this time, found himself unable to concentrate on his work. Instead he could think only about Woodrow Gaines, whom he had met on his first day at the bank, forty years earlier. Woodrow had come to the bank on the third day of a three-day drunk, wanting to change his will. The young Mr. Skeffington talked him out of it. Eleven days later, Woodrow died in Maine.

Mr. Skeffington pulled himself from 1951 long enough to telephone his wife. "Why am I thinking of Woodrow?" he asked.

"Who?" she asked, assuming that Woodrow was a Gaines of some sort.

"He died in 1951," said Mr. Skeffington, by way of explanation.

"Because you're obsessed," said Mrs. Skeffington. "That's why you're thinking about him. Will you be on the six-eighteen?"

"I just can't get him out of my head," Mr. Skeffington confessed.

"Just don't miss your train over it," Mrs. Skeffington replied.

"Yes, dear," Mr. Skeffington said absentmindedly. He hung up and went back to wondering why he was thinking so much about Woodrow.

•

Louis Gaines Shapolsky, the youngest member of Old Shap, was celebrated throughout the New York bar for billing twenty-seven hours in a single twenty-four-hour day to a single client. He had flown to the West Coast on behalf of a Gaines-related matter and charged for the time difference as well as for his efforts. He was legendary in state court for the day he billed three separate Gaineses for three separate matters that he performed all at the same time. While litigating a matter for Tess (client number one), he telephoned Sam David about a building he was selling for Sam David (client number two); then, on hold, he flipped through the file of Chester Alan, whom he would represent in court the next week (client number three). The Gaineses compared their legal bills and sensibly refused to pay, but it was the spirit of the thing that made Louis G. a self-described "billing animal" and, despite his extreme youth—he was still only twenty-seven—the unacknowledged driving force of the firm of Old Shap.

The driving force, along with the driven, sat around their elegant mahogany conference table, each with a copy of the Harry Gaines will and trust before them, each, in his or her own way, looking glum. In keeping with the slightly revised tradition of Old Shap attorney meetings, Moses Shapolsky, Louis G.'s father, spoke first.

"I don't like this trust business any more than any of you," Moses began. "But I don't see what choice we have."

His cousin Deborah and his father, Henry Clay, nodded. Moses cast a quick glance at his son, who was not paying attention to the discussion. Louis G. was studying his copy of the will, as if some mysterious secret might reveal itself if only Louis stared hard enough.

"I think our best shot is to go the usual Gaines routine," Moses concluded.

"Tell the court he was insane when he signed the will?" Deborah asked.

Moses nodded. "It's worked in the past. And we've got that nurse ready to testify that the bank people exerted undue influence. When she came into the room, Harry was gaga. He thought she was Winona and Amelia was Anne Frank."

"I don't think it'll work," said Deborah. "I spoke to Chester Alan. When he went in, Harry was perfectly fine. New Shap can claim he was having a lucid interval when he signed the agreement, and how can we prove that he wasn't?"

Moses frowned. "The court would probably listen to a cardiologist before they listened to a nurse," he said.

"We could argue that the nurse has more day-to-day contact with the patient," said Deborah. "She'd know better than Chester Alan. And besides, Chester Alan's a relative with a vested interest in his testimony. We might be able to keep him off the stand entirely."

"The whole thing's risky," said Henry Clay, speaking up for the first time. "You'd be betting the whole case on that one nurse's testimony. I don't think we should go the insanity route. And there's another thing. Clause Five. 'If any beneficiary under this Will . . . contests or attacks this Will—' " Henry Clay made a rapid cutting motion across his neck. "Which of our clients would be willing to risk that?"

"In that case," said Deborah, "I think we have to figure out how to make this will work for our side. We've got two votes already. We've got Sam David and Tess."

"Yeah, but you know they'll never vote together," said Moses. "They won't even talk to each other."

"Not even for a piece of sixty million dollars?" asked Deborah.

"Not even for six hundred million, if you want my opinion," said Henry Clay. "I think we have to pick one of them and try to get three more votes for that position."

Moses and Deborah looked first at one another and then at Louis, still engrossed in the will.

"The question is, who should we back?" Henry Clay asked. "Tess or Sam David?"

After a moment of reflection, Deborah spoke first. "I think we should go with Tess," she said. She worked most closely with Tess and secretly admired her.

"Why Tess?" Moses asked, surprised. "I think Sam David's the only one with a reasonable plan." Moses billed most of his hours to Sam David and had been handling his real estate transactions ever since Sam David had taken over what remained of the family business.

"Reasonable?" asked Deborah, rapidly tapping a pencil. "What makes Sam David's plan more reasonable than Tess's?"

"Well, for one thing," Moses said, "Sam David's is the only plan likely to maximize the asset value for the whole family. Sam David would become a major player in New York real estate if he builds those three office buildings. That would increase the value of the rest of the family's portfolio. It's prudent."

"You know, there's more to life than prudence and maximizing asset values," Deborah said sharply. "There's also caring for humanity."

"Since when do you care for humanity?" Moses asked, surprised. "You represent the Gaineses."

"I represent *Tess* Gaines." Deborah sniffed. "And *she* cares about people a lot more than Sam David does."

"Oh, that's ridiculous," Moses responded. "She's an heiress with a guilt complex. If she had any sense, she'd get a husband and just go to charity balls like the rest of her ilk. That's what she should do. Homeless people!"

"Don't start criticizing homeless people in front of me," said Deborah, eyes flashing. "And don't go calling the Gaineses 'ilk.' They're our clients."

"They're a bunch of lazy, good-for-nothing malcontents," said Moses, expressing feelings that had been building up inside him for years.

"Moses!" Henry Clay Shapolsky exclaimed. "I'm surprised at you!"

"Aw, Pop, I'm sorry," said Moses. "But Deborah's crazy! How is she ever going to get four Gaineses to vote for a homeless shelter? Tess has the weakest trust at the bank. Do you think the bank people will vote with her? Look, helping those people is all very nice and everything, but it costs money! Why should the whole Gaines family be subsidizing her wacko scheme? What does she think, she's going to stop homelessness? No! All she's going to do is waste the whole family's money, instead of just her own. I think it's ridiculous."

"Well, I think it's ridiculous for Sam David to want to build more buildings!" Deborah told the others. "I think he's the greediest man I've ever seen! He has zero social conscience! If I had my way, he wouldn't even be a client here!"

"If you don't want to represent Sam David Gaines," Moses said darkly, pointing to the reception area, "that's the door."

"Now, both of you, stop it," insisted Henry Clay, who had had enough. "Stop your bickering. You aren't five years old anymore. This is a law firm, not a nursery."

"Sorry, Dad," said Moses, staring at the floor. "But she started it."

"*I* started it?" Deborah replied, shocked. "You started it! You're the one who called Tess an heiress with a guilt complex!"

"Well, she is!" Moses responded in full voice. "Why can't she just screw up her life, like the rest of the Gaineses? What's she trying to prove anyway?"

"*I will not take that from you!*" Deborah shouted.

"*You're gonna take it and like it!*" Moses shouted back.

"Oh, God," said Henry Clay, shaking his head.

"I think I've got it," Louis G. said quietly.

"You think you've got what?" the rest asked, immediately forgetting their dispute.

"What's the real problem here?" Louis G. asked, playing law professor.

"How to get the money," offered Deborah.

"Thank you for playing," said Louis G. "Next contestant, please."

"Screwing over New Shap?" asked Moses.

"Getting warmer," said Louis G., who could be extremely annoying, especially when he thought he knew something the others did not.

"It has to do with Morris," Henry Clay opined.

"Ooooh," said Louis G. "Grandpa's hot!"

"What about Morris?" Moses asked, losing patience quickly with his son. If only Louis G. were not such a good lawyer and billing machine, Moses would never have tolerated his insolence.

"The question is," said Deborah, "why has Morris been so quiet? Why haven't we heard from him?"

Louis G. touched his nose. "Two points for Aunt Deborah," he said.

"You know," Deborah told him, "you're almost as much of a pain in the ass as Sam David."

"Please," Henry Clay said to Deborah. "Now, Louis, why don't you just spill the beans? I hate it when you play your little games."

"Sorry, Grandpa," said Louis G. "The question is, why is Morris so quiet? Normally, after somebody dies, he's lining up clients, filing motions, calling us six times a day. And so far, we haven't heard from him once."

"He's probably just lining up votes for Glenda or Keith," Deborah offered.

"Doubtful," said Louis G. "I called Chester Alan, and he says Rebecca told him nobody on Harry's side of the family has heard from Morris, either. They've been wondering the same thing I am, which is, why is Morris keeping such a low profile? It's not like him."

"True," said Henry Clay. "And you think it means—what?"

"I think it means," Louis G. began, leaning forward dramatically, "I think it means that Morris doesn't want the Trust Committee to work."

Consternation broke out. "What are you talking about?" Moses asked.

"You're crazy," said Deborah.

"But then his clients lose their money," said Henry Clay. "What good would that do him?"

"That's what I've been trying to figure out," Louis G. said, a knowing look on his face. "Look at the will again. Look at section four point seven."

The other members of Old Shap opened their copies of Harry's will to section four point seven, which contained the language turning the proceeds of Harry's estate over to the federal government in the event that the Trust Committee could not muster a four-vote majority.

"So what?" asked Deborah.

"Read it carefully," said Louis G.

Moses read the language aloud: " 'Seven. In the event that the Trust Committee is unable to agree as to the disposition of the Trust, the Trustee is hereby instructed to donate the proceeds of a sale of all assets of the Trust, as conducted by the law firm of Shapolsky and Shapolsky, less appropriate commissions and fees, to the Federal Government as a gift to reduce the Federal Deficit.' I agree with Deborah. For once. So what?"

" 'Less appropriate fees and commissions,' " Henry Clay repeated, his eyes narrowing.

"I think Grandpa's got it," said Louis G.

"What has Grandpa got?" asked Moses, still not getting it.

"I believe," said Henry Clay, "my grandson Louis is suggesting that Morris is not his usual whirlwind of activity at this time because he actually wants to see the Trust Committee fail at its task of getting a four-vote majority. I think Morris wants the committee to fail so that his firm can sell the assets—the theaters—and keep the real estate commission. That's what that 'less appropriate commissions and fees' language is all about. If we say the theaters will bring sixty million, what's six percent of that?"

"Three point six million dollars," said Louis G.

"Is that what you were thinking, Louis?" Henry Clay asked.

"Yes, Grandpa, it was," Louis G. said quietly. A Gaines family without its sixty million would need Old Shap's services much less frequently. There would be so little left to fight over.

Moses spoke first. "That's the sleaziest, most disgusting thing I've ever heard of," he said. "I'd like to see Morris get disbarred for this."

Deborah looked equally upset. "I hate to agree with Moses on anything, but I think it's awful. I think we should go right to Sam David, Tess, and the rest of our clients on Sam's side and tell them what Morris has done."

"I think we should call the bank," said Henry Clay. "They ought to know this. And I would be delighted to press charges against Morris. This is one of the most dastardly acts I've ever heard of at the bar."

"Ripping off your own clients," said Moses, bristling with anger. "And your own flesh and blood. After all, we're related to

Morris. He's stealing from their family and from ours. I think we should move immediately on this."

"And I don't," said Louis G., a slight smile playing across his face.

"Why not?" asked Deborah.

"Read it again," he said.

Deborah looked at the clause. " 'Seven,' " she began.

"Skip that part," said Louis G., licking his lips.

" ' . . . the Trustee is hereby instructed—' " Deborah read.

"Skip that part," commanded Louis G, barely containing his glee.

" ' . . . as conducted by the law firm of Shapolsky and Shapolsky'?"she read. "Is that the part?"

"That's the part," said Louis G., rubbing his hands together with joy. "Look. Morris wants the family to fight so his firm can sell the assets and keep the commission, right?"

"That's your thesis," said Henry Clay.

"But New Shap is written with an ampersand," said Louis G. He turned his copy of the will over and wrote, "Shapolsky & Shapolsky."

"But the will," Louis G. continued, "is written with an 'and.' 'Shapolsky *and* Shapolsky.' Get it?"

"Are you suggesting," said Deborah, thinking aloud, "that in the event the committee can't get four votes together, and the property has to be sold so the money can go to the government, *we* can make the sale?"

"And keep the commission?" Moses asked.

Louis G. looked expectantly from his father to his aunt to his grandfather. "That's exactly what I'm suggesting."

"You're saying we should rip off our clients before Morris rips off his?" Moses asked. "Is that it?"

"I'm not saying that at all," said Louis G. "I'm just saying that *if—if* the family cannot agree, and the money has to go to the government, then why should Morris sell it? Why shouldn't *we*?"

Silence.

"Is Morris more entitled to the money than we are?" Louis G. asked. "Does he have clean hands in this? He's ripping off his clients. That's unethical. We're just trying to rip off *him*. I think he deserves it."

The other Shapolskys nodded slowly. Louis G. had done it again.

"How much was the real estate commission on sixty million dollars?" Deborah asked.

"Three point six million," said Louis G. "Three point six million dollars divided four ways is—"

"Nine hundred thousand for each of us," Henry Clay said, his eyes steely. "All my life I've been waiting for an opportunity to pay Morris back for stabbing this firm in the back, stealing Harry and Harry's relatives from Father and Louis B. and myself. They never forgave Morris, and neither have I. I say *we go for it!*"

"Uncle Henry," Deborah asked, concerned, "you're not saying we subvert the intent of the will, are you?"

"Of course not," said Henry Clay. "We support all of our clients' efforts to have the committee reach an agreement. But if they don't agree, and the assets have to be sold . . . I give you my word of honor: it won't be Morris selling them."

Henry Clay's martial attitude stirred the other three Shapolskys.

"I guess that's the plan," said Moses, already beginning to think about the vacation houses he would buy with his nine hundred thousand.

"I guess that's it," Deborah said nervously, thinking about how her nine hundred thousand could be invested in Tess's homeless shelter.

"I'm going to draw up an injunction," said Louis G., "so that the minute the committee fails, we can go to court, keeping New Shap from selling the property."

"Good idea," said Henry Clay, thrilled with his opportunity to stick it to Morris once and for all. "But you'd better not do it on our word processing system. I wouldn't be surprised if Morris and the others could tap into it somehow."

Henry Clay trusted modern technology no more than he trusted his cousin Morris.

"Well, if you think it's necessary," said Louis G., "I could get somebody at some other law firm to draft it and keep it over there."

"No good," said Henry Clay, who attributed much of his success at the bar to paranoia. "I think you should find a lawyer in another state and have him draft it."

Louis G. frowned. He thought it was a dumb idea, but Grandpa was Grandpa. Louis G. thought for a moment. He tried to remember which of his law school classmates had gone far from New York to practice. Then he remembered someone.

"I've got a friend who's a lawyer in Los Angeles," Louis G. said. "He's with Tower and Gates in downtown L.A. Is that far enough away for you?"

Henry Clay nodded. "That's fine," he said. "Morris'll never find it out there."

"So that's the plan?" Louis G. asked rhetorically. Of course it was the plan. "We stop Morris?"

The others nodded.

"We stop Morris," Henry Clay Shapolsky said firmly, speaking for the rest of the firm. "We stop him cold."

28

AMELIA DID NOT even wait for the elevator. Instead she hurried down the stairs to Mr. Skeffington's office.

"Yes, Mr. Skeffington?" she asked, out of breath.

Mr. Skeffington looked tense, as though he had an unpleasant task before him.

"You know Mr. Scarpatti?" he said, keeping his emotions in check.

"Of course," said Amelia, surprised by the question. She thought back to Andre's rumor.

Mr. Skeffington sighed. "The bank has to let him go," he said sadly.

"Mr. Scarpatti?" Amelia asked, stunned. *Andre was right*, she thought. "But why? He's one of the hardest workers in the bank! You've said so yourself!"

"Amelia, this, as you know, is a trust department. Trust is our first name. Mr. Scarpatti . . . inflated certain achievements of his on his résumé."

"But he's been working here five years," Amelia protested.

"I'm aware of that," Mr. Skeffington said. "As I told you, though, the bank is going through something of a reorganization, and one of the things I've had to do is go through the résumés and personnel files of each of our employees. To make sure that everyone is trust-worthy." Mr. Skeffington pronounced the last word as though it were two words. "And most regrettably, Mr. Scarpatti has failed that test."

Amelia gasped. She looked as though she, and not Mr. Scarpatti, had failed that test. "What did he do?" she asked.

"He claimed he went to business school in Belgium," Mr. Skeffington explained. "It turns out that he did no such thing. I had no choice but to fire him. This memo explains everything." He handed Amelia a sheet of paper, which she studied bleakly. She looked stricken.

"Is anything wrong?" he asked. Granted, she and Mr. Scarpatti had been next-desk neighbors for several years, but they had never seemed especially close. Mr. Scarpatti was the sort of quiet person who had little contact with his colleagues. The thought crossed Mr. Skeffington's mind that perhaps Amelia and Mr. Scarpatti had been involved at one point. Why else would Amelia react so excessively?

"He must feel so ashamed," Amelia said. "I just feel sorry for him."

"Well, he should feel ashamed," Mr. Skeffington said curtly. "He violated our trust in him."

"Yes, sir," Amelia said, looking at the floor. "Was there something else?" she asked in her most professional voice, trying to pull herself together. She hoped to avoid arousing Mr. Skeffington's suspicions. She did not realize that she had already done so.

"Yes, there's just one more thing." He rummaged on his desk for the right pink message slip. "While you were away from your desk, you got a collect call this morning from a woman named Elizabeth Herder. I took the call. She said she was on a bus and that she'd be getting to New York tomorrow. I didn't know anyone rode the bus anymore. You know how I feel about taking personal messages, Amelia."

Amelia sank deep into her chair. "Oh, my God," she said, putting a hand over her eyes.

"Amelia, is everything all right?" Mr. Skeffington asked, concerned.

"Yes—uh, no—uh, I'm perfectly fine," said Amelia, trying to stand but finding her knees weak. With effort she rose up to full height, nodded at her boss, gave a wan smile, and said, "I'll be perfectly . . . Just an old friend. Someone I hadn't heard from in a while."

"All right, back to work," said Mr. Skeffington, who strongly disapproved of personal calls at the office.

"Yes, Mr. Skeffington," Amelia said, trying to sound business-like. She left his office and walked slowly back to her own desk, deep in thought.

Glenda, granddaughter-in-law of Harry, descended the stairs of the Gaines Shelter for Women and Children, to find Tess, granddaughter of Original Sam, folding sheets and towels with two other women after a long night of squalling babies and overcrowded rooms.

"Glenda?" said Tess, surprised. After all, her only contact with Glenda came at funerals and in Surrogate's Court—and, of late, at the Trust Committee.

Glenda looked nervously about her. She had never been inside a shelter before. If Glenda was nervous, it had nothing to do with her surroundings and everything to do with the committee. She had done some calculating of her own after dinner with her husband, Woodrow Sam, and her brother-in-law, Grover Sam. She had concluded that Morris was not trustworthy and that he would probably sell his vote to the highest bidder, which most likely meant Sam David, the family's king of cash.

Without Morris, she had only two votes for certain—her own and her father-in-law's. Glenda believed that Keith would go for the plan she had hatched with Woodrow Sam and Grover Sam—one Broadway theater, one vaudeville/film museum, and one theater to be sold. Glenda realized, however, that since Morris could not be counted on, she would need another vote. She did not consider Sam David approachable. She considered him the enemy. She had long known of Sam David's plans to destroy the three theaters Harry and Original Sam had built. Everyone in the Broadway theater community knew that such were Sam David's plans. If Glenda was to replace Morris with anyone, it would have to be with Tess.

"Nice of you to come by," Tess said warily.

"Well, I was in the neighborhood," Glenda said, forcing a smile. "You know how it is."

"Sure," said Tess, wondering why a member of Harry's side of the family would willingly speak to a member of Original Sam's without a lawyer present.

Glenda looked around. "Is there someplace we can be alone?"

Tess nodded. "Excuse me," she said to the volunteers. And to Glenda: "Come on, we can go to my office."

Tess led her to a room that was three parts nursery/play area and one part standard-issue desk and office chairs. Toys, building blocks, stuffed animals, dolls, and a few diapers littered the floor.

"This is your office?" Glenda asked, amazed.

"The maid hasn't been in yet," Tess said wryly. "Come on in."

They entered, and Glenda was overpowered by the smell of diapers.

"They use my desk as a changing table at night," Tess said. "We're kind of short on room. Can I get you something to drink?"

"Oh, no, that's okay," said Glenda, not knowing what to make of it all.

"Have a seat."

"Thank you."

The two women seated themselves, and Glenda looked around the room. "Isabella's eight," said Glenda, referring to her daughter and seeking common ground. "All these baby things really take me back."

"My little Marie is six," said Tess.

"We should get them together to play," said Glenda, wondering why the idea had not come to her before. The answer, of course, was that both Original Sam's and Harry's sides feared their offspring might give away some bit of legal strategy they might have overheard. Isabella had only seen Marie, or Sam David's children, Franklin Delano and Sarah, from across a crowded courtroom.

"That would be lovely," said Tess, not convinced.

"Yeah," said Glenda, still uncomfortable in the presence of a woman whose family she had entered, only to join in its many lawsuits, including, of course, some against Tess. Glenda wondered what approach to take. A Gaines by marriage and not by birth, her first thought was to tell the truth.

"I want you to know," Glenda practically blurted out, "that of everyone in this family, I admire you the most by far."

"Faint praise," Tess said ironically. "But thank you."

"I would admire you even if you weren't a Gaines," Glenda said. "I think what you do is amazing. Taking care of all these people."

Tess nodded thanks. "I once heard somewhere that there are two kinds of people in the world," she said, "nurses and patients. I guess I was born to be a nurse."

"Hmm," said Glenda. "You don't know how many times I've walked by this place and thought, I really ought to go in and say hello to Tess. I've appeared in shows within two blocks of this place—I don't know—three times in the last five years."

Tess smiled. "I know," she said. "I'm your biggest fan."

"Really?" Glenda asked, wanting to believe it.

Tess nodded. "The first time I went to see you act, I think it was in *Prison of His Days*. You were the—"

"Girlfriend," Glenda said, touched. "You saw that?"

"I saw it twice," Tess admitted. "I went the first time because I knew you were in it and I wanted to see what kind of horrible person you truly were. Marrying Woodrow Sam and then spending all your spare time suing my brother and me. *And* my parents."

"You should have come backstage," Glenda said. "It would have been wonderful."

"I guess, but you know, with all the family stuff . . . " Tess's voice trailed off.

"Yeah, I see what you mean."

"It's sad that it has to be this way," Glenda said. "I mean, you seem really nice."

"Out of court?" Tess asked, smiling.

"Out of court," said Glenda. "I know I've sued you and everything, but I just have to tell you: I think what you do is . . . pretty great. I wish I could do the things you do."

"Thank you," said Tess. "And I think you're one hell of an actress. I wish I could do the things you do."

Glenda was amazed. "I never thought you'd care about anything as, you know, unimportant as theater."

"That's not true," said Tess. "Ever since I was a little girl, and

Harry used to tell me about vaudeville, I always wanted to be an actress."

"So what happened?"

"I don't know," Tess admitted. "I think a combination of too little talent and too much guilt. Over being so rich."

Woodrow Sam had told Glenda of Tess's bluntness, but the statement took Glenda by surprise anyway.

"I think this whole idea of Harry's is brilliant," Glenda said suddenly. "If it weren't for the Trust Committee, we would never be talking right now."

"I guess you're right," Tess said doubtfully. "But I think if Harry believed he could somehow unify this family, he was a little misinformed."

"Well, we don't have to unify the *whole* family," Glenda said. "Just four votes." She outlined her secret plan to turn one theater into a homeless shelter, one into a Broadway theater that she, Glenda, would run, and the third into an entertainment museum that Keith and Grover Sam could manage together. Grover Sam and Woodrow Sam were going to see their father, to line up his vote. Then they would need either Morris or one of the people from the bank to vote their way, and they would be all set.

"Does that mean squeezing my brother out?" Tess asked, concerned.

Glenda held her breath. Fraternal loyalty remained the only obstacle to the plan.

"I'd do anything to squeeze my brother out," said Tess, whose instinct to help the homeless paled before her desire to stick it to Sam David. "Count me in."

"Oh, Tess!" said Glenda. "You're such a good person that sometimes I have trouble believing you're really a Gaines." She winced. "I'm sorry," she said. "That didn't come out the way I meant it to."

"It's okay," said Tess. "Sometimes I feel the same way about myself. Should we go to the bank? And talk to Amelia and Howard? Before my brother offers them millions for their votes?"

"Absolutely," said Glenda. She could not believe how easily the whole thing had gone. But then, she reminded herself, it was not for no reason that she had been almost nominated for a Tony for her work in *Prison of His Days*. In just a few months, she would have a Broadway theater to call her own.

"If you have time," Glenda added. "But I think we should keep the whole thing a secret. I wouldn't want Sam David tampering with Keith."

"I never have time," Tess said, giving a weary smile. "And if you want to keep the whole thing a secret, that's fine with me. Let's go to the bank."

GROVER SAM and Woodrow Sam had not seen their father in four years and five years, respectively. Grover Sam rarely left Los Angeles, unless on crash video business. Woodrow Sam, too consumed with his perennially unsuccessful Cars Out of New York organization and with raising his daughter, Isabella, did not make the time to travel. Keith tried not to leave Aspen except for golf. Now the two brothers made their way through the lobby of Keith and Babette's hotel in midtown, ascended, and knocked on their parents' door.

Babette answered. She and Keith were packing to go back to Aspen. They thought the whole Trust Committee idea was stupid and hopeless, and that no one in the family had the slightest chance of amassing four votes. The plan's greatest virtue, in Babette's opinion, was that if it failed, Keith would have to abandon his vaudeville museum memorial to his father. And none too soon, she decided.

"What a surprise!" she exclaimed upon seeing her two scowling sons. "Why, Keith, look who's here!"

Keith looked.

"Hello, boys," he said, as surprised as Babette to see Grover Sam and Woodrow Sam. The four had not been together since Woodrow Sam and Glenda's wedding, thirteen years earlier.

"Hello, Father," the boys chorused. Suddenly all felt transported back thirty years, to a time when Woodrow Sam was nine years old, Grover Sam thirteen, and Keith had just bought his first car dealership.

"What brings you boys up here?" Keith asked, his voice softening.

Grover Sam and Woodrow Sam exchanged embarrassed looks. Woodrow spoke up first. "We're here to talk about the Trust Committee," he said. "Glenda isn't here, is she?"

"No," said Babette. "We haven't seen her since the meeting at the bank."

"Good," said Woodrow Sam. "Can we all sit down for a minute?"

The four Gaineses took seats in the living room of Keith and Babette's hotel suite. Sidney the cat perched on Babette's lap, glared for a moment at Keith, and promptly went to sleep. Woodrow Sam thought bluntness the best way to relieve the awkwardness in the room. He skipped the small talk and spoke plainly.

"Father, you want to build a three-building museum of vaudeville, am I right?"

"That's right," Keith said, embarrassed by the grandiosity of his plans, which now seemed so far from fruition.

"You're never going to get it," Woodrow Sam said. "We all know that. But how would you feel about a one-building museum of vaudeville?"

Keith, dismayed at his son's sharp talk, pondered the matter. "I guess I could live with it," he allowed. "But I've only got one vote. In fact, your mother and I were going back to Aspen tomorrow."

"Well, we think you should stay here and fight," said Woodrow Sam, speaking for his brother as well. He outlined their plan.

"Let me make sure I understand this," Keith said. "I'm one vote, Morris is another, Tess is a third, and one of the people at the bank is four? And I get a theater, you"—he indicated Grover Sam—"get a theater, and Tess gets a theater? Well, what's in it for Morris? Why would he vote with me?"

"Father," Woodrow Sam began, "if we lose the money, Morris loses his biggest client. I mean, he'll still have us, but we won't have the sixty million."

"Mm," said Keith, agreeing. "Good point."

"But what about Glenda?" Babette asked. "Wouldn't she object?"

Grover Sam and Woodrow Sam looked at each other. "You leave her to us," Woodrow Sam said.

"I think we should go right to the bank," said Keith, excited for the first time since he had heard of the Trust Committee. His plans might be truncated, but they would go forward. Harry would get his monument. "I think we should go talk to those two people right now."

"Amelia and Howard?" asked Woodrow Sam.

"Let's get a cab," said Keith. "We've got to get to them before Sam David does. He'll buy their votes in a minute."

"That's exactly what we were thinking," said Woodrow Sam, delighted that their plan had been such an easy sell. "But not a word to Glenda. Or anyone else."

"Okay," said Keith. For the first time in years, they were a family. "Let's do it!"

30

Two TAXIS bearing six Gaineses arrived simultaneously at the bank.

Keith, seated up front next to the driver, was paying the fare when Grover Sam, seated nearest the curbside door, saw two family members emerging from a cab of their own.

"Hey, look! It's Tess and Glenda!" exclaimed Grover Sam.

"Where?" asked Babette, looking out the window.

"Together?" asked Keith, craning his neck to see.

"I don't believe it!" said Woodrow Sam. "What's she doing with Tess?"

"What's Tess doing with her?" Keith asked. "I didn't know they spoke."

"They don't," said Woodrow Sam. "At least they never did before."

"Well, they are now," said Grover Sam, stating the obvious.

"But why?" Keith asked.

Grover Sam's eyebrows furrowed. "I think she and Tess did a deal," he said. "I think they're trying to squeeze us out."

"A deal?" Woodrow Sam repeated angrily. "Are you accusing my wife of trying to screw us over?"

"Yeah," said Grover Sam. "Isn't that what we're trying to do to her?"

Keith thought quickly. "I don't think we should let them know we know about them," he said. "Where's Morris's office?"

"At 1620 Broadway," said Woodrow Sam.

"Let's get to him before they do," said Keith. "Driver, 1620 Broadway. And step on it."

As the taxi bearing Keith, Babette, and their two sons sped off, Tess and Glenda, oblivious of having been observed and by now fast friends, entered the bank. They made their way to the Trust Department and asked for Amelia. No one knew where Amelia had gone. Amelia, somewhat overwhelmed, had retreated to a small office in the Legal Department, where she had promised a delighted Aaron a date in exchange for his word not to tell anyone where she was. Meanwhile, in the Trust Department, Howard recognized Tess and Glenda as Gaineses and invited them into a small, tastefully appointed conference room. He offered them coffee.

Tess and Glenda outlined their plan, which delighted Howard because it achieved the exact goal Harry had set forth—to reunite the disparate and warring elements of his family after his death in a manner that had eluded him in his lifetime.

Howard liked the plan for another reason. Although he would never have told Amelia, he had been preparing for two full years to take over the Gaines account. He recognized quickly that neither Stone nor Vaccaro could handle the contentious personalities, the acrimonious will contests, or the constant assaults on the family's capital. Howard believed firmly that he and he alone, of anyone in the Trust Department, could manage the Gaineses. Thereby, his career path at the bank would take a steep upward turn. That Mr. Skeffington might hand the Gaineses to his girlfriend, Amelia, was a contingency for which he had never thought to prepare.

If Tess and Glenda's plan succeeded, and if he were viewed as its linchpin, Mr. Skeffington might still reward him by taking the Gaines account from Amelia and giving it to him. All those evenings and weekends he had spent reading the voluminous Gaines files, familiarizing himself with the family's history and legal warfare, might still pay off. He might still get control of the biggest account in the department. As much as he cared for Amelia, he believed that *he* deserved the Gaineses.

Howard was so pleased to accede to Tess and Glenda's wishes that he agreed to keep his decision to vote their way a secret from Amelia and the rest of the bank staff. If he told Amelia, she might tell Dwight David, who might tell his father, Chester Alan, who might tell his cousin Sam David, thereby endangering the plan. Secrecy was critical. If even one person found out, then who knew what would happen? Most likely Sam David and his checkbook would foul everything up for Tess and Glenda, or the committee would never find a majority, and the theaters, God forbid, would end up with the federal government.

The three shook hands on their secret agreement. Tess and Glenda left the bank to get a cab to Keith and Babette's hotel, hoping to catch them before they left for Aspen. They did not know, of course, that Keith and Babette were already on their way to see Morris and line up his vote. Howard realized with surprise that he had come to trust members of the Gaines family more than he trusted Amelia. He wondered what that said about their relationship.

Upstairs, in Legal, Amelia felt ill. She wanted to return home and crawl into bed and wait for the nightmare to end. Her discomfort stemmed less from the Gaineses or her late night with Dwight David than with the telephone message from Elizabeth Herder. A hidden part of her past had caught up with her, and she wanted only to run and hide from it. But going home was not an option. Amelia, unaware that Howard had cut a deal with two Gaineses, buried her personal worries in a marathon reading session of Gaines will contests. Aaron, who was thrilled at the prospect of an evening with Amelia, set out volume after volume before her.

She read the shortest one first:

Gaines et al. v. Chester Alan Gaines, 81-390874

May 16, 1987

In Surrogate's Court, New York, New York, Paul Martland III, Surrogate Judge.

Henry Clay Shapolsky and Deborah Shapolsky, Shapolsky and Shapolsky, New York, New York, for petitioners Annette Morris Gaines, Theodore Gaines, Sam David Gaines, and Nancy Frankel Gaines.

Morris Shapolsky and Barry Shapolsky-Kleinman, Shapolsky & Shapolsky, New York, New York, for petitioners Woodrow Sam Gaines, Glenda Monash Gaines, Grover Sam Gaines, Charles C. Gaines, Keith McNiven Gaines, Babette Reynolds Gaines, and Isabella McNiven.

Moses Shapolsky, Shapolsky and Shapolsky, New York, New York, for respondent Chester Alan Gaines.

JUDGE MARTLAND: This case results from the death of Gloria Coss Gaines in 1981 and has dragged on in my courtroom for the past six years. In that time, other Gaineses, including several who were parties to this action, have died or otherwise left the family. I speak of the late Theodore Gaines, who died earlier this year and whose will, it pains me if it does not surprise me to note, is also the subject of intense litigation in my courtroom. I speak also of the late Isabella McNiven, mistress of Harry Gaines, who died in 1982 and whose will was challenged in the case of *Keith McNiven Gaines v. Chester Alan Gaines and Sam David Gaines*, 406 N.Y.2d 382 (1983).

That's the case I got in the mail, Amelia told herself. She read on:

Also, Nancy Frankel Gaines, the estranged wife of petitioner Sam David Gaines, had the uncommon good sense to abandon this family in 1983, causing this judge to thank the good Lord that he does not handle cases of divorce.

Before I state the facts of this case, I will dispose quickly of the challenge of said Sam David Gaines to my fitness to serve as Surrogate Judge in the matter of his late aunt Gloria's will. I have been handling Gaines will cases for thirteen years, and I must sadly make the claim that no one on God's green earth or on the New York State bench knows this family better than I do. I hereby dismiss Mr. Gaines's challenge on the basis of prejudice. I am not prejudiced against any individual member of the Gaines family. The fact that I think all of them are out of their minds in no way influences my ability to decide their cases as a judge.

This particular installment of the Gaines saga involves a challenge to the will of Gloria Coss Gaines, widow of the late Woodrow Gaines. As the widow of Sam Gaines's eldest son, the decedent left behind a considerable estate, and her will gave it all to her son, Chester Alan Gaines, a noted cardiologist. By 1981 and the time of decedent's death, however, respondent Chester Alan (again I refer to the Gaineses by their first names not out of sentimentality or overfriendliness but merely for the sake of order) had been conducting a lengthy and, from evidence brought into court by various petitioners, continuing extramarital affair with one Rebecca Reynolds Gaines. Said Rebecca is the daughter of Edith Reynolds, Harry Gaines's second mistress. Rebecca is a Montague to Chester Alan's Capulet, and the proceedings in the instant matter are replete with expressions of disloyalty and disgust on the part of family members from both Harry's and Sam's side.

Why it should be that any Gaineses, let alone virtually all of the living adult Gaineses, consider it their business that two of their own have fallen in love is beyond the understanding or jurisdiction of this Court. Suffice it to say that the Gaineses, with the exception of Tess Gaines, who nobly refused to testify in this matter, owing to her friendship with respondent Chester Alan, *made* this relationship their business. Chester Alan's affections for Rebecca, and hers for him, were called "treason" (trial transcript at 827), "morally wrong" (t.t. at 1438), and "disloyal to the memory of Original Sam" (t.t. at 2830).

Amelia thought back to her brief conversation with Annette Morris Gaines, Theodore's widow, after the reading of Harry's will. Annette, Amelia remembered, had volunteered the information that no one in the family had ever interfered with Chester Alan and Rebecca. Once again, a Surrogate's Court decision told Amelia a different story. Amelia wondered what compelled the family to lie. To protect its secrets? To justify the unjustifiable? Amelia had no answer. She read on:

Despite the legal wrangling that delayed the conclusion of this case for six long years, I fail to find even the slightest bit of reasoning why any member of this family has the right to challenge a simple bequest from a mother to a son. As best as I can understand it, the sole purpose of the various legal stratagems employed by the two Shapolsky firms, both of which firms incidentally bring shame and discredit to the Surrogate's Court bar, was to tie up Chester Alan's bequest for years solely as a punishment for his relationship with Rebecca. The lawyers' fees for the contestants have been gross even by Shapolsky standards, and testimony in this Court on that matter hinted that the combined fees equaled forty percent of Chester Alan's bequest.

All challenges to the will of Gloria Coss Gaines are hereby DISMISSED, and the entire family should be ashamed of itself.

PAUL MARTLAND III, Surrogate Judge

"Wow," said Amelia. She closed the case reporter and opened the next one.

Aaron appeared in the doorway. "Everybody's looking for you downstairs," he said. "Some Gaineses showed up. Howard talked to them."

"I just want to read one more case," said Amelia, not ready to face the world yet.

"I didn't see you," said Aaron, smiling conspiratorially. "I don't know where you are."

"Exactly," said Amelia, and she opened one more case reporter to the index card that Aaron had thoughtfully provided. She read:

Actors' Home for the Aged v. Gaines et al., 61-38391
Gaines v. Vinograd, 61-38392

In Surrogate's Court, New York, New York, December 11, 1962. Paul Martland, Jr., Surrogate Judge.

Morris Shapolsky, Shapolsky & Shapolsky, for petitioner Charles C. Gaines.

Louis Brandeis Shapolsky and Henry Clay Shapolsky,

Shapolsky and Shapolsky, New York, New York, for petitioners Theodore Gaines and Sarah Gurrelts Gaines.

Jay Silberwine, Silberwine and Porwitz, Katonah, New York, for respondents Actors' Home for the Aged.

Sherman Kosciusko, New York, New York, for respondent Hillie Vinograd.

JUDGE MARTLAND: This action combines two lawsuits over two last wills and testaments that the respondents, Actors' Home for the Aged and Hillie Vinograd, respectively, sought to enter into probate after the death of decedent Winona Wilson Gaines.

We will first take up the matter of the will that respondent Vinograd has brought to this courtroom. The late Mrs. Gaines, married for forty-five years to the vaudeville actor Harry Gaines, died after a long bout with cancer last year at the age of sixty-two. The will under which Mrs. Vinograd stakes her claim (hereinafter the "Vinograd" will) leaves half Mrs. Gaines's estate to her two sons, Charles C. and Harold L. Gaines, and half to Mrs. Vinograd herself. Mrs. Vinograd served as decedent's housekeeper during the last three months of decedent's life. The will, evidence showed at trial, was written in Mrs. Vinograd's own handwriting, although expert testimony made clear to me that the signature belonged to the decedent, Mrs. Winona Gaines.

Testimony at trial further showed that throughout the last three months of her life, Mrs. Gaines suffered from dementia. Her doctors testified that at no time during the three months prior to her death could she have been lucid enough or of sound enough mind to understand a will, particularly one that left so much of her not inconsiderable wealth to her housekeeper of such short standing. I hereby declare the Vinograd will null and void and have recommended to the district attorney the prosecution of both Mrs. Vinograd and her legal counsel for the procurement of a will under false and fraudulent pretenses.

We come now to the prior will, one executed in 1953, eight years before Mrs. Gaines's death and, according to her physicians, four years before the onset of cancer or any mental defects resulting therefrom. The 1953 will (herein-

after the "1953 will" or simply the "will") reads, in pertinent part:

> ... 4. I hereby will, devise, and decree twenty-five
> percent of my estate to each of my two sons, Charles
> Chaplin Gaines and Harold Lloyd Gaines. I hereby
> will, devise, and decree fifty percent of my estate to be
> placed in a trust for the benefit of the Actors' Home
> for the Aged.

According to testimony at trial, Mrs. Gaines had expected, before her illness struck, that she would spend her
declining years at the Actors' Home. Instead, after her
illness struck, she remained at her Manhattan address,
where she had lived since the 1930s and her estrangement
from her husband, Harry. This explains the bequest to the
Actor's Home.

Come now petitioners Charles Chaplin Gaines, Theodore
Gaines, and Sarah Gurrelts Gaines to challenge that portion of decedent's will giving fifty percent of decedent's
estate to the Actors' Home. Petitioners argue that sharing
ownership of the theaters with the Actors' Home would
likely be detrimental to their own financial position. Petitioners therefore have adduced evidence in this Court that
in 1953, at the time decedent made her will, she was legally
insane. Conversely, the Actors' Home brought witnesses,
most notably decedent's personal physicians, to testify as
to her robust state of mental health in 1953.

Before the Court rules on the merits of petitioners'
motion to strike from the will the bequest to the Actors'
Home, I feel called upon to comment on the courtroom
behavior of certain members of the Gaines family. This is
the first time that I have presided over a Gaines will trial,
although their reputation precedes them. See my father's
decisions in *Gaines v. Gaines et al.*, 149 N.Y.S. 2d 34
(1951), *In re Estate of Grover Gaines*, 329 N.Y.S. 401
(1942), *In re Gaines*, 187 N.Y. 329 (1934), and *Essex Street
Orphanage v. Gaines*, 122 N.Y. 173 (1916). I refer here to
the behavior of Charles C. Gaines and Theodore Gaines.
These men are descended from the two opposing sides of
the Gaines family. Charles is the son of Harry Gaines, and
Theodore is Sam Gaines's son. I had to threaten both men
repeatedly with contempt of court citations in order to
have them present in the courtroom at the same time.
Whatever allergies the various Gaines family members

have developed to one another, I urge them to seek treatment outside the confines of my courtroom.

Amelia snorted. *Well, everybody was young once,* she thought.

I hope I have made my point clear. I turn now to the merits of petitioners Gaines's contentions. There are none. Mrs. Winona Wilson Gaines is hereby judged to have been of sound mind in 1953 at the time of the signing of her will leaving part of her estate to her sons and part to the Actors' Home. While the Court sympathizes with the desire of petitioners to keep all of the Gaines family business in Gaines hands, this Court will not interfere with the functioning of a perfectly valid will. Whether Harry Gaines chooses to leave all or part of his assets to his wife's estate, knowing as by now he surely must that half will go to the Actors' Home, is nobody's business but his own.

Case dismissed with costs to petitioners.

JUDGE PAUL MARTLAND, JR.

Amelia let out a sigh. Once again, she had been privy to the true dimensions of the war between the Gaineses. She closed the lawbook, promised herself to come back later to read the earlier cases, composed herself, and returned to the offices of the Trust Department.

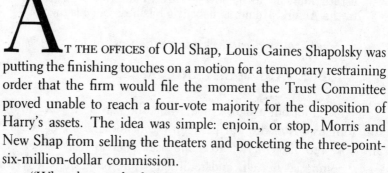

31

A T THE OFFICES of Old Shap, Louis Gaines Shapolsky was putting the finishing touches on a motion for a temporary restraining order that the firm would file the moment the Trust Committee proved unable to reach a four-vote majority for the disposition of Harry's assets. The idea was simple: enjoin, or stop, Morris and New Shap from selling the theaters and pocketing the three-point-six-million-dollar commission.

"What do you think?" Louis G. asked Moses Shapolsky, who had wandered into his son's office to watch the young man at work. Moses read the longhand draft and nodded.

"Looks good," he said. "It's a winner."

"Thanks, Dad," Louis G. said politely. Even if his father had not liked it, he would not have made any changes. Louis G. picked up the telephone and called Los Angeles directory information. He wrote down the number of Tower and Gates, the firm where his law school classmate worked. He called the number and was connected to his classmate's secretary. His friend was away on vacation until the following Monday, but the secretary would be happy to have the document go through word processing at the firm. She had seen too much paranoia on the part of lawyers to question one more display of it. She gave Louis G. the firm's fax number, and Louis G. thanked her and hung up. He went to the Old Shap fax machine (bought entirely at his insistence), dialed Tower and Gates, and sent the document.

"That thing really work?" asked Louis G.'s grandfather, Henry Clay, who had joined Louis and Moses in the fax and copying room. Deborah wandered in, and the whole firm was present.

"I hope so," said Louis G., who retrieved the draft of the temporary restraining order after it had passed through the fax machine and reproduced itself three thousand miles away in the offices of Tower and Gates. Louis G. then took his handwritten accomplishment and tore it into bits. He put the torn paper into an ashtray, took some matches from a nearby desk, and lit them. The family watched the draft burn.

"The only copy of that document is three thousand miles from here," Louis G. said. "Safe from the hands of any Gaineses."

"Or from Morris Shapolsky," added Henry Clay, the steely glint returning to his eyes.

"Or from Morris," repeated Louis. "Tower's word processing will type this out for us, and when we need it, all we have to do is have 'em fax it back."

"Wonderful," said Henry Clay, watching the fire consume the last of his grandson's handiwork. "Those ashes are going to be worth three point six million dollars!"

"That's right, Grandpa," said Louis, his eyes on the embers. "And all we have to do is just let the Gaines family take its natural course. Four votes. They couldn't even get two votes on that committee to agree."

Across town, in New Shap's offices, the mood was darker. Morris had returned from his lunch with Sam David a changed man. He entered the office with barely a greeting to his children, Edward and Samantha, or to his cousin Samuel G. He walked right by Barry Shapolsky-Kleinman, his devoted nephew, as though Barry had been a hatrack. The confused members of New Shap held an impromptu whispered conference outside Morris's door.

"Is he okay?" Samantha said.

"I've never seen him like that," said Edward. "He looked so upset," said Barry.

"It may be a delayed reaction to losing Harry," offered Samuel G.

"Makes sense," the others agreed. They never would have guessed that Morris was debating whether to sell them out for a million eight.

"You know, I'm worried about Old Shap," said Barry.

"How come?" asked Samantha. "We haven't heard anything from them."

"That's just what I mean," said Barry.

"You'd think they'd be bothering us with questions and phone calls and everything," said Edward, "the way they do before every will contest."

"Well, this one's different," replied Samantha. "If anyone goes to court to challenge the will, they're automatically cut out. Maybe that's why they're so quiet."

"I just don't know," said Barry. "It's that asshole Louis G. I'm worried about."

"Forget Louis," said Samantha. "In ninety days he'll be flat broke and without any clients. And we'll be on easy street."

"I guess so," Barry said uneasily. "I just wish Uncle Morris wasn't acting so odd. I've just never seen it before."

At that moment, the firm's receptionist came running. "A whole bunch of Gaineses!" she said. "They're outside, and they want to talk to Morris!"

The members of New Shap eyed each other nervously. Was Morris too overcome by the loss of Harry to meet with his clients?

"Tell them we'll be right there," said Barry. "Put them in the conference room."

The receptionist nodded and disappeared. Gingerly, Barry knocked on Morris's door. There was no answer. Barry opened the door slowly, to find Morris sitting at his desk, slowly shaking his head and saying, "I don't believe it," over and over.

"What don't you believe, Uncle Morris?" Barry said soothingly, as the rest of the family looked on. "Look, some of the Gaines family is here, and they want to meet with you. Should we tell them to come back later?"

"N-n-n-n-no," said Morris, rising catatonically. "Let's go talk to them."

"Are you sure, Dad?" asked Samantha. "We could reschedule."

"That's okay," said Morris, visions of Sam David's one point eight million dancing and swirling before him. "Let's go see what they have to say." He forced a smile as if to reassure his relatives and colleagues that he was well. They made their way down the hall to the conference room, where Keith, Babette, Grover Sam, and Woodrow Sam awaited them. After greetings and expressions of surprise and delight on the part of all the members of New Shap to see so many Gaineses under the same roof neither to bury nor to litigate, Keith got promptly down to business.

"We need your vote, Morris," Keith said earnestly. "It's all worked out. We get you and then we get Howard and Amelia from the bank, and it's all locked up. I get a theater for my vaudeville museum, Tess gets one for her homeless shelter—no, forget about Tess. She's in cahoots with Glenda. I don't think we can count on either of their votes. Anyway, the bank keeps us as clients, and we keep the theaters, and the whole thing's just jake. How about it, Morris? Can we count on your vote?"

Gaineses and Shapolskys alike turned toward Morris to see how he would react. He did not respond at once. What he heard was disastrous. If everything went Morris's way, then Sam David and only Sam David could muster the required four votes. Morris would then receive his one point eight million. Although, to be sure, Morris would ask for a certified check in advance. Morris had decided on the way back from lunch that he could choose his own Swiss bank—he did not need Sam David for that. In any event, this was Morris's Plan A. Plan B came into effect if Sam David could not round up the requisite third and fourth votes. Under Plan B, the committee would be forced to disband in failure and Morris's firm would sell the theaters. Morris would not get the one point eight million from Sam David—he, like the rest of the members of New Shap, would receive his $720,000 share of the real estate commission. Plan B clearly had its virtues, although it had one million eighty thousand less virtues than Plan A.

Now, to Morris's shock and horror, Plans C and D had come into existence. Plan C was Keith's proposition, in which Keith and Morris would be a voting bloc and in which Keith and the rest of the

Gaineses present would solicit the votes of the two bank representatives, Amelia and Howard. Plan D was the same as Plan C, except
that Glenda and Tess would replace Morris and Keith. Morris
wondered whether there was still time to try and cut a deal with
Glenda and Tess.

Morris was hardly the only Shapolsky at the table disquieted by
the sudden and surprising demonstration of Gaines family solidarity.
After all, if either the Keith-Morris-Howard-Amelia axis or the
Glenda-Tess-Amelia-Howard axis prevailed, New Shap would lose
its three point six million. The trick for Morris, all the other
Shapolskys present immediately recognized, was to give the four
Gaineses present the impression that Morris would vote with them
even though such was the opposite of the truth. Morris, his relatives
believed, would not vote for anyone. Morris himself knew that he
would not vote for anyone but Sam David.

Morris cleared his throat. He was in the unfortunate position of
facing eight of the people closest to him in life, all of whom he had
a great financial need to sell out.

"I just don't know what to say . . . it sounds like a good idea
. . . I need time to think," he began.

"What's to think about?" Keith asked, not understanding
Morris's hesitation. "I'm your client! I'm Harry's son! I'm on the
committee! Don't you want to vote with me?"

"Dad's overcome just now," Edward said, hoping to cover for
Morris and appease the Gaineses. "I think the whole fact of losing
Harry just hit him this afternoon."

"Oh," Keith said, nodding slowly. "Oh, I'm sorry. Gee, that
makes sense."

"We should come back later," Babette said sympathetically.
"Poor Morris just doesn't look himself at all."

"They were so close," added Grover Sam.

"We just wanted you to know how we felt," said Woodrow
Sam in a sympathetic tone. "Come on, everybody, let's go. Morris
is a little overcome. He and Grandfather were friends for so long."

Morris gave Woodrow Sam a look of gratitude for the younger
man's understanding. Morris was perfectly content to allow his
clients, and his relatives, to believe that the determinant for his
depressed state was not greed but grief.

With scraping of chairs and quiet goodbyes, the Gaineses took their leave of the New Shap attorneys. Morris, first exhausted by contemplation of a million eight and then displeased by all the peace breaking out in the Gaines family, excused himself and locked himself in his office, where he sat at his desk and closed his eyes. He meditated in order to eliminate his fear that the Gaineses could close ranks and gather four votes behind one position or another. He chose as his temporary mantra: "one point eight, one point eight, one point eight."

Downstairs, the Gaines family, feeling more and more like a family and less and less like a collection of litigants bound solely by a common progenitor, made plans to go on to the bank, once it could be established that Tess and Glenda had moved on. Grover Sam took this opportunity to bow out.

"I've got to get back to Los Angeles," he said. "I came out on a nonrefundable ticket."

"Tear the ticket up," said Keith, in the first-ever recorded act of impulsive Gaines generosity. "Stay longer. I'll buy you a ticket when this is all done. You can't leave now."

"Gee, thanks, Father," said Grover Sam, "but my plants need to be watered and I might get a call from my agent, and besides, I have to go back to work." Grover Sam was referring to his word processing job at the downtown law firm of Tower and Gates.

"Well, if you insist," said Keith. Grover Sam said goodbye to his father, mother, and brother. It was the first warm, genuine goodbye in the history of the Gaines family, making for two firsts in one conversation. Miracles were spreading like the dew.

"Why don't you come to Aspen this winter?" Babette asked. "We've got a lovely guest room for you. We have the nicest young man who'll pick you up at the airport. He loves Sidney."

"Okay, Mother," said Grover Sam. "Well, good luck at the meeting. Goodbye, everybody."

Grover Sam kissed his mother, shook his father's hand, shook his brother's hand, and, never taking his eyes from his family, stepped off the curb and into traffic. A car swerved to avoid him and smashed violently into a parked truck. A taxi driver, making a sudden left turn, never had a chance. He plowed into the back of the smashed-up car. Grover Sam didn't notice.

Keith, Babette, and Woodrow Sam watched and winced at the accident. Broken glass was everywhere. A crowd of bystanders gathered as a policeman helped the drivers and passengers out of the wrecked car and taxi. The cab driver was near tears. Keith, with his mechanic's innate abhorrence of car crashes, guarded his temper. He did not want to allow his son's destructive tendencies with regard to motor vehicles to ruin the warm glow of family feeling that had so recently descended upon the four of them. "Well," Keith said diplomatically, "that's my boy."

32

As Grover Sam arrived at Newark Airport for his flight back to the West Coast, Gil Thompson and Cynthia Crossen were arriving from Omaha. They took a cab directly to Wall Street, where they waited across the street from the main entrance to the New York Bank and Trust Company. Their objective: follow Amelia and learn all they could about her.

Amelia returned to her desk from the Legal Department, feeling no better, trying not to think about poor Mr. Scarpatti or the message from Elizabeth Herder. Amelia felt Mr. Skeffington's eyes upon her at all times. She sensed that he sought to understand why the Elizabeth Herder message should so disturb her. Amelia's desk was covered with pink slips—more and more Gaineses were trying to get in touch with her, hoping to land her vote. She swept all the pink slips off her desk and into the trash. Then Andre came by with another sheaf of pink slips. She accepted them without her customary good cheer, nor did she even say thank you. Andre attributed Amelia's new rudeness to her getting her own *Wall Street Journal*, which it was his duty to place on her desk early each morning. Once people got their own *Journal*, Andre had noted, they tended to get very full of themselves. Amelia, he noted sadly, had turned out to be no exception.

Amelia gave the message slips a cursory scan and threw out all of them except for one from Dwight David. She called him at his apartment in his father's building on Fifth Avenue.

"Last night was very meaningful," Dwight David told her.

"For me too," said Amelia.

"I want to see you tonight," Dwight David said. "I'll send a limo for you at the office."

That's all Howard has to see, Amelia thought. "That's okay," she said. "I have to go home and change first."

"Can I have him pick you up at eight?"

"Eight would be great," Amelia told him, and she hung up the telephone as Howard approached her desk. "Oh, hi, Howard."

"Have a sec?" Howard asked, unsure of where exactly he stood with Amelia.

"Sure," said Amelia, trying to dismiss all disturbing thoughts from her mind.

Howard seated himself opposite Amelia. "I feel like you've been ignoring me since Dwight David came to town," he said bluntly.

Amelia sighed. "Howard, this just isn't the best time—"

"What about tonight?" Howard asked. "Can we just, you know, have dinner?"

Amelia shook her head. "I already made plans," she said.

"With Dwight David," Howard guessed.

"With Dwight David," Amelia admitted.

Howard did not try to hide his feelings. He said, "You know I told you I couldn't, you know, make things official with you until our folks met. Well, I've been thinking it over, and maybe I was wrong. I promised my parents, and everything, that I wouldn't get engaged until they'd met your parents. But I feel, like, if only I hadn't been waiting for that, none of this would've happened. I love you. I want to marry you. I want to spend the rest of my life with you. And since you got the Gaineses, I can barely get to see you."

Tears formed in Amelia's eyes. "Oh, Howard," she began. "I didn't mean to hurt your feelings. It's just that—"

Mr. Skeffington interrupted her. "Excuse me," he said. "Howard, may I have a word with you?"

"Of course, Mr. Skeffington," said Howard, rising hastily to follow Mr. Skeffington. Howard turned back to Amelia. "Just tell me one thing. Why are you so—so *obsessed* with this family? Will you tell me that?"

"They're my clients," Amelia said defensively. "I'm supposed to be thinking about them."

"Night and day?" Howard asked, glancing toward Mr. Skeffington's office. "Just tell me why."

"I don't know what to say," Amelia admitted, lowering her voice. "This family . . . it's just—it's just *different*. It's so screwed up. It's so monumentally screwed up. The further back I go, the more screwed up it is. I just have to keep going further and further back."

"But why?" Howard said. "It's not normal."

"Well, maybe *I'm* not normal," said Amelia. "I mean, there are some things you don't know about me. I'm not exactly who you think I am. I have kind of a past."

"In Greenwood, Nebraska," Howard said, not understanding.

"Well, no. Not in Greenwood, Nebraska. I've kind of made up a few things about myself," Amelia admitted in a whisper.

Howard looked alarmed. "Things that Mr. Skeffington wouldn't like?"

Amelia gave a small nod. Howard did not understand what was happening. He feared for her job and for their relationship. Who was she, really? What was she hiding?

"Like what?" Howard whispered.

"I don't want to talk about it here." Amelia saw Mr. Skeffington observing their whispered conversation. "He's waiting for you," she added.

"Later?" Howard asked. And then, glumly: "Oh, I forgot. You're having dinner with Dwight David."

"Please don't start that again," Amelia said.

"I'm sorry," said Howard, although he could not deny a measure of jealousy for the young Gaines scion. "I just want to know what is it about that family, why you are so . . . *fascinated* by every little detail."

Mr. Skeffington had just asked her practically the same question.

"The answer," Amelia whispered, drawing her words out

slowly and seriously, "is that coming from where I'm coming from, next to them I just feel *normal*."

"Coming from where you're coming from?" Howard repeated, not understanding. "Greenwood, Nebraska?"

"No," Amelia whispered sadly. "Not Greenwood, Nebraska."

Andre loomed. "Mr. Person, Sam David's on line three for you."

"I'll call him back," said Howard. "I just don't get it, Amelia. I just don't understand."

Howard left Amelia at her desk and went to see Mr. Skeffington. He wondered what Sam David wanted. *Probably wants to increase his bribe for my vote,* he told himself. Of course, he was right.

33

As she left the bank that night, Amelia was thinking too deeply about the imminent arrival of Elizabeth Herder to notice that she was being followed.

Thirty yards behind her, inconspicuous in the rush hour crowd, crept Gil Thompson and Cynthia Crossen.

Twenty yards behind them, equally inconspicuous, was Richard Bickle.

Amelia walked along Broad Street to the subway. Gil and Cynthia followed her down to the uptown express platform. Bickle had to stop to buy a token. Fortunately for Bickle, the train was delayed, as usual, and he had time to find his target in the densely packed crowd. When the train arrived, Amelia entered the second car from the front, via the northernmost door.

Gil and Cynthia entered the same car at the middle door.

Bickle entered at the rear door.

The train pulled away, Amelia unaware of the intense scrutiny of her every breath. Gil, his moves honed during hours of practice in the lobby of Manhattan Hospital, watched Amelia over the top of his *New York Post*. Cynthia divided her attention between Amelia and Gil. She was savoring the renewed opportunity to watch a master spy go about his business. Bickle was by far the most nervous of the four. If he lost Amelia in the crowd, Sam David would say terrible things to him. Bickle thought it prudent to avoid this.

Amelia changed to the local at Grand Central, as did Gil, Cynthia, and Bickle. The train made its lugubrious, pitching journey uptown. Amelia emerged at the East Seventy-seventh Street station. So did Gil and Cynthia. So did Bickle.

Amelia followed the slow-footed crowd to the center of the platform, through the exit gate, to the stairs, and up to daylight. Gil and Cynthia remained ten to twelve bodies behind at all times. Bickle, unaccustomed to following people around the city, got jostled, lost his target, and went up the wrong stairway. Fortunately, he saw her across Lexington Avenue. He picked up the trail.

Amelia stopped in a Gristede's on Lexington at Seventy-fifth Street, two blocks from the station. Gil and Cynthia followed her in. Bickle, who, as it happened, shopped regularly at the store and feared losing her again in its familiar crowded, narrow aisles, waited outside.

Amelia made use of a handbasket and not a cart, Gil noted. He grabbed a handbasket and nodded briefly to Cynthia to do the same. They followed her through the aisles, grabbing an occasional item and putting it in their baskets. They were far more concerned with what Amelia was putting in *her* basket.

Flour. Butter. Eggs. Sugar. Walnuts. And chocolate chips. These were the contents of Amelia's basket as she took up position in one of the slow-moving checkout lines. Gil's basket of items chosen at random, to make it look to anyone watching that he was just another shopper and not a world-class spy, contained matzoh farfel, gourmet cheese popcorn, canned beets, and animal crackers. Cynthia's basket held a can of Diet 7-Up and a cucumber. They joined the line two shoppers behind Amelia. Gil memorized the contents of her basket.

Outside the store, looking in, Bickle watched her unload the items and also memorized them. A clue was a clue. Leave it to Sam David to unravel the deeper meaning.

Once Amelia chose paper instead of plastic and paid, Gil and Cynthia coolly put their baskets on the floor and followed her out of the store. Bickle picked up the trail, as well. At Seventy-third street, Amelia turned east, her entourage forty feet behind her, as inconspicuous as three extremely nervous New Yorkers can manage to look. At Third Avenue, the subject turned right, walked twenty yards, and disappeared into her apartment building.

Bickle and Gil raced each other to the phone at the corner. They had never met, so they did not realize that they had been tailing the same woman. Gil got to the phone first. He called Old Shap.

"Louis G.?" he said. "Gil. I followed her home. She's in her building. She stopped in the grocery store. . . . Eggs, flour, butter, sugar, and walnuts."

"Sidney, you forgot chocolate chips," Cynthia reminded him.

"Huh?" said Gil, forgetting that Cynthia still thought his name was Sidney. "Oh, yeah. And chocolate chips . . . No, I have no idea. You just told me to follow her and notice everything. That's all there was to notice. . . . I'm not yelling at you. . . . Okay. Okay. Yeah, I'll call you. Bye."

Gil hung up.

"What did he say?" Cynthia asked.

"He said he didn't care what Amelia bought in the store," Gil said. "He said I should only tell him what's important. Temper that guy has. Come on, there's a bar across the street. We can go sit there and wait for her to come out of the building." He recalled his undercover triumph in Nebraska. "And maybe they know something about her in there. Let's go."

Gil and Cynthia went off to the bar. Bickle, who had overheard their conversation, went to the pay phone and called Sam David.

"It's Bickle, sir. I followed her home. . . . Yes, she's home right now. . . . Anything unusual?" Bickle debated whether to mention Amelia's purchases in Gristede's. He did not want to subject himself to ridicule, as had Gil in his conversation with Louis Gaines Shapolsky.

Bickle opted for full disclosure nonetheless. "I don't think it means anything, sir, but she bought the things you need to bake walnut chocolate chip cookies. Flour, butter, sugar, walnuts, chocolate chips . . . I did, sir?" Bickle asked joyously. "Incredibly important information, sir? . . . . A raise, sir? Oh, no, you're too kind, sir. I was just . . ." Bickle blushed. "Why, thank you, sir. I certainly will. I'll stay right here and watch to see what happens next. . . . And I think you're excellent at your job too, sir," Bickle said, but then he was afraid that he had taken too personal and chummy a tone with his boss. He reverted to a more businesslike voice. "Absolutely, sir. You can count on me. Goodbye, sir."

Bickle hung up, delighted. He did not know why Sam David found it so useful to know that Amelia had purchased the ingredients for walnut chocolate chip cookies, but that was why Sam David was Sam David and Bickle was Bickle. Bickle stood outside the telephone booth and hoped that whatever that mysterious thing was that separated the Sam Davids of the world from the world's Bickles, it was somehow rubbing off on him.

Bickle crossed Third Avenue and went to a newsstand that offered an unobstructed view of Amelia's building. He slowly chose one magazine, and then a second, and then a third, his eyes constantly returning to the entrance of Amelia's apartment building. Gil successfully bribed the bartender across the street, only to learn that he, Gil, knew more about Amelia than did the bartender. Meanwhile, a white stretch limousine pulled up in front of Amelia's building. She emerged from her lobby, wearing a long blue evening gown. Under the watchful eyes of Gil, Cynthia, and the still beaming Bickle, she got into the limo.

W HERE ARE WE GOING?" asked Amelia, who had been in
limousines only when accompanying relatives of DLOLs to cemeteries.

"I'm not telling," said Dwight David, resplendent in his
father's tuxedo. It sagged a bit, since Chester Alan outweighed his
son by thirty-five pounds, but it looked good anyway. A bottle of
champagne, uncorked, rested in an ice-filled silver bucket between
them. "It's my last night in New York," Dwight David added, "and
I want to make it special."

"Great," said Amelia, thinking that the magic of the bank's
wallpaper was about to reveal itself. And just in time, she told
herself, convinced as she was that the outcome of the Elizabeth
Herder business would cost her her job. "But can we make one
quick stop first?"

"Um, sure," said Dwight David. "Just tell the driver."

Amelia picked up the intercom. "Take us to 15 Broad Street
downtown, please."

The address sounded vaguely familiar to Dwight David. "Is
that a club?" he asked.

Amelia shook her head.

Then Dwight David remembered what was at 15 Broad Street.
"We're going to the bank!" he said. "Why?"

"I want to show you some will cases," Amelia explained. "I didn't get to them today, when everything was so crazy."

"Will cases?" asked Dwight David, confused. "I don't get it. Whose will cases?"

"Gaines will cases," Amelia explained. "I may be out of a job soon, so if we don't go right now, I may never get another chance to see them."

"Is that what you really want to do?" Dwight David asked. It did not sound like his idea of a good time.

"That's what I want to do," said Amelia. "Afterwards we can go out and do something else. But that's what I really want to do right now."

"Okay," said Dwight David, looking disappointed. "If that's what you *really* want to do."

Twenty minutes later, the limousine pulled up at the night entrance to the bank. Amelia and Dwight David told the driver to wait. She showed her bank ID to the surprised security guard, and the two entered and took the elevator to the offices of the Legal Department. Their voices echoed strangely in the nighttime atmosphere of the bank.

"This place is kind of creepy at night," said Dwight David.

"It's not so bad," Amelia said agreeably. "I've spent a lot of time here at night. Not dressed like this, of course."

"So you come here, like, every day?" Dwight David said, reflecting on the nature of employment. "Monday through Friday?"

"That's what people with jobs do," Amelia said gently. "Sometimes we even come in on Saturdays."

"Then when does everybody work on their tans?" asked Dwight David.

They reached the third floor, flipped the lights on, and headed for the Legal Department. To Amelia's surprise and chagrin, Aaron was working late. He was visibly unhappy to see Amelia in the company of another man and asked in a sulking sort of way, "Who's your friend?"

"Aaron, I'd like you to meet Dwight David Gaines."

"Oh, the cash machine," Aaron said, extending a hand. "I've heard a lot about you."

"Not from me," Amelia said quickly.

"From Vaccaro and Stone," said Aaron. "Amelia's predecessors."

"You knew Vaccaro?" Dwight David asked. "What was with that guy?"

"Nothing that all the Valium in the state of Pennsylvania can't cure," said Aaron. "Your family was a little more than he could take."

"That's why we like Amelia," said Dwight David. "I think she can stand up to us."

"Off to a ball tonight?" Aaron asked. He eyed the ample and sagging waistline on Dwight David's borrowed tux. "You might have a word with your tailor. Or are you expecting to have seconds on dessert?"

"I just wanted to show Dwight David some of the will cases," Amelia explained nervously. She wanted the conversation with Aaron to come to an end before he could say something inappropriate about Amelia and Howard or Amelia and himself.

"Well, you don't need me for that anymore," Aaron said. "Excuse me," he said to Dwight David. "Some of us have to work for a living."

"That's too bad," Dwight David commiserated pleasantly.

"Don't forget our deal," Aaron told Amelia.

"My only hope is that I get fired *before* I ever see you again," Amelia told him.

She and Dwight David took their leave of Aaron and went into the law library.

"Strange dude," said Dwight David.

"Too much law," said Amelia. "I've seen it happen before. Destroys the personality."

"Bummer," said Dwight David. "But what are we doing in here?"

Amelia consulted the list of remaining Gaines will cases. "We're going to learn some early history of your family," she explained, pulling volumes of case reporters off the shelves.

"My family got written up in those books?" Dwight David asked, pride creeping into his voice. "Really?"

Amelia nodded. She opened the first of the three volumes and flipped to the page specified in the case citation. Something was wrong. The pages went 31, 32, 33, 34, 39. "That's strange," Amelia said, puzzled. Then she realized that someone had taken a razor blade or scissors to the book and neatly, almost surgically, excised the pages containing the Gaines case.

"I can't believe that," she said, looking up at Dwight David. "Somebody cut it out of the book."

Dwight David looked at the page numbers and the neatly clipped remainders of the missing pages. "Wow," he said.

"Who in your family would do something like that?" Amelia asked him.

Dwight David snorted. "Who *wouldn't*?" he asked. "But how do you know somebody from my family did it? Maybe someone from the bank cut it out."

"That's impossible," Amelia said, insulted. She took the honor of the Trust Department personally. "One of your relatives must have come in here with a pair of scissors. Let's look at another case. I want to show you what your family looks like in print."

"Okay," said Dwight David, and he handed her another volume. Amelia took it, checked her list, turned to the page—and found that this case also had been cut out.

"I can't believe this," she said. "Give me the other one."

Dwight David handed her another volume. Once again, Amelia checked the list of cases and turned to the appropriate page. Once again, the case was missing.

"Somebody's got something to hide," said Amelia, incensed equally at the secrecy and at the violence done the innocent lawbooks.

"I guess we'll never know what those cases said," Dwight David said, looking at his watch. "Come on, I've got something *I* want to show *you*."

Amelia stared at him. "Aren't you *curious*?" she asked. "Don't you want to know what the cases *said*?"

Dwight David looked uncomfortably at the floor. "Um, to be honest—"

"I can't believe you!" Amelia exclaimed. "These are your family secrets, and you don't even care!"

Dwight David shrugged. "Maybe family secrets are better off staying that way," he said. "Maybe there's stuff in there I don't *want* to know."

"Well, I've *got* to know," Amelia said. "Maybe *you* don't care, but *I* do. Where can we find another set of these lawbooks at this time of night?"

"Why do we have to do it right now?" Dwight David asked. "Why can't it wait for the morning?" He wondered again whether Amelia was perhaps *too* focused on his family.

"It can't wait for the morning," Amelia responded. She did not add that if Mr. Skeffington either discovered the meaning of the Elizabeth Herder message or subjected her résumé to the same inspection he had given Mr. Scarpatti's, she might not have a job in the morning. "I want to know right now."

Dwight David merely shrugged. The intensity of Amelia's curiosity about his family had begun to bother him. He looked around at the rows and rows of lawbooks on the shelves. "I wonder if you have to read all these books if you go to law school," he said. "I'd hate that."

"No, of course not," Amelia said, not really paying attention. She was trying to think of a law firm or bank that might be open at this hour. She could not think of any. "You get casebooks, and you just have to read those cases— Wait a minute! Dwight David, that's it! We could go to a law school library!"

"I thought we were going out to have fun," Dwight David said, disappointed. "I don't want to go to a library."

"Come on," she said. "It'll just take a few minutes. Then we can do whatever you want."

Amelia's eyes shone so brightly at the thought of tracking down the Gaines family secrets that Dwight David knew well he could not refuse. Dolefully he agreed. They left the bank and returned to the limousine.

"NYU Law Library," he told Acey, his driver. Acey, who had driven limousines in New York City for thirty years and who had been driving for Dwight David since the young man's seventeenth birthday, had never heard of the NYU Law Library and had certainly never been directed there by a smartly dressed young couple out for a night on the town. He looked it up in a book of maps.

Eventually the limo pulled away from the curb and headed up to the law school. Dwight David felt somewhat annoyed with this woman who seemed more interested in dead Gaineses than in the live one beside her in the back seat. Amelia, for her part, was fixated on the missing cases. What did they say about the family? Why would someone have cut them out?

They reached the law school in fifteen minutes, went inside, and found their way into the Law Library, which was packed with students. Every desk, every carrel, was occupied. The law students looked up from their casebooks and outlines with a mixture of envy and awe for their two elegantly dressed visitors, reminders that a world existed beyond their lawbooks, a world where people had fun.

"Why is it so crowded?" Amelia murmured, looking at the drawn, unhappy faces.

"Finals week," said a student passing by.

"It's creepy in here," said Dwight David. The blank, sleepless expressions of the law students reminded him of a cross between a horror film and the waiting area for a long-delayed international flight.

"Can you help us find these cases?" Amelia asked a student, who looked at the case citations Amelia showed her and pointed to a set of shelves against a far wall.

"Thanks," said Amelia.

"Let's just get the books and get out of here," Dwight David said, thoroughly spooked by the sight of all these people around his age who were doing something difficult with their lives.

Amelia and Dwight David felt the eyes of two hundred law students upon them, upon his tuxedo and her gown, as they made their way to the shelves holding the *New York Reporters* that contained the early Gaines cases. Amelia located the first book, turned to the right page, and, to her relief, found the case. It had not been cut out of the NYU Law Library's copy. She quickly gathered together the other volumes she needed. Just then the law librarian, a gray-haired woman in her seventies, approached Amelia. She wore a name badge that said "Miss Pander."

"Are you affiliated with the law school?" Miss Pander asked, looking suspiciously at Amelia's elegant appearance.

"Why, no, I—" Amelia began.

"Then I'll have to ask you and your friend to leave," Miss Pander said firmly. "The library is closed to anyone outside the law school community. It's finals week."

"But we just need to—" Amelia said. Dwight David picked up the stack of lawbooks Amelia had pulled from the shelves and took off. He headed for a nearby men's room.

"I'm sorry," Miss Pander said firmly.

"But I've got to read those cases!" Amelia said. "It's very important for my job."

"I'm sorry," Miss Pander said. "Rules are rules."

"Couldn't we just stay for ten minutes?" Amelia asked, looking around for Dwight David. She wondered where he had gone. "We just have to read a few cases, and then we'll be out of your way. I promise."

Miss Pander shook her head. "You're making my job very difficult," she said. "I don't like to have to do this, but unless you go right away, I'll have to call Security and—"

Dwight David suddenly reappeared. "It's okay," he said quickly. "Come on, Amelia, let's not bother anybody. We can read those cases in the morning, somewhere else."

"But, Dwight David," Amelia began, incensed that he would take the librarian's side in this.

"Amelia, I *insist*," Dwight David said firmly. Amelia had never heard him use that tone before. Then Dwight David bestowed a gracious smile on the librarian, who fluttered and smiled back.

Dwight David put his arm around Amelia's shoulders and gently turned her toward the door. Amelia, shocked, complied meekly.

"You're a nice young man," Miss Pander said to Dwight David, "but rules are rules."

"Of course," Dwight David said charmingly. "Good night." He gave the librarian another warm smile, and he and Amelia left the library.

Once they reached the corridor, Amelia's wrath ignited. "What was the *meaning* of that?" she asked angrily. "How come you took her side instead of mine? And how come you just disappeared, leaving me to deal with that woman? What's wrong with you?"

Dwight David said nothing. Instead he reached under his

cummerbund and pulled out a dozen pages freshly torn from lawbooks.

Amelia's eyes widened. "I can't believe you did that!" she said.

"I'll just send a donation to the library fund in the morning," he said. "Come on, let's read 'em in the limo. I don't want to get caught."

They returned quickly to the limousine. Once inside, they turned on the little reading light over the back seat. They started with the will of Woodrow Gaines, torn from volume 149 of New York Supplement 2d Series at page 34.

"It's Grandpa!" Dwight David explained. "Unbelievable!"

Amelia felt a chill as she introduced a present member of the Gaines family to an aspect of his past. And she had to know for her own sake what each of the earliest will battles contained.

"GAINES V. GAINES ET AL., 51-32893," Amelia and Dwight David read together. "Surrogate's Court, New York, October 13, 1951, Judge Paul Martland, Jr."

"The 51 there tells you it was filed in 1951," Amelia explained. Dwight David nodded. "Okay," he said.

Louis Brandeis Shapolsky, Shapolsky and Shapolsky, New York, New York, for petitioner Gloria Coss Gaines.

Henry Clay Shapolsky, Shapolsky and Shapolsky, New York, New York, for intervenor Theodore Gaines.

Morris Shapolsky and Samuel Gompers Shapolsky, Shapolsky & Shapolsky, New York, New York, for intervenor Charles Chaplin Gaines.

JUDGE MARTLAND: The widow Gloria Coss Gaines (hereinafter "Gloria") of decedent Woodrow Gaines (hereinafter "Woodrow") has come to this courtroom seeking a declaratory judgment to the effect that her husband was insane in 1936 at the time of the making and signing of his will.

"Grandmother did *that*?" Dwight David asked, stupefied. "Calling Grandfather insane?"

"Just keep reading," said Amelia, surprised that Dwight David did not know about the suit. Amelia had assumed that all the Gaineses knew everything about their legal history.

Her motion is opposed by Woodrow's only surviving brother, Theodore Gaines (hereinafter "Theodore") and by Woodrow's first cousin Charles Chaplin Gaines (hereinafter "Charles C.").

As in everything related to Gaines family matters, it all comes down to money and intrafamily squabbling. I have conducted four trials related to Gaines family wills, and never have I seen a family bear so many grudges over so little for so long. Nor have I ever seen a law firm such as Shapolsky and Shapolsky, which flirts so dangerously with conflict-of-interest issues. How can it be that members of the same firm feel free to represent competing family members in a will case? I bring the matter up only to state that I asked petitioner Gloria and intervenors Theodore and Charles C. at trial whether they were troubled by the potential for conflict of interest. They said they were not. If they are not troubled by it, then neither is the Court.

Decedent Woodrow left, by his 1936 last will and testament, three quarters of his estate to his wife, Gloria, and the other quarter to his uncle Harry Gaines (hereinafter "Harry"). Evidence was brought at trial showing that Harry and Woodrow enjoyed something approaching a father-and-son relationship after the death of Woodrow's own father, Sam Gaines, in 1933. See *In re Gaines, 187 N.Y. 329 (1934)*. Harry Gaines, as shall be demonstrated *infra*, once a successful vaudeville comedy actor, fell on hard times in the 1930s with the onset of talking movies.

"I never knew that," Amelia said.
"I did," said Dwight David. "Harry was poor for a long time."
"What about all his investments with Sam?" Amelia asked.
"He couldn't touch that money. Woodrow and Theodore had it all tied up in the buildings."
"So you know about that?" Amelia asked.
"We all do," said Dwight David. "We all know about the buildings."

They read on:

According to uncontroverted testimony at trial, Harry was institutionalized for depression in 1934 and again in 1936. He possessed little in savings. At this time, decedent Woodrow, on paper a wealthy man as a result of the large bequest from his father's estate, made and signed the will in question. Said will established a trust in Harry's behalf to provide for the hospital costs and old age of Woodrow's beloved uncle Harry. It is this bequest that petitioner Gloria Coss seeks in this action to disallow.

By the late 1940s, Harry's health and career had revived themselves. Harry appeared on radio and then in television dramas both here and in the British Isles. By the time of Woodrow's death, Harry had little need for the trust money his nephew Woodrow had arranged to leave him.

Interestingly, Harry Gaines himself did not seek to intervene in this trial on his own behalf. He testified only under subpoena and threat of contempt of court sanctions. He testified that he did not want "charity" from Gloria or from anyone in the family. (Trial transcript at 437.) He said that this was a matter of "honor and pride" with him. (T.t. at 441.) On cross-examination, however, he admitted that were the Court to find for him and declare the will valid, he would accept the bequest. (T.t. at 512.)

Theodore, decedent's brother, sought leave to intervene in this matter on Harry's behalf even though he was not a beneficiary of the will. Under cross-examination, he admitted that his sole purpose was to get back at Gloria for her role in the challenge to the will of the late Grover Gaines. See *In re Estate of Grover Gaines*, 329 N.Y.S. 401 (1942). Although this sort of behavior is typical of the Gaines family, I will not have it in my courtroom. Theodore's motion for leave to intervene is denied.

We come now to the issue of decedent Woodrow's alleged insanity at the time of the making and signing of his will in 1936. Doctors testified to Woodrow's alcoholism (t.t. at 312–331; t.t. at 379–386), and the coroner for the town of Oakwood, Maine, testified that the level of blood alcohol in decedent was 2.0 when his body was recovered after the fishing accident in which he died (t.t. at 342). Petitioner Gloria failed, however, to bring proof as to Woodrow's mental health in 1936 when he made the will. Nor did she prove that Woodrow's alcoholism ever affected his mental capacities. For this reason her challenge to the will is dismissed.

A side issue raised by intervenor Theodore, the decedent's brother, involves the possibility of foul play in the death of Woodrow. Theodore introduced evidence in the form of the 1951 motel register for the Oakwood Inn, Oakwood, Maine; receipts from a fishing tackle store, also in Oakwood; and a bill from an automobile rental agency in Augusta purporting to show the presence of one Albert Pocini in and around Oakwood at the time of Woodrow's death. Theodore brought before this Court records of a 1931 eviction by Woodrow Gaines for nonpayment of rent of Albert Pocini and his family from their home, an apartment on 108th Street, Jackson Heights, Queens, New York. Said apartment belonged to Sam Gaines, father of Woodrow and Theodore.

Counsel for Theodore speculate that Mr. Pocini harbored a longtime grudge against Woodrow (t.t. at 391) and that Mr. Pocini, upon discovering Woodrow in Oakwood, threatened him, in the lobby of the Oakwood Inn, with great bodily harm (t.t. at 392–393) only days before Woodrow's unexplained drowning in the fishing accident. Theodore is reminded that such facts have no bearing on the outcome of his brother's will and that if he suspects criminal behavior on the part of said Mr. Pocini or anyone else, he is advised to bring such suspicions to the proper authorities and not to this Court.

The final issue Gloria raised at trial is that of changed circumstance. Harry, on his feet financially and physically once again, cannot be said to "need" the money Woodrow's trust will provide him. Therefore, Gloria argues, the bequest to Harry, including, as it does, a portion of Woodrow's ownership of three theaters in the Broadway district of Manhattan, should be struck down. The Court disagrees. A beneficiary's need for a bequest has never been recognized in the law as a reason for limiting or striking a bequest. *Holmes v.*

Rowland, 123 N.Y.S.2d, 358 (1941). *In re McAndrews*, 101 N.Y. 121 (1902).

The will stands as written; the bequest to Harry stands as written; and the will is accepted into probate.

Paul Martland, Jr., Surrogate Judge

"So that's how Harry ended up with a majority interest in the theaters," Amelia said, as the limousine crossed the Brooklyn Bridge and made for the Brooklyn-Queens Expressway. "He had his own fifty percent, and then he got a quarter of Woodrow's share. Makes sense."

"I can't believe my own relatives are in those books," said Dwight David.

"Want to see another one?" Amelia asked.

"Um, sure," said Dwight David, wondering, as did Howard, whether Amelia's interest in the family was completely healthy. Dwight David certainly found the cases interesting reading, though.

Amelia reached for another will case. The pages had yellowed slightly, and the print was smaller. They read:

in re Estate of Grover GAINES, 42-3833

Surrogate's Court, New York, New York
Paul Martland, Sr., Surrogate Judge
March 3, 1943

Barry Shapolsky and Louis Brandeis Shapolsky, Shapolsky and Shapolsky, New York, New York, for petitioners Woodrow Gaines and Gloria Coss Gaines.

Capt. Joseph Brown, U.S. Navy Law Department, Washington, D.C., for respondents Esther Lampkin Gaines and Theodore Gaines.

"Grover!" Dwight David exclaimed. This was the relative whose memory he cherished. "I'm not sure I want to read this," he said soberly. "Maybe there's stuff in here I don't want to know." But he and Amelia immediately read the case.

> JUDGE MARTLAND: The facts are as follows: Grover Gaines, a promising young baseball player, was drafted into the Navy after Pearl Harbor and died in a shipboard accident in the Pacific shortly before the battle of Corregidor. Six weeks before his death, he wrote a letter to his wife, Esther Lampkin Gaines, that set forth what he wanted to happen to his estate in the event that he was killed in battle. That letter reads, in pertinent part:

>> "You get three quarters of everything, my love, and my brother Theodore gets one quarter. I don't want Woodrow to get a plugged nickel. Not after what he did to Pa and me."

"Woodrow's my grandfather," Dwight David said, struck by the conflict between his two relatives.

> Decedent Grover left no other will. The estate in question is considerable because Grover was the son of the real estate businessman Sam Gaines and inherited one third of Mr. Gaines's real estate business.

> Come now Woodrow Gaines and his wife, Gloria Coss Gaines, to challenge the admissibility of the letter from Grover to Esther as a valid will. If the letter is declared invalid as a will, the late Grover will be said to have died intestate. As a result, his estate would pass in its entirety to his wife, Esther. This case can be read most simply as an effort by Woodrow and Gloria to keep Theodore from receiving the one-quarter share of Grover's estate as specified in Grover's letter.

> Petitioners Woodrow and Gloria base their suit on the claim that Grover's letter does not constitute a will in the technical sense of the term. As Woodrow and Gloria point out, there were no witnesses. The decedent's signature was not notarized, in keeping with the traditional requirements of New York State law. There is none of the legal language such as "I, So-and-so, being of sound mind and body" or "give,

devise, and bequeath," or other phraseology of wills in use since time out of mind.

While petitioners are correct in a technical sense, they are reminded that on Navy vessels steaming to do battle with the enemy, there is a shortage of attorneys and notaries public ready to serve the men on board. No one has challenged that the letter in Grover's hand was written by anyone but Grover. Nor has anyone challenged Grover's mental or physical fitness at the time of the writing of the letter, dated as it was only six weeks prior to his death in the unfortunate shipboard accident. The letter clearly expresses its author's will with regard to the division of his property in the foreseeable event of his sudden demise. This Court therefore accepts the letter as the last will and testament of Grover Gaines.

Much of the testimony at trial related to the acrimonious relationship between petitioner Woodrow and his brother, the decedent Grover. Amity between brothers Woodrow and Grover apparently declined first in the summer of 1931, when, according to testimony adduced at trial, Woodrow, then nineteen, took Grover, then thirteen, on a fishing trip to Maine, contrary to the explicit commands of their father, Sam. (Trial transcript at 307.) Sam apparently never forgave Woodrow or Grover for Woodrow's "insubordination" (t.t. at 311). Grover proved unable to repair the breach of relations with his father, who died less than two years later. Grover never forgave Woodrow for "lousing things up between him and Pa," as Woodrow himself testified under cross-examination (t.t. at 349). Bad relations between Woodrow and the decedent Grover therefore date back at least to 1931.

Woodrow also admitted at trial that he remained in contact with his father's second wife, Marie Benedict Gaines, after the death of his father, Sam, in 1933. According to Woodrow's testimony, Marie lost, as a result of poor investing strategy, much of the bequest she received as a result of my decision in the case surrounding Sam Gaines's will. *In re Gaines*, 187 N.Y. 329 (1934). Woodrow therefore took it upon himself to provide Marie Benedict, as she called herself after Sam's death, with a significant amount of cash each year to supplement her own limited income.

Grover, by the testimony of his wife, Esther, considered this action of Woodrow's highly disrespectful to their mother, Sam's first wife, Sarah. (T.t. at 432.) Esther testified that Grover on more than one occasion accused Woodrow of paying Marie "hush money" to keep quiet the circumstances surrounding Sam's death. (T.t. at 423.) Esther further testified that Marie was "blackmail[ing]" the family (t.t. at 441) and that Woodrow was "wicked" and "a fool" for paying her any money (t.t. at 451; t.t. at 453).

On the only occasion when Grover and Woodrow discussed this matter, at the wedding of Grover and Esther (behind home plate between games of a Pawtucket Red Sox–Columbus Redbirds doubleheader at McCoy Stadium, in Pawtucket, R.I., according to testimony at trial), Woodrow told Grover that it was "none of his business" (t.t. at 371). A shoving match ensued and was broken up by Grover's Pawtucket teammates. The brothers never saw each other again. (T.t. at 374.)

"You were right about Grover," Amelia said. "He sounds pretty normal to me."

They returned to their reading of the will:

The Gaines family is reminded that Surrogate's Court is no place for the rehashing of old family business. The purpose of this courtroom is to decide will cases and nothing else. I hope never to see this family, or any other family, try to turn this courtroom into a battleground for the rehashing or even the resolution of ancient family quarrels.

Case dismissed with costs to petitioners Woodrow and Theodore Gaines.

PAUL MARTLAND, SR., Surrogate Judge

Amelia turned to Dwight David. "What do you think?" she said.

"I never knew how Grover died," Dwight David said solemnly. "I knew that Uncle Theodore—he's my great-uncle, I guess, but I called him Uncle Theodore—I knew he hated my grandfather, but I never knew why. I guess now I know."

"I didn't mean to disturb you with these things," said Amelia. "I honestly didn't know what we'd find. Do you want to stop?"

"No, no, no," said Dwight David. "I want to read another case."

"Good," Amelia said quickly, as the limo left the Belt Parkway and headed north on the Van Wyck. "I was hoping you'd say that. Where are we going?"

"You'll see," said Dwight David, not wanting to give away the surprise.

Amelia shrugged. She reached for another case. This was the oldest one. The stiff pages practically crumbled at her touch. They read:

ESSEX STREET ORPHANAGE V. GAINES, 16-438

In the Surrogate's Court, November 1, 1916
Surrogate Judge Paul Martland, Sr.

Barry Shapolsky, New York, New York, for petitioners Sam Gaines and Harry Gaines.

Isaac Solomon, Solomon and Solomon, New York, New York, for respondents Essex Street Orphanage.

"That gives me chills," said Amelia. "Look. This is Sam and Harry together, before they stopped being friends. And Barry Shapolsky representing both of them."

"You really know us Gaineses," said Dwight David, but he was not sure whether this was a good or a bad thing.

They read together:

JUDGE MARTLAND: Harry Gaines and Sam Gaines, sons of decedent Dov Ber Ginzburg of Pinsk, Russia, in this action challenge their father's will, which leaves one quarter of his estate to each of the sons and the other half to the Essex Street Orphanage in New York City, where the boys were raised.

Respondent, the Essex Street Orphanage (the "Orphanage"), seeks to have this will admitted to probate as the last will and testament of said Dov Ber Ginzburg. According to trial testimony, Dov Ber at the time of the execution of the will was a virtual pauper. At the time of his death, earlier this year, he was wealthy. Apparently Mr. Ginzburg forged documents noting his own death and the death of his wife in 1899, when the boys were sent to America as orphans.

Petitioners, Mr. Ginzburg's sons, now grown to manhood,

challenge their father's will on the grounds that anyone who claims to be dead and sends away his children to another country must be insane. If Mr. Ginzburg was insane at the time he made his will, the will would not stand and his estate would pass in its entirety to his two sons. Harry Gaines and Sam Gaines therefore have staked their case on proving that their father, at the time he made his will and sent the boys to America, was insane.

Counsel for respondent Orphanage brought evidence that Pinsk in 1899 was a dangerous and poverty-ridden place for Jews and that the greatest favor Mr. Ginzburg could have done for his sons was to send them to America, where they might live in peace and security. Indeed, Mr. Sam Gaines has found success already in this country as a builder of small houses in the Bushwick section of Brooklyn (trial transcript at 83), and Mr. Harry Gaines has found steady employment as a vaudeville comedian (trial transcript at 99; exhibits C, D, E, and F). Counsel for respondent Orphanage made the excellent point that both young men would have been impressed into the Tsar's army had they grown to adulthood in Russia. Given the rapid and dangerous changes now taking place in that foreign land, Harry and Sam Gaines could perhaps be said to owe their lives to their father's decision to send them away.

This action is particularly distasteful in light of uncontroverted testimony introduced by respondent Essex Street Orphanage. Such testimony demonstrated that Harry and Sam Gaines in 1915 had the opportunity to bring their father, decedent Dov Ber, to the United States for medical treatment for his heart condition. Harry Gaines admitted under direct examination that he and Sam had made arrangements with the Hebrew Immigrant Aid Society (hereinafter "HIAS") to transport the then ailing Dov Ber to New York for hospitalization and surgery then unavailable in Pinsk. Harry and Sam could easily have afforded to pay for their father's passage (t.t. at 117). Harry was prepared to do so, but Sam missed repeated appointments at HIAS to pay for the trip. As a result of Sam's procrastination, the deadline for Dov Ber's departure passed. Physicians in Pinsk subsequently pronounced Dov Ber unfit for travel, and he died of a heart attack a few months later, precipitating this action.

The will, as translated from the Russian by this Court's translator, is accepted into probate, and the challenge by petitioners Sam Gaines and Harry Gaines is hereby DISMISSED.

Costs to petitioners.

Paul Martland, Sr., Surrogate Judge

"That explains everything," Amelia said, shaking her head slowly.

"It does?" asked Dwight David, not understanding.

"Look. In Harry's diary from 1915"—Amelia took it out of her handbag, where she had kept it since the reading of the will—"Sam was supposed to show up three different times at HIAS. It didn't say why they were going there. It just said they were going to do something for Dov Ber. Okay? Now . . ." She rummaged through her bag and pulled out Theodore's letter to Tess and Sam David and flipped to the last page. Dwight David watched her in awe.

"And in this letter," Amelia continued, "Theodore tells Tess and Sam David not to judge Original Sam too harshly for what he did to his father, Dov Ber. That's the big family secret! Don't you get it? And Gaineses have been trying to prove each other insane ever since."

"That's so sick," Dwight David said sadly.

"One more?" Amelia asked.

"Must we?" asked Dwight David, as the limousine turned onto the Interborough Parkway. He had had enough of family secrets for one night.

Amelia turned to the last of the cases. They read:

IN RE GAINES, **33-749**

In Surrogate's Court, New York, New York
Judge Paul Martland, Sr., Surrogate Judge
February 9, 1933

Arthur Whitelaw, Saratoga Springs, New York, for petitioner Marie Benedict Gaines.

Barry Shapolsky, New York, New York, for respondents Sarah Gurrelts Gaines, Woodrow Gaines, Theodore Gaines, and Grover Gaines.

JUDGE MARTLAND: Sam Gaines, decedent, amassed during his forty-three years a sizable fortune in New York City real estate. In 1911 he married respondent Sarah Gurrelts Gaines; in 1929 he divorced her. In 1933 he married his second wife, petitioner Marie Benedict Gaines. Sam Gaines died of a heart attack on his wedding night in 1933. He had never changed his will, made in 1922, which left half of his estate to his first wife, Sarah, and one third in trust to each of his three sons, respondents Woodrow, Theodore, and Grover Gaines, who were twenty-one, nineteen, and fifteen, respectively, at the time of their father's death.

Despite repeated advice from counsel (trial transcript at 234), Sam never changed his will after his 1929 divorce from Sarah. Comes now the petitioner Marie Benedict Gaines to challenge Sam's 1922 will and to claim the entire estate of Sam Gaines. She reasons that by divorcing Sarah and marrying her, Sam demonstrated his intent to leave his entire estate to her.

Respondents Sarah, Woodrow, Theodore, and Grover naturally take issue with Marie's reasoning. They argue that Sam, an advanced alcoholic, was insane at the times he divorced Sarah and when he married Marie, and that Marie acted with undue influence in her seduction of the eventual marriage to Sam.

Sam Gaines had every right to divorce and remarry, regardless of the opinions of or consequences to members of his family. Proof of his alcoholism as brought by petitioner Sarah (trial transcript at 83, 122–129, 315–319, and 406) does not in and of itself demonstrate Sam's insanity. Although our sympathy lies with Sam's second wife, Marie, because Sam did not change his will in her favor, this Court has no choice but to admit the will to probate as it stands. An unchanged will is still valid, regardless of the testator's marital status at the time of his death. The petition of Mrs. Marie Benedict is hereby DISMISSED.

Costs to both parties.

Paul Martland, Sr., Surrogate Judge

"God bless our happy home," said Dwight David.

"Mm," said Amelia. "Now we know why somebody cut these cases out of the lawbooks."

"And the rest of the cases are like this?" Dwight David asked. "I mean, you know, Uncle Theodore and Great-Grandma Sarah and—"

"And Isabella McNiven and Winona and your grandmother Gloria."

"So it's the same thing every time?" Dwight David asked. "I mean, we really just wait for each other to die so we can go to court and say the person was insane?"

"Pretty much every time," said Amelia, thinking it over. "Sometimes it's something else, but this is basically it."

Dwight David looked sad. "I just thought it was a sick joke in the family, calling dead relatives insane and fighting for their money. I didn't think we actually did it."

"I'm surprised you've never been involved," said Amelia.

"I leave that stuff to the grownups," said Dwight David.

"But you're a grownup," said Amelia. "You're twenty-five."

"Yeah, I guess so," said Dwight David. "But if being a grownup means being like them, I'd rather be a kid."

"I guess I understand," said Amelia. She looked out the window and recognized nothing. "Where *are* we?" she asked.

"You'll see," said Dwight David. Then he remembered something. "What did you mean when you said before that you were going to get fired?" he asked.

Amelia thought back to the day's events: the message from Elizabeth Herder; the firing of Mr. Scarpatti. She sighed. "You have to be a certain kind of person to work in a trust department," she said. "You have to be trustworthy."

Dwight David grinned. "Boy, I think you were born to the job," he said.

"Well, that's what they've always thought too," Amelia said ruefully. "Won't it be a big surprise when they find out it's not true."

Dwight David was about to ask for an explanation when the limousine pulled off the Interborough and rolled down a pitted, poorly paved road.

"We're almost there," said Dwight David. "I want to show you something."

"Like what?"

"You'll see."

They sat in silence the rest of the way. Amelia wondered what sort of surprise lurked at the end of this unmarked, unlit back street. Dwight David and Acey apparently had been this route before. Then the limousine stopped. The driver got out, pushed back a rusted iron gate that squeaked as it moved over the road, and returned to the wheel. He drove, much more slowly now, on a road half as wide and twice as bumpy. Amelia looked out the window and, to her shock, saw tombstones. Old, broken, vandalized tombstones lined the path.

"What are we doing here?" she asked Dwight David, suddenly afraid.

"It's okay," he said soothingly. "You'll be glad we're here."

Amelia eyed him as though for the first time. What kind of sick individual was he? Did he intend to have a picnic dinner on a smashed-up grave site? She shuddered—did he want to make love here? Why a cemetery? And how did he, and his driver, know the way through that back entrance? How did he know the gate would be unlocked? Weren't cemeteries supposed to be closed at night?

Dwight David sensed her discomfort. "Just trust me," he said. Finally, the limousine bounced to a halt. Dwight David looked out his window, and then he looked up. "We're here," he said. "Come on."

Amelia feared for her physical safety. Anything could happen to her out here, and no one would know.

"Come on," Dwight David insisted. "There's something I want to show you."

Nervously Amelia followed him out of the limousine.

"If this is some kind of a joke. . ." she murmured. She slammed the limo door behind her, and the noise echoed off the surrounding tombstones. She shuddered again.

Then she saw it.

In the moonlight, it was unmistakable. Three stories high, the color of dirty alabaster, chipped in places where neighborhood boys had broken off pieces of the surface, it looked like a three-story model of the Washington Monument. At the base was a door. Over the door, engraved in foot-high letters in a style of relief both massive and foreboding, was the name Amelia had come to know from letters, photographs, will contests, obituaries, trust documents, and the memories of two dozen relatives. Amelia and Dwight David stood before the final, grandiose, moonlit resting place of Original Sam Gaines.

"Oh, God," murmured Amelia. She could feel Sam's presence as though he were stirring from a long, deep sleep behind the heavy marble door, ready to chase away the visitors who disturbed his rest. He would come through the marble door at any moment, a hand to his temple, nursing his eternal hangover.

He would recognize Dwight David immediately, because Dwight David had been here before. How else would Dwight David and his driver have known just where to find Sam? And then he would want to learn who Amelia was, whether she was a relative or a friend, a Gaines by birth or a Gaines-to-be. Amelia involuntarily drew a breath and held it, waiting fearfully for Sam to emerge.

She reached out for Dwight David's hand, found it, and held it tight. "I'm scared," she said.

"It's okay," said Dwight David, his eyes also on the marble door. "You can feel him, can't you?"

Amelia nodded, swallowing hard. "This must have cost a fortune," she said.

"Go first class or stay home," murmured Dwight David. "Want to go inside?"

"No!" Amelia said, horrified. And then: "Can we?"

"Sure, if you want," said Dwight David. "Acey, do you have the key? And the flashlight?"

The driver, whose presence Amelia had forgotten, came out of the darkness. "Got 'em both," he said. He stepped forward to unlock the mausoleum door. Amelia watched him, grateful that he was there. The ghost of Sam Gaines could be no match for the three of them. At least that's what she hoped.

The driver unlocked the door and handed Dwight David the flashlight.

"Thanks," Dwight David said to him. And to Amelia: "Ready?"

"Not really," Amelia admitted, genuinely scared. Then she told herself, *There are no such things as ghosts. There is nothing to be afraid of.*

Dwight David pulled the door open, turned on the flashlight, and took Amelia's hand again. Slowly, fearfully, a step at a time, they made their way into the crypt, as Dwight David's flashlight played eerily on the blue gneiss ceiling and back wall. Amelia's grip on his hand, and then his arm, grew tighter and tighter. The inside was better maintained than the outside. The floor was smooth, polished to a high gloss. The walls looked freshly painted, a robin's-egg blue. To be inside the tomb seemed safer, somehow, than to be outside. Dwight David turned the beam of the flashlight on the highest shelf, and there Amelia read again the name SAM GAINES.

Her heart raced, and her breathing became shallow. She could feel his control, his eyes on her, his anger for her having learned the secrets that in 1915 he had no compassion for his father and in 1931 he had no compassion for his son. She felt him looking at her with a combination of resentment and need. She felt that he needed her not to let anyone else know that Woodrow had gone to Maine anyway. He wanted all his secrets kept safe. He looked upon her as an interloper, an outsider who knew too much about him, his wives, his drinking, his dismal relations with his sons. He looked upon her as someone who knew the embarrassing, mortifying secret of his death, a heart grown hard (Gaines's syndrome), exploding in his chest as he reached his last climax in the body of his second wife. Amelia sensed him staring hard at her, wondering why she was so obsessed with him and his offspring and their way of life and their legal battles. And then the strangest thing happened: Amelia felt his stern mien change. His harsh features recomposed themselves into something approaching a smile.

Amelia gave him a questioning look: If you are so upset at me for knowing so much about you, why are you smiling at me? She looked perplexed, awaiting an explanation. The smile on Sam's face broadened until she could see his uneven white teeth. An odd thought possessed her: If Sam had lived today, he would certainly have gone for cosmetic orthodonture. And then she smiled back, and as Dwight David watched uncomprehendingly, Amelia saw Sam's face break into a grin, the decades of shame and anger melting before her, the worry lines on his forehead uncreasing themselves, warmth coming into his tired, cold eyes. Sam and Amelia exchanged beatific smiles, and Amelia suddenly realized why he looked so eternally happy.

Fifty-eight years after his death, ninety-two years after his arrival in America at the age of nine when he was separated from his beloved mother, no longer fearing the back of his father's hand, safe from the Russian army, safe from poverty, safe from Cossacks, safe from pogroms, Sam Gaines finally had the one thing that had eluded him in his brief, wealthy, and pain-filled lifetime. He had, in Amelia, someone who understood him thoroughly, someone who knew all his secrets, someone who could accept him as he was, without grudges, without rancor, without hatred for the choices that sadness and missing his mother and finally alcoholism forced him to take. Amelia had redeemed Sam. She had not forgiven him, because there was no need for forgiveness on her part. He had never done anything wrong to her. She simply understood him thoroughly and completely. For the first time in or since his life, Sam's life made sense to someone. And for that he would be eternally grateful.

"What's happening?" Dwight David asked.

Amelia just shook her head, never taking her eyes off the image of Sam Gaines that she saw. He looked just as he did in the formal portrait she had found in the file room at the bank, except, of course, for that smile, full of gratitude and relief.

"I think your great-grandfather is feeling better," Amelia told Dwight David in a calm, quite voice.

Dwight David did not exactly understand why this should be so, but he believed her anyway. He looked up at Sam's nameplate. "I told you you'd like her," he told Sam.

"Who else is in here?" Amelia asked.

Dwight David answered by lowering the beam of the flashlight to shine on other names. Amelia read: SARAH GURRELTS GAINES, 1893–1974. "Sam's first wife," she said. And then, below Sarah: WOODROW GAINES, 1912–1951. "His first son," Amelia said.

Dwight lowered the beam again. "Gloria Coss Gaines, 1916–1981," Amelia said. "Woodrow's wife."

"My grandparents," said Dwight David.

Amelia nodded. He fixed the beam on the uppermost rung on the other side of the tomb. There lay Theodore Gaines, 1914–1987. Below him was an empty tomb, reserved presumably for Theodore's widow, Annette Morris Gaines. Below that space, the next name down read: GROVER GAINES, U.S. NAVY, 1918–1942.

"Is his wife here too?"

Dwight David shook his head. "After Grover died, the family lost touch with her. She probably remarried."

Amelia nodded. It made sense. She would still have been young.

"Glad you came?" Dwight David asked.

Amelia's expression left no doubt that she was glad.

"I'd like to ask you something," said Dwight David.

Amelia's breath caught once again. She had been expecting this moment all evening, and now it was here. "Wait," she said. "Don't say anything."

"Huh?" asked Dwight David. This woman was very strange. First she was communing with the spirit of his great-grandfather, and now she was reading his mind.

"I know what you're going to ask me," she said, looking tenderly into his eyes.

"You do?" Dwight David asked, confused. He believed her.

Amelia nodded. "You're going to ask me to come back to France with you. You're going to ask me to leave my job, not that I may have a job to leave after tomorrow, but that's another story. You're going to ask me to come with you back to Antibes, and live in your house with you, and maybe one day marry you."

Dwight David watched, amazed. Amelia was completely wrong.

She continued. "But I don't want you to ask me," she said soberly.

"Why not?" Dwight David asked, his mouth suddenly going dry.

"Because I love someone else," Amelia said plainly. "Howard, at the bank. He may not be rich, and he may not be flashy—not that you're flashy. You're very understated for someone who spends as much money as you do. And he may be, you know, kind of boring sometimes, and he can never get his head out of his work, and he even takes spreadsheets to bed with him, but—but he's a good influence on me, and I think I'm good for him. We kind of balance each other. You and I . . . we have fun, and I like the way you handle your family—you know, living five thousand miles away from them and not getting involved in the will contests and just spending a lot of money—but I don't think we'd work out. I just want to be—I just want to be *normal*."

Dwight David stared cluelessly at Amelia.

"I know I'm not making sense," Amelia admitted. "I'm just trying to spare your feelings. Please don't say what you were going to say. Please don't invite me to France or ask me to marry you. I'm having fun with you, I really am. But it all just makes me realize that I'm really in love with Howard. You must be so hurt. Insulted. Please, don't be. I've had the best time with you, and I'll never forget it. Ever. Just don't ask me to come back with you to France."

Dwight David, numb, took it all in. Surrounded by his ancestors, he was listening to a trust officer babbling about marriage. Marriage? *Dwight David?* Maybe she could read Sam's thoughts, but she was doing a rotten job of reading his.

He guessed that perhaps she did not understand why he had brought her to the tomb. Then he realized *he* did not understand why they were there. He just wanted her to meet Original Sam, he supposed.

"I wasn't going to ask you to come back with me to France," he admitted.

"Oh," said Amelia, confused.

"I actually have a girlfriend there already."

"Oh," Amelia said, and her hand involuntarily brushed back her hair.

"I kind of like her," Dwight David said. "I didn't mean to get you to think I was going to marry you or anything. Last night just kind of happened."

"I feel the same way," Amelia hastened to add.

"What I was going to ask you was—" Dwight David looked sheepish. "Now I feel stupid," he said.

"You can say anything to me," Amelia said.

"I was kind of going to ask if you wanted to go back to my place and split a pizza."

"Oh," said Amelia, and she suddenly realized that she had completely misread the situation. "Oh," she said again. To her credit, she asked gamely, "What kind of pizza?"

"Gee, I don't know," said Dwight David. "I thought maybe meatball or sausage or something like that. You can't get good pizza in France. They just don't get the crust right. I always try to have a pizza whenever I'm in New York."

Amelia nodded quickly. "Pizza would be fine," she said. "Um, I like sausage."

"Great," said Dwight David. "Back to the city?"

"Back to the city," said Amelia, drained by the variety of emotions she had just experienced: fear of Sam's aura; warmth when she connected with it; affection for Dwight David; love for Howard; and utter embarrassment when she understood that she had totally misinterpreted Dwight David's intentions.

"We can call from the limo," said Dwight David. "The pizza'll get to the apartment the same time we do."

"How convenient," said Amelia, trying not to sound nonplussed by all that had just happened, between herself and Dwight David and between herself and Sam.

Acey locked the door of the tomb. Amelia and Dwight David settled in the back of the limousine and returned to Manhattan.

FOUR

Absolute

Dominion

35

IN PEEKSKILL, two hours later, Mr. Skeffington awoke suddenly and sat straight up in bed. He put on his glasses. "I finally figured it out," he said firmly.

"Oh, God," said Mrs. Skeffington, clutching her nightgown. "Frederic, you scared me."

"I finally figured out why I've been thinking about Woodrow so much. Do you want to hear why?"

Mrs. Skeffington did not particularly care to hear why, especially at this time of night, but after forty years of marriage, her husband was entitled to a few moments of obsessiveness.

"Tell me," she said sleepily.

"Any other family would have either killed each other or never spoken to each other as long as they lived after something like Woodrow's will trial."

"So what?" asked Mrs. Skeffington, yawning. She hoped her husband's explanation would not take long and that she would not fall asleep in the middle of it. Then she decided that she would not mind falling asleep in the middle of it.

"The Gaineses didn't fall apart," Mr. Skeffington said, a hint of admiration in his voice. "They *thrived.* No matter how great the challenge, they always rise above it. They sue each other, but they stick together. They can go on suing each other forever. If they survived Woodrow's will, they'll survive Harry's."

"Which means—" Mrs. Skeffington began.

"Which means"—Mr. Skeffington sighed—"I'll never be rid of them. They'll find a way to keep together. They *need* to hate each other. It keeps them healthy, somehow."

"That's the silliest thing I ever heard of," said Mrs. Skeffington.

"No, it isn't," said Mr. Skeffington, hurt. His wife clearly did not appreciate the brilliance of his logic. "It means they're going to find a way to get the four votes. I can *feel* it. I'll *never* be rid of them."

"It's just as well," said Mrs. Skeffington. "If you lost them, you'd miss them so much you'd go crazy."

Mr. Skeffington harrumphed. He was about to argue, when he realized that she was right. He pulled the covers back over himself and Mrs. Skeffington, curled up, and went back to sleep. Resigned to his fate, he slept soundly for the first night since Harry's death. Mrs. Skeffington watched him sleep for a bit, realized she wasn't tired anymore, and went to the kitchen to warm herself some milk.

"Ironic, isn't it, Donald?" Sam David asked a wallet-size photograph of his sandy-brown-haired spiritual leader. He was dressed in jogging clothes and hid in a doorway past which, Bickle had discovered, Amelia ran every morning. "Harry's will said 'get along.' But the family is trying harder than ever to screw each other over. But by trying to screw each other over, we're talking to each other for the first time in years. So by subverting the will's terms, we're fulfilling it. What do you think of that, Donald?"

Sam David could not wait for a reply. Just then, Amelia, jogging to clear her head, ran by. Her evening with Dwight David had ended only four hours earlier, over pizza and champagne. Sam David, wordlessly, fell in step beside her.

"You don't return my phone calls," he said by way of greeting.

Amelia gasped. She had not noticed him lying in wait for her.

"What do you want?" she said, too drained emotionally to deal with him. "Why are you here now? Can't it wait till the office?"

" 'And Moses went to Pharaoh in the early morning and made him an offer before the rest of Egypt was awake,' " Sam David said, misquoting Exodus. "I want your vote. I'll give you a million dollars for it."

"Leave me alone," said Amelia, jogging faster, but Sam David easily matched her stride.

"A million one hundred thousand," said Sam David.

"Get away from me."

"A million two."

She said nothing.

"Two and a half million for your vote and Howard's," Sam David said. He had budgeted himself for two million apiece for Howard's and Amelia's votes. He had a lot of negotiating room left. Amelia and Sam David by now had reached Lexington Avenue.

"What makes you think I'd sell you my vote for *any* amount of money?" Amelia asked.

"Because I know who you are," Sam David said calmly.

Amelia stopped in her tracks. "What are you talking about?"

"Your name is not Amelia Vanderbilt," said Sam David, as Amelia's eyes widened. "You did not go to the University of Chicago. You did not grow up in Greenwood, Nebraska. There are no Vanderbilts in Greenwood, Nebraska. And *you* make the walnut chocolate chip cookies that you claim your Granny Vanderbilt makes." Sam David delivered the clinching blow: "And there *is* no Granny Vanderbilt."

Amelia eyed him. Her worst nightmare had come true. She had been found out.

"You know all this, and you'll still pay me for my vote? Why don't you just tell me you'll go to Mr. Skeffington and get me fired if I don't vote your way?"

"Because I'm a nice guy," said Sam David, but Amelia did not believe it. "Okay," he admitted. "I'm not a nice guy. But if I get you fired, what good does that do me? I need your vote more than I need you fired. Don't you understand that? And I thought maybe we could help each other. You get some nice money, I get my buildings, and maybe Mr. Skeffington never finds out that Amelia isn't really Amelia. That she's actually someone else."

Amelia considered the offer. "What if I say yes?" she asked.

"Then I forget everything I've learned about you," Sam David said. "It's that simple."

"And if I say no?" Amelia asked, considering her options.

Sam David smiled his sharklike smile. "You won't say no," he told her.

"Why did you cut the cases out of the lawbooks at the bank?" Amelia asked suddenly. "Because Sam wouldn't help Dov Ber come to America? Because he wouldn't let Woodrow go to Maine? Or because he bought it on his wedding night?"

Sam David snorted. Amelia had done as good a job investigating his family as he had done investigating hers. She had done such a good job, in fact, that he thought for a moment about offering her a job in his office.

He hailed a passing cab. "Every family has its secrets," he admitted. "But if I don't get your vote, I'll tell everyone *yours.*"

Sam David got into the cab and slammed the door. Amelia, shaking her head slowly, watched the cab drive off. Sam David turned back to look at her, to give her one last stern warning. He looked a lot like Original Sam.

"We've got an hour until the meeting," Mr. Skeffington told Amelia as he hurried past her desk on the way to his office. "Have you read my memo?"

"I'm about to," said Amelia.

"See that you do," said Mr. Skeffington.

Amelia sighed and read his memo.

```
TO: Amelia Vanderbilt and Howard Person
FROM: Skeffington
REP: Gaines meeting, noon, Mtg. Room A

I have decided to open today's Trust Committee
meeting to all Gaineses and all Shapolskys, not
just the ones on the Committee. I have therefore
arranged for Meeting Room A to have a medium-sized
table placed in the middle, for the seven com-
mittee members, to be surrounded by a circle of
chairs for those Gaineses and Shapolskys who wish
to attend. I expect perfect attendance, to be
frank. Only Committee members may participate,
however. I am taking this step to avoid litigation
later on; you both are familiar with the Shapol-
skys' tendency to sue first and ask questions
later.
     Sixty million dollars is a lot of money. It is
```

```
fair to say that jobs in this department ride on
your ability to keep it in the bank.
```

Skef.

"Read the memo?" Howard asked, sitting across from Amelia. Whatever anger he felt toward her had dissipated. He assumed the game between them had ended and that Dwight David had won. Worry lines creased his forehead, however.

"Just finished it," Amelia said. "Why?"

"C'mere," said Howard. To Amelia's surprise, he led her off to the stairwell, away from the Trust Department. He brought the memo with him.

"Read that last line again," said Howard. He read it aloud for her: " 'It is fair to say that jobs in this department ride on your ability to keep it in the bank.' Whose job? Not my job. I just got promoted. Not Mr. Skeffington's job. He's safe."

"Then whose job is he talking about?" Amelia asked.

"I think *yours*," said Howard. "I've been thinking about it. I think giving you the Gaineses was just a setup to get you fired."

"What are you talking about?" Amelia asked in disbelief. "Mr. Skeffington thinks I'm wonderful! I even got my own *Wall Street Journal!*"

"If you're so wonderful," Howard asked, "how come he took away all your clients?"

"The DLOLs?" Amelia asked. "Because they don't bring in enough money."

"Well, there's more to the story," said Howard. "How come you lose the DLOLs the same week you get the Gaineses? Look what happened to Stone and Vaccaro. They got the Gaineses, and then they left the bank. Look, I think it's like this. I think Mr. Skeffington was told to cut out a certain number of people in the department. So what does he do? He looks for the most vulnerable people. He checks out people's résumés. Like Mr. Scarpatti. And Scarpatti's gone. That means you have the least seniority in the department. Then he takes away your DLOLs, which are basically the only clients you've had since you got here. Then he gives you the Gaineses, which is practically like asking you to fire yourself. No one can manage the Gaineses. I thought maybe I could, but I must have been crazy. I think he's trying to find a delicate way of firing you without having to fire you!"

"Why would he do that?" Amelia asked, not wanting to believe him.

"I don't know," said Howard. "Maybe firing you would ruin that 'family feeling' he's always talking about. Or maybe he's afraid you'd sue for sex discrimination. Or maybe he isn't good at firing people."

"He did a good job of firing Mr. Scarpatti," Amelia said.

"Well, I don't know, then," said Howard. "Maybe he doesn't want to fire you because he likes you. He just took away your clients and gave you the worst account in the department."

Amelia did not want to admit that there might be some truth in Howard's argument.

"So you're saying," Amelia began, "that if we don't get four votes for *something* at that meeting, I'm going to get fired?"

Howard thought it through and nodded. "I think that's exactly what's going to happen."

"I can't believe Mr. Skeffington would *do* this to me!" Amelia said, her tone betraying her dismay. "I've worked so hard for him!"

"Maybe it's not up to him," said Howard. "Maybe it's the bank's new management."

"But still."

"Well, it just means we have to get four Gaineses to agree on something."

Amelia considered for a moment. "Sam David offered us two and a half million dollars for our votes," she said.

"I know," said Howard. "He said the same thing to me."

"Howard," Amelia asked abruptly, "would you still like me if my name wasn't Amelia?"

The question surprised Howard. "I thought we were through," he said. "I thought you were more interested in Dwight David."

"How could you ever think that?" she asked. Then she remembered Howard's surmise that she had spent the night with Dwight David two nights earlier. "Don't answer that," she said. "Look, I'll admit I was . . . interested in him. But I think that's just because he's a Gaines. And you know how I feel about the Gaineses."

"Yeah, you're obsessed," said Howard.

Amelia sighed. "Okay, I admit I'm obsessed," she said. "But obsession isn't love. It's just . . . curiosity. Taken to an unhealthy extreme. But I don't love Dwight David, and I don't love any of the Gaineses. Except Sam and Harry, and they're both dead. What I'm trying to say is that I still love you."

"Oh, Amelia," said Howard, taking her hand. "And I still love you!"

"But could you still love me if I wasn't Amelia?" she asked.

"I—I just don't understand what you're talking about!" said Howard, confused.

"Stick around," said Amelia, thinking about Sam David. "You'll find out."

Howard sighed. They embraced, left the stairwell, and returned to their desks. Just then Andre approached Amelia with a pink message sheet. "Somebody called Mrs. Herder just called," he told her. "She says she's in the coffee shop by the Trailways counter in Port Authority."

Amelia froze.

"Is everything okay?" Andre asked, concerned.

Amelia did not answer. Instead she sped out of the department and out of the bank.

36

A
T THIS TIME of day, Amelia realized, the subway would be quicker than a taxi from Wall Street to the Port Authority Bus Terminal. She stopped at a cash machine and withdrew two hundred dollars, jumped into the uptown subway, and arrived at the bus station twenty minutes later. Quickly losing her way in the labyrinthine terminal, one of the few New York landmarks she had never visited, she asked a policeman to direct her to the coffee shop specified in the message. Amelia, fearful, descended two flights of escalator stairs and found the object of her haste, a large, disheveled, and confused-looking woman twenty years her senior, sitting uncomfortably at the counter, the remains of a piece of lemon meringue pie on a plate in front of her.

Amelia saw her. She could think of nothing to say.

"I'm not going to bite," said the woman, studying Amelia's clothing and looking quite impressed.

"How did you find me?" Amelia asked, approaching slowly.

"You're thinner," said the woman.

"I work out a lot," Amelia said mechanically. "You're thinner too."

"No I'm not," said the woman. "I'm heavier than ever. What do you think of that?"

"How did you find me?" Amelia repeated.

"I paid a *detective*," she said with great satisfaction. "You can run, but you can't hide."

"What do you want from me?" Amelia asked, staring at her.

"Why, I want you to come home with me," she said, as if it were the most natural thing in the world.

"Oh, Mother, that's just not possible," said Amelia, shaking her head. "I have a . . . I have a whole life here."

"Well, what about my whole life?" the woman asked. "Doesn't that mean anything to you?"

"Yes, but . . ." Amelia sighed. "Where are you going to stay?"

"I'm not going to stay," she said. "I came to bring you back."

Oh, God, thought Amelia, running a hand through her hair. She reached into her purse. "Look, here are the keys to my apartment. Why don't you just go there, and we can talk tonight? I've got a lot of work I've got to get back to."

The woman stared at the keys as if they represented something evil. "Apartment, huh?" she said suspiciously.

Amelia, trying hard to remain composed, took out a pen and wrote down her address on the back of a napkin. "You just give this to a taxi driver, and go inside and wait for me. We'll work something out."

The woman looked at the address on the napkin. The location meant nothing to her.

"I don't have any more money," she said.

Amelia sighed. The whole experience reminded her of lunch with one of the DLOLs. She tried to imagine her mother at the Exquisite Tulip, eating cucumber sandwiches. She opened her purse again and removed forty dollars. "Here's some money," said Amelia. "Maybe you can go shopping, if you want to. Or eat a regular meal. Or whatever."

The woman looked with great surprise at the money. "How'd you get that? she asked. "You hooked up with something, like that other time?"

"I have to get back to the office," said Amelia. "Just go to my place, and I'll call you. Okay?"

"Are you coming home with me?" the woman asked plaintively.

Amelia sighed again. "Just go to my place, and we'll work something out, okay?"

"Okay," the woman said reluctantly, accepting the money, the keys, and the address.

Amelia felt herself on the verge of tears. "I'm leaving," she said. "I'll call you later."

She turned her back on the woman and left the coffee shop.

"Don't you want to hear about your father?" the woman called after her. "He's getting out next month."

"Later," Amelia called back. "Everything later."

Tears forming in her eyes, she walked quickly to the subway.

In Los Angeles, Grover Sam, on his way to his first day back at the office after his New York sojourn, stepped off the bus, walked to the corner, waited for the light to change, crossed the street, and headed for his firm's building without creating a single accident.

On board the Concorde, Dwight David, having abandoned his newly purchased elegant clothing on the floor of his father's spare apartment, was nibbling at the last slice of pepperoni pizza that he and Amelia had shared the night before. He could think only of Amelia. Once he finished the pizza, though, he could think only of his Scandinavian girlfriend, who would be waiting for him at the airport in Antibes.

In room 607 of Manhattan Hospital, Chester Alan and Rebecca, in full surgical scrubs, anxiously monitored the dimming vital signs of their patient and relative, veteran of countless will battles, Charles C.

As Charles C. declined, Chester Alan turned to Rebecca. They had barely spoken to each other since their falling out.

"I'm sorry I was so thoughtless," Chester Alan said. "I'm sorry for all the things I said."

"You don't have to apologize," said Rebecca, taking his gloved hand in hers. "I'm the one who said all the terrible things. And I'm sorry I sent the bankers copies of the Keith versus you and Sam David case."

Chester Alan stared blankly at her. "You did *what?*" he asked.

All other living Gaineses, and all the living Shapolskys, Old and New, were making their way to the offices of the New York Bank and Trust Company, each nervously awaiting the Trust Committee meeting that would enrich him or her and impoverish all of his or her relatives. The four Gaines children—Sam David's twelve-year-old Franklin Delano and ten-year-old Sarah, Tess's six-year-old Marie, and Woodrow Sam and Glenda's eight-year-old Isabella, present so that they could get their first taste of family tradition—could sense their respective parent's or parents' unease as the various taxis approached the bank.

Gil Thompson and Cynthia Crossen were also en route to the bank, where they would attend the meeting as guests of Louis Gaines Shapolsky of the law firm of Old Shap. Gil had still found no reason to disabuse Cynthia of her belief that he was a member of the Gaines family and that his first name was Sidney.

Taxis arrived and Gaineses and Shapolskys piled out. Soon Meeting Room A was abuzz with family members and their lawyers, all convinced that their grand plans were about to swing into effect. A knowing smile played across the face of Sam David, present with Richard Bickle, certain as he was that Morris's vote was in his pocket, along with the votes of Amelia and Howard. Morris could not resist the money; Amelia would fear losing her job; and Howard would act out of loyalty to Amelia to throw his vote Sam David's way. To Sam David's mind, the committee vote enabling him to take control of the three theaters, so that he could tear them down and build his massive office towers, was practically a done deal.

Woodrow Sam gave his wife Glenda's hand a gentle squeeze. Woodrow Sam had every reason to be happy. He could count on her vote and Keith's vote. No other Gaines could claim two votes for a given plan. One of the bank people, or perhaps Morris, would have to go along with their idea to create one combination film institute/vaudeville museum (to satisfy Keith and Grover Sam), to give one theater to Glenda to restore to its prior Broadway glory, and to sell one theater, as he, Woodrow Sam, wanted, to increase family cash flow and to pay for the projects of his wife, brother, and father. The Woodrow Sam bloc of votes, he believed, was impregnable.

Glenda turned to her mother-in-law, Babette, who sat with her cat on her lap, and asked, within earshot of the newly arriving Gil and Cynthia, "Does Sidney have a pedigree?"

"Oh, no." Babette laughed, trying not to move so as to avoid waking the sleeping feline. "We found him behind a supermarket."

Cynthia gave Gil/Sidney a look of enormous surprise.

"I was adopted," Gil/Sidney said, thinking quickly.

"Oh," said Cynthia. She would never understand this family, she told herself.

Tess and Glenda exchanged the tiniest of smiles. After all, the decision would be made by secret ballot. They could count on Keith's vote, because he would get his monument to Harry, and they would each get a theater of their own—one for Tess's greatly expanded homeless shelter and one for Glenda's nascent theater empire. With three votes behind them, someone from the bank would have to go along. Or perhaps Morris would vote with them—after all, he represented Glenda and Keith and yet he was friendly with Tess. And Woodrow Sam and Grover Sam would never know that Tess and Glenda had sold them out.

Keith looked content because he thought the deal among himself, Glenda, and Woodrow Sam was still in effect. He had no idea that Glenda, working with Tess, planned to sell out Woodrow Sam and Grover Sam.

The sole Shapolsky seated at the center table, reserved for the committee members, Morris Shapolsky, sat slumped in his chair, his eyes on the floor. The temptation to sell out his family for one point eight million dollars was too great to ignore. He had decided to sell his vote to Sam David.

The rest of the New Shap Shapolskys—Edward, Barry, Samantha, and Samuel G.—sat together, indifferent to Morris's discomfort and concentrating solely on how they would spend their share of the three point six million dollars in real estate commissions once the committee failed to agree on the disposition of Harry's assets. They still believed wholeheartedly that the committee was doomed to failure. After all, how could four Gaineses ever agree on *anything*?

The Old Shap Shapolskys—Deborah, Moses, Henry Clay, and young Louis Gaines—could barely contain their glee. Once the committee failed to reach agreement (itself a given), Morris would try to sell the theaters, and Old Shap would ride to its own rescue, filing with the appropriate court the injunction papers that Louis Gaines Shapolsky had drafted and then transmitted by fax to his friend at the law firm of Tower and Gates in Los Angeles—far away, the Old Shap Shapolskys believed, from the inquiring eyes of any member of the Gaines clan.

Amelia, back from the bus station, her mind on her unexpected guest, took her seat next to Howard. Amelia looked more nervous than anyone in the room.

At that moment, in Los Angeles, Ernest Davis, law student and word processor, who sat one terminal away from Grover Sam at the law offices of Tower and Gates, asked Grover Sam how his trip to New York had gone. "Just fine," he said, smiling knowingly, aware as he was that the Trust Committee meeting was about to begin. Within one hour, it would present him with a theater for his film museum. Grover Sam put on his headphones and activated his word processor for what he hoped would be the last time in his life.

"Injunction," said the voice on the tape, which belonged to one of the high-level associates in the firm. "To halt the sale of properties pursuant to a will and trust agreement."

Typical boring legalese, Grover Sam thought, as he began to type.

At Manhattan Hospital, an extremely anxious Chester Alan Gaines ordered an unconscious Charles Chaplin Gaines prepped for surgery. Dr. Braunstein had graciously yielded to his colleague, now that Charles C. was too far out of it to know the difference.

On the Concorde, Dwight David Gaines struck up a conversation with the twenty-two-year-old daughter of an Italian olive oil magnate, who had come to New York to buy herself a small brownstone in the East Seventies.

"That's funny," said Dwight David, wondering whether there was still time to wire his Scandinavian girlfriend not to meet him at the airport. "My family owns a lot of buildings in New York too. How long did you say you were going to be in France?"

Mr. Skeffington entered Meeting Room A, and a hush fell upon Trust Committee members and spectators. The time had come to begin the meeting. Since this was only the second time the group had met, no protocol existed, and no one knew who was supposed to speak first. All eyes eventually fell upon Amelia and Howard. Amelia, too consumed with her own problems even to think of leading the meeting, looked hopefully to Howard, who cleared his throat, frowned slightly, and began.

"Fellow members of the Trust Committee," Howard said, in a quavering voice that eventually grew to its usual confident if businesslike tone, "Gaines family members, and members of the law firms of Shapolsky and Shapolsky and Shapolsky & Shapolsky. Welcome. We hope that at our meeting today we will be able to meet the terms of the will and trust of the late Harry Gaines. Of course, if we are unable, during our remaining days, to reach a four-vote majority, the value of those assets will be given as a gift to the federal government, in keeping with Harry's wishes."

The New Shap lawyers gave each other knowing smiles. The Old Shap lawyers observed the knowing smiles on the New Shap lawyers' faces and elbowed each other ever so slightly in the ribs. It was like a dream for them.

"So our work today is quite serious," Howard concluded. "Um, is there a motion among the members of the committee for how to proceed?"

The seven committee members looked at one another. No one wanted to go first. Finally, Keith raised his hand.

"Yes, Keith?" Howard asked.

"I move," said Keith, full of misplaced confidence in the outcome, and delighted that the whole work of the committee could be over in a flash, "that the three theaters be divided this way: One will be a combination film institute and museum of vaudeville, run by my son Grover Sam and myself. One will be a Broadway theater, run by Glenda. And the third will be sold to an existing Broadway theater chain at the best possible terms. The money will be used to run the film and vaudeville museum and to get Glenda's first theater production off the ground, and the rest will be divided equally among all living Gaineses."

"The motion is on the floor," said Howard. "Is there a second?"

Glenda nodded. "I second it," she said. Babette, holding her cat, Sidney, in her lap, closed her eyes. She couldn't look.

"Discussion?" Howard asked.

Silence. Glenda looked away from Keith and Woodrow Sam. Morris looked away from all the Gaineses. Amelia looked away from Howard.

"In front of each of you is a pad of paper and a pen," said Howard. "We've agreed to do this by secret ballot. Please write 'yes' or 'no.' Again, we're voting on Keith's motion."

Everyone in the meeting room leaned forward. Each of the committee members wrote his or her vote on the piece of paper supplied. Glenda shielded her sheet from Keith's eyes.

"Mr. Skeffington, would you come here and count the votes?" Howard asked.

"Certainly," said Mr. Skeffington. He collected the ballots from each of the seven committee members. He read off the votes one at a time: "Yes," he said. "Yes."

The Shapolskys, Old and New, held their breath: Had the family actually managed to agree? Were they, the Shapolskys, out three point six million dollars?

"No," intoned Mr. Skeffington, reading the third ballot. "No," he repeated, reading the fourth. And then: "No," again. All present realized that one more negative vote doomed the proposal. Keith remained confident. Two of the noes were probably from Tess and Sam David. He could still count on Glenda's vote, Keith told himself. And then he would only need to pick up one from Amelia, Howard, or his own side of the family's attorney, Morris. It still looked good.

"No," said a tense Mr. Skeffington. "The motion fails."

"What about the last vote?" Keith asked, crestfallen.

Mr. Skeffington looked at the remaining ballot. "No," he said.

A gasp went up from the family. Keith, stunned, turned

quickly to Glenda. Her eyes told the whole story. She had voted against him. Keith was speechless.

As one, all the Shapolskys sighed with relief. The rest of the Gaineses grew slightly more nervous. If the committee could not agree on a proposal that seemed to benefit so many Gaineses, could they ever agree on a different proposal?

"Does any committee member wish to make another proposal?" Howard asked cautiously. He also found the five-to-two defeat of Keith's proposal a dismal sign, even though he had contributed to that defeat by voting against the proposal. Howard had done so because it was accepted by only half of the Gaines family, Harry's half. It did not benefit even a single member of Sam's side, and this, Howard, believed, was neither fair nor good for the family. Harry's will was intended to bring his family together by means of the committee, not to split them irrevocably apart.

"I do," said Tess. "I have a proposal."

All eyes fell upon Tess. Her daughter, Marie, seated directly behind her mother, crossed her fingers and toes.

"I move," Tess said, speaking slowly and deliberately, "that the assets be divided this way: one theater will be converted into a homeless shelter, to be named the Gaines Shelter, which I will run."

Sam David rolled his eyes. Tess ignored him.

"A second theater," she said, looking directly at Keith, "will be called the Harry Gaines Museum of Vaudeville."

Keith, surprised, looked gratefully at Tess. Howard, especially, was pleased. Here was a proposal with the potential to satisfy members of Harry's *and* Sam's sides. This could be a proposal he could support.

Woodrow Sam felt the ax coming.

"The third theater," said Tess, averting Woodrow Sam's questioning gaze, "will become a Broadway theater to be run by Glenda."

"*You sold me out!*" Woodrow Sam yelped to Glenda. "You sold me out to her!"

"Oh, stop it," said Glenda, who looked guilty despite herself. "Calm down."

"My own wife sold me out!" a pained Woodrow Sam cried out. "I can't believe this!"

"Order," said Howard, highly disturbed at Glenda's action. How could he, Howard, vote for a proposal that alienated husband and wife? "Is there a second?" he asked, the distaste evident in his tone.

"I second it," said Glenda.

"The motion is seconded," said Howard. "Discussion?"

"You're terrible!" Woodrow Sam told Glenda. "I can't believe I ever married you!"

"Could we please confine the discussion to the merits of the proposal?" asked Howard.

"I just can't believe it," said Woodrow Sam, utterly appalled. "I just can't believe it."

"If there is no further discussion," said Howard, "let's vote."

Once again, the seven committee members took pens in hand to record their votes. Each covered his or her writing hand with his or her free hand so as not to let anyone else see the ballot. Mr. Skeffington came and collected the votes from the seven members. Woodrow Sam stared wildly at Glenda. Glenda would not even look at him.

"N-no," said Mr. Skeffington, reading the first vote, his voice catching unexpectedly. "No," he said, reading the second one. Then: "Yes." "Yes." "Yes." "No." All present held their breath as he read the seventh and deciding ballot: "No." Tess, Glenda, and Keith slumped in their seats.

"Ha!" Woodrow Sam cried triumphantly.

The Shapolskys, New and Old, began to perspire. Three point six million dollars had nearly slipped through their outstretched hands.

"Does anyone else have a proposal?" Howard asked, beginning to believe that the whole exercise was pointless. It seemed highly unlikely to Howard that anyone could suggest something that would unify the committee.

"I do," said Sam David. The entire room grew still. Everyone wondered why Sam David had remained silent for so long. His strategy had been to allow the committee to reject a few proposals and then recognize that if it did not act quickly, it would lose all the money.

All eyes turned to Sam David, except for those of Morris, which were focused squarely on the floor.

"We're talking about sixty million dollars in assets," said Sam David, his voice sly and seductive. "There are eighteen of us in this whole family. That works out to three point three million dollars for each of you, from Charles C. down to little Marie. Three point three million for little Marie. Three point three million for little Isabella over there. Three point three million for each of you. I just can't believe that this family would be willing to let that kind of money get away just out of stubbornness and selfish, foolish pride."

His words hit home.

"And that's only what the theaters are worth if you sell 'em today," Sam David continued, aware that his argument—and his numbers—held his audience rapt. "If you tore those old suckers down and put up some decent state-of-the-art office buildings, you could have ten times that amount. *Thirty-three* million dollars for little Isabella. *Thirty-three* million dollars for little Marie. Thirty-three million dollars for each of you."

The Shapolskys in the audience grew tense. So did Mr. Skeffington. Was Sam David getting through to any of his fellow committee members?

"Gee, Glenda," said Sam David. "You could sure buy a lot of Broadway theaters for thirty-three million dollars. And Keith. You could build your father one hell of a vaudeville museum with that kind of money. And Tess. You could—you could—"

Sam David found himself unable to finish the sentence. He could not even verbalize for a moment the thought of his hard-earned money going to homeless people.

"You could do a lot of—of good works," he concluded. "My proposal is a real estate investment trust, with each of you as limited partners and myself as the general partner. I guarantee you could have ten times your money in five years. That's my proposal for the theaters."

"Second?" asked Howard, who had to admit to himself that the plan had merits.

Silence. None of the committee members wanted to admit publicly to supporting Sam David.

"*Morris*," Sam David whispered.

"Second," Morris said guiltily.

The five other members of the committee stared at Morris. Was he in cahoots with Sam David? The members of his firm and the members of Old Shap all leaned forward in their seats. So did Mr. Skeffington. What was Morris up to?

"It's just so we can have a discussion," Morris said lamely.

"Discussion," said Howard.

"We're talking about Harry's theaters," said Keith. "We're not talking about some vacant lots. Harry wouldn't have wanted office buildings. If he did, he'd already have built 'em."

"We're not talking about what Harry wants," said Sam David. "We're talking about what's best for the family. Including little Marie and little Isabella."

"I wish you'd cut that crap about little Isabella," said Glenda. "I don't like you using my daughter as a pawn in this thing."

"I'm just saying we have to look at everyone's best interest," Sam David said coolly. "Not just our own."

"You're assuming you can actually make money on those buildings," said Tess. "Everything I've read about the real estate market in New York says the market's glutted already. You're throwing a lot of figures around, but how do we know what they're based on? If the real estate market really got depressed in this city, we'd be losing money, not making it."

"Bickle," commanded Sam David.

"Yes, sir?" said Bickle, snapping to attention.

"Read my sister the projections," Sam David said.

Bickle cleared his throat. "In five years—"

Keith cut him off. "You're not a member of this committee," Keith said. "You have no right to speak."

Bickle looked to his mentor for direction. Embarrassed, Sam David looked at Howard.

"I think Keith's right," Howard said gently. "I think only committee members can speak. Otherwise it would get out of hand."

Sam David, displeased, did not seek to argue the point. "What Bickle would have told you is that the projections are sound and that thirty-three million is a conservative estimate."

"What do our bankers advise about this investment scheme?" Keith asked. "That's what we pay you for."

Howard and Amelia exchanged glances. Amelia looked imploringly at Howard. Howard paused thoughtfully before he spoke.

"To be honest," he said, "from a fiscally prudent standpoint, I'm not so sure it's a good idea to put all this family's eggs in the commercial real estate basket. Tess is right. The market's shaky, and it could easily tank."

"But you've got to take some risks if you're going to make real money!" Sam David protested. "That's how Original Sam would have done it!"

"Taking risks?" Glenda asked pointedly. "With money that belongs to little Marie and little Isabella?"

"If your motion failed, everyone else's has to also?" Sam David asked darkly. "Is that it?"

Glenda exploded. "I resent your insinuation that my decision was based on anything other than reason and clear thinking—" she began.

"Please," said Howard. "Both of you. Are there any other comments on Sam David's plan, or should we put it to a vote?"

"Let's vote," said Sam David, glaring at Glenda, confident that he had a four-vote majority without her. After all, he had his own vote, that of Morris, that of Amelia, and, despite that nonsense about being "fiscally prudent," that of Howard, as well. His family could go hang. He was getting his three office buildings.

"We're voting on Sam David's proposal to tear down the theaters and put up office buildings," said Howard, as the seven reached for their pens.

"Over my dead body," Glenda muttered.

"You're not even a Gaines," said Sam David.

"Thank God for little things," Glenda snapped back.

"Please," said Howard. "This is serious business."

The seven members cast their votes. Morris, who, aside from seconding Sam David's proposal, had not said a word at the entire meeting, crouched low over his ballot and wrote with his free arm shielding the ballot. He looked to the others like a fourth-grade student taking a spelling test.

Amelia looked at Sam David with something approaching loathing in her eyes. And then she remembered: he was a Gaines, and he was only doing what came naturally. She felt lighter than she had in days. And then she wrote out her vote.

Mr. Skeffington collected the ballots. He shuffled them and slowly read the results: "Yes," he said. Sam David looked pleased. "Yes," he said again, reading the second ballot. Sam David looked even more pleased. "No," said Mr. Skeffington, reading the third ballot. Sam David gave Glenda a dirty look, to which she responded in kind. "No," said Mr. Skeffington, reading the fourth ballot. Sam David glanced at Keith, who returned Sam David's gaze with an expression that said, *I voted against you and I'm glad I voted against you.*

Mr. Skeffington picked up the fifth ballot. He was as nervous as anyone in the room. Sam David's proposal was the bank's last best hope of keeping the sixty million out of the hands of the Federal Treasury. If it passed, Mr. Skeffington would never know how it felt to run a trust department that the Gaineses did not dominate. "No," he said, his heart pounding.

Sam David looked around nervously. Who had voted against him? It must have been Tess. Tess looked noncommittally at the floor. Two votes left. Sam David needed them both. It was time for Amelia and Howard to come through for him.

Mr. Skeffington closed his eyes, turned to the sixth ballot, and frowned mightily.

"What is it?" Glenda asked.

"No," said Mr. Skeffington. A gasp went up. Sam David had lost. Sixty million seemed on its way to Washington.

"What about the seventh ballot?" Sam David asked quickly.

"Mr. Skeffington opened the seventh ballot. "No," he said. "The proposal is defeated, five to two."

Sam David looked darkly at Amelia. Morris had voted for him, but she had not. Her frank expression made it clear. She had defied him. Sam David had no choice but to strike back.

"Does anyone else wish to make a proposal?" Howard asked forlornly. Even if anyone did, no one would vote for it. Everyone was already too disappointed and angry that his or her own proposal had failed to garner the requisite four votes.

"I don't have a proposal," said Sam David, rising to his feet. "But I do have to challenge the fitness of one of the members of this committee to serve on it."

Amelia's eyes widened. He was really going to do it. He was going to expose her.

"What are you talking about?" Mr. Skeffington asked sharply.

"What am I talking about?" Sam David repeated, too far gone to turn back. "I'm talking about—"

"Me," Amelia interrupted. "He's talking about me."

"What?" everyone shouted at once. "What is this?" "What's going on?"

"Amelia," Mr. Skeffington said sternly. "Explain."

Amelia stood. "If I have the floor, then he has to sit down," she said, pointing to Sam David.

"Have a seat, young man," ordered Mr. Skeffington.

To everyone's surprise, Sam David meekly sat down.

"I have a confession to make," Amelia began, her expression contrite. "My name isn't really Amelia Vanderbilt."

Everyone present gasped, even the children, who did so only because they saw everyone else doing so.

"My name is Margaret Herder."

Everyone in the room stared at Amelia in disbelief. None stared harder, or with more stupefaction, than Mr. Skeffington.

"I didn't grow up in Greenwood, Nebraska," Amelia admitted.

Gil Thompson gave Cynthia Crossen a knowing look. He cocked an eyebrow, as if to say, *we figured that out a long time ago.*

Howard stared at his girlfriend in utter disbelief.

"There is no Granny Vanderbilt," Amelia continued. "I bake my own cookies."

Bickle nodded, proud of himself. This was the part that he had uncovered.

Amelia found some calm within her, and she spoke from that calm place. Honesty felt good, somehow. "I grew up in a bunch of trailer parks," she said. "In Nebraska, in Kansas, in Oklahoma, in a bunch of places. My mother is completely insane, and I haven't seen my father since I was five years old. I don't mean she's in an institution. I just mean she's off the wall, irresponsible, messed up, fat, ugly, weird. I grew up completely afraid of her, and all I wanted to do was run away and change my name and change everything about me and *never be like her*.

"I never went to college."

Mr. Skeffington's jaw dropped. Finagling a résumé was grounds for dismissal, as he had so recently demonstrated with Mr. Scarpatti.

"I mean, I went to college," Amelia said, "but only to the career counseling office. I was working as a waitress, and I'd go into the career counseling office and tell them I was a student at the University of Chicago and that I had a perfect GPA and great extracurricular activities and all that other bullshit. And they bought it." She turned to face an incredulous Mr. Skeffington. "And so did *you*.

"And so did *all* of you. I just pretended I was this perfect little girl from this perfect family, and you all bought it. Maybe you wanted to buy it, because you'd never seen anyone from a happy family. Look at you all. You're ridiculous. You've been fighting for . . . forever, and why? Over what? Don't you think it's ridiculous?"

Amelia stopped. "I'm sorry. I should be talking about myself, not about you. I can't blame you for believing me. You all wanted to believe me because it was such a nice *fantasy*. A girl from a happy home. Well, that's all it is. A fantasy."

Amelia sighed and looked at Howard. "Oh, Howard, I'm so sorry," she said. "But if I'd said my name was Margaret Herder and I grew up in a bunch of trailer parks and my father was a drunk and in jail someplace and my mother was a wacko, would we have ever gotten together? I couldn't have even gotten a job here. I'm sorry I lied. I'm sorry I lied to all of you. I feel terrible."

Amelia slumped into a chair and started to cry.

"Get her some water!" someone cried out.

"The poor thing," Glenda said sympathetically.

"It's okay," said Tess.

"There, there," said Keith.

"She'll be okay," said Morris, who was relieved to have someone or something take the spotlight away from him. He gave Amelia his handkerchief. He did not want anyone to know that he had gone down with Sam David's sinking ship. And in any event, he was still entitled to the one point eight million dollars, he told himself. Just because Sam David didn't win didn't mean he didn't owe Morris, Morris told himself.

"Is all of this true?" Mr. Skeffington asked Amelia.

She nodded sadly.

"Then I have no choice but to fire you," he said, equally unhappy. It was true that he had intended her to leave the bank, because of the personnel cuts he had been forced to carry out, but he never meant for it to happen this way. "I'm sorry, but that's the policy."

"It's okay," said Amelia, sniffling into Morris's handkerchief. "I understand."

"Amelia," said Howard, until now dumbstruck by her revelations, "is this what you were talking about before?"

She nodded and began to cry again.

"It's okay," said Howard. "I don't care what your name is or where you come from. I still love you."

"Isn't that sweet?" asked Glenda, touched by the emotional scene.

"Delightful," muttered Sam David, disappointed that Amelia had stolen his thunder but pleased because justice nonetheless had been served. In truth, he felt a measure of remorse for plotting Amelia's downfall, but business was business.

"Amelia, I must ask you to leave the bank at once," said Mr. Skeffington. "You know the rules."

"Yes, sir, Mr. Skeffington," Amelia said tearfully.

"Just a minute, Mr. Skeffington!" said Howard. "Amelia, or Margaret, or whatever her name is, is still a member of this committee. She's entitled to stay as long as this meeting is going on!"

"Hang on!" snapped Sam David. "The committee includes an Amelia Vanderbilt, not a Margaret Something-or-other! She's got to go!"

"Not so fast," Howard replied heatedly. "It was Harry Gaines's intent that this woman serve on his committee, whatever her name was! For a while he thought she was Anne Frank! Right, Morris?"

Morris reluctantly agreed. "I think that's what Harry wanted," he said.

"Then she can stay as long as the meeting is going on," said Howard. Amelia looked gratefully at Howard. She had never seen him take charge this way before.

"Well, I guess she can stay," Mr. Skeffington said reluctantly.

"But the meeting is over!" protested Sam David, tired of the whole thing. "We haven't come to an agreement, so we're done!"

"You hear that?" Morris said suddenly. He was thrilled. Not only would he collect the one point eight million dollars from Sam David for his vote, but he would also get his share of the three point six million dollars for the real estate commission when his firm sold the theaters. Today was turning into a very lucrative day for him.

"We have not adjourned," thundered Keith, in the most powerful voice anyone present had ever heard him employ. "We have not taken a vote to adjourn. We have not taken a vote to disband. This meeting is still going, and this woman Margaret or Amelia or whatever is still a member, and I oppose any effort by Sam David to wrap this up!"

"I agree with Father!" said Woodrow Sam.

"So do I," Tess said.

"I guess the meeting is still open," said Howard. "Would anyone object to a ten-minute recess so that Amelia, or Margaret, can catch her breath?"

Not even Sam David could object to that. "Ten-minute recess," declared Howard.

Amelia rushed out of the room, Howard following behind her.

"I'm so sorry," she said, sobbing and falling into his arms.

"It's okay," Howard told her, and he could feel her hot tears against his cheek. "I love you no matter who you are." He paused for a moment. "Who did you say you were?"

At that moment in Los Angeles, Grover Sam, his mind on the invitation list for the opening gala ball of his film museum, unconsciously typed the terms of the Application for Temporary

Restraining Order into his computer. He was halfway through the order when suddenly he realized he was typing a familiar family name.

It was his own family's name.

"That's funny," he said aloud. "Gaineses in L.A. too." He read back over what he had typed so far.

> . . . Hereby petition the Court to restrain the firm of Shapolsky & Shapolsky from selling any and all assets pursuant to the will of the testator, Harry Gaines. We will show the Court that said firm of Shapolsky & Shapolsky was endeavoring to subvert the financial interests of its clients in avaricious pursuit of its own gain.
>
> The language of the trust makes clear that the law firm entitled to sell the assets, and keep the real estate commissions appurtenant thereto, indicates not their firm of Shapolsky & Shapolsky, but *our* firm of Shapolsky and Shapolsky. This is clear meaning of the language of the will of Harry Gaines.

Grover Sam said, "What the . . .?" and typed in the rest of the document:

> Therefore we petition the Court to enjoin Morris Shapolsky of the law firm of Shapolsky & Shapolsky from selling the late Harry Gaines's assets, primarily three Broadway theaters, and we hereby petition the Court to allow our firm of Shapolsky and Shapolsky to sell those same assets.
>
> Respectfully submitted,
> Louis Gaines Shapolsky
> Shapolsky and Shapolsky
> New York, New York

Grover Sam, highly alarmed, pushed the Print button on his computer, and the laser printer produced the order in seconds. Grover Sam turned to Ernest Davis.

"What does this mean?" Grover Sam asked nervously, shoving the document in front of his colleague's face. Ernest, looking displeased to have his own work interrupted, read the document. He was familiar with Harry's trust and Grover Sam's family's relationships with the Shapolskys—anyone who knew Grover Sam heard all the stories about the Gaineses. The meaning of the document revealed itself to him in short order.

Ernest snorted. "It means your lawyers were fucking you over, but now *their* lawyers are trying to fuck *them* over."

"That's what I thought it meant," said Grover Sam, and he raced out of his chair to the fax machine. A lengthy draft of an appellate brief was grinding through the machine on its way to Sacramento.

Grover Sam ripped it out of the fax machine.

"What the fuck you think you're doing?" asked the fax operator.

"Take it easy," said a tense Grover Sam. He knew the bank's fax number from memory, because he had sent first Stone, and then Vaccaro, and now Amelia so many copies of his plans for the film museum. "Just give me a minute."

Grover Sam punched in the number. There was not a moment to lose, he told himself. He got a go-ahead signal and placed the injunction into the machine. The only thing that concerned him was whether anyone at the bank would see the thing and get it to the Trust Committee meeting before it was too late. Grover Sam watched the injunction pass through the fax machine, watched the OK signal indicating that it had been received at the bank, and held his breath.

At Manhattan Hospital, Charles Chaplin Gaines was being prepared for an emergency quadruple bypass operation. As risky as it was for a man of Charles C.'s age and condition, Chester Alan and Dr. Braunstein had jointly concluded that it was Charles C.'s last and only hope.

At the bank, Howard continued to dry Amelia's eyes with Morris's handkerchief, but the tears would not stop. Howard sighed. He looked around for tissues. "Maybe there's some tissues in the mailroom," he said. "Come on."

Amelia and Howard crossed the corridor and went into the mailroom. Andre was sorting the mail. "Hi, guys," he said. Then he noticed Amelia's tearful countenance. "What's wrong?" he asked.

"Nothing," said Howard, who found a box of tissues on the counter. He opened it and handed a few to Amelia.

At that moment, Andre noticed the incoming fax. In keeping with bank policy, he stopped sorting the mail to see what the fax was all about. He observed that it said "Gaines" and "Shapolsky." When it came out of the machine, Andre handed it to Howard. "I guess this is for you," he said, and went back to sorting the mail.

Howard, still holding a tearful Amelia, read it, and his eyes practically bugged out of his head.

"I don't—I can't—I—" he stammered.

"What is it?" Amelia asked.

"Read this," he said, stupefied with anger for the Shapolskys. Amelia read it. She stared at Howard in disbelief.

"Andre," Howard barked. "Can you make me thirty copies of this, right now?"

"In a minute," Andre said. "Soon as I get done with the—"

"*Now!*"

Andre, taken aback, relented. "Okay, okay," he said. "Didn't realize it was so important. Geez."

Andre took the fax, several words blurred by Amelia's tears, and made thirty photocopies. Howard snatched the copies from the machine, remembered to thank Andre, grabbed Amelia's arm, and pulled her out of the mailroom.

"Come on!" he shouted.

They ran across the hall and back into the meeting room, where Gaineses, Shapolskys, and Mr. Skeffington were arguing about what, if anything, was supposed to happen next. Howard did not even try to find words. Instead he just threw the copies of the injunction around the room like confetti.

"What is the *meaning* of this?" he bellowed. Gaineses and Shapolskys, stunned by his act, grabbed copies of the injunction from the air. Louis Gaines Shapolsky recognized it first. "Oh, my God," he groaned.

The others read it in mounting disbelief.

"You tried to screw us over!" Morris yelled at his cousins in Old Shap.

"*You* tried to screw *us* over!" Louis Gaines Shapolsky yelled back at Morris and the lawyers of New Shap.

"YOU tried to screw US over!" Gaineses yelled at Morris and New Shap.

"*He*," Sam David shouted, pointing at Morris, addressing himself to the other members of New Shap, "*he* tried to screw you over!"

"What in the name of Sam Gaines is going on here?" Mr. Skeffington shouted over the din. No one heard, because everyone was yelling at someone else.

The children, at first afraid, were then delighted. Everyone was so excited. Maybe there would be soda and cake. Soon they realized that it was just another family dustup and an uncatered one at that. The children settled back in their chairs and waited for their elders to come either to terms or to blows.

Fifteen minutes later, calm had been restored. The Gaineses and Shapolskys had simply yelled themselves out. Those who had been sold out had gotten satisfaction from verbalizing their dismay; those who had tried to sell out others received the tongue-lashings they deserved.

"I'd like to make a motion," Keith said repeatedly, until all fell completely silent.

"I'd like to make a motion," Keith said again.

"What's your motion?" asked Howard, seizing the possibility of a return to order.

"I move," said Keith, as the others finally gave him their attention, "that we take all of Harry's assets and put them in a new Gaines Family Trust, for the benefit of each and every member of the Gaines family, the disposition of which assets can be decided, um, at a later date."

"Second," said Tess.

"Wait, there's more," said Keith. "I further move that, to paraphrase Shakespeare, the first thing we do is fire all the lawyers. I never want to see another Shapolsky as long as I live!"

"Second!" shouted Glenda, delighted to have the Shapolskys put to shame and the spotlight removed from her own attempted sellout of Woodrow Sam.

"I'm not done yet!" said Keith. "I further move that this Gaines Family Trust be maintained here at the New York Bank and Trust Company—"

"Second!" Howard called out.

"Oh, thank God," muttered Mr. Skeffington, who had feared

the family would leave the bank in reprisal for the assignment of an uneducated, dishonest trust officer to their account.

"There's more," Keith told the others. "Would you please let me finish? The trust will be maintained at this bank only on condition that it is managed by the only person who has ever understood this family or, dare I say, appreciated it—"

Keith turned to Amelia. "What did you say your name was, honey?"

Amelia, sunk in shame, looked up in surprise at Keith. "My name?" she repeated, as though she could not understand why Keith was addressing her. "My name is Margaret Herder."

"To be managed by Margaret Herder," said Keith, indicating Margaret with a sweep of his arm.

"Second!" shouted Tess.

"But she doesn't work at this bank anymore!" said Mr. Skeffington.

"Well, she better get a job here real fast," Tess informed Mr. Skeffington, "because otherwise it's going to cost you sixty million big ones."

Mr. Skeffington gasped. Clients were dictating hiring policy. It would not do. On the other hand, it gave him a way to explain his rehiring of Margaret. Or Amelia. Or whoever she was.

"This is most irregular," said Mr. Skeffington. "It would require the approval of my superiors."

"And she gets to keep the DLOLs," Howard demanded, pressing their brief advantage.

"I'll see what I can do about the DLOLs," said a beaten Mr. Skeffington.

"Well, that's the deal," said Keith, as Margaret and Howard exchanged looks of uncertainty and relief.

"The motion is on the floor," Howard shouted. "Can we take a vote?"

"I vote yes," said Tess. "We don't need a secret ballot."

"I vote yes," said Sam David. Now there would be more time to convince the family of the rightness of his plan.

"I vote yes," said Glenda, who had already begun to plan her apologies to Woodrow Sam.

"So do I," said Keith. "For chrissake, it's my proposal."

"I vote yes," said Howard.

"I vote yes," said Margaret.

"I might as well make it unanimous," said a defeated Morris Shapolsky. "Yes."

A roar went up from the assembled Gaineses. They had complied with the terms of Harry's will, and the theaters would stay in the family. The Shapolskys looked beaten, glum, and thoroughly pathetic. For the first time in American legal history, the clients had come out ahead of the lawyers.

Mr. Skeffington, resigned to a future bright with Gaineses, called for Andre to bring champagne. Andre could not uncork the bottles fast enough for the celebrating. He also brought soda and cake from the bank commissary for the children. The most amazing result had to do with the adult Gaineses. Sam David chatted amiably with Keith. Tess and Babette exchanged telephone numbers. Annette, mother of Tess and Sam David, sat on the floor and talked with Isabella, daughter of Glenda and Woodrow Sam, about school. Glenda and Woodrow Sam kissed and made up. Woodrow Sam apologized for his disparaging remarks about Glenda's carpet-bagging and his jealousy over her stage career. Glenda apologized for making a secret deal to sell him out, and she promised she would never do it again.

On Sam's side, too, amity reigned. Tess went so far as to commend Sam David on the architectural design of his latest skyscrapers, ignoring for the moment that the buildings had displaced a hundred and eight-seven low-income families. Sam David praised Tess for her good works and grudgingly admitted that "maybe the homeless weren't as bad as I've always made them out to be." He even volunteered to spend an evening or two in the Gaines Shelter, serving dinner. Annette, overhearing all this familial devotion, nearly fainted.

The children followed their parents' lead. Marie, Tess's daughter, came over to invite Isabella to her next birthday party. The birthday party was eleven months away, but it was the thought that counted. Franklin Delano and Marie, first cousins, introduced themselves. In short, Harry had achieved by means of his last will and testament the one thing he had never been able to do in his lifetime—he brought together his entire family. The descendants of Sam were getting to know the descendants of Harry in a setting devoid of rancor and old family arguments. The lion was lying down with the other lion.

Mr. Skeffington, Howard, and Margaret watched with quiet pleasure as Gaineses, under the influence of champagne, unity, and mobilization against the Shapolskys, got friendly.

"I really don't know what to say," Mr. Skeffington told Margaret.

"Neither do I," said Margaret. "Let's just worry about it later."

In a corner of the room, the two sides of the Shapolsky family were shaking hands for the first time since Morris and Samuel G. had left Barry, Louis, and Henry Clay back in 1946. They were discussing, in fact, the possibility of a merger of their two firms, now that they would have to be like regular lawyers and pursue clients. In fact, they had agreed in principle on every issue except one— whether to call the combined firm "Shapolsky and Shapolsky" or "Shapolsky & Shapolsky."

The era of good feeling among Gaineses and Shapolskys was entering its second half hour when Andre returned to the conference room and motioned Mr. Skeffington to a telephone.

Amelia/Margaret and Howard could hear his end of the conversation: "Yes, Chester Alan, it's Mr. Skeffington. . . . Oh, I'm so sorry. . . . Yes, I'm sure you did everything you could for him. . . . What time did it happen?. . . . Just fifteen minutes ago?. . . Of course I'll tell the family. . . . Yes. My best to Rebecca. . . . Of course. Goodbye."

Mr. Skeffington hung up. "It's Charles C.," he told Margaret and Howard. "He—he died on the way to the operating table. Never felt a thing. No pain. An easy death. I suppose I ought to tell the family."

Mr. Skeffington looked at all the happy faces and gathered himself to deliver the sad news. He did not want to say or do anything that might disturb their peace, but as the head of the Trust Department, he knew that the responsibility for informing the family of Charles C.'s passing rested on his shoulders.

"Ladies and gentlemen, may I have your attention?" Mr. Skeffington asked. The Gaineses and Shapolskys ignored him. "Ladies and gentlemen, I need your attention, if you please."

Gradually, reluctantly, those present turned to Mr. Skeffington to hear what he might have to say.

"I hate to rain on this most wonderful parade," he began, "but I just received a call from Chester Alan at Manhattan Hospital. We lost our beloved Charles Chaplin Gaines fifteen minutes ago. He did not suffer."

A moment of silence greeted the news. The silence turned to apprehension when Sam David asked the question that had rapidly formed in the minds of all the adults present.

"Mr. Skeffington," Sam David asked, "does that mean that Charles C. is one of the Gaineses for the purpose of the Gaines Trust Fund we just set up?"

Mr. Skeffington pondered the matter. "I suppose so," he said. "We concluded the agreement thirty-five minutes ago. Charles C. was still alive."

"So his estate contains one share of the sixty million?" Sam David asked.

"How can he talk about things like that at a time like this?" Margaret whispered to Howard.

"I thought you were the expert on the Gaineses," Howard whispered back. "You tell me."

"That's not all he left," said Keith. "When Harold L. died last year, he left everything to Charles C."

"Who's got the will?" Woodrow Sam asked. There might be something for him in it. After all, Charles C. was his uncle.

"As it so happens," said Morris, glad to be of use again after his brief disgrace, "I have the will."

There were shouts of "What's it say?" "Read it!" "Let me see it, Morris!"

"I've been carrying it with me," Morris explained, "ever since Charles C. went back into the hospital. It contains a few . . . surprises. Mr. Skeffington, may I read it?"

"Of course," said Mr. Skeffington, who waited for someone in the family to object. After all, Charles C. had not been dead for more than twenty minutes. Another family might have accorded the departed member a little more dignity before turning to the matter of his estate, but another family would not have been the Gaineses.

All eyes turned to Morris, who took his glasses from his pocket and then removed Charles Chaplin Gaines's last will and testament. Slowly, dramatically, he began: " 'I, Charles Chaplin Gaines, being of sound mind and body—' "

"Skip that part," said an impatient Sam David, speaking for the rest of the family. "Get to the bequests."

Morris frowned, his thunder stolen. "Okay, okay," he said. "I was just trying to prepare you."

Morris read: " 'Fifth. I hereby give, devise, and bequeath all of my estate, both real and personal, of every nature and wherever situated, of which I may die seized or possessed, including, without limitation, all property acquired by me or to which . . .' "

Two entire families—the Gaineses and the Shapolskys—hung on every word. Who could believe that the Gaineses had come into a sixty-million-dollar windfall only moments before? Decades of training had honed their interest in the current will, not the last one. Harry was old news. The action had moved to the estate of Charles C., including, as it did, his life savings, his brother Harold L.'s life savings, and one share of the estate of Harry Gaines.

" '. . . or to which,' " Morris continued to intone, " 'I may become entitled after the execution of this will to one of my most beloved companions and delightful friends—' "

"Friends?" Gaineses asked each other. Had Charles failed to leave his estate to his relatives? That would not be cricket.

Morris put down the will and dramatically swept the room with his eyes. He knew that the next two words he would speak would cause an explosion greater than any the Gaineses had witnessed so far. He concluded in his most powerful voice: " 'Sidney Gaines!' "

Utter pandemonium broke out. Cynthia Crossen, sitting in the back all this time with Gil Thompson, turned to him and screamed, "Sidney, we're rich!"

"Not so fast," said Gil/Sidney, shaking his head. "I'm not the one."

"You're not?" Cynthia asked, not understanding.

"*He left his estate to a cat?*" Sam David thundered, hitting the nail on the head.

"To *our* cat!" Babette screamed, unable to contain her surprise. Sidney, unaware of his good fortune, awoke and stretched.

"He did love Sidney," Keith admitted. "Maybe even more than he—oh, skip it."

"That's ridiculous!" shouted Glenda. On the other hand, it *was* her in-laws' cat. And cats don't live forever.

"It's absurd!" said Tess. How could a cat enjoy several million dollars when there were so many homeless people in the world who could use the money? she asked herself. This bequest could not go unchallenged.

"I've never heard anything like that in my life!" exclaimed Woodrow Sam. "But you know, Sidney and I have been good friends for years. I petted him only the other night."

"Why did Charles do that?" Howard asked Amelia/Margaret.

"I don't know," she said. "I get the feeling he was trying to make a point."

Howard nodded. "I think you're right," he said.

"You can't really expect a bequest to a cat to stand up in court," Sam David told Keith and Babette.

"Who said anything about court?" Keith asked anxiously. "You're not going to *challenge* this, are you?"

The Shapolskys held their collective breath. Maybe there was hope.

"Of course you don't want me to challenge it," said Sam David. "When Sidney dies, you get it all!"

"He's our cat!" Babette protested. "Get your own cat!"

"They think you're a cat?" Cynthia asked Gil, confused.

"I'll explain later," Gil replied.

"Sidney *is* their cat," Annette told her son, Sam David.

"You can't leave money to a cat!" Sam David said.

"Why the hell not?" asked Keith. "Morris, can't you leave money to a cat?"

"I don't know," Morris admitted. "I'd have to do some research."

"Well, maybe you should," said Keith. "I mean, just to keep Sam David from attacking us."

"If that's the way you feel about it," said Sam David. "Louis, what are you doing for lunch?"

Louis Gaines Shapolsky, late of the law firm of Shapolsky and Shapolsky and currently of the law firm of either Shapolsky and Shapolsky or Shapolsky & Shapolsky, knew an opening when he saw it. "Eating with you and Bickle?" he asked. "Planning our method of attack in the estate of Charles Gaines?"

"You're goddamned right that's what you're doing!" thundered Sam David. "Leaving his money to a cat!"

Keith, dumbfounded, stared at Sam David. "Is that the way you want it?" he sputtered. "You're going to take my cat to court?"

"You're goddamned right I'm taking your cat to court!" said Sam David. "Come, Bickle."

Bickle came.

Keith looked around the room for help. "Morris, Edward, Samantha, Barry, isn't there something we can do? He can't take my cat to court, can he?"

The firm of New Shap reconstituted itself. "Do you want to come by our office this afternoon?" Morris asked. "We can plan Sidney's defense."

"I don't believe this is happening," said Howard.

"It doesn't surprise me in the least," Margaret told him. "I think Charles C. did it on purpose. Just to make a point about this family."

"You bet I'll be there," Keith told Morris.

"Me too," said an indignant Babette. "Poor Sidney!"

Woodrow Sam and Glenda looked at each other. "We'll be there too," said Woodrow Sam, taking his wife's hand.

"The merger's off," Morris told Henry Clay and the rest of the Old Shap Shapolskys. "See you in Surrogate's Court."

The descendants of Harry Gaines stared sullenly at the descendants of Sam Gaines, who stared back with equal malice. The members of Old Shap glared at the members of New Shap. Neither side could believe they actually had contemplated joining forces. The era of good feeling for both families had ended almost as quickly as it had begun.

"Gaines versus Gaines versus Gaines," said Andre, who had brought more champagne. "I guess you won't be needing any more of this stuff."

"I guess not," Mr. Skeffington said sadly. He turned to Amelia/Margaret. "Are you sure you want to stay with these people?"

"Oh, absolutely," she said, and Howard took her hand. "They're more like family to me than my own family!"

"If you say so," said Mr. Skeffington, and the three members of the Trust Department sighed and left the meeting room to the Gaineses and Shapolskys, who had already begun to plot legal move and countermove.

"Just another day at the bank," said Margaret. "Just another day for the Gaines family."

"If they couldn't sue each other," Howard reasoned, "they probably wouldn't be very happy. What do you think Sidney's going to do with all that money?"

"Good question," said Margaret. Then she grinned. "Let's not forget he *is* a Gaines," she added. "He'll probably just blow it all on catnip."

"You're the greatest, do you know that?" said Howard, smiling. Then he looked concerned again. "What did you say your name was?"

"Margaret," said Margaret.

"Okay," said Howard. "Margaret."

"By the way," she said, "my mother's in town. Care to have dinner with us tonight?"

"She came in from Greenwood?" Howard asked.

"Not exactly," said Margaret, who wondered where exactly her mother had come in from.

"Sure," said Howard. "Of course I want to meet your mother." He grinned. "I've been wanting to meet your parents for I don't know how long."

"Seven-thirty at my place?" Margaret asked. She wondered what Howard and her mother would make of each other. She shuddered and tried not to think about it.

"Sounds okay to me," said Howard

They gave each other a quick peck on the cheek, and then they went back to work.

Author's Note

This novel grew out of discussions with my wonderful agent, Kristine Dahl of ICM. Were it not for Kris, this book simply would not exist. I am very grateful to be working with her and to benefit from her creativity, enthusiasm, instincts, and, as the expression goes, uncommon common sense.

I gratefully acknowledge the kind assistance of John C. Davidson, vice president and trust officer of the Santa Monica Bank, Santa Monica, California, who gave generously of his time and explained to me some of the inner workings of trust departments.

My thanks also to Joe Muto of the L.A. County Coroner's Office, Mike Wendell of the National Baseball Library at the Baseball Hall of Fame, Cooperstown, New York, the reference librarians of the Beverly Hills Public Library, and the reference staff of the UCLA Law School Library, all of whom shared generously of their time and research skills.

My friends Tom Braunstein, Judi Elterman, Jonathan Fink, Dick Hannes, Brad and Wendy Justus, Andrew Lewin, Tom and Audrey McLaughlin and David Schreiger kindly took the time to read early drafts and offer comments and criticisms that are reflected throughout the final draft. Michael Flood remains Michael Flood, and for that, I thank him.

Errors and inaccuracies remain strictly my own. Two historical notes: The development of the theater district in the Times Square area of Manhattan preceded by a decade or so Original Sam Gaines's time as a developer. I took a little poetic license to go along with Sam's real estate license. Also, certain old-timers in Pawtucket, Rhode Island, may recall

349

that in 1938 and 1939 there were no Pawtucket Red Sox. I make mention of that city's McCoy stadium in this novel for strictly sentimental reasons. People who have actually been to McCoy Stadium, especially on windy afternoons, might wonder what there is to be sentimental about. My lips are sealed.

One of the best things about getting to write novels is getting to work with Robert Asahina, my editor at Simon & Schuster for this and my first two novels. Bob is everything one could possibly hope for in an editor: brilliant, demanding, imaginative, patient, and thoughtful. I've grown so much under his stern but affectionate tutelage, and I owe what I am as a writer to him. Bob and I have been working together for seven years now, and I hope we go on together forever. Thanks are also due to Sarah Pinckney for all her careful work.

On a sadder note, the writing of this book was bracketed by the untimely deaths of two wonderful Susans in my life. My aunt, Susan Silverman, passed away a week after I started the first draft. She was a wonderful human being taken from us far too soon, and her family and friends love her and miss her. During the final rewrite came word that Susan Fisher Beckwith, one of the most thoroughly lovely people I've ever known, a skiing and drinking buddy, a great student of the English language, and a woman very much in love with life, died under tragic circumstances. I miss them both, and I hope that where they are, there's a good library.

MICHAEL LEVIN

Santa Monica, California
August 1992

About the Author

MICHAEL LEVIN studied Ancient Greek and English at Amherst College and is a graduate of Columbia Law School. He has published four books: *Alive and Kicking* (1993); *Settling the Score* (1989), a comic novel about classical music; *The Socratic Method* (1987), a comic novel about law school; and *Journey to Tradition* (1986), a nonfiction study of Judaism. Levin has also written for *The New York Times*, CBS News, *The Wall Street Journal*, and the *Jerusalem Post*. He has taught writing at UCLA Extension, in public high schools, on an inpatient psychiatric unit, and in a homeless shelter. He lives in Brookline, Massachusetts, and is a member of the Massachusetts Bar.